Readers' Comments on *Cross Sections*:

"A great story…congratulations on a most creative work, well researched and most engagingly presented. As my father would have said: "It's a rattling good tale!""   W. Allen, Michigan

"…Literate…absorbing…" R.Kelley, New Jersey

"…Absorbing reading…" N. Aronson, Pennsylvania

Cross Sections

Thomas Knobel

PK Publishing

Princeton

Cross Sections, a Novel
Published by PK Publishing
649 Princeton-Lawrenceville Road
Princeton, New Jersey 08540 U.S.A.

Cover designs by Nhieu Vo
Author's photograph by Tu-Anh Pham

Publisher's Cataloging-in-Publication
(Provided by Quality Books, Inc.)

Knobel, Thomas.
     Cross sections / Thomas Knobel. – 1st ed.
     p. cm.
     Includes bibliographical references.
     ISBN: 0-615-11690-6

          1. Germany—History—1933-1945—Fiction.
     2. Spies—Fiction. 3. Espionage—Fiction.
     I. Title.

PS3561.N615C76 2000   813.6
                                       QBI00-493

Printed in the United States of America

Cross Sections

The author would like to acknowledge the support and contributions of the following friends: Mrs. Tasha O'Neill of Princeton, New Jersey; Mrs. Margaret Quetel of St. Thomas, U.S.V.I.; and Mr. Wickham Allen of Midland, Michigan. Their help with content, editing, story flow, and German language elements was crucial to any success this novel might have.

TMK
6/1/2000

Preface

"The Nazis wanted an atomic bomb; we knew that. They had as good a chance at it as we had...(But) their war organization was a botch. Palace politics, bemedaled nincompoops playing expert on subjects on which they were ignoramuses, overlapping power in the hands of parallel agencies – these were some of its characteristics...Finally, the whole structure was clogged with the suspicion, the intrigue and chicanery, and the constant poisonous fears that are to be expected in any system that functions at the whim of a dictator."

Dr. Vannevar Bush, Director, Manhattan Project, speaking in June 1949

All of that, and something more...

Author's Notes

When my journalism advisor cursed me for congenital laziness, I figured, what does he know? Them that does, does; them that can't, teach. He said I "wouldn't know a good story unless it bit me on the ass." In college I could afford to ignore the old fart. Two years down the road and I heard the exact same words from an equally smelly old bastard. But unfortunately this one signed paychecks and decided to teach me a lesson by assigning all the drudge work around the paper; you know, flower shows, PTA meetings, funerals, and charity bazaars. In a small town like Princeton, it was hard to cut corners. If I bagged a late night zoning board meeting and tried to work from its secretary's minutes, inevitably the editor's mother or idiot brother had attended, whining about some minor deal that the secretary was too embarrassed to record. So I was busted and screwed...daily.

I learned fast what was most important to small-town subscribers: death. I envied big city reporters assigned to society pages, crafting seductive stories around lists of weekend partygoers. Here at the end of the track, funerals substitute for masked balls, raves, cotillions, and coke-dusted movie premier bashes.

So I developed a system of sorts: a kind of *fill-in-the-blanks* format for the paper's obits and funeral coverage. First came a quick scan through the paper's morgue: old issues going back a hundred years. If somebody died young, it was easy since stories from the last twenty years were computerized and cross-referenced. With older folk it was tougher but manageable. And it was a good place to hide when there's real work lurking about.

If the newly deceased was connected with the university, frequently the case in Princeton, I'd phone the campus library and press office for a fax of whatever they might have. Then it's off to the funeral or memorial service, scribble a few rough notes about the eulogies, count cars in the procession, then back to the office to...fill in the blanks, as I said.

Cross Sections

Princeton's a pretty odd place. Lots of famous and rich, and famously rich people live there but keep really low profiles. So occasionally I'd get a surprise, when someone I'd never heard of died, then turned out to have invented penicillin or rubber bicycle tires or something like that. It got to be a game where I'd dig deep to find tidbits no one else knew. Well, maybe nobody realized they were playing the game with me, but that didn't detract much from my fun. God, I must have been really bored!

Other times there was nothing, a life so hollow and insubstantial that the accomplishments of ancestors and children took up more of his obituary than his own. I once wrote one that looked just like that...

William H. Petersen, Professor of Chemistry, Longtime Resident

Professor William H. Petersen, of Princeton, New Jersey, died Wednesday at Princeton Medical Center following a long struggle with cancer. He was 81 years old and had lived in Princeton since 1942. Before retiring ten years ago, Professor Petersen held the Lawrence Chair for Chemistry at the University. Author of many scholarly papers and a textbook on thermodynamics, Professor Petersen was well respected and well liked by both his peers and students.

Born in Ringle, Wisconsin, William Petersen earned his bachelor's degree at Marquette University in 1938. Afterwards he spent two years in studies and research at the National University in Munich, Germany. Progress towards his doctorate was interrupted by the outbreak of World War Two and he returned to complete a doctorate at Princeton in 1943 where his thesis committee included Nobel Laureate Albert Einstein. Afterwards Dr. Petersen joined the Chemistry Department, attaining full Professorship in 1955. He chaired the Chemistry Department twice, once between 1959 and 1962, and again between 1966 and 1970. Professor Petersen transferred to emeritus status in 1977 and despite his illness, continued to write and lecture until late last year.

Professor Petersen is survived by his wife of 48 years, Elise Wagner Petersen, and two adult children, Dr. Franklin J. Petersen, MD, of Phoenix, Arizona, and two-term U.S. Representative Mary Petersen Voigt (R-Ohio). Professor and Mrs. Petersen have four grandchildren and one great-grandchild. A memorial service will be held at 10:30 a.m. Saturday, October 24, at the Princeton University Chapel. Details of the internment have not been announced.

Not bad, if I say so myself, but I could find nothing more. *Nada. Zilch.* Just another dingy old guy, I figured, a whole life spent with his test tubes and Bunsen burners, evaporating at the end like so much vapor leaking from a freshman's lab apparatus.

Well, I figured I'd turned up at the wrong building when five hundred people showed up for Petersen's memorial, including an ex-president (of the United States, for Christ's sake). Mourners materialized from Russia, England, Germany, and even places like India and China. What was going on? The ex-president was whisked away by his secret service detachment without comment and the eulogies seemed somehow obtuse. One of the speakers (I didn't catch the name) spoke respectfully of his courageous friend and colleague, declaring him a hero and patriot. And what was that all about?

Afterwards no one would pause, even a second, to answer the simplest of questions, and a few scattered at the sight of my camera, like they were worried someone would find out they attended Petersen's funeral. Weird, isn't it?

Deadlines are deadlines and when the paper was delivered the next morning, Professor Petersen's funeral got eight sad lines.

It slipped my mind completely until the end of December when the boss needed copy for a year-end issue, a review of newsworthy scraps from the past year. My *Book of the Dead* for that year was fairly long and picking through my files I'd decided not to include Professor Petersen among the immortals. Then I stopped at Starbucks for coffee one morning and recognized Mrs. Petersen seated alone, reading our newspaper, at a rear table beside the fireplace. One could hardly miss her: tall, lean, straight-backed, and well dressed.

I felt a pang of guilt, took a deep breath, and stepped up to her table.

11

Cross Sections

"Mrs. Petersen?"

"Yes?" she offered cheerfully.

"I hesitated to bother you, but my name is Knobel and I write for the newspaper here in town. I attended the memorial service for your husband at the chapel and wrote the short article that we published.

"It's late in coming, but let me offer my sincere condolences at your husband's death."

"Thank you, young man," she smiled pleasantly. "Some ways it seems like Willy's been gone more than just a few weeks. Yet I'm starting to feel it now, especially since everyone's stopped calling and visiting."

"Must have been nice with people like President Bush coming to help remember your husband."

"Yes, but that's one problem of living to be very old like Willy and I: you risk outliving all your friends, indeed the history of your times. Please sit down, Mr. Knobel."

"Thanks. You and your husband were married for more than fifty years?"

"Fifty-two years. But I first met Willy almost eight years before that, when I was very, very young."

"How did you meet?"

"In Munich. My father was Professor of Chemistry at Munich University. Vati brought Willy home for dinner one evening. He was my father's research assistant but had been living in some sort of hostel for several months and was nearly starved. But he was so tall and beautiful; and he was an American! He was always smiling, not like we Germans who were so desperately serious in those days. I was quite taken on that first night, though I still had to fend off my friends who were all equally infatuated with him.

"We were separated after the war began and I thought he must be dead until some years later. We were married in New York after the war and he brought me back to Princeton."

"You spoke about history. I have to admit I was puzzled by Dr. Petersen's biography. One of the speakers at the memorial called your husband a hero and patriot, but his bio doesn't mention his war record. The university's write-up made your husband seem like another dusty academic. I'm sorry too, if my story didn't do him credit or justice."

"Young man, if you only knew the truth." She paused and was silent for a few moments, remembering. "Before he died, Albertle told

12

me that Willy had saved the world."

"Alberdle?"

"Albertle. Professor Einstein, of course."

I tried to swallow but my throat was dry. My next question was almost a croak: "Mrs. Petersen, how did your husband save the world?" She stared into my eyes intently for several seconds, measuring me carefully.

"I suppose the story is long, though I remember it all like yesterday. But it's a secret, one bound up with many promises and some particularly nasty threats."

"Threats? Threats from whom?"

She smiled ironically. "That's a good point, Mr. Knobel. You know, I mailed thank-you notes to everyone who attended the memorial or sent flowers. None of the men who made those threats were on the list. Most are long dead I suppose, and maybe others have forgotten in time. In any case the world is quite different today than forty or fifty years ago. Perhaps Willy had something important to do with these changes. Or at the very least, the world would be a very different place today if it weren't because of Willy."

"I don't know what to say, Mrs. Petersen. It all seems very mysterious."

"Maybe more of an adventure than a mystery, young man," she mused. "But you don't need to say anything if you know how to listen and take notes. You said you were a writer, didn't you?" she teased. "If you come by our house one evening, you can listen, and *I* will talk."

"Would tonight be convenient for you?" I asked, my ass bitten.

It took many, many evenings.

Munich, Germany – *Oktoberfest* 1938

Willy awoke stiff, sore, and very, very cold, his mouth and stomach sour from strong beer and stronger French cigarettes. His legs were cramped and one shoulder and hip throbbed dully after sleeping all night without shifting position. As he inched himself upright, there was a whooshing in his ears and Willy's head spun round like a top, his eyeballs headed in the opposite direction. *Whoa, give it another minute.*

Burying his head deep in the grimy pillow afforded some temporary sense of equilibrium, but he was reluctant to try sitting up again. At least not yet. On this Monday morning he was lying fully dressed in Friday's clothes, and even with his overcoat as a blanket and his woolen scarf wrapped round his head, his fingers and toes were numb in the unheated room. Stumbling home from the beerhall last night, it was probably fortunate he didn't try to light the coalgas jet on the tiny wall heater. He would have set himself and the entire student hostel ablaze.

None of his three roommates had made it back to the hostel. Their cots were empty, and if it appeared they'd been slept in, well, that was the way they always looked. Willy supposed this could be a good or bad sign depending on where his friends wound up, however he was sure to hear outlandish stories about the women they'd conquered last night: older women, married women, acrobatic women, or multiple women. Women who always materialized magically moments after the group broke up for the night. Everyone would offer something colorful to explain his absence. Needless to say, all the tales would be good, and as each was recounted, successive stories would evolve to outdo the preceding one. Incredible stuff maybe, but captivating to a small-town boy. *Certainly more interesting than the truth*, Willy smiled weakly to himself.

On the way home last night Willy had been stopped twice by city police, pushed around, berated, and sent packing with some ill-defined warning about better behavior.

"*Junge*, puppy, where are you off to? What kind of German are you? Where do you live? *Himmel*, he smells like a gypsy. You're an embarrassment to the Reich. I know how to sober you up." They circled around him shouting questions and insults, poking him with their batons, making him even dizzier. He'd been too drunk to be afraid, but embarrassed enough to not raise a stink. The police were just doing their jobs he supposed. With *Oktoberfest* in full swing, they certainly had their hands full. And the police were everywhere, patrolling alongside the brown-shirt *Sicherheitsdienst*, the *SD*, a junior branch of the *SS*, Hitler's personal army, and the *Gestapo*, the *secret* state police. The SD's job was to enforce Nazi party rule on the streets.

If his new friends, who seemed quite incapable of keeping their mouths shut, had run afoul of the same patrols, there's a good chance they ended their weekend in a cell, if they were lucky, or beaten and unconscious in the gutter somewhere between the *Rathaus* and the hostel. Willy had fled the *Biergarten* when a brawl erupted in front of the band platform, not so much from fear, but for the need to escape the noise and confusion. As he headed out the door, his friends were joining the melee. He hadn't felt afraid, just tired and disconnected. He was sure he wasn't missed.

As his body slowly reanimated, he realized that his throat was raw, doubtless from all the shouting and singing; though he seemed to recall a bout of explosive vomiting sometime on…Saturday afternoon. As further evidence, a very unpleasant sensation lingered in back of his palate and up into his nose. A bruised knee reminded him about a tumble from atop a wooden dining table where he was attempting to recreate a Bavarian folk dance. That must have been Saturday night, he was almost sure.

These sensations were unexpected and worrisome. Beer in Wisconsin somehow didn't seem as potent, and the American recreation of *Oktoberfest* tamer. Willy had never smoked a cigarette until last Thursday night, but even now had a deep craving for one. The student crowd in Milwaukee was loud and raucous and something to avoid, but this...this was something far beyond anything he'd ever imagined.

Die Gedanken sind frei, they had sung: thoughts are free! But this morning any thought came with a heavy cost. The thought of food made Willy retch; the thought of standing made him nauseous; and the thought of his first meeting tomorrow with Professor Wagner and his staff filled him with apprehension and dread.

Cross Sections

Over the last few days he'd put off thinking about school: well, he had to admit, that wasn't really true. He had completely forgotten about school. Four days reserved for sightseeing and relaxation: that was the original idea. But since his arrival in Munich the previous Thursday, he'd seen the train station, the hostel, and the smoky, dank insides of a half dozen beer gardens and beer halls. He and his new friends slept all morning in strangers' apartments and had sang and drank and talked and drank all afternoon and night, every night. He assumed they must have classes and lectures to attend but no one mentioned such trivial matters. *Beer* was their encompassing philosophy, one had proclaimed, and their science, too. Beer halls were the laboratories and endless arguments about which served the best brew led to bloody fistfights as readily as any left-wing, right-wing street confrontation. Beer to stave off the lingering summer heat in the daytime, and beer with schnapps to fight off the cool autumn nights.

Arrival at the climax of the *Fest*, plunked Willy in the midst of the annual, nation-wide binge, though his new drinking comrades assured him that among students, *Oktoberfest* lasted year round; or at least as long as one of them still had pocket money from *Vati und Mutti* or textbooks that could be hocked. If puritanical restraint was really the new by-word in Germany then his friends and their friends had made it a mission to compensate for any general increase in sobriety.

Willy had set aside some clothes for his debut tomorrow at the university, but he definitely needed a bath. Lying in his bed, he thought he smelled vomit and hoped it was in his own nose and not on his clothes. He hadn't thought to inquire about arrangements for laundry.

There were no bathing facilities in the hostel. The nearest public shower bath was at the university's athletic center. But to get there would require him to sit up, stand, and walk a mile across the city, in the bright sun. *Lie still for just a few more minutes*, he told himself.

Free thinking and free talking. In bits and pieces and intermingled with singing and mindless carousing, Willy recalled snatches of endless shouted discussions over the last several days: pro-nationalist, pro-Communist, atheist, and moralist, anarchist, and pacifist. Willy had noticed that German students seemed reticent and close until they got into a beer hall. There, everyone had strong opinions and seemed almost desperate to express them loudly, albeit in anonymity.

Willy and his new best friend Walther, a history major and self-proclaimed social pundit, had held court at a large table in the back corner of the *Hofbrauhaus* with a constant turnover of people and a continual flow of ideas, some strikingly naïve, others stunningly profound. Every speaker had his detractors, indeed many of his fellow drinkers considered it their role to attack, oppose, and assail every idea regardless its proponent or position. The audience was more patient with babbling drunks than with more sober types. The more lucid and well-spoken the argument, the louder and more riotous the objections. If the ideas couldn't be readily debunked then the attack became personal:

"How can such a small man have such big ideas?"

"*Liebchen*, come back when you grow up!"

Others were deathly serious, presenting points like cold-blooded lawyers, sarcastic and even threatening if someone tried to make light of their opinions: "Just you wait," "You'll see," or "You'll get yours!"

One major topic was British Prime Minister Chamberlain's meeting two weeks before, here in Munich with Herr Hitler. It didn't matter what anyone thought about *Der Führer*, the Englishman was universally derided and despised as a prissy, weak fool.

Walther provided running commentary and translation when Willy's fluent German failed. His fellow drinkers and philosophers came from all over the country and when drunk all lapsed back to local dialects. Of course their mothers couldn't have understood many of the worst and even Walther had trouble. After one particularly adamant diatribe by a pudgy, balding, and unintelligible student, Walther leaned over to Willy.

"I can't be sure, Willy. This fellow here, one Hermann Müller from Münster, either believes Chancellor Hitler is the anti-Christ or the Second Coming of Christ," Walther shouted directly into Willy's ear. "I can't tell what he's getting at, but if he's from Münster, he's a farmer of pigs and probably a fornicator of pigs as well. There's pig shit between his toes and between his ears, too! I can smell it from here!" Everyone within earshot oinked their agreement and then the *oinking* spread around the hall like a wave until even the band stopped playing and started squealing. Müller from Münster ran from the hall, hands over his ears, like a madman pursued by demons. Three hundred people broke into derisive laughter, though few had any idea what it was all about.

Walther craved an audience and had singled out Willy at the hostel as a fresh face and an unsophisticated American who lacked schooling in continental philosophy, politics, and low living. In the first few hours

Walther had told Willy his entire life story, or at least a life story, since even befuddled by beer, Willy thought Walther's stories were mostly fiction. No one wanted to admit who they really were, few even had last names, and when asked about themselves, however innocently, they quickly changed subjects or recounted stories so off-the-wall that anyone could tell they weren't true.

Likewise, no one *wanted* to know much about anyone else. As a foreigner and recent arrival, Willy thought his new acquaintances might be interested in where he came from and what he was doing in Germany. But few such questions were asked. Older Germans he'd been brought up with home in Wisconsin could be very close, but Willy thought there was something else here. Wariness, perhaps maybe fear of something.

Among jumbled memories Willy could remember girls seated at the table, blond, brunette, short, and tall, but mostly quiet, sensible to the difficulties and dangers of trying to be heard over the clamor of shouts, singing, table-pounding, om-paah music, and crashing dishes. Some wore these incredibly tight dresses and Willy found himself uncontrollably aroused, the table hiding his discomfiture. But these visions would no sooner appear than they'd be whisked away, before he had a chance to even attempt to talk to them, difficult as that might be amid the oppressive noise of the hall. This morning all that remained was a single, homogenized image of bright red lips, pale, creamy skin, short blond hair, and deep blue eyes. Had there really been a girl like that at his table last night, he wondered? What happened to her? Where did she go and what did she do? Who was she with right now? *Will I see her again*?

Since Willy arrived the week before, the drinking, debating, and other debauchery had gone on non-stop with an intensity Willy had only witnessed on football homecoming weekends back in Wisconsin. His father was an elder in the German-American community around Wausau and Ringle and projected an image of temperance and responsibility that reflected deep-rooted Lutheran ethos. Home-brewed beer was an indulgence limited to special occasions and then consumed only in stern moderation, with no philosophical or scientific implications. Prohibition was repealed while Willy was an undergraduate. Nothing like that had apparently inhibited his German peers.

Four years of undergraduate chemistry studies at Marquette University in Milwaukee had afforded Willy a brief glimpse of a wilder side of life, but this, Munich, was almost otherworldly. Leastwise during

Oktoberfest, everyone here seemed to be enjoying himself or herself immensely, though they must be somehow immune to hangovers. Willy certainly wasn't enjoying the aftermath of a four-day binge and without clearer recollections it was hard to calculate a balance of cost and benefit. And there were supposedly four days left to go of the *official* celebration!

Regardless, the first installment payment was now due in full. Willy slowly sat up, feet flat on the floor, hands on knees to steady himself. His vision tunneled and he could only concentrate on things directly in front. He really didn't want to risk turning his head. Lining up on the door latch, he stood and covered the distance in three shaky steps. Beyond the door was the deserted hallway with a filthy toilet at the end, its door twisted off its hinges. Ten steps and he was in. After relieving himself, he slowly made his way back to his room, collected his toiletry kit, and headed for the stairs. Both hands on the banisters, he descended one step at a time out onto the street. The bright midmorning sunshine was painful at first, but the cool, dry air helped immeasurably to clear his head.

Willy teetered precariously at the first two intersections, where he had to stop, watch and consider the brisk Monday morning traffic in front of the main railway station, the *Hauptbahnhof*. He just managed to make it across unscathed, but within a few blocks he had begun to feel...better. At least he would survive and could safely take some interest in the rest of the world and this new city.

The sidewalks were crowded with weekday shoppers, street vendors, and loiterers as Willy made his way through the *Maximiliansplatz* on his way to the university, north of the city center where the gothic *Rathaus*, Munich's ornate city hall, towered over *Marienplatz*. He'd spent a week at a scientific conference in Chicago and he'd explored Manhattan one afternoon while waiting for his steamship's departure for Hamburg. To that small-town boy, everything was interesting. But Munich was unlike anything he'd even imagined. All the churches in Milwaukee would fit comfortably inside just the *Frauenkirche* cathedral. And its exotic onion-shaped domed spires made Willy think of pictures he'd seen of Russia or Poland.

Germany seemed to Willy a country of unresolved paradox. During the train trip south from Hamburg he'd seen castles and walled estates suggesting great wealth and power. At one unpaved railroad crossing a skinny man held his bony horse and a wagon piled with roofing thatch; at the next crossing, a long streamlined overpass carried four wide lanes of the new *Autobahn*, already crowded with large, fast cars.

Stations had been crowded with ragged, crippled veterans begging for food and packed with foreigners and emigrants on their way out of Germany with their families, all their worldly goods in boxes, trunks, and suitcases tied with twine, bursting at every seam. Willy had witnessed a shoving match and fistfight between a group of waiting passengers and the railway police, indicative of the desperation that prevailed. Fellow passengers aboard the train looked up only for a moment before returning to their newspapers or books.

Some things stood out that were strikingly familiar in a weird way. The marquee of one cinema announced that *Meuterie auf der Bounty* was held over for another week and Clark Gable's face stared down at him from a twenty-meter wide billboard. In a country where *Germanness* was so important, fashionable shops promised the latest in Paris couture and American cosmetics.

Midway along the *Theatinerstrasse*, the gold-on-red sign of F.W. Woolworth and Company was identical to the one on Maple Street in Milwaukee and the huge multi-story department stores in Munich rivaled anything he'd seen in New York and Chicago. While he hoped to see inside the churches and experience a performance at the Opera House, things that were definitively German, in the confusion and rush of his arrival, Gable and Woolworth were comfortable benchmarks that made him feel less the hayseed. It's a big city, he told himself, with more differences between Milwaukee and Chicago than between Chicago and Munich. Except, that is, for the history and traditions of an *ancient* city, which were apparent on nearly every block.

But across the street from eight-hundred year old churches, ultramodern apartment and business complexes sprouted as part of vast programs to clear slums and provide better quality housing for everyday Germans. Change was another by-word.

Germany's universities were respected the world over, but students ignored their studies and top professors and scientists were all moving to America and England. Yet adjacent to the university's library stood the *Amerika-Institut*, the Roosevelt Library, and Munich offices of the Rockefeller Foundation.

German newspapers were full of reports of foreign conspiracy that seemed a little paranoid, yet the country was obviously in the process of reasserting itself after two decades of dominance by France and England.

There seemed to be so much hope, countered by a sense of trepidation or uneasiness. "The new Germany is exciting…like a train with no brakes," someone had said last night.

Rumors of war abounded, but with no precise sense of whom the enemy might be. The papers railed against everyone, the Dutch, the Czechs, the French, the Poles. According to the papers and many of his fellow beer drinkers, the common factor was an international cabal of Jewish bankers who had their hands in everyone's pocket and were rich from people's labor and sweat. Willy kept to himself his thought that this was an odd proposition from these middle and upper class German students, themselves unfamiliar with *labor* as a form of livelihood. Willy had come to adulthood during the American Depression and had tried to inject into the argument that it was *all* bankers and not just Jewish ones who were stealing and hoarding peoples' monies, but he was laughed and shouted down, and after this episode he kept silent and drunk. "How can you be so naïve?" someone had asked sympathetically.

Regardless the political rhetoric, the everyday, working German took more interest in the giant national lottery, with its promise of instant wealth, than he did in international politics or the tumult and intrigue in Berlin. Their northern cousins had always seen themselves as separate and superior to Bavarians, who were whispered to lack culture and certain sophistication.

But as he walked across the city, he had to be impressed. Munich was beautiful. In early autumn, the landscaped gardens and palaces were like something out of a storybook. Everything was so clean. If he were careful to balance the temptations and opportunities, this will be heaven on earth, he told himself.

Willy was blocked for several minutes at the next intersection as a large troop of uniformed young boys marched down the avenue toward the *Englischer Garten*, Munich's main park. A small tinny brass band led the way playing what Willy recognized to be the German National Anthem. The boys were singing along with the music, but many of the voices were still changing, falsetto one minute and baritone the next. One moment children, the next young men.

Willy had been active in the Boy Scouts until he was fourteen. These uniforms were similar, but these boys seemed so very serious. No smiles in anticipation of a day in the park, none of the joking or shoving you'd expect from free-spirited American boys. Most looked straight ahead, watching and listening intently for commands from their troop leaders. *"Deutschland, Deutschland über alles!"* was the refrain. *"Für das Deutsche Vaterland!"* The leaders, tall young men wearing the same uniforms, sang loudest of all, their united voices reaching far beyond the street, resonating off surrounding buildings.

When the troop had passed, Willy and the other people who had held at the crosswalk went about their businesses. He studied them closely. What kind of German would *he* become over the next three years? The uniformed patriot, the besotted student, the detached burgher, or the non-citizen, one of the foreigners or non-Christians stuck somewhere on the fringes of German society and life? He could already sense an underlying structure that required men and women to shoehorn themselves into one of these roles. Indeed someone had told him that in Germany for years after the Great War, shoes were available only in odd sizes: 5, 7, 9, 11, and 13. That meant only half of the people had comfortable shoes and Willy wondered whether the major challenge for Germans was unchanged: making sure who fit comfortably into this new German social order.

What other roles might there be? Willy suspected Professor Wagner would present him with another. Hopefully, his beer-sour breath, week-old underclothes, bleary eyes, and hopelessly nonchalant American attitude wasn't going to formulate the Professor's opinion and plans. *Well, too late now. If I just get rid of the smell…*

Professor Ernst Wagner came from the old school, before the Great War, back to the era of Bismarck and Kaiser Wilhelm the Second. Impeccably dressed in an elegant suit with wing-collar shirt, waistcoat, and watch chain, his back remained straight and his build thin. He was the quintessential Prussian, precise in his speech, commanding in bearing. But at seventy-two he was on a slow decline.

Willy's researchship had been arranged through an ancient family connection, though his undergraduate advisors had strongly suggested Willy solicit and consider other offers. Things are very bad in Germany and getting worse, they said. All valuable, original work was done in the United States nowadays. But Willy knew his own predilection and his strength as a researcher underscored his determination to go to original sources. Willy read and absorbed everything he could find that Professor Wagner and his students had written and published over the years. While Professor Wagner's groundbreaking experiments were first reported in the 1890's, his reputation for thoroughness, accuracy, and scientific integrity had carried forward for fifty years. While the Professor's primary field of study dovetailed perfectly with Willy's interest in thermodynamics, the Professor hadn't published research reports of special merit for a number of years. But such things had become difficult to follow, as the German scientific community was increasingly isolated from the rest of the world. Though some professional and career risk was inherent in his German *adventure*, Willy hoped to learn much at the great man's feet. For the next three years, Professor Wagner would wield inordinate influence on Willy's professional and personal life. Beyond obtaining his doctorate, letters of recommendation from the Professor would say everything about if and where Willy would work. He'd heard from other academic contacts that Professor Wagner was formal but approachable. The university's facilities and laboratories were also reputed to be among the best in the world.

"We are quite pleased to have you with us, young man," the Professor offered after formal introductions and family greetings were politely passed along. "It is difficult these days to capture the interest of young men in science. There are many distractions."

"Munich seems such a thriving city," Willy suggested. "Everyone I've met is a student."

The Professor replied with some acid. "They may call themselves students, but few are enrolled in the university and even fewer attend lectures regularly. This is a national shame. The brightest of them are drawn to the military schools, which are very popular right now, however I hear very little time there is spent on science or even mechanics, mostly on marching and political indoctrination. I have to wonder where skilled artillery officers will come from if this is allowed to continue.

"The majority of this city's students use their status as an excuse for endless celebration and drinking," the Professor said, looking a little more closely at Willy. As he peered intently at Willy through his monocle, his *Einglas*, the Professor's thin, pointed nose went up slightly. Willy wavered a little but managed to maintain the appearance of attentiveness. Despite his cold shower bath yesterday afternoon, Willy was certain he still carried the stale smell of the beer hall with him, even if his bloodshot eyes didn't give him away. *I'm screwed.*

But the Professor continued: "Several of my senior students have sought positions with I.G. Farben and other chemical companies, abandoning their graduate studies. I suspect they are aware of the history of the last war, when jobs in those critical industries shielded young men from conscription. I am sure they will all aspire to be highly competent technicians," he said with undisguised irony.

"For the most part, the rest of the lot is worthless: political duties come ahead of lecture attendance; no one has enough time or interest to complete laboratory exercises.

"The current political leadership emphasizes the physical over the mental, empiricism over scholarship. They have small use for formal academic training and I am much afraid that German dominance in chemistry and other disciplines will soon be lost forever.

"As it stands, you will be my only assistant this year, Herr Petersen. Since you are not a German citizen, I expect you to remain free of *political* responsibilities. I consider myself fortunate, though you might not feel the same. This will mean much hard and tedious work for you." Willy stood passively, unsure how to respond.

Professor Wagner was friendly again, and smiled ironically. "I find that it is no longer safe to have me working round the lab. Indeed former assistants, at my daughter's insistence, barred my entrance unless all the equipment was shut down and stored away," he said affably. Willy tried not to react outwardly, unsure whether the Professor might be sensitive to such treatment, but the Professor continued to smile.

"I admit to becoming forgetful and clumsy at times. You must forgive the weaknesses and foibles of an old man."

"Herr Professor, I sincerely hope you'll come to understand how much I appreciate the opportunity to work with you and to learn from you. However I can be of assistance. Where can I begin?"

"Herr Petersen, your letters and thesis proposal suggested that your primary interest is organic chemical purification, especially those related to metallic compounds used for dyes and pigments. These have always been research and commercial fields where Germany leads the world. Most of my laboratory's work over the last ten years has focused on this area, but I am afraid that our experimental notes and reports are in considerable disarray. Perhaps if you could spend some weeks going over them with me, we can identify the best point for you to begin your independent thesis research. No need to reinvent the wheel. Creativity is the keystone of scholarship, but the foundation stems from the past. In the last twenty years, I suppose I've become more foundation than keystone, but let us find out where you may also fit into that edifice.

"If you can help me put my correspondence in order, it will also provide means to establish precedence for any of your own work that follows. I have been loath to attend scientific meetings over the last years because I have fallen so far behind. In a few months perhaps we can make the rounds in Berlin and Heidelberg and introduce you to some of my senior colleagues. We are a dying breed in Germany but need to work together in order to keep the science moving forward. Germany is losing its dominance in chemistry but must continue to contribute. It is important for the history of the nation."

"I can begin today if that is possible, Herr Professor," Willy said. "If you can show me some space where I might work."

"For now I suggest we have the porters move a table into this office, so we can consult frequently. Have no fears; recently I've tried to work at home most days and rarely come to the university or the Chemistry Institute. My fellow faculty members are obsessed with political intrigues for which I have little patience. They spend their time deciding appointments and directorships based on a man's politics rather than his success and skill as a researcher or teacher. It's nonsense and I'll have nothing to do with it.

"As I mentioned, there is little demand for me as a lecturer these days. On rare occasions when undergraduates have shown interest in my dusty ideas, their numbers are so few that we meet at my home or in this office. Regardless, what used to seem a brisk walk from my house near the *Englisher Gartens*, has become a tedious and exhausting cross-country journey most mornings. You will have as much peace and privacy as you need in this office or the adjacent laboratory. Treasure it. It is at a premium in this city nowadays."

Retrieving an envelope from a desk drawer, he passed it to Willy. The Professor was apparently uncomfortable and for the first time didn't meet Willy eye-to-eye. "I have prepared a note for you to carry to the bursar's office. I am sorry if your stipend seems trifling; I hope it will suffice. The current government has cut back funding to the Chemistry Institute. You have found suitable and adequate lodging and board?"

"Yes, Herr Professor. Quite adequate, thank you," Willy lied.

"Excellent. If you will fetch the porter from the gatehouse, we will see if we can arrange for your furniture."

On this basis, Willy began sorting through the Professor's notes and data, as the Professor described their rough organization. Over the next several weeks, Willy made significant progress. While few reports and articles for scientific journals had been authored, notes had been kept in careful order, each experiment's records bundled together and tied with red ribbon.

Willy's first task was to organize the Professor's correspondence. Everyday letters arrived from all over the world asking for advice or comments on experimental results or new theories. When the Professor visited his office, Willy would quickly and efficiently review the more important inquiries, taking notes on the Professor's comments, suggesting details of responses, and later typewriting letters for the Professor to sign. Replies were sent to America, Russia, England, Japan, India, and even South Africa. In his nominal retirement, Professor Wagner was still an 'Authority,' his earlier work cited frequently in new scientific papers.

Willy's tasks were far more than secretarial: solid comprehension of the science was crucial to the job at hand. It fell to him to decide which ideas were relevant and which theories deserved comment or action. As he mined his way through the laboratory's stacks of notes and data, he was able to segregate work into collections that might form the basis for future publications. It was readily apparent that much of the laboratory's work was still valuable and some groundbreaking. The Professor himself showed little interest in publishing scientific papers, but Willy convinced him that some of the data needed to be shared to help researchers and students in other parts of the world and to uphold the reputation of the Chemistry Institute. Willy began to draft a series of articles and worked with the Professor to tie them all together logically.

But during that first month, Willy observed a further decline in the Professor's health and mental acumen. Usually sharp and insightful, sometimes he was especially forgetful and would suddenly become detached and distant for minutes at a time. He always arrived dressed perfectly with his bowler hat and umbrella at hand, his white hair parted and moustache combed with Prussian precision. But one day, with considerable embarrassment, he admitted to Willy trouble that morning finding his own office, and how he relied heavily on his daughters to take charge of his buttons and studs. Then, beginning in early November, one of the widowed Professor's two daughters, Gabrielle or Elise, would accompany him to the office and return later for the walk home. Usually they would not enter the building, obviously to keep from further embarrassing their father. Through the window Willy observed that both girls were very pretty with dark hair and stylish clothes.

He played a mental game and tried to guess what they were like, creating an imaginary personae for each. From a distance at least, they didn't act like young girls at all, but rather seemed very serious, confident, and mature. The elder daughter, Gabrielle, was taller and elegant and sometimes perhaps a little impatient with her father. Outside the window one morning, Willy caught Gabrielle lighting a cigarette after her father had gone inside. Willy found this very exotic and sophisticated.

Elise Wagner was sixteen years old, but sometimes appeared to treat her father like her own child, fussing with his buttons and scarf, taking inventory of his gloves, *Einglas*, books, files, walking stick, or umbrella before she would kiss him on the cheek and release him to the world.

Truth be told, Willy could have found some ready excuse in the first month to meet either girl and introduce himself. But despite his curiosity, he was embarrassed by his own appearance. There were few enough opportunities to keep his clothes clean or even to shave properly. He needed a haircut and a shoeshine and knew he looked like a scarecrow from back home on the farm. In his imaginary world, Gabrielle would look down on him with haughty disdain; Elise would cluck at him with a cold critical eye. In either case, he would be so humiliated that he'd run away and hide. He took to watching for the daughters every morning to refresh his vision at a safe distance, but mostly to be forewarned if they ever came inside. He had an escape plan ready, at least in his head.

In the real world beyond the comfort and quiet of the laboratory, Willy had other problems of his own. The bursar's office was perpetually shuttered, and Willy was loath to loiter around the entrance along with several dozen similarly concerned and hungry senior students. His father had provided several hundred dollars to tide him over, but too much of that money had gone to buy beer for utter strangers during his first week. He vowed to make the remainder last at least until the end of February when university classes would break for several months and he might find more time to camp at the bursar's office. Every week or so rumor would spread that the office would open on such a day at such a time. Things would look hopeful and of course the disappointment was therefore more profound. And the group that gathered each time was a hotbed of gossip and sometimes-delirious opinion on university politics.

Lurid stories circulated concerning the famous Werner Heisenberg, winner of the 1932 Nobel Prize for Physics. Heisenberg and his friends expected an appointment by the Reich Ministry of Education to head the Physics Institute in Munich replacing old Professor Sommerfeld. But there was some sort of controversy. Current 'wisdom' held that Heisenberg was some sort of demon, knowing what can't be known, privy to cabalistic secrets and rituals. Heisenberg was accused by militant students of being a master of 'Jewish science,' a branch Willy wryly thought to include *anything* drunken undergraduates couldn't comprehend.

While one mean-spirited faction demanded that Heisenberg be detained or deported, others whispered that Heisenberg was under the direct protection of the SS and *Heinrich Himmler himself!* The Student League waffled back and forth, first condemning then supporting Heisenberg. The Physics Institute was in total disarray.

Everywhere in Nazi Germany, ambitious academics were drooling over prospects of promotion to the positions vacated by recent émigrés. The University of Munich was predominantly Catholic and there had been a dearth of non-Germans and Jews holding civil appointments there in any case. But men who felt they had suffered, particularly during the Depression, and had supported and voted for the current government now demanded their reward. They were impatient and increasingly hostile to the remnants of old guard authority. Standing quietly to the side, Willy sometimes could not distinguish between these men, once serious scholars and budding scientists, and the loud rabble that filled the streets and beerhalls every afternoon and night.

Even after six weeks, this was all Willy really knew of Germany and Germans. He worked sixteen hours a day, collapsing on his cot at the hostel, often with an empty stomach, oblivious to the comings and goings of his roommates. He'd eat a single daily meal at the canteen during the week and purchase a half loaf of black bread to tide him over the weekends. No more cigarettes or beer. Willy learned which alleys and neighborhoods had shops with the best deals, husbanding his money like a miser.

Willy also discovered which back streets to navigate to avoid trouble spots between his room and the university. And there was often trouble, yelling heard down alleyways, sometimes followed by screaming, sometimes by silence. Small fires burned. Windows were smashed and shops looted, apparently at random. At night in particular, he sensed a common frenzy, an almost hysterical feeling that Armageddon neared. Men shouted instead of speaking, quick to come to blows over the slightest disrespect; free will seemed to be lost; there was no self-consciousness. Apprehension and fear were palpable. Away from the main plazas and other gathering places, thousands of people hid themselves. When absolutely necessary they walked the streets with heads down, willing themselves to be invisible. Their neighborhoods appeared deserted day and night.

The successful and wealthy among them vanished. Familiar figures in the community left on annual vacations and never returned. But the poor had few options. The Nazi's Emigration Tax would leave them with nothing in a new land. How would they be better off? This too will pass.

Willy saw all this like a photograph with no perspective and little hint whether this was a normal or abnormal state of affairs. It was not his business and hadn't touched him personally. He grew up no more or less anti-Semitic than any mid-western American but he had witnessed the upheavals of the Depression in America, the tent cities, the WPA camps, lines at soup kitchens. Was Munich different from Milwaukee? Except that Milwaukee hadn't lost a war and been stripped to bare bones by reparation payments and the exodus of a significant portion of the national wealth. Everyone was quick to point this out to Willy.

Strong leadership and collective sacrifice was saving America. Were things in Germany really so different? In contrast to America's itinerant rabble, he couldn't ignore the thousands of clean-cut, uniformed Hitler Youth parading double-time through the city, helping with public works, and projecting an image of self-discipline and dedication that begged admiration.

When mob rule seemed ready to prevail at any moment, the National Socialists, the Nazis, were elected democratically, and then *had* effected change.

The unavoidable finally happened, though it wasn't because of any failure of will on his part. If he could have chosen the time and place Willy would have felt he had done his best under the circumstances. A modicum of pride might have been salvaged.

Fräulein Gabrielle had walked the Professor to the institute one morning, arriving like clockwork at ten. Willy had been busy since just after dawn and sitting at his table with a view down the avenue, he watched them strolling arm in arm under the leaf-bare trees along the sidewalk. Professor Wagner appeared to be struggling a little and the pair paused to rest several times over the last hundred meters. As was their routine, Gabrielle left her father with a kiss on the cheek at the foot of the stone steps. This time she watched intently as the Professor made his way slowly up the stairs. As her father passed inside, Willy, standing back from the window where he couldn't be seen, saw her shake her head, turn, and walk back up the street.

Willy met the Professor at the office door and helped him off with his coat. He was panting and shaking, exhausted from the stairs.

"I must apologize, Herr Petersen. I know we planned to complete the final draft of the paper for the *Physical Chemistry Journal*, but I'm not feeling very well today. My daughters tried to keep me at home this morning, but I insisted on coming in any case. A mistake perhaps, but I can't allow them to believe I'm totally under their control."

"Your daughters are only concerned for your health, Professor."

"I know and I'm grateful. But I haven't forgotten that we have a submission deadline Friday and must complete the review today."

"Professor, I'm sure the editors would understand. I can send them a telegram asking for a few more days."

"I won't have that! We have deadlines and schedules for a reason and I will not take advantage of their tolerance in regards to weak and helpless old men."

"Perhaps we'll be able to finish the review tomorrow and arrange for a railway courier to carry the package to Berlin instead of using the post."

"Your suggestions are excellent as usual, Herr Petersen, but in truth, I can't guarantee I'll feel better tomorrow. The opposite is more likely the case. So I have a suggestion of my own. Collect all the papers and materials we need and we'll return to my home and work together in my study. Bring your typewriter, too, and when we finish the review, you can type the final version and I'll proofread as you complete each page. My daughter Lise will force me to drink endless cups of herbal tea, wrapped like an Egyptian mummy in quilts, sweating in front of the roaring fireplace. You'll stay for tea and dinner and we'll finish this evening. I can't promise you a fancy meal on short notice, but I hope you don't mind.

"I beg you to ignore the ministrations of my daughters. I'll assure you that it will be much more embarrassing for me than for you. Perhaps together we can reestablish male primacy in my house, at least for one afternoon."

The Professor was obviously struggling with the idea of letting a junior colleague penetrate this corner of his life, but his approach was self-deprecating and disarming. Willy had been grasping for some reason to refuse or an alternative that might buy him time to bathe and shave, but once Professor Wagner had made up his mind, resistance was useless. And he caught Willy's glance at the heavy typewriter.

"Why don't you run down to the porter and ask him to fetch us a taxi? My reputation as a slave master aside, I wouldn't expect you to carry the typewriter all the way to the *Englischer Garten.*"

The Wagner home was a formidable stone edifice in a row of equally elegant townhouses that faced out across *Königenstrasse* to the *Englischer Garten* and its Greek Pavilion. As he stood on the steps, typewriter cradled in both arms, Willy turned and looked across the board open field, covered with a light snowfall. Even on this nippy November morning dozens of people were taking their daily walks or riding horses along the bridle paths.

The Professor was fumbling for his key, forgetting that he no longer had a need to carry one. Fräulein Elise heard the commotion and came to open the door, admitting a parade of the Professor, Willy hugging his typewriter, and the taxi driver bearing a large box of papers and books. While Elise hurried off to find money for the taxi, the Professor led them down the hallway to his ground floor study. With the typewriter safely on the corner of the massive oak desk, Willy followed the Professor back to the hallway to hang their coats on the ornate rack near the door. The hangers were the spikes of deer antlers. The floors were polished limestone cut to expose fossil imprints. Elise had reappeared with silver coins for the driver. She was dressed neatly in an old-fashioned skirt and blouse with a scarf around her head and rags sticking from her pockets. It was apparent that she'd been cleaning house. Willy smiled mischievously to himself. *I'll score that a tie*, he thought.

A voice called from the top of the stairs that ran to the first floor from the hallway. "Lise, what's going on?" Willy looked up and saw

Cross Sections

Fräulein Gabrielle at the top of the stairs, bleary-eyed, in a sheer nightgown, back-lit with sunlight from a window behind her. Lise answered without looking up.

"It's all right, Gabi. Vati's come home early. Everything's fine." Before Willy could look away, Gabrielle caught his eye and smiled at him, oblivious to the fact that a stranger was seeing her undressed. Her stare was intense and when she finally broke off and disappeared, Willy grimaced and mentally kicked himself. Fräulein Gabrielle, nearly naked, had made Willy self-conscious again about his ragged clothing.

"Thank you, Lise," the Professor said as his daughter helped him with his heavy coat. "I thought it would be sensible to work at home today. It's unusually cold in the office, so I've brought along Herr Petersen and we expect to work through the day. He has been invited to stay for dinner. Please ask Erna to set an extra place."

"Of course, Vati…Herr Petersen, it's very nice to meet you at last," Lise offered her hand in the fashion of a man. Her handshake was firm. "My father says many good things about you and your work."

"Don't embarrass the man, Lise dear."

"In any case, Herr Petersen, we all appreciate the help you give him."

"It's my pleasure, Fräulein Wagner."

"Vati, may I bring you tea? Herr Petersen? And I'll fetch your slippers and lap blanket. I'll have Erna light the fire in the study. Herr Petersen, if you'll excuse me." And she was gone, rushing back to the kitchen and pantry. As Willy and the Professor settled down to work in the study, the housekeeper rebuilt and lit the fireplace. Lise returned with an armful of woolen blankets, slippers, and a hot water bottle. She fussed over her father for several minutes, stripping him of his suit coat, replacing it with a heavy smoking jacket, and bundling him up as he sat in his big leather desk chair. She ignored all his protests and at last stood back looking critically at her work, decided that it was the best she could do for now, and retired from the study without comment.

The Professor sighed, "Shall we start again?"

Late that afternoon, after a pleasant lunch of thick soup and exquisitely fresh bread, Professor Wagner dozed while Willy clacked away at his typewriter. Finishing a page, Willy sat back for a moment, stretching and twisting in his chair. For the first time he looked around the study. It was wondrous and telling. Shelves were stacked and packed with books, not just about science and mathematics, but contemporary fiction, Greek and Roman classics, and Elizabethan plays. His eyes came across copies of Harriet Beecher Stowe and Mark Twain, the latter in German translation. A giant Marconi all-band radio rested on a heavy side table near the desk. Everything was perfectly organized and neat, quite unlike the Professor's office at the Chemistry Institute.

Filling one set of shelves was a collection of rocks and crystals. One wall was covered with framed certificates, diplomas, and awards from technical societies all over Europe. The oaken floor was partly covered with lush, dark red China carpets. On the mantelpiece, under an Impressionist landscape depicting the high Alps, were family photographs of the Professor's wife and eldest daughter, perhaps four or five years-old at the time. Frau Wagner was very beautiful, obviously much younger than her husband, with dark hair and eyes. Willy could see where the daughters inherited their exotic looks. He'd never asked and the Professor had never volunteered, but Willy wondered whether Frau Wagner might have been French or Spanish. He added that new element to his evolving fantasies about the Professor's daughters.

Throughout the day, Lise sneaked into the study hourly to check that her father was still covered and warm, that the fire was burning properly, and to refill their teacups. Willy had seen and heard no further sign of the older daughter, Gabrielle. Apparently after she had dropped her father at his office before ten o'clock, she'd returned home and gone back to bed. Perhaps she wasn't feeling well either. Gabrielle had materialized like some vision in a movie as she stood at the top of the stairs and Willy stirred uncomfortably at the memory. Before he was carried away by his own daydreams, Lise opened the door and stepped into the study. Smiling at Willy, she moved to rearrange the blankets that had fallen off the Professor's knees. She added a log to the fire and collected the tea service from the desk and side table. As she made to leave, she caught Willy's eye and gestured with her head. Willy pushed back his chair and followed, closing the door quietly behind him.

"You two have been working all day without a break. I think it would be good for my father to nap undisturbed for awhile, if you don't mind. Could you help me move him upstairs to his bedroom?"

"Of course."

Lise reentered the study with Willy behind and shook the Professor's shoulder firmly until he woke. "Vati. Vati. You should go up to your room if you're going to sleep."

"Yes. Yes. Thank you," he said groggily and with Willy and Lise at each elbow, they maneuvered him up the broad stairs to his room.

"Thank you, Herr Petersen," Lise said. "I'll be down in a few minutes." Willy went back to the study.

She returned ten minutes later. "Thank you again, Herr Petersen, not just for today but for all the assistance and support you've given my father over the last month. Since you arrived, my father has shown a renewed enthusiasm for his researches. As you must be aware, his health has not been the best for some time and until recently Gabi and I were afraid he would just sit home, growing more depressed and sullen every day. Most days his mind is clear and he desperately needs stimulation, something you provide that's quite beyond either of us."

"I only need to do my job, Fräulein. The research is compelling in itself. But if it weren't for the Professor, I would be the one who's sullen and depressed. I'm more thankful for the opportunity to be here than you might imagine."

"Thank you then for that sentiment. I don't think my father would be able to express his appreciation; it's not his way. But he thinks about it all the time and talks to us endlessly about you and your work."

"Perhaps you should take a pause yourself. Vati will probably sleep until six o'clock."

"Thank you for an excuse to stretch and walk around outside for a few minutes."

Lise suddenly seemed a little shy. "I was going to suggest that you join us for tea and cake in the dining room."

"Thank you, Fräulein," Willy answered, suddenly in a panic, "but there's still a great deal of work to do."

"Nonsense. Please take a short break," she said and Willy realized there was something else going on here. She read his look. "I admit to selfish reasons. Two of my friends have stopped by and they insist that I introduce you. They threaten never to speak to me again if I refuse, though it's really up to you."

"But Fräulein, I'm hardly presentable. I dressed this morning for the lab. I don't want to embarrass you."

"Don't concern yourself about that for a single second, Herr Petersen. I can assure you that Annamarie and Hannah won't notice and they'll be the ones who embarrass themselves. They're being quite silly. Please join us for a few minutes at least." Willy could see that Lise was uncomfortable.

"For a few minutes. But you'll have to promise not to talk about me after I've gone."

Lise actually blushed, but she recovered quickly and counterattacked with an easy smile. "I won't promise that. If it's really important to you, you'll just have to stay until the end."

His fantasies about Gabrielle and Elise Wagner were whole-cloth creations of his own imagination. He had never spoken to them and had used his own references and limited experience to form their imaginary personae. It somehow hadn't occurred to Willy that Lise was still a teenager. Though she was obviously far more mature than her friends, afternoon tea was not what he might have expected.

Annamarie was the daughter of Professor Schumann, a neighbor and old friend of Professor Wagner. She was short, dimpled, and plump and shook as she laughed. When she blushed she turned red as a beet. Hannah was blond, lean, and athletic. Lise introduced Hannah as the champion runner in school. At first both girls studied Willy like a bug, but later competed with each other for his attention. And Willy responded shamelessly, bowing slightly over their handshakes and pretending to hang on their every word, excited to participate in their girlish game.

He wasn't sure when the dam actually broke, but after a few minutes of formal, adult, and calm discussion, the girls' excited interest got the better of them and questions began to flow, sweeping Willy from one topic to another until he was actually dizzy.

"Is Jean Harlow's hair color natural?"

"Have you ever met a wild Indian?"

"How much does lipstick cost in American stores?"

"How tall are the skyscrapers in New York?"

"Do any movie stars live in your town?"

"Are all American men as tall as you?"

"How many men did Al Capone kill?"

"At what age do American girls get married?"

Sorting through the questions later that night as he lay on his bed, still exhilarated about the day, Willy remembered that while Lise giggled shamelessly at some of Willy's stories, her own questions had been more serious and pointed:

"Are your houses different from ours?"

"Do you have brothers and sisters?"

At first he had tried to answer the girls' questions as simply as possible, even minimizing the differences between America and Germany. He struggled to play the jaded and worldly sophisticate. But after a while, their unbridled interest and attention got to him and he started to spice it up for them. Hannah and Annamarie would giggle about an answer and then whisper conspiratorially before asking another question on a completely different topic. It was the first time in two months that Willy had found himself in the company of women, or of girls in this case. He was light-headed and light-hearted.

At one point he asked after Fräulein Gabrielle: "I hope she's not sick to bed." The two visitors exchanged glances and started to giggle uncontrollably until a terrible look from Lise cut them off like an ax.

"Thank you, Herr Petersen. Yes, I'm afraid Gabi wasn't feeling well earlier, but she'll be up and about for dinner." Hannah choked back another titter and took a sip of her tea. But Annamarie was determined and willing to defy Lise.

Ignoring Lise's unspoken warning, she asked, "Herr Petersen, do American women smoke cigarettes and drink champagne?" Willy's answer was a model of tact and non-committal.

"No more than the German women I've met," Willy equivocated, trying to guess what answer the girls were fishing for. "Champagne is expensive in America and is reserved for special occasions. American women generally prefer gin drinks, like dry martinis." Truthfully, Willy drew this conclusion from the same source the German girls used themselves: Hollywood movies. Neither his mother nor sister would touch the beer his father brewed at home. The Fathers had closely monitored coeds at Catholic Marquette University. Willy only heard rumors about their drinking habits. He realized he might leave the wrong impression.

"In America, like most places, women are expected to behave like ladies…." Now both girls were grinning wickedly. "…That's how they find the good husbands." Silence. What did he say wrong? Willy stole a glance at Lise, who was looking daggers at her friends.

"Did I say something wrong?"

"No, Herr Petersen. There was nothing wrong with your answer," Lise replied, "only with silly questions from silly girls. I hope you will forgive them."

Willy was confused and suddenly self-conscious again. *These girls must be making fun of me. What did I say that's so funny? Or is it because I look funny?* He remembered where he was and whom he was talking to. He was definitely out of bounds. *What is Lise thinking about me?* This question was suddenly very important to him.

Her face was still stern and lips pressed tightly together. *She must think I'm a clown,* he thought. He'd made the mistake of flirting with her friends like a high school boy. *How stupid can I be?* Panic set in again and he spilled a little tea as he clumsily fumbled to finish and excuse himself. He had to get back to work in the study, he claimed.

Back at the desk, he resumed his typing, but found himself squirming in his chair. He felt like a gawky kid who would run and hide when embarrassed by an adult. *I'm the adult,* he tried to remind himself, but all he could think about was finding some way to excuse himself so he wouldn't have to face Fräulein Elise again at dinner. He took a deep breath and rushed ahead with his work and found that if he kept at it, just as fast as possible, his mind wouldn't stray back to the tea party.

After an hour Willy figured that he wasn't going to finish before dinner. The Professor hadn't returned from his nap. Maybe Willy should just say that he would work right through dinner. Frankly that wasn't likely to go over well and he was afraid that the Wagner family might take that as a slight of some sort. *This is all too complicated.*

At precisely six, Lise knocked quietly and opened the door.

"Am I disturbing you?"

"No. No, not at all."

"My father's still asleep and I think it might be best to let him rest until dinner. Does that cause any problems?"

"No, Fräulein, I've made lots of progress. If the Professor can spend some time after dinner reviewing the final draft, we'll finish tonight."

"Is there anything I can do to help? Until you arrived last month, I'd been handling much of my father's correspondence. I'm familiar with the terminology and have become a competent typist. Would it help if I typed while you marked corrections?"

Willy was uncomfortable with the idea, partly from his already injured pride and partly concerned that regardless her motives, she might actually slow things down and close off his avenues of escape. But she simply stood there, hands folded in front, waiting patiently for him to decide. It was easier to accept her suggestion that to keep her waiting while he fabricated a lame excuse.

"It would be very helpful, Fräulein. But I don't want to take you away from your regular activities."

Now she smiled brightly. "As I said, this used to be my regular activity. I would welcome the chance to stay involved. In any case, Frau Erna is busy preparing dinner, and she'd just as soon I was in your way rather than hers. If you'll let me take that seat and show me where you've left off, you can sit in my father's chair."

Willy was doubtful for a moment about usurping the Professor's throne, but the only alternative was to sit right beside Lise. He quickly decided to put the desk between them. Something about this girl made him very nervous and his feelings weren't improved when after several minutes of typing, she interrupted him with a question about one of his conclusions. Her question and instant comprehension of his concise, technical reply left Willy stunned as she went back to the typewriting.

This girl was an enigma, one moment a teenage schoolgirl, the next a competent, serious, and mature young woman. Lise was tall for her age and exceptionally slim, with a long face and sharp nose. Her hair and eyes were dark, not uncommon in southern Germany, but in any group of young German women, she would stand out as unique and striking. You might expect her to be gangly and awkward at sixteen but Willy had noticed that she moved deliberately and held herself very erect whether standing or sitting. Even when he had interrupted her housekeeping chores, Lise was neatly and modestly dressed.

"Excuse me, Herr Petersen. In the third paragraph, do you mean to imply that the reaction was completed to one hundred percent conversion or was allowed to progress until an end-point?" Willy walked around to stand over her.

"The reaction was carried to its end-point. Yes, you're correct. The first interpretation would have been misleading. Thanks. The journal editors might have caught the mistake, but in any case, you've saved us time and trouble." She turned up to him with a measured look and Willy realized that he sounded condescending. He quickly escaped back to his side of the desk.

She's testy, too, he thought to himself. *Wouldn't want to get on her bad side.*

Night of Glass

Working late into the evening, Willy had foregone his lunch and tea. He knew several food shops that remained open until nine o'clock and as he locked the lab, Willy needed to rush lest he'd go without dinner, too. He'd been alone in the lab all day, the Professor "working" at home, and the huge building had seemed even quieter than usual.

As he made his way onto the street, the boulevard was also oddly deserted. Even on chilly autumn nights, the sidewalks were usually crowded with students on the prowl to the beer halls and workers returning home from late shifts. Willy stared at his watch and wondered whether it had stopped; it was more like midnight than nine o'clock. Along the residential blocks, curtains had already been drawn and door lamps extinguished.

As Willy hurried past the Opera House and crossed the wide *Maximiliansplatz*, he noticed how no streetcars were running and only two automobiles were in sight, both racing north on *Ludwigstrasse*, disregarding several red traffic lights. It was very eerie. Something must be going on that he wasn't aware of, probably some big party rally. He could imagine nothing else that would clear the streets like this and shut down the city center.

He'd seen newsreels at the cinema of the giant rallies recently held in Nürnburg and Berlin. Tens of thousands of party faithful decked out in full regalia. Parades of torches and banners like something Willy thought mirrored ancient Rome at its most imperious. *At least as portrayed in Mr. De Mille's movies,* Willy smiled nervously and picked up his pace.

As he turned down *Schillerstrasse* he nearly bowled over a shopkeeper who was standing in front of his shoe store. As they exchanged apologies, Willy saw that the shopkeeper had been lettering a white board nailed to his storefront, using a brush and a small can of black paint.

The sign read simply, "GERMAN-OWNED STORE!"

Willy continued to apologize and bow as he backed away down the street. What an odd sign to have on one's shop? But as he hastened along the well lit street he noticed for the first time that most of the shops had such signs, some on discrete, smallish placards in the windows, others with bold, black-on-white signs hanging prominently from their marquees. Most shops appeared to be closed, though Willy was certain that on previous weekday evenings many of the same shops were open and bustling with customers.

Rounding the next corner to a narrow street he frequently used to cut across to the hostel, he made his way to a small bakery where he often bought the day-old pastries that comprised his Spartan dinner. The proprietors, an elderly couple, had been very kind to Willy and other students residing at the nearby hostel and there always seemed to be something tasty left over at the end of the day. Indeed the pastries were never stale and Willy suspected that they might be made special for the students, even if they were priced as *day-old*.

As he reached the door, he noted uneasily that the bakery also had a sign in the window. Perhaps it had been there all along. Maybe it was new, but it read: "JEWISH-OWNED STORE."

Willy tried the doorknob: it was locked and only a single dim lamp shown through the window. As far as he could recall, he had never seen the bakery closed so early in the six weeks he'd lived nearby. It was always busy when he walked past in the morning on the way to the university. Sometimes the husband or the wife might be outside sweeping the walk or cleaning the large plate glass window and they would exchange simple greetings.

Willy shrugged and turned away, losing hope now that any of the other shops along the street would be opened for whatever the reason. But he heard a key rattle in the lock and turned back. The door cracked open a few inches. From behind the door a nervous voice asked, "Yes?"

"So very sorry, sir, I thought you might still be open." The man hesitated for a few moments.

"Yes, yes, we are open. You must forgive me. I must have locked the door accidentally. Please come in."

As Willy stepped inside the darkened shop and went to the counter, he heard the proprietor click the lock behind him.

"I was hoping to get a small loaf of black bread and a pastry if you have any left from today," Willy asked sheepishly. However as he looked over the display cases and racks behind the counter he was amazed that the shop was still fully stocked. He would have expected them to be empty this late in the evening. His day-old purchases were usually brought out from the back.

"You've an unlimited choice this evening, sir. As you see, business was very slow today."

Willy looked over the selection and was wondering whether he could afford to buy enough bread to last him for tonight and tomorrow.

"Excuse me sir, you are the American who lives at the hostelry, are you not?"

Willy was not surprised. It was no secret after all, and the neighborhood was small and friendly.

"Yes, sir."

"My wife and I have many relatives in America, in the city of Brooklyn, near New York. Do you know Brooklyn?"

"Sorry, I don't. I come from the mid-west, closer to Chicago. I stopped in New York for a single day before boarding the steamship for Hamburg, but I didn't have enough spare time to visit many of the sights."

"Chicago? Isn't that where all the gangsters live? Isn't it very dangerous there?"

"That's only what you see at the cinema, I'm afraid. Chicago is actually more famous for its stockyards and slaughter houses." The old man looked almost disappointed, so Willy added: "Of course there are real gangsters in Chicago and in New York and Brooklyn, too."

"I believe there are gangsters everywhere in the world, even in Germany, I think."

"That would surprise me," Willy replied. "The government and police in Germany seem very strong and efficient. I can't see them tolerating gangsters...If I might have these two loaves of black bread and two pieces of the mince strudel?"

"Of course, sir," but the shopkeeper still wanted to talk, almost like he wished Willy to linger. "There are gangsters here in any case, and many people are very frightened of them."

"Can't you ask the police to help?"

The old man looked past Willy through the window to the street outside. "My young friend, you've been in Germany only a short time. But I thought by now you'd understand that the police and the gangsters are one and the same."

"Are you saying that the police are corrupt?" Willy asked curiously.

"More than that. Much more than that. They come in here, the uniformed police or the young thugs from the SD that work beside them. They come in broad daylight. Steal from the cash box. Take whatever they like. Threaten my wife and intimidate my customers, good men and women who've been buying my bread for twenty years. They are told that they shouldn't be shopping at Jewish-owned stores, that if they do, my customers are not patriotic Germans and will be watched in the future."

"What's the difference between your store and any other?"

"They say we steal customers' monies and poison the food; that our food is unclean because we're Jews. We're non-German. It isn't true. I volunteered and fought in the Great War, surviving two years in the trenches and dugouts in Belgium. I breathed the mustard gas at Ypres and helped put down the Bolshevik rebellion after the armistice. I have ribbons and a medal to prove it. But now, suddenly and without recourse, I am designated as non-German and my rights as a German citizen are challenged."

"Surely the justice courts...."

"No longer. My complaints are now thrown back at me with sneers and insults."

"I'm sorry. I don't know what to say."

"Would such things happen in America?"

"I suppose there are always conflicts between different peoples even in America where so many mix together. Sometimes our government is clumsy and slow, but President Roosevelt is renowned for his stand on civil rights and equal opportunities for every man. I guess most Americans find ways to work around differences, though it's still difficult for many people.

"But honestly, I'm obviously not the person to ask. I'm usually so absorbed in my work, I'm oblivious to what's going on around me. I hope things get better for you."

"For now we only pray that things will go back to how they were before the Nazis were voted into power," the baker sighed heavily.

"What's going on today? I haven't seen a newspaper for a week. Where is everyone? The streets are deserted and most shops closed early."

"I don't know, sir. I saw nothing in my newspaper except that Herr Hitler is visiting Munich today. But yesterday there was much printed about the shooting of a Nazi diplomat in Paris, supposedly by a German-

Jew. There's no way to know the real truth, but it will mean more troubles for us, I am sure.

"Today my regular customers passed me on the street without meeting my eyes or acknowledging my greetings. A half-dozen party thugs in their brown shirts and swastikas stood outside all afternoon, just across the street. They wandered off somewhere else at sundown. They didn't say or do anything. It wasn't necessary. I haven't had a solitary customer all afternoon, and my beautiful breads are cold and stale. My wife is in the back kneading dough for tomorrow, but what if the SD comes back again? Contrary to what party propaganda claims about Jews, I am not a wealthy man. They will drive me out of business very quickly."

Willy began fumbling for his coins. "How much do I owe you for the bread and pastries?"

"My American friend, tonight everything is free. Here, please take another piece of the strudel. I owe *you* something for staying here and listening to the paranoid ravings of an old man. You've helped me recover some perspective. These things have happened before and will happen again. If I am patient and continue to bake excellent bread and pastries, why shouldn't I be welcome in this city."

Willy carried his bread back to his room. Even this late, there was no sign of any other residents. The night porter poured Willy a glass of weak tea and in his room, Willy treated himself to two portions of strudel after finishing one loaf of the hard bread. The others he carefully rewrapped and hid beneath his cot. When it came to food, his roommates were all socialists who didn't believe in private ownership. Willy was asleep before eleven o'clock, as usual, wrapped tightly in his blankets and great coat against the chilly November night.

Willy's lingering fear of fire in the ancient wooden hostel alerted him to the smoke. He must have been dreaming about food and home, because the first thing he thought was that his sister had left something in the oven too long. Then he was instantly awake and sitting upright and alert on the edge of his cot. His wristwatch said it was just midnight.

He could see smoke wafting past the gas light in the hallway outside his open door, but it didn't smell much like he imagined the decrepit building would stink if it burned. It was more like something burning in the kitchen. But it was best to take no chances. He debated packing his bag and carrying it to the lobby with him: nearly everything he owned in the world was on the shelves and hooks above his cot. Maybe the porter has just burned some toast on his hot plate. Willy made his way down four flights of stairs to the tiny lobby. He saw no sign of the night porter whom he would have expected to be asleep in his chair at this hour.

The building's lobby door was propped open and apparently the thick, acrid smoke was coming from outside. As he stepped through the door he was startled by the loud crash of breaking glass, as if a thousand beer bottles had been dropped from a nearby roof. Cheers and shouts came from all directions.

On the street he was drawn toward the noise and could see immediately that the little bakery shop was on fire. As Willy first walked and then ran down the sidewalk, he could see men carrying things out of the shop on to the street. He wanted to help, too. The old man didn't seem to have much but we must help him save whatever possible. *Has someone called the Fire Company?*

He reached the front of the shop just in time to watch a man pour gasoline from a small can over a pile of bread, furniture, and clothing tossed into the middle of the street. Another man used a torch he was carrying to ignite the gasoline and everyone jumped back as the pile burst explosively into flame. There were more cheers. Between the two fires, the street and sidewalk sparkled with the broken glass from the bakery's window.

Satisfied that their work was finished here, the men, all dressed in everyday clothes, ran off down the street and around the first corner.

Willy stood outside the shop for several minutes as flame and black smoke poured from upper windows. There was no sign of the old man and his wife. He feared they lived in an apartment on the floor above the shop, but everything was engulfed in fire. He felt helpless and worthless. As he stared up at the fire, two uniformed men hurried down the street to the shop.

After a moment's consideration, Willy heard one say, "Dieter, run and fetch the fire brigade, otherwise the fire will spread to neighboring buildings. Hurry!" The second man ran off. While he waited the first man, who Willy now recognized as a SD officer, pulled a list from his pocket and made several marks with his pencil. He was calm and businesslike, incongruous in the face of the raging fire and littered street.

When he noticed Willy standing on the sidewalk opposite the bonfire, he walked over and berated Willy angrily, "I hope you're not one of those responsible for the fire in this building. Your instructions were quite specific. Dump everything in the street and destroy whatever you don't want to take with you. If the building burns it becomes worthless and threatens surrounding properties. What do you have to say for yourself?"

"I...I...I only...arrived after the fire was already burning." Willy didn't know what to say but feared that a wrong answer would have consequences.

"Lucky for you then. But what are you waiting here for?" He consulted the list in his hand. "Next one is the butcher shop at *Thalerstrasse*, number 134. Get over there right now or I'll take your name and report you to your section leader. There are ten more stops to visit before dawn. So move on."

The man stood between Willy and his path back to the hostel and he desperately wanted to get back there as quickly as possible. Horrible things were happening here that he could not stop and didn't want to see. He decided that he'd go to the corner and work his away completely around the block, but as he reached the corner, down along *Thalerstrasse* he could see a line of fires burning in the street, the nearest only a hundred feet ahead. Keeping to the opposite side of the street he walked straight along, eyes ahead, trying to remain inconspicuous and purposeful.

The window of the butcher shop had been smashed along with all the upstairs windows above the storefront. Men were raging through the building tossing things from the upper windows that other men carried to the blazing pile in the center of the street. Mattresses and bedding, coats and shoes, framed pictures and books, all came raining down from above. Some of the bedding and clothing fluttered away in the cold wind and caught in the trees and bushes that lined the street nearby.

Someone had neatly arranged a row of items along the curb opposite the butcher shop: a sewing machine, a gramophone, a typewriter, and several gilt-frame oil paintings. As another painting was added to the row, the man who brought it from the house shouted to his comrades nearby: "This one's mine. Keep your bloody hands off it or I'll kill you!"

As Willy hurried by the butcher shop, he passed an open foyer and a commotion inside drew his attention before he could think. Four or five men with truncheons were bent down examining a body lying on the floor at the foot of a broad marble stairway leading to the expensive apartments above. Willy could only see the man's legs and feet, but he could tell what had happened. In his brief stay in Munich, he'd already witnessed what the police could and would do with their truncheons.

"What do you want?" One man sneered as he saw Willy staring inside. Another looked up from the body.

"Who are you? I don't recognize you. What section are you with?"

"Halt right there!" The group ran from the lobby and quickly surrounded Willy.

"I said, who are you? What are you doing here?"

"I...I was just walking by, trying to get back to my room."

"No one is just walking by tonight. Who are you?"

"My name is Petersen. I'm a student at the university."

"Another worthless parasite, evading your duty to your country, is that it?"

"It's not my country. I'm an American."

"*Ach so*, then just what are you doing? Are you spying on us? This is none of your business."

"If we let him go he'll talk about what he saw. Americans are all in love with their Jews and blacks. You're all half-breeds and cowards and yours is a country without culture." Several of the men started forward, their clubs held horizontal forming an impenetrable fence. Willy was trapped.

"No, comrades, hold up," said one. "We have orders, remember. Leave foreigners alone and that includes this American swine. Just move along, Herr Petersen. Climb back into whatever hole you came from and stay there for the rest of the night. Forget what you've seen. It has nothing to do with you. And feel lucky that you ran into soldiers who remember their orders and know how to follow them to the letter.

"Go *now*. Corporal Fritch, escort this tall fool back to his room and make sure no one mistakes him for a true German. Then meet up with us at the cinema on *Constanzplatz*. We have an appointment with its owner and we don't want to disappoint."

The circle of men reluctantly opened and Willy rushed off down the street circling the block back to the hostel. He could hear the steps of the soldier following him but never looked back, left or right. But while he could control his eyes, his ears could hear more shattering of glass, more cheers, and one time a long drawn, heartwrenching scream; woman's scream that Willy could still hear echoing in his head as he buried it in his blanket and tiny pillow. No matter how hard he tried, the scream lingered at the edge of his awareness. Sleep was impossible and as morning broke, smoke continued to fill the building and Willy's consciousness. *What kind of place is this? What kind of people are these men?* Willy did not dare venture out until well after sunrise, though usually he was off to the lab early. Like the prior evening, the streets were empty. Whatever had happened the previous night, no one had come out to investigate or question. As he walked beside residential blocks, he could sense that people were peeking from behind their drapes, but he didn't pass a single soul on his way to the university.

It took him a long time to reach the lab for whenever he saw wreckage in the streets or piles of smoldering ashes from the bonfires, he would turn around and try to find another way. But seemingly every street and alley had been touched.

Later as he sat at the lab bench, he heard footsteps in the hallway and was suddenly very scared. *Did the SD men report my name? Will I be questioned about last night?*

But it was Lise Wagner who pushed the door open.

"Good morning, Herr Petersen, " she said with a nervous smile.

"Good morning, Fräulein Wagner."

"I'm glad to see that you're safe. Gabi and I were concerned. We heard that there were riots last night near the *Bahnhof*, and I.... I mean, we were both afraid for you. Vati says you always work late here at the lab. We thought you might have been in danger when you tried to return to your room."

"Thank you for your concern, Fräulein Wagner, but I fell asleep at my desk here last night and slept right through the night. I didn't see or hear anything."

"That's wonderful. Gabi wanted me to tell you that if anything like that happens again, you are welcome to stay at our house. I'm sure my father would approve. We have plenty of room. Your help is very important to our father and we want to make sure you're comfortable and safe." Lise considered for a moment what she'd said. "You don't think we're completely selfish do you? Oh, please, I wouldn't want you to think that."

"Never," said Willy, "and I greatly appreciate your offer."

"I came also to tell you that Vati will not be in today. He's not feeling well and his medicine is nearly exhausted. I stopped by Doctor

Blum's surgery on the way over. No one is answering the bell. I hope
he's not left the city on holiday. Vati would never be happy with anyone
but Doctor Blum: they've been friends for fifty years."

By five o'clock Willy was exhausted. He buried his consciousness
and heart in his work and the day had passed. But every time he paused,
even for the briefest moment, vivid memories of last night resurfaced.
At one point he thought he could hear the woman still screaming down
the deserted corridor outside the lab. When he could stand it no more
and reluctantly went to investigate, he found a noisy steam valve leaking
in an empty lab. Back at his desk, it still sounded like the woman.

Staggering out of the chemistry building toward his room at the
hostel, he reached the first crosswalk and stopped, stunned and confused.
The street was jammed with cars and trucks and bicycles. Hundreds of
people filled the sidewalks, some taking their late afternoon exercise in
the parks and gardens.

As he approached the *Bahnhof* and his own street, it was as if nothing
had happened. The trash and piles of ash had disappeared. Only his
sense of smell and sooty black marks on the pavement were evidence of
last night's bonfires. While he avoided the street in front of the bakery,
he passed several shops that were neatly boarded up. For the life of him
he couldn't recall which businesses had been marked as 'GERMAN-
OWNED' and which 'JEWISH-OWNED,' but it was not necessary to
guess. Business was brisk at the remaining stores.

Back in his room, he unfolded the wrappings from his bread and
pastries. They still smelled fresh and delicious. He took a bite from the
strudel and its tart sweetness tickled his mouth and made his eyes water.
Willy began to sob uncontrollably and fell back on his cot. He wanted to
go home.

Three weeks passed before Willy, distracted by his own thoughts,
found himself on the street in front of the bakery again. Remarkably the
shattered window had been replaced and though the upper windows were
boarded and smoke stains discolored the bricks, the shop appeared to be
open. The old baker and his wife were rebuilding. This was a wondrous
thing. Willy wanted to see them again and burst in the door, smiling ear
to ear.

The man behind the counter was grossly obese with red hair and the small, square moustache that many men were now affecting. Willy was speechless.

"What do you want?" the man grunted impatiently.

"I was hoping to get a small loaf and a pastry if you have any left from today."

"We don't sell pastries," the man replied, "and all loaves are twenty *Pfennig*."

That was twice the former price and four-fold what Willy had paid at the end of the day.

"Pardon me," Willy said, searching for an excuse to escape this madness. "I seem to have forgotten my pocketbook. I'll have to return later." He began to back toward the door.

"If you come back again, remember to bring money," the man snarled. "Damn students," he said to himself, scratching his fat stomach.

Outside the shop, Willy took one last look through the window, and could not miss the sign: "GERMAN-OWNED STORE."

Heisenberg

Professor Wagner's laboratory comprised a long narrow room with slate-topped benches extending down the middle and along each wall, usually one bench for each graduate student. Above each bench top ran shelves stacked three-high, every centimeter taken up with amber bottles, jars, beakers, and carboys of liquid and solid chemicals. Carefully labeled, some were deadly poisons, others harmless salts. And from this collection, almost any other compound could be prepared or rare elements extracted and purified. Water, steam, and gas pipes ran all along the ceiling and ventilated exhaust hoods took up both ends of the room. But with only Willy at work, the lab was empty and eerily silent most days.

When the door from the hallway into the lab opened, Willy looked up from his desk startled. Visitors were rare and usually meant trouble: someone soliciting donations for a party-supported charity or youth camp, or a functionary from the student committee making another mysterious headcount. But the man standing before him looked out of place against the clutter. He was tall and well built, like a laborer or upland farmer, but stylishly dressed and carrying a thin, expensive-looking attaché case. His blond hair was swept back as if he'd just come indoors on a windy day and his hair and wide-set eyes made his face appear open and friendly.

"Good morning. My name's Heisenberg. I was hoping to catch Professor Wagner in his office. No one's there, so I guessed he might be in the lab getting his hands dirty," he said with a breezy smile.

Willy flushed and jumped to his feet. While he didn't recognize the man's face, the name was known the world over. He had never met a Nobel Prize winner before. Heisenberg was the most famous scientist in Germany. What could he possibly say to such a man?

"I'm sorry, Professor Heisenberg," Willy stammered. "Professor Wagner's not coming to the university this morning. Is there anything…anything, I can help you with? I'm Willy Petersen, the Professor's assistant."

Heisenberg offered his hand. His grip was firm. "Thank you, Herr Petersen. I've come to enlist his help with some...troublesome calculations. How's he doing these days?"

Willy hesitated for a moment. He didn't want to be caught in a boldfaced lie. But Heisenberg's question sounded innocent enough. "Oh, quite well. He still walks to the office from his house on *Königenstrasse* most days, but this morning his daughter sent word that he'd work in his study today. Is it important that you talk to him immediately? If you like, I can run over to his house with a message," Willy offered.

"I'd hoped to take the train back to Leipzig this afternoon and would prefer to speak with Professor Wagner this morning, if only for a few minutes. Let me suggest that we walk over to his house together. You can show me the way, if I'm not interrupting your work. No? Then excellent. It's been fifteen years since I last visited his home. I was a young man then, very much like you. We can talk along the way."

"Certainly, Herr Professor. I'm sure Professor Wagner would be delighted to see you. Let me get my coat."

The December weather was crisp with patches of ice and snow left over from another early season snowfall the previous week. The sky was crystal clear and as they crossed the wide plaza outside the Chemistry Building, they could just glimpse the snow-covered Alps far off to the south.

"So, Herr Petersen, tell me about the work you're doing with Professor Wagner," Heisenberg asked.

"My original plan was to focus on purifying industrial pigments based on heavy metal elements, Herr Professor. But I have to admit to a slow start. Many students left the university over the last year and like most of the faculty, Professor Wagner hasn't had anyone to assist him for months. Most of my time is spent helping catch up with correspondence and with completing and documenting experiments already underway."

"I suppose that's actually an excellent way to become familiar with the Professor's work. What is your background? Where did you attend gymnasium?"

"Actually, in America, Herr Professor. I was born in northern Wisconsin. My undergraduate degree is from Marquette University in Milwaukee."

Cross Sections

Heisenberg pulled up suddenly and turned to face Willy. "Remarkable! Your German is perfect. I never would have guessed. How long have you been in Germany?" They continued along the sidewalk.

"Only two months, sir. However my father and mother immigrated to the United States from Regensberg before the Great War. We speak only German at home. My hometown is predominantly German-American."

"Well, you look and sound every bit the new German man, Herr Petersen. How long do you plan to stay?"

"At the present rate of progress, it might be ten years," Willy smiled and shrugged, "but we'd planned for two to three years."

The two men had paused at the intersection across from the National Library on *Ludwigstrasse*, waiting for the control officer to halt traffic. The wide street was busy, full of private and government cars, trucks, buses, and hundreds of bicycles.

"I hope you're enjoying yourself. What do you think of the *new Germany?*"

"It's difficult to make any comparison, Professor. I've only read about the *old* Germany, after all, and heard stories from my parents and neighbors back home. But no one could help being impressed by all the energy and industry. The building and construction. People on the move. Goods in the shops. In some ways things are a better here than back home in Wisconsin. I've heard horror stories about how bad things were in Germany during the early twenties and again in the early thirties. But right now, there seem to be more people here with better, productive jobs. No soup kitchens like we have in Milwaukee. And there are certainly *different* things happening in Munich than I would not expect to see in the United States."

Even with his short time in Germany, Willy had learned to be circumspect in conversation with strangers. He knew who Heisenberg was, but not what he was or where he stood. Willy recalled rumors about the Professor's family connection with Heinrich Himmler. This would be scary to any sane German. Willy's experience on *Kristallnacht* had effected him greatly. This was a polite term Germans were using now as the burghers coldly discussed the billion Reichmarks the Jewish community was fined for damages and clean-up costs related to that night. Crazy, irrational things *were* occurring here that would never

52

happen in Milwaukee. Heisenberg continued, oblivious to Willy's allusion. "I appreciate your perspective. I'll be visiting the United States in a few months myself for an international conference on cosmic rays. Perhaps we can compare notes again when I return."

"Where are you staying in the States?"

"Many places." Heisenberg ticked them off on his fingers: "Michigan, California, New York, Indiana, Chicago. Something of a whirlwind tour. But I'll get to see many old friends and hear updates on research in the States." The two walked silently for a time. The Professor was thoughtful and serious. Willy guessed Heisenberg was asking himself analogous questions about Willy: *Can he be trusted?* He must have reached a conclusion.

"It seems like half of German science was instantly transported halfway around the world. Theoretical work can continue to advance as fast as ever if we remain in touch and cooperate. It's a very competitive game you know, this theoretical physics. Not at all like your chemical researches, where cooperation is the rule. Many of our greatest discoveries derive from casual conversation, over beer and sausage, with pencil scribblings on napkins, or on long walks along the beach. We don't require expensive laboratories and a complex apparatus. Theoretical science transcends boundaries and politics, but distance is now an obstacle. Day to day we test ideas by arguing them out. People take contrary viewpoints, often just for the sake of argument and we debate. But all the good debaters have moved to America. I miss them."

Willy knew there was more to this story. Most of the scientists who'd left were driven away after losing faculty seats or government jobs five years ago in the wake of the new regime's Civil Service reforms. Whether it was their politics or their religion, they'd been mercilessly hounded and left with little choice and few options. Willy could not read Professor Heisenberg's feelings and opinions on this matter. It was best not to ask for elaboration. But it was stimulating to have someone finally break the unspoken rules and talk about such matters, no matter how abstruse he might be.

"I don't claim to comprehend your discoveries, Herr Professor, certainly not enough to debate with anyone about them. Perhaps I'm an excellent example of your *Uncertainty Principle*: I am completely *uncertain* about the principle!" They laughed together. "How do these ideas originate?"

Cross Sections

"Oh, Herr Petersen, I have come to believe that these important concepts are just out there fully formed; they're simply descriptions of physical systems. *Discovery* is recognizing them and *success* come from describing them.

"Formulating these concepts is like writing a poem. It's a struggle sometimes to choose just the right words to express what you see in your mind or what you've sketched on the blackboard. Like a poem, when the words are correct and they're in the right order, the harmony and rhythm is obvious to everyone. The result will be elegant and simple at the same time. My father was a professor of Greek philosophy and I guess I absorbed these Platonic perspectives as a child."

As they came down a side street intersecting *Königenstrasse*, the English Gardens spread out in front of them. They paused at the edge of the frozen grass. In the distance, the trees were leafless, but the vast expanse of the gardens and lawns, right in the middle of the busy city, was still surprising and exhilarating.

"Ideas can come to me while I'm playing the piano or while I'm hiking in the mountains or when I'm walking in a park like this." Heisenberg patted Willy on the back: "Then I'll leave it to energetic experimentalists like you to figure out how to make the discoveries practical…and blame it on you if they aren't!" They turned right and walked along the sidewalk bordering the gardens.

"Sometimes we theorists are accused of straying too far afield. That's happened this time and I need Professor Wagner to bring us back to earth. I believe he's still Europe's greatest empiricist. We need his experience and insight."

"What exactly are you working on?" asked Willy.

"How much do you know about nuclear physics and radioactivity?"

"In the chemistry department back home, our seminars reviewed recent publications on Bohr's atomic theory, particularly as it relates to chemical reactivity. I suppose I have a working knowledge of alpha and beta radiation related to naturally occurring substances like radium and polonium. But I'll admit with no embarrassment that this business of quantum theory that you propose is far over my head. And with all the changes here at the university, I'm afraid I've been out of touch for a few months. What can you tell me, please, that I can understand, about recent developments?"

"Let me suggest that you sit in on my discussions with Professor

Wagner, if he doesn't mind. I'll give you both a little background first: a status report of sorts. We'll talk about the practical applications of our little theories. And finally I think it's only fair that I alert Professor Wagner to some of the potential political complications of involvement in this project."

"Politics?"

Heisenberg hesitated for a long moment, then offered, "You know, Herr Petersen, scientists spend half our careers trying to find patrons to support our work and our families. This process is rife with frustration and humiliation. Regardless how much esteem we have from our peers, most of us, unless we're wealthy by birth, manage to stay one short step ahead of the moneylenders.

"But I'm learning a new lesson I'll pass on to you. In matters of patronage, keep in mind that if you wish too hard, your wish might come true!

"I recognize this house," Heisenberg said gazing up at the impressive façade. "Let's hope we get an opportunity to continue this conversation. I still have more questions about life in the United States."

"I look forward to it, Herr Professor," said Willy sincerely. They shook hands warmly and climbed the steps to knock on the door.

Willy led the way in. Lise Wagner had answered the door herself and as Willy introduced Professor Heisenberg, Willy watched for a sign from Lise. They had developed a set of code words and gestures that would steer Willy or other visitors away if the Professor was feeling badly or was having one of his episodes. But today, Lise nodded subtly to Willy and greeted Heisenberg with a curtsy.

"Could this be little Elise? The last time I saw you, you were just taking your first step. You seem much steadier now! And even more pretty, if that is possible."

"Thank you, Professor," she blushed.

"And how is your sister? Gabrielle? She must be quite the young woman by now."

"She's indisposed at the moment, Professor. But I'll tell her that you're here."

Willy knew that 'indisposed' meant that Gabi was still in bed and behind her smile and tact, Willy sensed Lise's impatience and embarrassment.

Cross Sections

"If you please, Professor, let me take you right to the study. I'm sure my father will be both surprised and pleased to see you." Lise took Heisenberg by the hand and lead the way. Willy tagged along behind.

Lise rapped several times on the library door and then drew Heisenberg in.

"Vati, I have a surprise for you. Look whom Herr Petersen brought by for a visit."

Willy watched Professor Wagner's face as he looked Heisenberg up and down, then stared at his face for a moment. An instant of doubt started to knot his brow, then he recognized his visitor.

"Werner, my boy. It's wonderful to see you. I thought perhaps you'd gotten too famous to come visit old friends."

"Only too busy, sir, too busy. And we've missed you at all the recent society meetings."

"Too old, Werner, too old. I don't like to travel any more. You can't get me away from the comforts of home. In any case, unless someone like you is lecturing, I admit I have a difficult time staying awake. Very embarrassing for all concerned."

"Nonsense. As a matter of fact, there's an important symposium scheduled in Berlin next April and I insist you attend. I'll give Herr Petersen the details before I leave, but you must come. We need, or I should say, I need, your advice and counsel on some very weighty matters."

"Of course, any way I can be of assistance," Professor said. "How is your wife? And did I hear that you've twin boys? How exciting and challenging that must be? I only have my useless girls," he said with a wink. Lise was standing quietly just inside the door and seemed to ignore the jab.

"Oh, I don't know about that Professor. My wife would certainly disagree with you. You have the flowers of Germany and I the weeds!"

Lise took this as a cue. "Father, should I make tea and will the Professor please stay for lunch?"

"Thank you, Elise," Heisenberg responded, "but I must get over to the station by two. Perhaps the next time I'm in Munich." Lise smiled and closed the study door behind her.

"I wish you could stay longer," Professor Wagner said. "We've so much to catch up about. How is that rogue Otto Hahn?"

"Otto is fine, Professor, and making some remarkable breakthroughs in his experiments. This is partly why I wanted to speak to you

56

informally."

"Certainly. Would it be all right with you if Petersen took notes for me? I'm afraid that like everything else about me, my handwriting's becoming completely illegible."

"Of course. As a matter a fact, I've already suggested that Herr Petersen sit in on our discussion. How should I begin?"

At first Heisenberg relaxed in the Professor's high-back stuffed chair, but within a few minutes he was on his feet pacing around the room as he talked animatedly. Willy tried to take detailed notes and kept an eye on Professor Wagner to catch if he began to fade or wander. Lise brought in a tea set and poured for each of them before leaving quietly with a questioning glance to Willy, who nodded reassuringly. Heisenberg was a captivating speaker even in the confines of Professor Wagner's small study.

"You may not have heard yet, but the Physics Institutes have been taken over by the Ministry of Education and the Army Ordnance Department. On one hand, our access to funds, equipment, and other resources has increased dramatically. We can at last, after talking and planning for ten years, begin to construct the experimental facilities we need to test our theories on atomic energy. The institute's staff is convinced that we have the ability to develop science and engineering that will unleash the power inherent in the forces that bind matter together. Einstein's germinal work is thirty years old now and at last we'll have the computational tools and experimental facilities that might allow us to reduce his theories to practice.

"And in practice, these atomic processes could be sources of unimaginable energy that would sever our ties to coal, oil, and wood, resources that dwindle with every passing year. The life of every human would be enriched and an era of prosperity and peace would result.

"With this in mind it's imperative that research and development work expand," Professor Heisenberg said with intensity. Then he paused and shrugged, "But we shouldn't completely ignore the equally inconceivable *risks* if this science is misused.

"Because, as I said, now our support comes with strings attached. First, the Army has interest in military applications of the technology. One day in the future, this will pose some ethical dilemmas for those of us involved in pure research, but we will continue to control the science

57

because of the Army's limited comprehension of fundamental theoretical precepts. Of this I am confident.

"Secondly, within the Education Ministry lurk enemies of science itself; men who believe that *theories*, products of minds and imaginations, are inherently unsound and even dangerous. Hegelian philosophies run amok. Paradoxically, these men have demanded what amounts to *experimental data* before they will support our *experimental research*. It is necessary for us to provide them with simplified descriptions of our work to date, presented using mathematics that they can understand, review, and verify.

"We've attempted several times to break through the wall of dim-wittiness that pervades the Ministry with little success. The chief reviewer seems to have trouble with the calculus, and I don't think a suggestion that he return for a term to the gymnasium would be well received," Heisenberg smiled bitterly.

"That brings me to you, Professor Wagner. One of the crucial concepts involves the calculation of the absorption cross-sections of uranium atoms when bombarded by neutrons, and the propagation of that reaction to the point where it becomes self-sustaining.

"Otto Hahn recalled your work forty years ago on serial calculations related to element purifications and we agree that the same series of *algebraic* calculations can be used to verify our more esoteric mathematics. We understand that these calculations are extraordinarily lengthy and tedious, but we believed they would be acceptable to the Ministry lunkheads. A proposal was presented and accepted with a single qualification: the Ministry will accept these new calculations only if they come *directly* from the great Professor Ernst Wagner.

"Otto and I tried to explain that our staff or any number of Ministry drones with sufficient time could do the work reliably. But once your name surfaced, nothing less would satisfy them.

"I've come to beg your help, though I'm afraid the task is so trivial that it might be insulting to you and a misuse of your valuable time. I can only repeat that I believe it is a matter of significant national and international importance."

"Werner, my boy, of course you can count on me. I'll help in any way I can," Professor Wagner reassured him. "Please tell me more about the parameters…"

Heisenberg spent a further twenty minutes running through the various factors and variables, pointing out how and where they related to more general terms in Professor Wagner's classic work.

"If you please, Professor, Otto and I prepared a brief paper for the Ministry that includes many of these details. I've a copy here for you to consider. The Ministry agreed that this is proper, however they've warned me not to try and influence your independent findings. I've been instructed not to provide you the results we've already calculated." He pulled a thick binder from his case.

"I've absolute confidence that you will reach conclusions identical to our own but if this is what it takes to untangle the Ministry's purse strings, so be it." Heisenberg passed the binder to Professor Wagner who hefted it in his hands.

"As you said, Werner, these calculations will take some time. At present, I have only Herr Petersen here, to help me."

"Given our long-term plans at the Physics Institute, if the Ministry can have your results next summer, all our schedules can be sustained. I'm leaving in April for a long visit to the United States, but I wouldn't expect the Ministry to complete its review until sometime just before I return. Otto will get the go-ahead and start to collect and order the equipment we need. We're proceeding with the design work already."

"That allows me some six months," Professor Wagner considered. "It should be sufficient. I can commit to you that the report will be complete by early summer."

Willy had written *early summer*, and raised his head to look closely at Professor Wagner. His eyes were bright and his whole body alert, even excited. But Willy had strong doubts. Should he share them with Heisenberg privately? How many days between now and July would Professor Wagner actually be able to get to his desk? Perhaps the challenge would help the Professor resist his episodes, Willy thought hopefully, but he had been trying to interest Professor Wagner in all sorts of new ideas for several months with little lasting effect. Willy needed to talk to Lise as soon as possible.

"I have to run along to the rail station now," Heisenberg said, glancing at his wristwatch. "I apologize again for the sudden visit and for my inconsiderate absences. My family will be visiting Munich during the Christmas holidays and perhaps we can get together again under more festive circumstances."

"An excellent idea. Werner, I insist that you and your wife spend at least one evening with us. And please bring your sons. Herr Petersen, will you arrange these things with my daughters?"

"Yes, Professor. Professor Heisenberg, might I walk you back to the station?"

"Certainly, I'd enjoy the company."

Willy waited on the platform until Heisenberg's train to Leipzig departed. During the walk to the station, Willy had listened for an opening, for some way to hint to Heisenberg about how difficult this assignment might prove for Professor Wagner. Willy had little confidence that he could cover for the Professor. This was quite different from answering letters, few of which required even the slightest technical acumen, or abstracting results from experimental work long since completed and confirmed.

Willy tried to get some clue from Heisenberg about his expectations.

"As you'll read in the project brief," Heisenberg offered, "we're trying to predict what mass of uranium will be needed for an atomic reaction to become self-sustaining. This is the key to everything. The contrarians think the mass is infinitely large and equally impractical. We believe the critical mass is much smaller. Once we have the funding to construct our test reactor at the new Physics Institute in Dahlem, we can then begin to collect purified uranium samples, stack them together in a pile, and try to measure the output of free neutrons and heat.

"But this is the underlying problem: purified uranium is rare and expensive. We need the total backing of the government to gather enough together. You may already be aware that the best ores are found in Czechoslovakia and Africa. Secondly, we believe we need some sort of moderator to enhance neutron capture once the reaction begins. The simplest thing to use is deuterated water; the students call it *heavy water*. Heavy water is a natural component of all water but again it must be laboriously separated using immense amounts of electric power. We have only three hundred kilos of heavy water in Germany today, barely enough for our modest experiments. We've heard that the Norwegians are planning an expanded separation facility, but our respective governments are not on the best of terms and there's no assurance that we'll have ready access to this source at any price.

"As you'll appreciate, Herr Petersen, since it's your field of specialization, the issue of purity is crucial. There are many common elements that will act to inhibit or halt the self-sustaining reaction and their presence in either the uranium or the heavy water as impurities will result in complete failure. Keep at your own studies and research: if we can substantiate the practicality of these atomic processes, *purification* will be the enabling technology. It will be a field with tremendous professional promise."

"Thank you, Professor."

"When I get back to Leipzig, I'll have my secretary mail you details of the April symposium in Berlin. Please prevail on Professor Wagner to attend. He'll have the place of honor he deserves, and his presence will lend significant credibility to the proceedings."

"I will try, Professor."

"And by all means come along yourself, Herr Petersen. I assure you that the meetings will not merely comprise our usual enigmatic and codified theoretical musings. People will attend from many disciplines: chemistry, engineering, shipbuilding, and even commercial interests like banking. You can make many contacts that might prove valuable for your career.

"Many of the most promising students in the country are invited. This will also give you a chance to share ideas, experiences, and probably a substantial volume of beer with your peers."

"Thank you again, Professor. I appreciate your interest and consideration. And I'll try hard to get Professor Wagner to attend."

"And thank you, Herr Petersen. I hope to see you again soon."

Christmas - 1938

"I fear this will be the last Christmas we'll enjoy at peace for a long time to come," Professor Schumann suggested. "I see preparations for war everywhere. Factories in the Ruhr Valley are building tanks and airplanes. My grandson visited Kiel last month on a business trip and saw it for himself. He says new U-boats and warships are launched weekly, despite official claims to the contrary. My concern is that such extreme efforts are always accompanied by a certain momentum and inevitability."

Ever the lawyer, Herr Studer, equivocated: "Surely, Herr Professor, this is not unreasonable. Remember. After the last war the Versailles treaty completely gutted our army and navy. We lost the means to protect German interests on the continent and around the world. Only luck has kept us from being overrun by Communists in the interim. I suspect it will take another five years to reach parity with the French, English, or Russians. Might I remind you that to be safe, we must be stronger than any one of these, since they are likely to ally against us again in any conflict that develops? Parity with any single country is not sufficient. The government has my support in these matters."

"I don't mean to disagree with you, Herr Studer, not at all. I'm only saying that it's sad. With war comes disruption and separation. I look around this room and see everyone gathered together: families, friends, and neighbors. The lights are bright and cheerful. Good food and *Glühwein* are plentiful. The worries of the world are very far away," Professor Schumann sighed, his cup of spiced wine in one hand, a thick slice of plum torte in the other.

The Wagner's parlor had become the Christmas Room decorated with Advent wreaths and colorful bunting, an antique crèche arranged on a tabletop opposite the tree. The gaslights were dimmed and the room was filled with candles that lent a warm, soft light. The fireplace crackled and sent sparks up the chimney as the logs shifted and settled. Candles in the windows on all three floors greeted both visitors and passers-by.

In their father's name, Lise and Gabi had invited their neighbors and their father's friends and colleagues to the party, several days before Christmas, and people had been coming and going all evening, many making the rounds of several gatherings and dinners.

Every guest brought small gifts and the tall tree was surrounded with a wall of bottles and decorative boxes of cakes and sweets.

Gabi and Lise spent the evening answering the door, hanging winter coats, making introductions, and providing distraction for a half dozen mischievous children who weren't satisfied until they were allowed to light some of the tree candles, despite a tradition they remain unlit until *Heligabend*, Christmas Eve. The tall spruce tree brushed the high ceiling and was trimmed with gold, silver, and brightly colored balls, small cakes and candies, tinsel, and elegantly carved ornamental figurines. These traditions had been carried to America and reminded Willy how far he was from home.

Willy had been drafted as waiter and barman, but rather than a sense that he was hired staff, Willy was elated. It was the first time he'd felt a member of Professor Wagner's family. In the bustle, Lise had begun to call him Willy, rather than Herr Petersen, and she insisted that *Willy* be introduced to every guest:

"Herr and Frau Schultz, this is Willy Petersen. He works with my father at the university. He's from America and this is his first German Christmas. Willy, Herr Schultz is a famous art collector."

"Nonsense, Fräulein Wagner, I'm a collector of famous art!"

Lise seemed to know everyone and dazzled Willy with her grace, tact, and control of the chaos. Gabi remained at her father's side through the evening. He had been excited and completely lucid earlier, but as the evening passed, Professor Wagner became progressively forgetful, short-tempered, and argumentative. Gabi, uncharacteristically demure in her long blue dress and simple make-up, would prompt her father when he couldn't recall a guest's name, and redirect the conversation if he became agitated. At nine o'clock, Gabi and Lise made excuses for their father and bundled him upstairs to bed.

"Is the Professor all right?" Willy asked Gabi privately when she returned. He had felt uncomfortable playing host on his own.

"He'll be fine, thank you, Willy. Lise prepared his medicine and will sit with him until he's asleep. I think he had a very good time this evening." She reached out, took his hand, and held it for several moments. "Thank you for your help, Willy."

Willy returned to the parlor. Everyone wanted to know about America.

"Do you know Al Capone…Jean Harlow…any Red Indians?"

He couldn't accept that these well-educated and sophisticated men and women would know so little about America until it struck him that they were pulling his leg. He flushed red as a beet and couldn't help but smile at himself. He'd been very neatly put in his place.

Willy was adding a log to the fire when a friendly hand squeezed his shoulder.

"Professor Heisenberg, it's good to see you again."

"And you, Herr Petersen, how are you getting along?"

"Very well, thank you."

"Come, let me introduce you to my family," Heisenberg took Willy's arm.

"Darling, this is William Petersen, Professor Wagner's research assistant. He's from America, but don't pester him with questions: I'm sure he's been repeating himself all evening. And Herr Petersen, those are my sons." The young twins, dressed identically, were kneeling on the carpet with Lise, hovering restlessly over a pair of presents she'd selected from beneath the tree.

Frau Heisenberg shook her head and smiled, "I must say, Werner, the Wagner girls are both so beautiful and poised. It's amazing that they were raised without their mother. I would have expected either tomboys or bespectacled, inhuman calculating machines. To the contrary: they are both quite charming...Don't you agree, Herr Petersen?"

Willy blushed and cringed. Frau Heisenberg had caught him watching Lise with a rapt look on his face. She and her husband both laughed and she joined the boys who were pleading for permission to open their gifts.

"I was sorry to miss Professor Wagner, Willy. We've just come from my father's house and dinner was late. Have you convinced the Professor to join us in Berlin for the April symposium?"

"Yes, but he is genuinely enthusiastic. Barring any complications, we'll be there. It was more difficult to convince his daughters. Fräulein Elise offered to accompany her father to Berlin, but I think I've persuaded her that her father will be fine with me. I've been threatened with dire consequences if I somehow fail in my duties, but such are risks inherent in dealing with such strong-willed women."

"Well, the symposium has already generated considerable excitement and anticipation. Discussions are likely to be pretty lively. I've been forewarned that important politicians and bureaucrats are anxious for a report. Indeed, some of the military representatives are *over-excited*, if I might be tactful, and there's talk that proceedings and reports from the meeting should be limited as top military secrets."

This made Willy wonder whether he might be turned away at the door. But Heisenberg was unconcerned. He continued.

"I've argued that this is not the time for choking critical lines of communications to scientists elsewhere in the world. We need to bring to bear every able mind if we are to be successful.

"So they asked me for a roster of men I thought should be kept informed and I scribbled down about a dozen names. Several days later the list was returned to me with almost every name struck off. When I confronted the SS officer in charge, he accused me of *purposely* providing a list of Jews, communists, and enemy agents. Did I think they were stupid? Was I playing some sort of joke on them?

"Willy, they had struck off Niels Bohr in Copenhagen. It's insane. I tried to explain how Niels is the father of atomic theory, how he continues to be the world's greatest theorist, and even how he's been my friend and mentor for twenty years. Denmark is not a belligerent nation, and so on, and so on. I made argument after argument, but to little avail.

"As far as Berlin is concerned, Bohr is a man with dangerous, contagious pacifist and socialist ideas. He's been active in finding employment for scientists who've lost their academic positions in Germany and Austria. This man waved a thick file at me and accused Bohr of conspiring with others to spirit Lise Meitner out of Germany across the Dutch border, and arranging a research position for her in Sweden. He dared suggest that I was implicated along with Otto Hahn. Otto and Lise worked together for years at the Physics Institute. Her contributions had been remarkable. I tried to assure the SS that Otto is suffering her absence more than anyone. They weren't sympathetic or convinced.

"So in the end, they ordered me to break off all contact with the men on the list and I'm in a worse position than if I'd kept my mouth closed. There's another lesson for all of us. Be more circumspect in the future. Not everyone we're working for shares our perspectives and altruism.

For now we have other immediate problems." He raised his empty glass. "Do you think we can find more of this excellent cognac?"

A great commotion arose on the street in front of the Professor's house. It was *Klöpfelnacht*, Knocking Night, and a group of masked children, watched closely by their parents, was running up and down, ringing cow bells and rattling tin cans filled with pebbles. The young Heisenberg boys pretended to be frightened at the grotesque masks and costumes in order to glean more attention from Gabi and Lise, then as the group passed on down the street, they begged the sisters to let them follow.

Throughout the evening, Willy's conversation with Heisenberg would resume when they found themselves standing together alone. "My greatest fear is that your countrymen won't understand the unique situation here in Germany. Our government has always taken a close hand in research. Governments come and go, but their support has always been critical to our progress and in the transfer of technology to German industry. There's always a chance our discoveries might be misused in the short-term. Predation and corruption exist everywhere in the world.

"You've lived and worked in Germany for only a short time, but you must be aware of how things work here. Will your colleagues in America understand? What can I say to convince them? I'm also worried that German scientists who've immigrated recently will influence opinion. They've every right to be bitter."

"Willy, what will your government do in the event of war in Europe? Our military believes they can defeat France and Britain, but if they knew America would join against Germany, there might be no war. On the other hand, if America waits and later allies itself with Britain and the tide turns against Germany, the military's drive for new, powerful weapons will increase exponentially. Why does your government hesitate?"

"Sometimes I think I should abandon this work altogether. Lise Meitner is gone. Otto Hahn talks of suicide rather than work for the military. Bohr is treating me like a stranger: we've been friends for twenty years, yet even he doesn't seem to understand. If he were to turn against us, so will the rest of the world, and everything we've accomplished will be demonized. I will lose effective control of our work and the dangers will be magnified, the very thing they all fear. If I could only speak with him directly, I can make him understand."

At midnight, as the party wound down, Professor Heisenberg was persuaded to take to the piano. At first he played familiar Christmas carols, including *Stille Nacht, Heilige Nacht*, the local favorite. Lise and Gabi struggled to get the Heisenberg twins to sing, prompting them with the lyrics, and singing along themselves. Even some of the adults joined self-consciously with the refrains.

Later, the parlor was serene and dreamy as Heisenberg played Chopin and Schubert from memory. The boys had fallen asleep on the settee with their heads in their mother's lap, clutching matching toy trucks. As he sat on a cushion, his back against the wall, his long legs stretched out in front, Willy was hypnotized by the music, the flickering candles, and the glowing fireplace embers.

He had overheard Professor Schumann speculating about war and had considered Heisenberg's comments about the growing influence of the military on his uranium work. Combined with the horrific events he'd witnessed, there was a lot to think about. This place, this new Germany, was so different than he had imagined, so unlike the quaint and harmless stories his parents had recounted. So much here engaged him: his own research, a chance to be involved with Professor Heisenberg's work, and even his growing responsibilities regarding Professor Wagner's failing health and his daughters. He watched the girls, out the corner of his eye lest they or Frau Heisenberg catch him staring again. Lise sat on another large pillow, her legs curled underneath. Gabi lay with her head cradled in Lise's lap, snoring quietly. A forbidden thought crept up on him and he looked away with a jerk. Best to think about other things.

He looked to the half-eaten slice of *Knörpletorte* on the plate in his lap and thought about his missing friend, the old baker on *Hochstrasse*. How could a nation that produced and nurtured Beethoven and the poet Schiller, allow the depredations of *Kristallnacht*? How could people so kind and protective of their own children, make life so miserable for the children of others only because their parents were Jewish? Would he ever figure it all out? He didn't wish to remain an outsider, but what's the price paid to be part of this new Germany?

As Lise and Gabi helped the sleepy boys with their coat buttons, Professor Heisenberg remained pensive: "There is no simple answer, I suppose. It's not an issue of physics anymore. Thank you for listening, Herr Petersen. Few men remain in Germany with whom I can air these notions. Please give our best regards to Professor Wagner and we hope he's feeling better soon. I look forward to seeing you both in Berlin in the spring."

Listening as the sisters gossiped and laughed in the kitchen, Willy carefully extinguished the candles on the tree and banked the fire. His parents had always spoken of the Petersen family as *German* even after thirty years in the states. But despite his ready acceptance and the idyllic scene enveloping him in this wonderful home, he again felt pangs of isolation and loneliness. And at this very moment, Willy realized that he was thinking of himself as *American*, as un-German, and he knew he shared the fears and doubts of those other outsiders.

When Professor Wagner arrived early that morning, the first work day in the New Year, instead of Lise, Gabrielle accompanied him. Willy thought it out of character for the older sister, but perhaps he had judged prematurely. Coming inside, Gabrielle helped the Professor with his boots and coat while Willy fetched hot tea from the porter's pantry. As the Professor sorted his correspondence, Willy returned to the laboratory. But before he'd settled back to his reading, Gabrielle appeared, pausing just inside the room. Her long winter coat was unbuttoned and an electric blue silk dress peeked out. Her careful makeup looked odd so early in the day, but nonetheless, she was striking. Gabi's complexion was pale and contrasted dramatically with her raven black hair and bright red lipstick, rouge, and nail polish. She reminded Willy of women in cigarette advertisements back home: beautiful, sophisticated, and unapproachable. Willy couldn't take his eyes off her lips but knew her eyes were boring in on him.

"Willy, I came with Vati this morning so I could see you. I hope you don't mind. We haven't had any chance to talk with Vati and Lise around all the time. They're so nosy. Is it all right with you? You're not too busy?"

"Sure. Of course not. Certainly, you're welcome," said Willy nervously, watching her lips move as she spoke. She seemed to sense that his attention was captured and moved closer.

"There's so much I need to know about America, Willy. I want to know about American clubs and dances and parties and movie stars. It's all so fascinating. I plan to go to America as soon as I can, so I want to know everything there is to know. You must help me." He knew he should respond with something sophisticated and witty, but in the confusion of fantasies and realities, he fumbled and could only mutter boring truths.

"I'll tell you everything I can, Gabi, but I'm no expert on dancing or movie stars. I'm sorry, but I've been studying so hard that I haven't really had time for these things, in America or in Munich."

She hopped up and perched herself on the corner of his desk. Her coat fell away as she crossed her legs. Her short blue silk dress rose to expose her knees and a hint of thigh only inches from Willy as he sat in his low chair. He flushed and in order to keep from staring at her legs, he leaned back and raised his gaze until their eyes met. That was even worse! Gabi seemed amused by his discomfort and smiled.

"Perhaps we can make a bargain. I'll take you to clubs and parties around town and you tell me about America and teach me to speak better English."

"I guess that would be all right," Willy offered doubtfully.

"But you must promise not to tell Vati or to tell Lise either. They'll try to spoil everything. They're so boring. You don't like being bored, do you Willy? You like to have fun, don't you?" She leaned forward and touched his knee. Her nails were long and painted red to match her lipstick.

"Yes, of course," Willy insisted.

"But you have to promise. Vati doesn't approve of my friends. Promise me."

"I promise."

"Great! This is going to be great. Why don't you meet me tonight? Do you know the *Black Cat Club?*"

"Yes, I think so. Over by *Isartor?*"

"Yes, yes. Meet me inside at ten o'clock."

"Tonight? So late?"

Gabi shrugged. "I have to wait for Vati to go to bed before I can sneak out. Go home and take a nap if you must, but I insist that you come tonight and be ready to have fun. Can I count on you? You won't be late? Don't disappoint me."

"Never. I'll be there."

Gabi leaned back and raised her arms to stretch provocatively like a cat. Her skirt climbed up a little further.

"Wonderful! And I'm going to buy a new dress for tonight," she said climbing down from Willy's desk. She reached down and straightened and smoothed her clothes, running her hands across her breasts down to her thighs. "What's your favorite color?"

"I don't know. Red, I suppose," Willy said, his eyes still fixed on Gabi's lips.

"I'll find a red dress then, just for you. You'd better show up or else I'll never forgive you." She wagged a finger in his face.

"Don't worry. I'll be there."

Gabi bent down suddenly and kissed Willy on the cheek. He tried to jump back but she had him cornered in his chair.

"See you tonight," she said as she turned and breezed out of the room.

Willy's cheek was on fire. He sat frozen for several seconds and felt the hot wetness from her kiss as it evaporated. Gabi's perfume hung in the air. It wasn't the flowery rose and lavender he was used to. The scent was dusky and feral and made him dizzy.

When he finally stirred in his chair he realized he was aroused and guiltily rolled his chair close to the desk in case anyone should come in and surprise him. But it wouldn't go away and for once he didn't fight the feelings, adjusting his trousers and relishing the sensation. He concentrated on recalling every detail of Gabi's visit, every nuance, lingering on her words, trying to divine her meaning. Taken at face value, their bargain was uncomplicated, but Willy knew, Willy wished, there was more.

A self-accusation of disloyalty to the Professor was not allowed to take root. It was only dancing after all. If something else happens, Willy promised himself, then he would decide at that time where he stood. Why aggravate over something that was just…a possibility? Of course when that time came, Willy could allow himself to be swept along and not worry about commitments he'd made to himself.

In the puritan work ethic of the new Germany, old-style nightclubs and people who frequented them were considered decadent and anti-Party. Most of the clientele were foreigners or antisocial elements who were either insane or stupid. But beautiful girls were always welcome. Absolutely everyone knew Gabi.

While the *Black Cat's* doormen had given him a difficult time, suspecting a shabbily-dressed SD agent, when they were told that Willy was meeting someone and someone was Fräulein Wagner, doors were thrown wide for him. It was Herr Petersen this, Herr Petersen that, and "will you have champagne, Herr Petersen?"

Except for the bandstand and dance floor, every inch of the dark club was filled with small tables, each with a dim, shaded electric lamp and a telephone. Despite its ban from German radio since 1935, a quartet was playing a jazz piece. Willy didn't recognize the tune. The stage was built for a much larger orchestra or band, perhaps a reminder of grander times. Half the tables were occupied, some people talking animatedly, others attending to the music. The musty air reeked of cigarettes and perfume.

Gabi's table was at the center edge of the dance floor. As he wove his way through, led by one of the waiters, he could only see Gabi, her red dress a beacon from across the hall. Everything else was a gray, colorless blur.

She was flirting with one of the men at her table and didn't see Willy at first as he stood awkwardly behind her chair. She was talking and gesturing animatedly, punctuating with a silver and pearl cigarette holder. Her long dress was loose as a slip and flowed like mercury with every move she made. Her shoulders were bare except for a single narrow strap, and as Willy looked over her shoulder, he could see her breasts quiver as she laughed.

"Willy, darling, you're late. I was afraid you weren't coming. Don't stand there like an old tree, sit down here," she patted the chair next to her and stood so Willy could squeeze in beside her. Gabi pressed her body against his and when she sat back down she took his hand in hers. This was fortunate because Willy wouldn't have known what to do with his hand otherwise.

"Willy, these are my friends. This is Karl and Renate from Zurich. This dashing fellow is Emilio, my friend from Milan, and this is…I'm sorry, Emilio?"

Cross Sections

"This is my friend Fräulein Presta. I'm sorry Presta doesn't speak very much German as yet. She's only just arrived from Roma to work as a secretary at our legation in Munich." Emilio was a dark, swarthy man, with gray streaks in his hair and moustache, three times the age of the others at the table. His friend Presta seemed confused and uneasy as he pawed her. Perhaps this was not a usual part of the responsibilities of an Italian legation secretary.

"Everyone, this is my friend Willy. He is a famous scientist from America who is here working with my father at the university. Reni, darling, isn't he beautiful? Just like I told you?"

Gabi explained how Karl and Renate were children of a Swiss banking official with a Munich office. While Karl and Emilio were unimpressed and sat smoking endless cigarettes, Renate and Presta began to ply Willy with questions, mostly in broken English, vying with Gabi for his attention. His head was spinning though he hadn't taken a single sip of his champagne.

At the first opportunity, Renate grabbed Willy's hand and hauled him bodily out on to the dance floor. Tall and gangly, Willy knew he was a poor and hopelessly awkward dancer, but as long as the band played a fox trot, he thought he could just manage.

Renate held him tightly, her head reaching only to his shoulders, so that as she put her arm around his shoulder she was stretched out provocatively full-length against his body. She didn't seem to care about the dance steps and Willy simply shifted his weight from foot to foot trying to keep time with the band's beat.

As he looked down on her, Renate's eyes were dreamy and distant. Willy wondered whether she might be drunk or taking narcotics. After two numbers, Willy steered her back to the table. Despite the club's inadequate heating system, Willy was sweating and had to wipe his face and the back of his neck with a handkerchief.

No escape now as Gabi yanked Willy back up on his feet. A slow song was playing and a dozen couples crowded the small dance floor. This time it was Gabi who pressed insistently against him. His left hand was on her back, and through the thin silk of her dress; Willy couldn't feel any underclothes.

"Willy, you're such a cad," she clucked as they danced. "I thought I could trust you. You must stay away from that Renate. I insist. You promise me. She's the worst kind of whore and she has her eyes on you.

All she cares about is lovemaking and her cocaine, and she doesn't care where she gets either.

"You're not to dance with her again. I invited you here and you must stay with me. Whatever she promised you, I can do better," she insisted. Willy was a little confused and very shocked.

"Gabi, she didn't say a word. I thought she might be asleep," he replied, hoping to be funny. "Don't lie to save my feelings. I know all about her. Don't you even look at her again tonight, you bastard," Gabi said squeezing him even tighter. They danced several numbers; Willy pushing Gabi from the floor only as a jitterbug started to play. "Please, please, Gabi, let me sit for just a few moments. You're wearing me out."

But Gabi had just started. In two minutes she was dragging Karl out to the floor to jitterbug. Karl was a good dancer, but Gabi wasn't dressed for this type of dancing. She had to pull up her dress hem and tuck it in her belt. As she swayed to the music and as Karl lifted her and swung her around, the entire room paused to watch. She was a wild animal, her breasts and long hair loose and alive. Willy was mesmerized and found he was getting excited. At first he was simply envious of Karl but as the two continued to dance, Willy began to feel jealous himself. Without thinking he finished off one bottle of champagne.

"Gabrielle, my dear, you're spectacular," Emilio offered when she and Karl finally returned to the table sweaty and breathless. People around the room had applauded at the finish. Several men shouted her name. Karl kissed her on both cheeks and sat back wiping perspiration from his hands. Presta and Renate sulked and pretended to ignore the attention everyone was giving Gabi.

She squeezed past Willy to take her chair, reaching up to kiss him on the lips. "Isn't it wonderful! Thank you, Karl." And to Willy, "And what did you think?" He was speechless. "Did I do the steps properly?" she pouted. Willy's heart was still pounding as if he'd been out there.

"Gabi, I have never seen anyone, anywhere in the world jitterbug so well. Not even in Chicago!" She kissed him again this time long and very hard.

"Willy, I'm so glad you're here. You must come every night. I want to hear you say such things every night."

And so it went for the remainder of the night. Willy only managed to convince Gabi to quit at two o'clock insisting that he had work to do early in the morning and that he must escort her home. They walked arm in arm, Gabi still bubbling.

"You remember what I told you about Renate. I know her and she'll try to find out where you live. Just stay away from her."

Willy thought he'd try to get back at her just a little: one little gibe to salvage some pride.

"Well, what about Karl? You two were a very sexy couple out there tonight. Perhaps you'd rather be with Karl than me. I'll never learn to dance like that."

"You silly man. Karl is a homosexual. Can't you tell? He's only hanging around with us since the SD began rounding up his German boyfriends and sending them off to labor camps. He's Swiss. He has nothing to worry about, but can't you see how lonely and depressed he is?" She started to laugh: "Listen, you watch out for him, too. Don't get too friendly with Karl. He is charming and very rich. So you just better stay away from the entire family."

"This is all very complex, but I shall, I promise," he laughed, nonplussed. They walked quietly for a few minutes. The streets were empty but the streetlights on *Leopoldstrasse* were bright.

"Willy, do you really think I'm sexy?" she asked.

"Yes."

"Like Jean Harlow?"

"No. You're more beautiful than Jean Harlow. And I'm sure she can't dance like you do." Willy was trying to be gallant and not salacious.

"Thank you, Willy," she said and hugged his arm tighter.

She halted just before the last street corner from her door.

"Let me go alone from here. Lise might still be awake and I don't want her to see us together. Now kiss me goodnight, Willy." He bent down and both her arms wrapped tightly around his neck. Her lips were warm despite the winter cold. She kissed his cheeks and neck and traced his lips with her tongue before breaking off with a low moan. A shudder swept him head to toes. Gabi was smiling mischievously.

"Will you watch me until I'm inside?"

"Of course."

"Tomorrow night?"

"Yes."

"Then *ciao*, Willy. Remember, the *Black Cat* at ten o'clock."

"Ciao, Gabi.*"*

Willy stood and watched from the end of the block as Gabi walked up the steps in front of her father's house and let herself in with her key. He turned slowly and wandered back toward his hostel.

He lay awake for hours, confused and conflicted about his longings and dubious intentions, but certain of one thing: he would be at the *Black Cat* again tonight.

"Your identity cards please, gentlemen," the SD officer demanded. Willy and Karl passed him their passports. He examined them carefully, in no hurry to complete his inspection. "American and Swiss. I would assume that you gentlemen have more important business in Germany than this," his gesture encompassing the cabaret and everyone in it.

Other uniformed and plainclothes officers were going from table to table intent on causing maximum disruption and interruption. One officer had climbed the stage and was questioning band members one by one. SD patrolmen led off two who could not produce proper documents.

"You come here and you will leave with the wrong impression of Germany. These women," and he plainly meant to include Gabi, Renate, and their friend Erika, "do not represent German womanhood. These women are lascivious and I see through their tasteless parody. They mean to arouse and not to inspire. And it is certainly not a place to bring young ladies, if there are actually any present tonight." This was directed directly at Gabi and Erika.

"Oh, I recognize both of you and I can assure you that reports are being prepared for your fathers. These foreigners are not proper company for girls with your upbringing and advantages. You should be setting examples for your younger sisters."

Erika listened to the officer with feigned interest and even had the audacity to bow her head and make it appear that his words had struck home. But Willy could see a glint in her eyes that belied an excellent performance.

Gabi simply ignored the man, looking away at nothing, drawing frequently from her cigarette, and tapping her feet in time with the dance tune that had been interrupted when the SD burst in. Willy thought this was dangerously reckless. Gabi was just trying to show off. Willy had been hassled by the police enough times staggering home from beer halls to appreciate a rational approach: hold your hat in your hand, bow your head, and nod subserviently on cue.

He suspected that this officer had given Gabi the same lecture before, with equal effect. Responding in kind, he went on as if she weren't present. "Yes, you see gentleman that Fräulein *Wagner*, believes she is somehow better that the rest of us. Conventions and rules don't apply to her. But I can assure you…and her…that this won't last forever. The party is establishing camps where wayward young women can be reeducated about their responsibilities as modern German women. Tonight she is just one step away from one of those camps."

"And as for you two *gentlemen*," he handed back their papers and glared back and forth between Willy and Karl, "on another night when I'm not so busy, I might want to satisfy myself that your papers are in absolutely perfect order. That would involve a lengthy visit to my headquarters and contact with your embassies. Our facility affords few comforts for gentlemen like you. Consider this a friendly warning." He turned, giving Gabi one last stare, shook his head in disgust and passed on to another table. Gabi blew a smoke ring after him.

"Gabi, I really think that Captain Werner has a crush on you," Erika giggled. "He always singles you out and ignores the rest of us. I'm very jealous and feel quite desolate."

"Well, he is your type, Erika, dear," Gabi retorted. "He's old, fat, and dull, just like your last boyfriend. If his cock's as stiff as the flagpole up his ass, you couldn't ask for more."

Willy was shocked. It embarrassed him when male friends talked this way, but to hear such vulgarity from Gabi was still stunning. Karl sat passively staring off into space.

"Oh, don't worry, Gabi, dear," Erika came back cattily, "unlike you, I do ask for more than that." The two glared at each other for a moment and then burst into fits of laughter clapping hands.

"Oh, Willy, don't be such a stooge," Gabi said, reading his worried expression. "These pests wouldn't dare do anything. They barge into a different club every night. The swine get to leer at naked dancers and avoid paying admission.

"Anyway, cabarets are quite legal, you know. Even Herr Hitler and Reichsminister Goebbels are said to attend shows at the *Scala* and *Wintergarten* in Berlin.

"And watch them as they go round the room. See the tables they avoid. Half the city government is here tonight with their mistresses and whores, and the police won't dare make a scene."

"They know your name, Gabi," Willy protested.

"Good. Then they'll remember how everything stands. Vati has many important friends and the police know whom."

The SD had finished their sweep, conversation returned to its normal roar, and the band started to play another tune. Several instruments were now missing and the sound was noticeably more hollow and tinny.

"Willy, if our waiter hasn't been hauled off to the concentration camp, could you see if you can find me more champagne?"

The apartment belonged to the friend of a friend, Gabi claimed, and Willy never lost his fear that someone would burst in on them. At first he was afraid he'd be embarrassed, discovered naked and aroused. But when the thought last occurred to him, he was only afraid that they would be interrupted. He didn't want it to stop, to pause, to relent, in any way.

Gabi took the lead, not because of Willy's clumsiness or caution, but because she was wicked and desperate. She wanted to try everything all at once and switched from one thing to the next so quickly and randomly that Willy ached for completion. Willy had thought that experience would come to him one step at a time over years. Instead it all came in a flash, faster than he could have read about it, faster than he could have fantasized each successive thing.

When he finally cornered her on her back, her ankles crossed tightly behind his back, he tried to take control. But Gabi was wild. She wouldn't hold still and regardless how hard he tried, her pace was double his. At the end he simply held still as she twisted and thrashed and squeezed until she emptied him completely. Even as he deflated, she refused to let go, holding him close.

When she finally began to relax, Willy rolled off to the side, uncertain about what to do next, what to say.

"Willy, will you get me a cigarette, please?" He took his time fumbling through Gabi's coat pockets and when he came back to the bed he struck the lighter and offered her the flame. This seemed like a very sophisticated thing to do, and for the first time in two hours, Willy felt a glimmer of self-confidence.

The bedroom was lit only by light coming from the tiny living room at the end of the hallway, and the flame from the lighter illuminated Gabi's face in an eerie way with colorless shadows. Willy sat the lighter carefully on the bedside table and still blinded by the bright flame, he slowly slipped back into bed. He had to say something, but was at a total loss for words.

"Gabi, you're so beautiful," he offered, moaning to himself about how hollow and lame he must sound. But Gabi was all appreciation. She wiggled over to his side, her head pillowing on his shoulder.

"Oh, Willy, I wanted you so much. I couldn't stand it any longer. I thought I would explode. You teased me terribly: you're a heartless man." What could he possibly say to that?

"It's getting very late, Gabi, I must get you home. It will be dawn by the time we reach *Königenstrasse*."

"Damn you, Willy! You're doing it again. Teasing me." She rolled onto Willy's chest and reached over, dropping her cigarette into a dirty coffee cup.

"You're trying to make me crazy, so I'll do what you want! But I'll show you. I won't stop until you're crazy, too." She pushed herself upright, straddling his hips, and began to search below with her hand.

Tweedledum/Tweedledee

The two young *Wehrmacht* officers looked like twins with their identical uniforms, badges, kit, and cropped, blond hair. As Willy led them down the hallway toward Professor Wagner's office, he tried to keep track of who was on the left and who on the right. He hadn't taken a long enough look to differentiate between the two. He had their names: on the left was Lieutenant Posen, on the right Lieutenant Bose. But if they were to switch position passing through a door, he'd be forced to let them introduce themselves, a minor breech of etiquette, but the kind that sometimes set off the Professor.

Professor Wagner seemed more himself today though he was touchy and unpredictable. Even when the Professor came to the office, Willy did his best to deflect casual visitors. "The Professor is in conference…Professor Wagner has a visitor…The Professor asked to not be disturbed…He's in the midst of an important experiment." But these gentlemen had been quite insistent. When Willy suggested that they didn't have an appointment, an identical look passed across their faces that left Willy stuttering an unnecessary apology. Willy decided *not* to ask them their business with the Professor.

All he could hope was that the two soldiers wouldn't say something to upset Professor Wagner or stay too long. Gabi had agreed to return today at three o'clock: any longer and fatigue would bring on a spell. The new doctor had urged that the Professor's schedule be rigidly maintained, modest meals at the same time everyday, a nap late in the afternoon, and bed by nine o'clock. But he'd also warned Gabi and Lise that their father's episodes would inevitably become more frequent and dramatic. His dementia was progressive, and while they could expect sustained periods of lucidity and normal behavior, there was no known treatment. He provided an opiate to make sure the Professor slept soundly through the night. The girls never left their father alone, though Gabi was emboldened by the new routine. She no longer had to sneak past her father's room on her way to meet with Willy and her friends. Gabi dealt easily with her sister's scorn and Willy was now her co-conspirator.

While Posen and Bose were abrupt and condescending with Willy, once in the Professor's presence, they removed their hats, begged his pardon for the interruption, and introduced themselves humbly. As usual, Willy took a chair in the corner prepared to take notes. The two paid him no more attention.

"Herr Professor, Lieutenant Bose and I work in the Ordnance Research Department in Berlin. Colonel Fromm is our chief and Major Platin is his deputy. Major Platin is the one who ordered us to visit Munich and to call on you."

"Yes, I remember Platin," Professor Wagner said without expression, though Willy thought he sensed impatience or dislike in the Professor's voice. *Not a good start*, Willy thought.

"Yes, sir," Bose continued, "the Major asked us to speak with you concerning the project you're working on for Dr. Heisenberg."

"And how does it concern *Major* Platin?"

"Ordnance Research has been funding the Physics Institute's efforts for several years now. Colonel Fromm is a strong advocate of Heisenberg's theories though they still remain untested and unproven. However, many scientists within our Department have serious doubts about these theories and their practical applications."

The Professor nodded to Willy. "Yes, Werner explained this all to us several months ago."

"Oh, that's excellent, excellent," Posen said. "We couldn't be sure what you've been told."

"Are you suggesting that Werner Heisenberg would lie to me?" The Professor demanded angrily, leaping to his feet and leaning across the desk, the monocle dropping from his eye. Willy sat forward ready to intervene.

"No, no, not at all," Bose leaned back, cowering in his chair, the Professor's sudden reaction as imperious as any senior General.

"No, of course not. I'm sorry if I've not made myself clear," Posen offered apologetically. The Professor straightened and began to pace behind his desk. "We also understand how important this work is to all science, but we were sent to explain our Department's interests and stake. Our objective is to make sure you understand how important your contribution will be to the government and the army."

The Professor rounded on them again. Willy could see how his complexion had gone gray. "The quality of my laboratory's report will be the same regardless of *your* interests. The same is true for its contents. Werner's request and his explanations are quite sufficient for me." "Certainly, Professor, no one in Berlin expects anything else. When Professor Heisenberg suggested your name for the review, the chief agreed instantly. Your reputation is unimpeachable and your loyalty unquestioned." Professor Wagner had regained control and sat back in his chair.

"Then why are you two here?" he peered at them doubtfully.

"Only to emphasize how much importance Berlin puts on this project."

"And by *Berlin*, whom precisely are you referring to?"

"Ordnance Research, of course," Bose offered, but the Professor's glare was unrelenting. "The General Staff." Still the stare. "The *Führer*."

Professor Wagner sat back and sighed, and color began to come back to his face. "Now at last the truth. The report has *political* implications. Werner warned us and also predicted there were groups that might try to influence our findings.

"Gentlemen, this is a scientific institute established before your fathers were born. We have only one way of doing things: applying scientific method backed by careful experimentation, analyses, and calculation. The system's results are free of politics and other such considerations. Any attempt to influence science politically will ultimately fail or will result in the complete destruction of science. Take that message from me back to *Berlin*, to your *scientists* and your politicians."

"Thank you, Professor. We will," assured Posen, anxious to escape his wrath. But Bose knew that they couldn't return to Berlin empty-handed.

"It is politics that worries us also, Professor, if you'll excuse me." The Professor was waiting impatiently.

"The Gestapo is concerned that Professor Heisenberg's politics and loyalties are not aligned with Berlin."

"Professor Heisenberg's politics? What has his politics to do with his discoveries and his current investigations?"

"Professor Wagner, some people believe Heisenberg is a pacifist, sympathetic to Jews, and tolerant of communists."

"I've known Werner for twenty-five years. He has no *politics*. He

81

is a humanist who is sympathetic and tolerant of everyone. Since when is that a political stand?"

There was no way for Bose or Posen to answer that question.

"But his loyalty to the Reich?"

"Werner's loyalty is to the truth and the objective pursuit of deeper truth."

"Professor, the world has changed. Germany requires more of its citizens now."

"And how does someone your age acquire such insight?"

Posen knew his answer would not be satisfactory. Willy could predict the Professor's response.

"I am a loyal Party member," Posen said meekly.

"The Party. The Party. The Party. You imply that the Party and the nation are synonymous?"

"Yes, Professor."

"But not every German is a member of the Party. *I* am not a member of the Party. So you also imply that Party membership is some measure of my loyalty or my German-ness?"

"No, of course not, Professor. As we said, your loyalty is not in question."

"Well, doesn't it suggest your reasoning might be flawed. If your suppositions don't apply to me, perhaps they don't apply to Werner or anyone else. Something more for Berlin to consider.

"Return to *Berlin*. You can report that I now appreciate how important this project is to the Party and its leadership. The report will be completed as promised and forwarded to the Ministry of Education. If its findings are disappointing or different from your expectations, that's one possible outcome of the search for fundamental truth. The answer will be the same in Germany as it will be in Russia or in Brazil. There can be no uniquely German answer. Can you understand this?"

"Yes, Professor."

"Yes, sir."

"Herr Petersen, will you be so kind as to help these young men find their coats and their way to the door? Please return here afterwards."

"Yes, Professor Wagner."

"Thank you, sir," the two lieutenants said together. The Professor did not offer his hand. They hesitated just for a moment before following Willy to the door. As they looked back one last time, Professor Wagner had returned to his reading.

Willy was stunned. In all these months, Professor Wagner had never talked about politics or current events. Willy had wrongly assumed the ailing Professor was unaware of what was going on in Germany and in Europe. His daughters sought to insulate him from news that might enrage or depress him, like the deaths of old friends or the dismissals of old colleagues. Perhaps they weren't as successful as they thought. But despite all this and his erratic mental state, the Professor could expound and argue his views rationally. Never had Willy heard another German attack the Nazi Party's motives and primacy. Willy's friends would joke and mumble and sigh profoundly, but never had one dared to speak his mind clearly and directly, even in private.

The two young officers were quiet as they collected their greatcoats. Willy escorted them to the main doorway.

"Herr Petersen, you've worked for the Professor for some time?"

"No, not really. Since last October. Four months."

"Is he always so...opinionated?" Posen asked, groping for the right word.

The best answer was a truthful one. "On the contrary, Lieutenant. This is the first time I've ever heard him speak of such matters...to anyone," Willy added when he realized he was being subtly interrogated about the Professor's activism. "He's been working very hard lately and I'm sure that's made him impatient. I suspect he's been challenging students in this manner for fifty years."

"Well, we certainly received a lecture today. I felt I was back in grammar school," Bose laughed nervously. He reached into his valise and handed Willy several sheets of paper. "We brought a long list of questions to ask the Professor. Perhaps you would discuss these with him when his mood...improves. You can mail us his responses. This would be very helpful."

"The Professor is a very senior man, Herr Petersen, and is doubtless nearing retirement," Posen said. "Older people sometimes begin to say things they wouldn't if their minds were clearer. There are people in Berlin who would like to make sure the Professor's reputation remains spotless. As Bose noted, you can help him in this." He reached in his pocket and gave Willy his calling card. "If it reaches a point where you believe the Professor is speaking to the wrong people or is inappropriately expressing his views, please feel free to contact me in Berlin. I would refer you to others who can resolve matters quickly. Your help would be appreciated and rewarded. Am I clear?"

"Yes, thank you." And they were gone, out into the cold and snow.

It *was* very clear: *Gestapo.* Willy had just been recruited to spy and inform on his teacher. As Willy stood at the door watching Posen and Bose waiting to cross the busy street, he smiled wryly to himself. *They don't know I'm American: Alice in Wunderland. They simply made assumptions about my politics and nationality. What'll they think when they get back to Berlin and make their report? Will some clerk, cross-referencing their notes, uncover their mistake? That won't go over well...in Berlin. Bad for their careers. Will it come back on me? On the Professor?*

Willy shrugged and shivered in the cold air leaking through the old doors. Walking back to the lab, he thought again about Professor Wagner. He had grown to respect the Professor immensely. When his mind was clear, his genius was obvious. He saw patterns in data that Willy would never divine. During these times the Professor could recall details of technical papers and unpublished experiments forty years past. But most of all, the Professor was a wonderful teacher who showed Willy how to think as well as how to perform the experiments and other lab work.

When Willy reentered the office, he walked very quietly up to the desk, reluctant to disturb the Professor's concentration. Willy had never had a real life hero. Tom Mix was every American boy's hero, but as Willy had matured, that ideal had faded. A hero is an ideal that's simple and distinct but doesn't suffer irony and paradox very well. This elderly and fading man, rapidly falling prey to dementia, was the one truly rational man he'd met in Germany, a nation and society where paranoia and obsession were becoming institutionalized.

Spy on Professor Wagner? More than ever Willy was determined to protect his teacher...and hero. It was also meant to mitigate his conscience about *his* disloyalty: Willy's on-going affair with Gabi.

"You needed something, sir?"

"There was something, I suppose, but I guess it's slipped my mind. What time is it now?"

"Just coming up on three o'clock, sir." Willy walked around to stand next to the Professor. "If I can suggest that you mark your place, Professor," he said, offering a piece of scrap paper, "Fräulein Wagner will be here shortly. She said she hoped you'd get a chance to rest before dinner."

"Thank you, Herr Petersen."

Willy needed to tell someone about today's meeting, his troubled and confused feelings welling up in his chest. He knew Gabrielle wouldn't understand and couldn't resist making fun of him if he opened up. She tended to treat Willy like a man-child despite their intimacy. Willy would find a chance to talk to Lise: she would understand and sympathize. She needed to hear about the threats implied in Posen's parting comment.

Cross Sections

The Uranium Club

The elegant new lecture hall at the *Kaiser Wilhelm-Institut* was packed to the rafters, dozens of students jostling for standing room along the back wall. Rumors about the symposium's presentations had circulated widely and the large room was filled with undergraduates from Berlin's universities and the technical *Hochschule*. Academic luminaries sat in the first rows, joined by representatives of the Education Ministry and senior officers from Army Ordnance. Willy had managed to secure a seat immediately behind Professor Wagner, glad to be nearby if the old man needed assistance. Hopefully a good night's sleep had helped.

Willy had put the Professor to bed early the night before, acting as both valet and nurse. The Professor, exhausted by the eight-hour train ride from Munich, was barely able to walk or undress himself. He'd lost track of where he was.

"Willy, please tell Lise and Gabi to come say good-night. I wish to hear them say their prayers. Tell them to come up now."

"Of course, Herr Professor. I'm sure they'll be up in just a few minutes. Here, please take your medicine, sir." By the time Willy had hung up the Professor's suit and finished unpacking his bag, the old man had quietly dozed off. Willy hoped the Professor would sleep soundly through the night, but he would have to be sure the concierge roused him early so he'd be handy when the Professor awoke.

Rooms at the Kaiser Wilhelm-Institute's Harnack House were large and comfortable, reserved for distinguished visitors. Lise had insisted that Willy request, over the Professor's signature, a second, adjacent room so he could stay close.

At first Lise had announced that she would accompany her father, but Willy had argued how her presence might embarrass an old man who was increasingly quick to take offense to innocent comments. Anxious to sample Berlin's nightlife, Gabi wanted to go, too, but Willy had just managed to resist her entreaties. If one daughter came along, how could he argue that the other shouldn't? Despite the craving she provoked, Gabi would be nothing but trouble. Even the thought of accompanying Lise on the long trip made Willy very uncomfortable. She always stared at him so earnestly. Willy suspected that Lise knew something of his adventures with Gabi and he was embarrassed. The two sisters would talk about him. He squirmed when he thought about that. It was nearly impossible to deny either daughter, and this was the first time he'd been able to stand up to either of them, admittedly for selfish reasons.

Gabi was still steaming when Willy left with the Professor in a taxi for the *Hauptbahnhof*. Willy had urged her to stay home and not to go out at night by herself, but didn't believe for a moment that he had any influence on her, despite how *close* they'd become. She would probably go out just to make him angry. Since the beginning of the year, the police had stepped up its harassment of club owners and patrons. Willy sensed danger and worried that Gabi didn't.

When he returned to his own room, Willy found a crude invitation shoved under the door. An association of research fellows and graduate students was hosting an informal reception downstairs. Beer and food were promised, no professors allowed. *Why not?* He'd earned a respite and knew very well that if he retired early to his room, he'd lie there and obsess about Gabi, making himself crazy with desire.

A makeshift beer garden had been opened in a large reception room off the main lobby. Thirty or forty rowdy young men were milling about, those with a sufficient head start on the beer, already talking loudly. A red-nosed student with a stupid grin intercepted Willy as he came through the door. He had a hand-written sign sticking from his breast pocket that read simply *Cu*, an odd name. Willy extended his hand and began to introduce himself.

"No, no, no! No names tonight friend. I'm writing tags for everyone that simply gives your chemical element of choice. If you don't have a preference, I'll pick one. No duplications! So far all the lighter elements have been claimed. And don't choose an inert gas: we'll reserve those for any Prof that shows up! We're seeking anonymity. Only way anyone will speak their mind anymore." Copper dropped his voice. "Between you and me, I've managed to assign toxic elements to all the party members and hard-asses here tonight. Watch out for them. If you don't know your *chemistry*, you'll end up in concentration camp. How's that for a grading system?

"So what's your pick?"

"You choose for me," Willy smiled back.

Copper checked his list, a crumpled copy of the periodic table torn from a textbook.

"With that yellow hair you ought to be sulfur, but I already gave that to some guy who farted while we were talking.

"Tell you what, I was saving silver and gold in case any women showed up, but that's not likely anymore. Prevailing dogma is to keep women pregnant in the kitchen. My entire life up until now was dedicated to the idea of keeping women in the bedroom and unpregnant. Now I have to give up that quest. What a shame!

"What few females remain at the institute can't handle the attention and are so ugly they should wear masks.

"You can have *Gold*," he offered and began to scribble the letters *Au* on a piece of scratch paper that he crammed into Willy's front pocket. He then shook Willy's hand and said, "Herr *Gold*, my name is Herr *Copper*. It's a pleasure to make your acquaintance. I'm sure we have much in common: we're both group One B!" With that, *Copper* moved on to some new arrivals. Willy wandered towards a table where beer bottles were being uncorked and passed around.

"Welcome, Herr *Gold*. *Weizbier* or *Pilsner*?" asked the self-appointed barman offering one of each. Willy accepted one and began to pour it into a clean glass.

"Watch out, *Sodium*," said another drinker standing nearby, "Better not be seen talking to *Gold*. That's a Jewish name if ever I heard one!"

"Nonsense. It surely refers to his shiny disposition and yellow hair. Herr *Gold*, just make sure you stay clear of *Arsenic* and *Antimony* if you don't want trouble!" Everyone laughed, though some more nervously than others did. Those that weren't yet drunk were still wary that this shield of anonymity was tenuous.

"*Prost!*" the barman proclaimed.

Throughout the rest of the evening, the nametags proved to be an effective and humorous way of introducing oneself. The chemists in the group were at something of an advantage over the physicists present, who didn't always remember their compounds correctly. Informal factions of gases and metals were formed and broken, and certain impossible bonding combinations and positions were proposed and debated at length.

As the volume of beer consumed increased, conversation ranged from obsessive tediousness to outright absurdity: "Whatever you do, don't pass out and fall down. The SS has special orders to haul the dull-witted off to camps."

"Then why haven't they picked you up already?"

"Look, I'm not fooling around," the young man said conspiratorially. "I overheard uncle telling my father that the government has plans to collect up everyone who's brain-damaged, retarded or senile and make them...*disappear*. I didn't even want to imagine what that might mean. But *euthanasia* in the name of efficiency and productivity, that's what I see."

"What horseshit you talk, Herr *Calcium*. Catholics would never stand for it. Germany is still a democracy and from what I can see, the current regime needs every idiot alive and voting National Socialist!"

"Fuck you, too, *Lithium*. But just wait and see. Uncle's a clerk at Gestapo headquarters on *Prinz Albrecht Strasse*, and he's seen all this stuff. On orders from the very top, plans have been set since last autumn. It has a code name: *Aktion T4* and will be run from the Reich Health Ministry. Every private doctor will be required to register patients with certain symptoms and then it's just a question of when the trucks start rolling. Of course it will be kept quiet. The top guy's not stupid, you know. He's cautious when it comes to public opinion."

Willy took it all in, drunken ravings, vicious gossip, and frightened rumor. In six months Willy had witnessed things that led him to believe even the most horrific was possible. A few students made bold, inflammatory statements, spouting what Willy thought was red rhetoric. But these young men had a certain desperateness about them that others whispered was a death wish. Most present were content to watch and listen, unwilling to comment or otherwise join the debates.

In Munich Gabi waited impatiently for Karl and Renate, growing angrier by the minute. The bandstand was empty and the *Black Cat* was deserted except for a few staff members scurrying around pointlessly. The champagne was warm and served clumsily by a busboy. She saw no sign of the regular waiters.

Word had gone round the city how the SD was determined to close clubs and cabarets they considered subversive to Party preachings. The *Blue Angel* had burned on Friday night as the Fire Brigade idly stood by to prevent flames from spreading to nearby businesses. It had been proscribed for featuring 'barbaric and degenerate' Negro music.

In the past twelve months, two of Gabi's favorite night spots had been bought by new investors, party members all, rumored to be using monies embezzled from the *Winterhilfwerk*, the ubiquitous Winteraid charity, established to help poor Germans with coal for heating. All the old staff and performers vanished overnight, popular acts replaced by long, tedious programs of folk songs and cruel, unfunny comedians skewering Jews and foreigners, interspersed with naked-dancing tableaus presented with classical music background to honor the purity of German womanhood.

On opening night, Gabi was part of a crowd of jaded customers who laughed at the wrong moments, heckled the comics, and accompanied the folk singers, loudly providing their own obscene lyrics. They were roused from their tables early in the evening and the new management made it clear that they would not be welcome in the future.

Though most of the dancehalls, cabarets, and revue theatres were now shuttered, Gabi wasn't going to give up easily. She thought she could count on her pals, but now it looked like they were as cowardly as most Germans. She sat smoking cigarettes, sipping tepid champagne, plotting revenge on her weak-willed friends.

Twelve o'clock came and it was obvious the manager wanted to close the club down for the night. He had expected some sort of intrusion by the SD and hoped his own presence might remind them about past *generosities*. He harbored little faith the SD would let him remain open any longer, despite his *contributions*, but he wanted desperately to salvage the club's fixtures and supplies, to sell to new owners, who would appear inevitably in the SD's wake. If he simply walked away he'd have nothing. He moved from table to table switching off the lamps, leaving Gabi's until the last.

"Fräulein Wagner? Fräulein Wagner? I'm so sorry, but I must close up now."

She stared at him blankly, smashed out her cigarette, and stalked out of the club without saying a word. She claimed her own coat and found herself in the empty street in front of the club. The neon marquee was dark and even the street lights had been extinguished.

Gabi was determined not to return home so soon. Lise would still be awake and with Vati and Willy off in Berlin, her earlier return would pique Lise's interest and criticism.

Late in the evening as Willy polished off a plate of cold, greasy sausage, his first bite since a late lunch aboard the train, a small, dark man with a receding hairline and thick wire-rim glasses sat down next to him. His tag said he was *Fluorine*.

"Excuse me," he started quietly. "I don't mean to violate the spirit of the party, but someone from Munich pointed you out. Pardon me, but you're Herr Petersen from America, aren't you?" Willy nodded and accepted *Fluorine's* limp handshake.

"My name is Tellerman, Edward Tellerman. I've been studying in Potsdam with Professor Kraus in some of the same areas as you and Professor Wagner, thermal separation and gas-phase fractionation."

"I've just finished reading your laboratory's latest paper, Herr Tellerman," Willy said truthfully. "Professor Wagner was very complimentary," he lied politely.

"That means a great deal to us, thank you. But I wanted to introduce myself to see if we might talk for awhile. You see, I'm leaving for America, for Minnesota, in a few days. Perhaps you wouldn't mind tutoring me a little on what to expect. It will be my first trip to America."

"I'll be happy to help any way I can. Perhaps it will be easier to hear if we step outside."

It was a pleasantly cool spring evening, the babble of animated conversation and raucous laughter spilling through the open windows. The two young men talked for an hour, Willy returning frequently to the hall to refill his glass. Edward nursed a single glass the whole evening. His manner was both nervous and intense.

Tellerman was from the Sudetenland, Willy learned, the ethnic German region of Czechoslovakia annexed by the Reich six weeks before. His father was an engineer managing several German-owned coalmines. Tellerman seemed very pleased and excited by recent political changes and mentioned proudly how his new German passport would relieve him of the stigma of being a foreign national in Germany, the country he considered his own. Many opportunities and academic appointments would now open for him without restriction.

He had acquired his new German passport that very afternoon at the Foreign Ministry in Berlin. Tellerman kept reaching in his pocket, reassured by its feel. When alone, he'd sneak it out and slowly leaf through the pages as if it were some rare book. They'd suggested he retain his old Czech passport with its American visa already affixed, otherwise he'd have torn it to bits and flushed them down the toilet.

Willy answered Edward's questions about academic life at American universities, emphasizing the free expression, open dialog, and collegiality he thought would be attractive to any student constrained under the current German system. But Willy came to suspect that Edward, instead of being heartened about prospects, seemed shocked and concerned.

Similarly, when Willy tried to describe the social life on American campuses, the drinking, dancing, music, and parties, he watched the German's eyes glaze over. Edward continued to ask but didn't seem to believe all Willy's answers.

"Are there really communists teaching at American universities? How can this be tolerated? Why aren't they arrested?"

Edward was joining a department headed by Professor Ralph Emmett at the University of Minnesota in St. Paul.

"I know Ralph Emmett pretty well," Willy told Edward. "Great guy. He was the faculty advisor for last year's graduate student symposia in Madison. A theoretician. Watch out, though, he's not much of a hand in the lab. His students tell me he's a *klutz* and will blow himself up someday. Trick is not to be around when it happens! But if you like that kind of thing, you'll have the complete run of the lab. Emmett rarely sets foot there.

"Watch out for his wife, too! She enjoys playing matchmaker and the choices will be hers. You might not be happy with her selection." A look of horror came over Tellerman's face. Willy groped for something that might make Edward comfortable again.

"Food. Don't worry about food. With large German communities in Minnesota and Wisconsin, you'll see lots of German restaurants and shops in St. Paul. My mother and father still speak German at home. In my town even the church service is in German. Big Polish community in Minnesota, too. And Swedes. And Czechs. A real melting pot and always lots of fun. It's not like here in Europe where everyone's always squabbling all the time. In the states everyone tries to get along."

In Tellerman's opinion, most of what Petersen said was inane and stupid. The part about Poles and Czechs was distressing, but Edward was happy to hear about the big German community in Minnesota. In Berlin, newspapers and party literature was full of stories and photographs trumpeting the dedication and loyalty of the American Nazi Party, the 'Bund,' especially its support and promotion of the Reich's positions on German hegemony in Europe. Nazi Party members had even campaigned for elected office in some American cities.

"Are German-Americans loyal to their Fatherland?" Edward asked tentatively.

"Very patriotic," Willy responded, completely misinterpreting Edward's question.

Willy was pretty tipsy by the time the reception broke up at two in the morning. Edward was not greatly impressed. Despite his prompting, Willy had shown little interest in discussing Professor Wagner's research projects. Edward wondered whether Willy was competent. If he was representative of American scholarship, it was likely Edward would have a difficult time in Minnesota.

Willy, for his part, was happy to have made a new acquaintance; at least one young German who didn't threaten to involve Willy in some drunken adventure. Maybe this Tellerman was just another stiff-necked Nazi, Willy chuckled to himself, but two weeks with Ralph Emmett and his merry band of lunatics would loosen him up. He'd certainly learn to drink more beer. *And maybe I'll learn not to drink so much,* Willy considered as he collapsed dizzily into his bed.

To escape his pestering, Gabi had promised Willy that she would not go out alone, *as if it were any of his business.* Since the New Year, almost every night they'd been accosted by roving bands of toughs, some in uniform, others not. But as long as they'd stayed in groups, the jackals had kept their distance, shouting insults and once tossing a bottle at them as they were getting into a cab.

Gabi had argued that she should accompany them to Berlin. She wanted desperately to sample its nightlife. Gabi heard there were fewer restrictions in the lively and decadent capital, so unlike the uncouth farmers and dreary churchmen who ran Munich. Willy must convince her father, she plead, rubbing his crotch provocatively with her foot. "Willy, we'll have such a good time, I promise."

Willy had insisted that it just wasn't practical. The meeting schedule in Berlin was full and he doubted there would be spare time to see the city. They'd be gone only three days. Surely she could relax and stay home for the two nights. Then Willy would make it up to her. *But that isn't the point, is it*? If Willy was going to enjoy himself in Berlin, she certainly wasn't going to sit home staring at the walls. She knew men were all pigs and had no doubt at all that Willy was plotting some erotic adventure in her absence. Was it envy or jealousy?

As she walked aimlessly through the dark streets beyond the *Isartor*, the old east gate of the city, she became disoriented and found herself transformed. She had set out in an angry huff, but now was lonely and frightened. She couldn't locate a familiar street name or landmark to steer her back toward home. It was a dingy commercial district and no one lived here, even above the empty shops.

Damn police! They were everywhere in your business until you needed help from one. At each successive corner she sought to choose the wider street, but they seemed to be getting narrower and darker at each turn. She felt vulnerable for the first time in years and remembered being lost in the forest once as a little girl. Then, she had screamed for her Vati, who had heard her cries and rescued her within minutes. She wanted to cry out now for her Vati or for her Willy, but knew that they were both far away. *How can they leave me like this?*

As she peeked around another corner, Gabi could hear music and singing; at least there were people nearby. She wove from one side of the narrow street to the other stopping and listening, afraid that the song would finish and she'd be isolated again. Then a dim red light shown from a street-level window with heavy drapes. As she stood beneath a tattered awning, she could see that it marked the door to a small tavern. The windows were filthy and she couldn't see inside. The singing was loud and boisterous, accompanied by a raw accordion. She hesitated for a moment with her hand on the door latch. Just enough light came from the door's small, barred window, that she lost her night vision and looking back over her shoulder the street appeared even darker and more foreboding. Whatever was inside would be better than the shadows outside. The door was not locked.

The celebration had begun at sundown, shifting from beer hall to beer hall and tavern to tavern as the group got smaller, until only six young men remained. The six had been comrades since childhood, all from good families and promising students at the *Gymnasium*. But they'd all come to share the fervor of National Socialism and aspired to important positions in the Party. Together they had known the animal excitement of *Kristallnacht*, had stood guard duty at a labor camp, and had watched enviously as more senior men carried to the streets the Party's brutal policies. Today they had graduated together from cadet training at the SD center north of the city.

It wasn't the grand entrance she always endeavored to make. Inside the door, she stood quietly in the entry. Except for a single table with a half dozen uniformed young men, the tavern was deserted. They were finishing a ragged and discordant twentieth rendition of the *Horst Wessel Song*, one man trying to keep pace with an old, wheezy accordion, half its keys broken. An old barman peeked nervously from the back room through a torn curtain, wary about providing his last customers with more drinks, but unwilling to risk their ire if he refused or hesitated. Gabi stepped forward into the light hoping to catch the barman's attention: perhaps he could help her find her way home.

"Gunter, I've had too much beer. No more for me. I'm starting to hallucinate. Look there," he gasped, pointing a finger at the vision near the door.

Gabi was standing beneath a bare bulb. Her long simmering blue silk dress showed below the hem of her fur coat. Jewels in her earrings and necklace caught the cold light and sparkled incongruously.

"*Gott in Himmel*, a gift from heaven."

"Please Fräulein, come closer, we must see if you're real."

Despite the filthy floor and crude furniture, the young men appeared clean-cut and sounded well educated. Gabi felt a thrill of relief. These youngsters were of a type she was used to handling with confident ease. She stepped boldly forward.

"Good evening, *meine Herren*. Am I interrupting your party?"

One man looked round the table at his speechless friends, sitting with mouths agape, stood and removed his uniform cap. "On the contrary, Fräulein, I think you've just revived it. Would you join us for a drink?"

"I had actually stepped in just to get directions. Perhaps one of you could point me to *Eigerstrasse* or *Isartor*?"

"Of course, Fräulein, but please brighten our celebration for a few minutes, then I will personally escort you to your destination."

"Dieter is right, Fräulein. No woman should travel alone at night nowadays. The streets are full of rough characters."

"That's most kind of you all. Perhaps a single glass of champagne."
Everyone laughed.

"No champagne here, I'm afraid. Maybe a cognac for a lady, though
I won't vouch for its quality. Joseph, you worthless child, get another
chair, and everyone make room for the lady.

"Bartender," he shouted towards the back room. "A cognac for the
lady. And make sure the glass is clean."

"May I take your coat?" offered one of the boys. Gabi hesitated.
She didn't want to linger in this place.

"No thank you, sir, I still feel the chill from the street and I really
must be getting home soon. My family will be worried."

"Oh, but they should have no worries. You are now under the
protection of B Squad of the Munich SD, graduated today at the top of
our class."

"Very impressive," she offered politely, suppressing a sardonic smile.
"Does that mean that you'll be police officers?"

"Yes, Fräulein. But that's just the beginning. In two years we will
all make application to join the Party and then transfer to the SS."

"Yes, Fräulein, then we will exchange these dull brown uniforms
for tailored black ones. Imagine us then."

"I'm sure you'll be too handsome for any girl to resist."

"Could you tell us your name, Fräulein, if I'm not being too
forward?"

"...Or sound too much like a policeman, you dunce." They all
laughed and pounded each other's shoulders.

The bent old man brought Gabi's drink, trying to set it on the table
without drawing any attention. He didn't succeed. "Another round of
beer for everyone," the one name Gunter commanded. "Can't you see
our glasses are almost empty, you worthless old turd?"

How charming, Gabi thought. She took a sip. It was musty and
foul. "My name is Gabrielle, Gabrielle...Beck," she answered with a
thin smile, reluctant to give these strangers her real name. She didn't
need one of these babies knocking unexpectedly at her door one afternoon,
flowers in hand. *How embarrassing would that be?*

"How did you come to be in this neighborhood so late? Did you get
separated from friends?"

"Yes. That's right. We became separated."

"How could any man let you out of his sight for even an instant?

Your boyfriend must be blind or a fool."

"That's very flattering, thank you. Not a boyfriend, just friends."

She bit her tongue: Perhaps *that was the wrong thing to say.*

"Well, you were lucky to come in here. Most of the ghetto's businesses have been closed or burned out. All owned by Jews, they were. Abandoned now. The former owners simply *wandered* off somewhere." The other men chuckled at his suggestion.

"We come here to guard it for them. In case they should decide to come back."

"Old Bilder, who owns this place, claims he's a devout Catholic," one of the men said loudly, so he'd be heard beyond the curtain. "We haven't checked his pedigree yet, but if he's lived among Jews for all these years, he needs to be watched closely."

"That's so, Fräulein. It's just as Goo...Goo...Gunter says," another stuttered drunkenly, desperate for a bit of her attention. "We're here to protect Jew propity...property, and keep old Bilder...out of trouble."

"And now, Fräulein, you can count on us to keep you out of trouble also," Gunter said as he reached over and patted her hand paternalistically. But his look was severe and Gabi thought she sensed some accusation in his voice. Her fuse began to smolder.

"Thank you all for you considerations and company. But I'm quite able to take care of myself."

"Oh, I'm sure you are. Fräulein Gabrielle, you obviously are not a typical, modest German girl. We see your rich clothes and jewels and can smell your imported perfume. And then we find you on the empty streets in a Jewish ghetto, alone, late at night. Why shouldn't we be suspicious?

"Perhaps you're here to visit your Jewish boyfriend. Perhaps you're a Jewess. I suspect it's one thing or the other, Fräulein. Which is it?"

"I don't have a boyfriend, Jewish or otherwise," she began angrily, incredulous that the tone of the conversation had changed so quickly.

"So you're saying then that you are a Jewess...." he offered calmly.

"Of course not and you're a drunken pig to suggest such a thing," she said speaking directly to her accuser. He ignored her insult.

"Gentlemen," Gunter sat back in his chair, "let's consider the evidence."

"I don't need to listen to this," Gabi shrugged and started to rise, gathering her handbag and gloves.

"I think you should. Heinrich, please make sure this thing doesn't leave." Hesitating for a moment, the largest of the group stood behind Gabi, put knurled hands on her shoulders, and forced her back down in her chair.

So they want to play some little game, she thought. She looked around the group. While Gunter stared at her with red-faced hostility, several of others looked uncomfortable or embarrassed, refusing to meet her eyes. They stared at their beer glasses, their own hands, or the tabletop. She was breathing hard and her heart was racing. She took a deep breath and fumbled for a cigarette. No one offered her a light so she fumbled again for her own lighter, took a deep draw, and fought to regain control. These piglets were just like the SD police she'd dealt with for a year, playing little games, trying to intimidate her and her friends. She was very angry and now wanted to draw them out as fair as possible. That way, when they came to appreciate her connections and father's contacts, they could experience the same fear she had.

"Let's see, first off, I see a black-haired female. Now some Bavarian women are black-haired, all Jew females have black hair, unless of course their bitch mothers have succeeded in deceiving and seducing Aryan men. Only now are we becoming aware of how often that's happened in the past, and how important it is to prevent such interspecies breeding in the future.

"This female's hair appears to be quite kinky. This is a fashion among some of our own woman, particularly those of loose morals who aspire to decadent foreign fashion. However curly, kinky hair is very common among Jewish females.

"As for the rest, what is she doing in this neighborhood? The SD has cleared out most of the kikes but there are bound to be some hiding in their rat holes. I think this female was coming to meet her Jewish lover, one who's used money cheated from true Germans to buy her these silks and furs."

"You're a fool," she blew smoke at him.

"I don't think so," Gunter said looking at his men. "What about you men?" He stared at each until they met his eyes in tacit agreement. Gunter was a bully and had been all his life. These boys had been under his thumb for years. The ideals of discipline and command pounded into them as cadets only increased their compliance.

"She *is* here, after all," one of them offered.

"Oh, I know that I'm right. As far as I'm concerned, it doesn't matter whether she's a Jew or merely a filthy whore who ruts with one. I think it's our duty to recover the rightful property of the German people. I propose that we strip her, confiscate her silks, gems, and fur, and throw her back out onto the street." Gunter stood in front of his chair, with his palms flat on the table, leaning across towards her.

Gabi couldn't believe what she was hearing. The room was quiet, and she thought for a moment that suddenly everyone one would break into laughter and the game would be over. But one by one each of the men looked up at her and she began to recognize a hunger in their eyes and for the first time she was terrified. Since she was fourteen, she'd sensed the desire and lust in men around her. As she grew older Gabi had learned to manipulate boys and men to her own ends and eventually to her own enjoyment.

To her core, this time she could tell this was more than desire and she would not be able to control it. She was a fawn, cornered in the dark forest, surrounded by a pack of dogs. One by one each man stood, pushing his chair back.

She sat frozen. Her cigarette dropped from her fingers to the floor. No one moved. Suddenly Gunter straightened to attention. Gabi leaped to her feet thinking only about getting to the door, but the big man, Heinrich, seized her in a bear hug before she could spin around. She squirmed and kicked, knocking over several chairs. The other men all backed away, startled by the violence of her struggle. Heinrich had his hands full and tightened his grip to keep her from twisting around, but her heels were smashing painfully into his shins. He lifted her bodily and threw her facedown onto the top of the table. Gabi was stunned for a moment and lay gasping for breath, but when she started to move, the men all pounced on the table, pinning her legs, arms, and head. She continued to thrash around and now able to breathe, she began to scream, "No…"

Now that they had touched her at last, their animal lust knew no bounds. The men holding her legs allowed their hands to creep up her legs under her dress, under the pretense of improving their holds.

Gunter grabbed Gabi's hair in both hands, twisted her head, and pressed her face into the tabletop to try to silence her screams. When it didn't work the first time, he lifted her head by the hair and smashed her face even harder. The impact stunned her in the midst of a scream and broke her nose. As Gunter continued to hold her head down, he ordered, "Get her coat off."

They were clumsy and disorganized and it took several minutes just to remove the heavy coat. Everyone was tugging with one hand on a different part of the coat while holding her down with their other hand, fighting against one another like a pack of hyenas.

Wrapped in her coat, Gabi had looked larger and somehow less approachable. Now she lay on the tabletop, spread-eagled facedown in her tight blue silk dress. In her struggle the skirt had ridden up above the tops of her silk stockings and every man's eyes seem drawn to this spot. Like some sort of tableau, all movement stopped again, except for Gabi's tense trembling and hysterical whimpers.

"Take off her dress," Gunter ordered still holding her head, hands buried and twisted in her hair. The men worked slower this time, each man taking turns, the first undoing buttons and fasteners down the back, another pulling one side of the dress off one shoulder, and a third man stripping the sleeve off the other arm. When the dress was loose around her waist, one of the men holding her legs pulled the dress down her legs.

When that man released her one leg for a split second, Gabi started to kick out again and even after another man caught her ankle, she continued to fight. The man held her ankle with both hands like it was the head of a dangerous constricting snake. When he had the snake by the throat, he crashed it on the edge of the table, breaking the bone. Gabi spasmed in pain and straining against Gunter's grip, raised her head to scream in pain. Gunter banged her face down again, knocking her senseless. Again, things stopped. Everyone was panting loudly.

"Is…is…is she da…da…dead?" asked the stutterer. Without another word they rolled Gabi over on to her back and stepped away from the table. Her chest was bare and she lay still with only her short bloomers, stockings, and one shoe. Her face was bloody from her broken nose.

"She's still breathing. She's just knocked out," Gunter remarked casually. He picked up a half-empty beer glass and poured it slowly over Gabi's face, washing away much of the blood. Beer and blood dripped onto the floor below her battered head.

"Take everything off. Let's see if her hair is naturally kinky, " he snickered. "Watch her feet. If she comes to, she'll kick you in the balls. You might just need them in awhile." Her stockings and underwear were thrown into a corner.

Gunter came around the table to stand between Gabi's legs.

"Well, boys, I can't say that I've ever seen a Jewess up this close, but I don't think this is a good example of one." He reached out, roughly planted a hand into Gabi's pubic hair, and dragged her down the table towards him. Her legs hung limply over the table edge. He loosened his belt and began to unfasten his trouser buttons that strained against his arousal. When he was finally free, he glared around at his comrades who had backed away. He was stroking his member as he talked.

"Joseph, *Liebchen*, get yourself ready. This will be your second graduation today. This afternoon they made you a soldier, now you'll be a man, too." He lifted Gabi's legs by her ankles and tried to force himself inside. The tabletop was too tall and he had to stand on tiptoes. "Somebody hold her down," he growled, still flailing himself to stay erect. When at last he was inside and began to move back and forth, he lasted only a few thrusts before he climaxed. But he didn't want his friends to think he was premature so he didn't give any outward sign and continued to rock back and forth for several minutes. When he was afraid he would slip out and show them all that he was already limp, he pretended to orgasm, made a big show of his last thrusts, and pulled away in mock triumph.

"Your turn, Joseph," he ordered, pulling his pant up from around his knees.

"But Gunter, what about *der Tripper*? I don't want to catch a disease."

"If you were really worried about that then you would have warned me, wouldn't you? Or are you a disloyal traitor as well as a homo? Do it now, the others are waiting.

"Dieter, find that Jew-lover, Bilder, and get me another glass of beer."

The youngest of the squad moved forward reluctantly and undid his belt and buttons. But when his underwear was down, it was apparent that he wasn't going to be able to perform. Everyone laughed, some angrily, others anxiously. At last Heinrich grabbed him by the shirt collar and threw him back across the room like a rag doll. Joseph crashed into some empty chairs and lay on the floor sobbing.

Heinrich didn't hesitate a second and he assaulted Gabi with clumsy violence, his heavy weight pressing breath and life out of her. Afterwards each of the other three mechanically took his turn, their sole thought to avoid the wrath or scorn of their comrades.

Gabi dreamt she was on a train as it rumbled, clacked, and swayed. The train was carrying her to America. She was puzzled by the dream: you had to take a ship to get to America. A train just wouldn't do. But she was looking out the train window at the same tall buildings she'd seen in the magazines and newsreels. And even aboard the train, she could hear the music, clarinets and drums. She wanted to be able to recognize the song, to impress Willy with how much she knew about America. But the melody kept changing. Or maybe many songs were playing at the same time. Willy knew everything. He was so smart, like Vati. *I have to remember that song. I'll show them I'm smart, too.*

But the train and its passengers were noisy and kept distracting her. One moment she thought she knew the song, the next moment she didn't. If the train would only stop for a minute...

The last man was too short to reach Gabi on the tabletop, so he pulled her towards him until her hips were well over the edge of the table. As he struggled with her limp body, holding her by the thighs, the table slid away and she slipped off the table, the back of her head thumping on the sticky floor. Her whole body quivered and shook, exciting the man even more. But a moment after he started, the tremors stopped and her body made a croaking sound as a last breath was expelled through her constricted throat.

The man stopped, propped on his hands and knees, and looked down at her face. Slowly her eyes opened. *Watch out! She's waking up*, he thought. But as the lids fell back he saw only the whites of her eyes, blank and hideous. He pulled away quickly, jumped to his feet, and retreated to a corner of the room. Gunter, who'd been sitting, nursing a glass of beer nearby, stood and walked over to Gabi's body. He tested it with the toe of his boot.

"Dieter, you ass, look what you've done. I was hoping for another round. What a waste. You're such an ox. Now there's bound to be questions. Let's get back to the barracks." Gunter straightened his tie and neatly arranged his belts and lanyards.

"One last thing: Freddi, I can hear Herr Bilder sniveling somewhere in the backroom. We can't have him telling any stories. Will you find him and break his neck for me? Joseph, perhaps you ought to go help him. Do *something* manly tonight."

Reluctantly, but without comment, Freddi took Joseph by the arm and shoved him along in front toward the curtained door leading to the back of the tavern.

When the cadets left five minutes later, they switched off the lights, and locked the door behind them. Dark and quiet, it was just like all the other buildings on the block. Deserted and abandoned.

Early next morning, the lecture hall crowd was boisterous. Professor Wagner was the preeminent scholar present and at his chair of honor, a dozen senior men paused briefly to shake hands and exchange best regards. Willy was sure the Professor did not recognize many of them any longer, but the room was so noisy that no conversation was possible or expected. With the exception of the small contingent from the physics department in Munich, Willy didn't recognize any of the men in the front of the hall, though by their demeanor he could tell there was something special about them. He had come to know the names of men who might be present: Hahn, Debye, von Weizsächer, and Heisenberg, perhaps even Max Planck and Gustav Hertz. Willy had seen photographs of some of these men; Planck's picture was in the frontispiece of Willy's thermodynamics textbook back home. But stare as he might, he couldn't connect any faces to names.

Waiting for the symposium to begin, he did spot Edward Tellerman standing in the back by the main door, and seated by themselves near the rear of the hall, Willy recognized his two visitors from Army Ordnance, poised to take notes. Even with the hall packed, no one wanted to sit next to them. Willy guessed that many of the men in this room had similar, disturbing experiences with Lieutenant Posen and his companion, Bose. He looked away quickly and settled lower in his seat. He had an uneasy feeling that they might think Willy's presence inappropriate and have him expelled from the hall if they recognized him.

The buzz in the hall subsided as Werner Heisenberg made his way to the podium from a side door, nodding to some of the men seated in the front row, pausing to shake hands and exchange a word or two with others. He seemed relaxed and totally at home.

"Please let me welcome you to the Conference's General Session. If you can be patient for a few minutes, I'll have some opening remarks.

Then Colonel Diebner has asked for a few minutes of your time this morning. Finally, Otto Hahn has agreed to provide us with both general background and an update of recent work relevant to this meeting. At ten o'clock we'll break up into smaller groups for specific technical topics that will continue after lunch, which will be served in the garden at one o'clock. My plan is for everyone to reconvene here at five o'clock to hear highlights of the working group sessions and perhaps for some closing remarks.

"It isn't always possible to assemble…" Heisenberg launched into an airy and friendly opening speech that included all the right words and sentiments. He mentioned cooperation, collegiality, free exchange of ideas, interaction, the past, the present, and the future. Willy had attended a dozen such conferences and in form and format this one appeared no different than any covering butterfly taxonomy or cotton bleaching. It was almost surreal.

Colonel Diebner was more succinct. His drab gray uniform was unadorned except for the stark contrast of the black swastika and white circle on his left sleeve. Willy's eyes were drawn to it. It seemed so alien at a scientific meeting.

"The Army is sponsoring this meeting with the purpose of gathering scientists and engineers into a single forum to learn about new concepts and processes that could have tremendous importance for the future of the Reich. Our government has been following these developments closely over the last ten years, and believes, as many of you do, that harnessing and controlling these fundamental forces of nature has practical and political implications beyond most of our imaginations. For twenty years now the Fatherland has been the helpless hostage of foreign politicians, after their pound of flesh. Restrictions on our sovereign right to expand and colonize have allowed them to blackmail the Fatherland economically. And foreign support of divisive elements within the Fatherland has lead to a mongrelization of our culture and our science.

"The Führer recognized this a decade ago and when the National Socialist Party came to power six years ago, he set out to restore purity and clarity to German science. We believe that we have succeeded. These new scientific efforts, of such monumental importance to the Fatherland and to the world, can now go forward unencumbered by personal political or social agendas. We can break the power these foreigners hold over us.

"You who become involved directly in this work have a responsibility to the German people to make it successful in whatever applications our leadership decides are needed. Your loyalties must be to the Fatherland and to the Führer. Pettiness and personal aggrandizement must be set aside. We expect you all to behave and perform as patriots. On this basis the Party and the German people will continue to support and monitor these valuable developments."

The audience's applause was restrained and polite. And no one relaxed until Professor Hahn rose and nervously began his presentation. Hahn was aware that many people in the audience had not been following recent progress nor did they comprehend how the theories of Einstein, Bohr, and Heisenberg tied the package up nicely. He was careful to explain each subject thoroughly and when he was finished Willy felt exhilarated. The bits and pieces he'd picked up in Munich and from Professors Wagner and Heisenberg now coalesced into a whole.

Standing out in Willy's mind were what Hahn defined as the most crucial elements and their interrelationships. Simply, how much uranium was needed to form a critical mass that would sustain the atomic reaction? What is the critical relationship between neutron energies and the ability of another uranium atom to capture that free neutron and then break up spontaneously, initiating a chain-reaction? What's its nuclear cross-section? From Hahn's vivid description, this was no longer simply the series of tedious calculations, but rather a real phenomenon, one that could be tested and confirmed in a laboratory. Hahn spent several minutes describing the new facility under construction at Dahlem in the Berlin suburbs. Here they would finally attempt to demonstrate their concepts. The new physics institute was to be named after Max Planck himself.

Willy came to understand that despite Heisenberg's casual request for Professor Wagner's review of his calculations, the value derived was fundamental to the understanding and application of this nuclear technology. It was thrilling to be participating with breakthrough technology, regardless how close to the fringes Willy might be. As he listened he was caught up in the excitement. This would look good in Willy's *vitae*, a document that would say a great deal about future professional and career opportunities.

Willy and Professor Wagner attended a smaller, informal technical session on uranium purification technology. The participants had focused on their special expertise and there was considerable friendly debate over whether gas diffusion or thermal processes would be the most effective and economical means to separate and purify the most active isotopes of uranium. Everyone agreed it could be done if no one cared about cost. At this point in the discussions, no one did, so some of the ideas were pretty wild. But the basic questions remained at the workshop's conclusion: What was the neutron absorption cross-section and how many kilograms of uranium isotope would be needed? In theory at least, the purification could be accomplished. That was merely an engineering problem.

Whenever discussion turned to his areas of interest, Professor Wagner emerged from his haze and contributed lucidly to the exchange. The remainder of the time, he sat in quiet dignity, nodding whenever a new speaker acknowledged his presence. He would occasionally fix his gaze on a speaker at the lectern and his stare and his reputation was such that no one questioned him or tried to draw him out. After lunch Willy managed to convince the Professor to return to his room for a nap, promising the Professor he'd return and waken him for the closing remarks. When Willy was sure the Professor was settled in, he returned to the symposium and joined a second technical workshop on engineering requirements for purification plants.

By the end of the afternoon, putting aside Diebner's troubling comments in the morning, Willy could see little difference between this conference and a dozen others he'd attended since he was an undergraduate. The event was partially social and fraternal. Most of these scientists and researchers had known each other for decades. Teachers were present, and teachers of teachers like Professor Wagner. It was an opportunity for researchers at less prestigious institutes to rub elbows with more famous colleagues. Most of the younger scientists saw the meeting as a chance to make personal contacts and position themselves in line for new fellowships and vacant teaching jobs. With the upheavals of the last five years, some of the institutes had lost half of their staffs to emigration. Regardless the true motives of the Nazi Exclusion Laws, many of these men were direct beneficiaries of laws stripping Jews and non-German ethnics of their jobs.

All through the technical discussions in the morning and afternoon, subtle references would be made to some bit of knowledge or experience to which they no longer had access: "It's unfortunate we can't ask Isaac Beckerman: he worked with stainless steel pump impellers and seals in the '20's." Everyone in the room knew how Beckerman and his family had disappeared mysteriously one night. Rumor said he was working in England. Regrets were neither emphasized or used as excuses, but after bumping up against this wall several times, the impact of the loss of these men, some great scientists and others just competent experimentalists, was fully appreciated. The loss would impede progress, particularly when this new technology needed to be reduced to practice.

Not a single speaker or participant would risk personalizing these changes, even though men like Otto Hahn had suffered great personal loss. When his coworker and friend Lise Meitner escaped to Sweden, he thought his world had ended. The Gestapo had been angry and threatening, suspecting his complicity. And Hahn knew that he'd never be allowed to leave Germany again. Many others had similar stories and experiences: senior men who had tried to defend Jewish coworkers after Hitler came to power in 1933. Some knew the Gestapo was closely watching them. Most suspected and feared so. Unless one was prepared to give up everything and join former friends in forced exile, it was best to remain silent and show enthusiasm whether feigned or genuine.

Late in the afternoon everyone reassembled in the main hall, Professor Wagner reclaiming his seat of honor. Heisenberg again took the podium.

"I've spoken with all the working group chairmen and it certainly sounds like significant progress was made in identifying what we know and what we don't know, what we can do and what we can't currently achieve. Each chairman has been asked to prepare minutes of his session and circulate them among the participants for comment and revision. Please respond promptly. Summaries will be prepared for our hosts at the Ministry of Education and the Ordnance Department. I sincerely hope they will be able to publish proceedings of this meeting and get them out to all of you. Progress in this nuclear technology is made daily and it's crucial that we all continue to communicate with one another and with other workers outside of Germany. We are a community of scientists and we have a responsibility to each other as well as to our institutions and nation.

"Some of you have approached me with concerns about the potential applications of this science. There is talk about powerful weapons of war. I hope you all agree with me that we don't know enough to speculate whether such weapons could be made or should be made. Regardless, these decisions are years away and will be made against a background of political and social circumstances we can't predict. Our individual and collective responsibility is to the search for knowledge. These are the careers we've chosen.

"The task ahead is complex and daunting. While we theoreticians conceptualize and ruminate, the experimental and engineering work required will become more and more important. We can't currently know who will play what roles and I've suggested to Minister Rust that we're still not at a point where formal organizations can be usefully established. For the time being then, let's think of ourselves as an informal fraternity of friends and colleagues with common interests. Someone suggested we call ourselves the *Uranium Club*. I think that is very appropriate," Heisenberg said with a smile.

"Let me say on behalf of the *Kaiser Wilhelm-Institut* and the Ministry of Education, how pleased we were that you could attend. If there are no further comments from the floor…thank you for coming."

During the train ride back to Munich the next morning, with the Professor napping in his seat, Willy jotted notes on scrap paper to provide an outline for what he'd heard the previous day. At first he concentrated on problems associated with isotope purification in the laboratory. Professor Wagner and his former assistants had been working on some unique chemical techniques for the purification of metallic pigments that might be applicable. Willy was thinking about simple experiments he should run to test his ideas. Certain references should be checked first and he made of notes of which ones.

The lively debate about industrial-scale purification was intriguing. One participant had talked about computations that suggested costs could exceed a hundred million marks and require two thousand technicians to operate. Surely no one foresees a need for anything on this scale. Who had that kind of money? Who could take such financial risks?

According to one speaker, the critical mass of uranium required might be over thirty thousand cubic meters in size and weigh over 10 million kilos. "Is there that much uranium in the world?" someone had asked.

"While I can't vouch for its purity," another man offered, "I understand the Belgians have large stockpiles from Katanga Province in the Congo stored here in Europe. Millions of kilograms, I've heard. I've no idea how much the Belgians would want to charge us for it."

"If they think we need it, the Belgians will hold out forever. The entire country is made up of petty merchants and money-lenders," sneered a young man at the end of the table. He was tall and blonde with a swastika pin in his lapel.

Looking around the room nervously, another man added, "I've read reports that there are rich deposits of uranium-bearing ore in Czechoslovakia. I suppose they are accessible now at little more than the cost of the labor." The man wasn't sure how other people would interpret his suggestion. Czechoslovakia had been part of the Reich now for only six weeks, but no one in this room really knew what that might mean.

Willy penciled some rough calculations comparing the scale of a purification plant against various levels of purification, but in the end he was convinced that such an operation would be beyond the scope of any institute or company anywhere in the world, including the United States.

Other senior scientists present had voiced strong opinions. A researcher from Potsdam had pointed out that a uranium pile of that massive size could never be a practical source of heat for the generation of electricity. He argued it was so huge that it would necessarily be located distant from factories and cities that need the power. Line losses would make it less economical than the current coal-fired generation plants. He then recounted a story about some visitors to his laboratory from the German Navy who were inquiring whether a pile could be installed in a ship as small as a submarine. He had told them, "Yes, as long as your ship is the size of a small city!" Several around the room snickered. Others stared thoughtfully at the tabletop.

He continued recklessly, "These two sailors then wanted to know if an explosive device could be assembled using the same principles. I told them in no uncertain terms that their city-sized pile was likely to blow up in any case, if that's what they meant. No, they wanted a device that could be carried by a ship or even dropped from an airplane. Their ideas were total nonsense. No ship would be large enough to carry it, certainly no aircraft."

"But Ludwig, if the nuclear cross-sections are found to be high enough and the uranium is sufficiently purified to concentrate active isotope, then…"

"No, no. Think about it, Johann. If the cross-section is ten times what Werner believes and we purify the uranium to ninety-percent active isotope, the pile still weighs what? A hundred thousand kilos! At a cost of what? Twenty million marks for one explosive device: for a single bomb? A bomb that couldn't be tested? Someone in the Navy has his head in the clouds. Or perhaps in some darker place as I understand is the predilection of some sailors!" Most everyone in the room smiled at his colorful comments. There were exceptions. *Bombs,* Willy thought. It was the first time Willy had heard this prospect mentioned so directly, despite the ridicule heaped on the idea.

Willy wasn't so sure, though he didn't make any comments during the workshops. In December Heisenberg had shrugged and told Willy that his calculations might be off by a factor of ten or a factor of a million. On his scratch paper Willy roughed out the numbers. If Heisenberg was off by a million fold from those worst case examples, then the critical mass of uranium isotope needed might be *five kilograms: ten pounds!* Split the difference and allow that Heisenberg is off by a factor of ten thousand and the critical mass weighs a thousand pounds! Even a small airplane could carry this weight. The pile would be dangerously radioactive and Willy didn't know how to calculate what shielding would be needed to protect airmen or sailors, but perhaps such a bomb with its trigger mechanism might weigh two thousand pounds. Bombs that large had been dropped from airships on London during the Great War.

During his presentation Otto Hahn had said that the uranium fission would be very efficient in terms of the conversion of mass to energy. He had used the chalkboard to illustrate some of the calculations. One equation stood out as integral to all the others and though Hahn wisely did not invoke his name, every scientist in the room recognized Einstein's formula, $E = mc^2$. The total amount of energy available from every pound of uranium was phenomenal: enough indeed for a city's heat and lights.

"Professor Hahn, how fast will the reaction occur?" asked someone from the audience.

"We believe the release of neutrons from each succeeding nuclear fission will occur instantaneously. We can't envision anything that would slow this process down. Unmediated, the chain reaction would theoretically cascade through a million steps in a few seconds. All the energy from the mass would be converted and released in the blink of an eye. Uncontrolled, this reaction would run away like many chemical reactions and cause an explosion. While this is something of great concern to us," he said, glancing over at Heisenberg leaning against a nearby door sill, "we don't see how we'll ever be able to eliminate all impurities from the uranium mass. Any contaminants will act to absorb the neutrons without splitting themselves and quench the reaction. We envision using long rods of non-reactive materials which when shoved into the pile will capture and control the neutron flux."

As Willy sat back in his train seat, watching the trees and poles quickly appear and recede, he came to his own conclusion that uranium fission was possible, even probable. Part of Willy's conclusion was based on a confidence that men like Einstein, Heisenberg, and Hahn wouldn't have gone this far if it weren't true and if they didn't believe it was true. Willy remembered what Heisenberg had told him during their stroll to the Professor's house before Christmas. These ideas are like poetry: suddenly all the right words fall into place and the poem is complete. Willy hadn't been involved for twenty years in this particular quest and as a newcomer with a different background and unjaundiced eye maybe he could see how simply this all fit together. Men from the German Navy and Army were like Willy: they didn't understand enough to worry about what couldn't be done, only what was possible.

Willy put his notes away and stared thoughtfully at the Bavarian countryside. This stretch of rolling hills, farms, and villages was not very different from Wisconsin. If a bomb could be constructed using this uranium fission technology, what would it mean to these little towns? What would it mean to similar towns in Wisconsin?

Heisenberg had taken Willy aside during tea break the previous afternoon.

"Herr Petersen, I hope you've found the symposium of some interest."

"Yes, Professor, very much so."

"I'm sorry I won't have time for that talk we promised about America. I would feel much better if I knew more about how opinion is running there. I fear my reception might not be a warm one. Some people will be quick to doubt our motives.

"In any case, I'm also sorry that Professor Wagner is still under the weather. I wanted to have a few words with him about the cross-section calculations. You work with him: has he had an opportunity to get started? Does he have questions that either I or Otto Hahn can answer before you two return to Munich tomorrow morning?"

Willy looked over Heisenberg's broad shoulder, avoiding his eyes, and told the lie. "Everything seems to be going well, Professor. The project is well underway. Professor Wagner works on them for several hours everyday. He hasn't asked me to help to this point, but I can repeat his assurances that the report will be complete by mid-June, early August at the latest."

"Marvelous. But again, if he has any questions please contact me immediately, and after I've left for the states, call Hahn or von Weizsächer. And please find time to visit the new facility in Dahlem later in the year. You'll certainly find it interesting and your independent account of our efforts might be important someday."

"Thank you again for your help, Herr Petersen. Afraid I have to run now. Lots of ruffled feathers to smooth. I hope to see you again soon."

As their taxi pulled to curb late that evening, Willy noted two official-looking black cars parked along the street near Professor Wagner's house. It flashed in through his mind that the Gestapo or Army had finally caught on to his nationality. Well, he hadn't actually lied. *No one had asked*. Willy helped the Professor out of the taxi and almost carried him up the steps. Willy knew in his heart that Professor Wagner had attended his last conference. The physical and mental strain had aged him another ten years in just three days. It was going to take weeks for him to recover his strength. Willy could be frank with Lise. Together they would have to convince Gabi how more of her help was needed to nurse her father and keep him active and hopeful. And he would ask them to help decide what to do about the Professor's ongoing work. As soon as they could get the Professor settled in his bed, Willy was determined to open and press the topic.

But as they reached the top step, Lise threw open the door. There were tears in her eyes and her face was flushed and contorted.

"Vati, Vati, the police are here…She didn't come home last night or the night before. I didn't know whom to call…"

The horrors of the next months were almost more than even Willy and Lise could bear.

112

Tellerman

A tall, burly man at the front door looked first at Edward's nametag and only then at his face. The big man sported an open collar shirt and tattered wool sweater.

"Ed, welcome!" Professor Emmett nearly shouted, slapping Edward on the shoulder. "I'm Professor Emmett, but please call me Ralph. Sorry no one told you about our parties here, but we try to be as informal as possible." Edward was wearing a formal black suit and old-fashioned collar and tie. These were his very best clothes and he was complete with waistcoat and watch fob. Edward's black shoes shone like mirrors. He had taken extraordinary care with his appearance for this first meeting with his new colleagues. *Ralph* was wearing filthy canvas shoes and no socks and hadn't shaved that morning.

Edward had left his new dormitory room with a little vain pride at his clothes, hoping to make the very best impression. Now, looking down the hallway at the other men and women chatting in the living room, he felt embarrassed and quite ridiculous.

"You'll find that American college life is much less formal than what I've witnessed in Europe. We try to be less stuffy. Helps everyone to be more creative."

"Yes, I understand," Edward replied lamely.

"Come in the living room and I'll introduce you around," Professor Emmett steered Edward down the hallway and into the large airy room. A servant handed Edward a glass of beer. The twenty people in the room were all dressed similarly in brightly colored clothes, talking and laughing. It was impossible to distinguish between professors and students. Jazz music blared from a phonograph in the next room.

Edward noted several women present, evidently students, wives, or girlfriends. But they were talking loudly, mixed in the groups with men. This struck Edward as inappropriate.

"I'm pleased to meet you at last, Ed. Your letters of recommendation speak for themselves. I'm sure we've got lots of interesting work for you here." He reached into one cluster of guests and grabbed the elbow of a blond, buxom woman gaudily dressed in some sort of tropical outfit with flowers in her frizzy hair.

"Ed, this is my wife, Peggy. Peg, this is Ed Tellerman…from Czechoslovakia. I told you about him. He taking up one of my assistantships."

"It's nice to meet you, Frau Emmett," Edward offered with a little bow. It would be rude to correct Professor Emmett for his mistake about Edward's citizenship in front of his wife.

"Please, Ed, all the kids call me Peggy. No reason to be formal." Edward could sense that the Professor's wife was looking him over critically.

"You make sure that my worthless husband remembers to bring you home for dinner. I love to hear what's going on over at the lab. I was a chemistry student here myself until I hooked up with this old pervert," she said giving her husband an affectionate shove. "You can spy on my husband for me. Help keep him away from the prettier coeds!" Everyone laughed at these remarks. "Fat chance!" somebody called out. Edward could only pretend to smile. He found this all very uncomfortable and painfully personal.

"Step this way, Ed," Emmett took him by the arm. "Let me introduce you to these folks. Don't worry if you can't remember all the names. In no time we'll all be like family." Emmett went quickly around the room: "This is Frank Maring and his wife Sandra; this is Joey Cipriano; Matt and Felicity Miller; and Fred Smalt." Each person or couple paused in their animated conversation to nod and shake Edward's hand. Even the women had strong handshakes and he knew everyone taking measure of him.

"Folks, this is Ed Tellerman. He just arrived this morning from Czechoslovakia. He's one of our new assistants. Please, everybody make him welcome. He's a long way from home. Joey, make sure you keep his glass full. One of you girls convince him to loosen his collar and stay awhile. Excuse me for a second, Ed, somebody's at the door."

Edward was suddenly surrounded by a group of younger guests. He understood that these were his fellow student assistants, colleagues for the next several years.

"In case you missed it, I'm Fred Smalt. It's nice to meet you, Ed.

Did you have a chance to settle in at the dorm?"

"Yes, thank you for asking."

A short, pudgy girl with thick glasses pressed forward, demanding attention. "I'm Linda Trout. We'll be sharing Lab Six over at Warner Hall. I've got a desk and bench space all cleaned out for you."

An older man shouldered his way into the group and offered his hand.

"Mr. Tellerman, I'm Dean Andersen. I head up the Institute of Technology here."

"I am honored, Herr Andersen."

"And it's nice to meet you, Mr. Tellerman. Ralph's been telling me how glad he is that you managed to get here despite all the troubles back home. Let me assure you right off the bat, that when you need help extending your student visa, the entire department and university will stand behind your application to Washington. Tragically, I can't see any way the situation in Europe will improve before it gets worse. Consider yourself part of our family here at Minnesota. You're welcome as long as you want to stay."

"Thank you very much, Herr Andersen," said Edward, confused about some of what Dean Andersen had been saying. Why should he have any trouble with the American government in Washington? *My papers are in perfect order.* Edward hoped to complete his graduate studies in two years, perhaps eighteen months if he worked diligently. If he stayed away from Germany too long he feared he'd miss many opportunities as science and technology continued to strengthen under the new regime. Universities all over Germany had broken up the Jewish cabal that had controlled many faculties, so appointments were opening up for true Germans.

Dean Andersen was continuing: "Dr. Leo Szilard was here visiting just a couple of months ago. He's Hungarian and in the same boat as you and your fellow countrymen. He made a speech at the faculty senate. Described the plight of non-Germans and Jews at German universities. Szilard's something of a mountebank, I gather, but he convinced our administration to find appointments for students like you. Szilard has lots of other crazy deals he's pushing about bombs and such, but no one's listening to that stuff."

Edward didn't really understand what Dean Andersen was getting at, but he was having a difficult time concentrating on his English with so many people talking at once. If Herr Andersen meant that an influx of Jews was expected, all the more reason to complete his research and return to Germany as quickly as possible, before those Jews began to entrench themselves and Jew science at this university.

"Herr Andersen, your support is deeply appreciated. I am grateful to be here and promise to work hard and make important contributions."

Linda wanted his attention again. "What can you tell us about your research back home?" she began, standing much too close for Edward's comfort. Dean Andersen drifted off to another group of students.

Edward's glass was never empty, and he ended the afternoon with a generally poor opinion of his new colleagues. They all seemed very naïve and harmless. Others were curious, but not well informed. The four-day train trip from New York impressed him with the expanse and variety of the countryside, the vast farmlands, and the factories in Ohio and Indiana. But it seemed as if all these great resources were wasted on a shallow and silly people.

One elderly professor disarmed him with his question: "So, sonny, tell me about *Yugoslobenia*, or wherever all this commotion is taking place. Can't you folks over there just settle down and get along?"

Hard work and his superior undergraduate training would put him above them all in short order. Monday would be the first day.

Conspiracy

In the month following Gabi's murder Willy's visits to *Königenstrasse* were infrequent and difficult. The police had been reluctant to release her body and only intervention by one of the Professor's influential and sympathetic neighbors had prevented the authorities from cremating the remains against the family's wishes.

When the state trial of the six cadets began, Willy offered to attend, driven partly by his own guilt and partly to protect Lise from the cold-blooded and shocking testimony he expected. She promised to stay away only if Willy came each evening to report what had transpired. Professor Wagner heard none of this and after the initial shock, invented his own delusions about where Gabi had gone and when she would return. Somewhere deep in his confused mind, he understood the truth and suffered some violent spells that had left Lise physically exhausted. In the deep sleep that followed, she found her only escape from the horrifying images that haunted her waking moments.

When the trial was over and the judges had sentenced the cadets to ten years hard labor, Willy sought closure, burying himself again in his solitary research.

But every day his eyes were drawn to Professor Heisenberg's project file, as it sat untouched in the office. After Christmas Professor Wagner had written out the long, complex series of calculations that would be used as the basis for the report and spent several days reviewing their subtleties with Willy who would have worked the more repetitive and tedious sections. But now Willy doubted Professor Wagner would ever return to his beloved laboratory.

No further work on the project had been done since April. And as part of his living nightmare, Willy began to perceive within the file the seeds and roots of more murder, on a scale so hideous that it was beyond comprehension. Nazis were capable of anything. In the back of his mind, despite the evidence of his own eyes, he'd clung to the idea that everything he'd witnessed earlier stemmed from a country and people in transition to something new. Ends might justify means and individual acts of brutality and terror would end as the regime prevailed. But at the trial, the Nazi judges and prosecutors had been calculating, callous, and cold, treating Gabi's life and murder as the mere sum of small, insignificant parts. And they applied this calculus to the sentences, where for the good of this and the benefit of that, the government decided. It was all so rational and inhuman. Individual acts were now part and parcel to an institutional authority which showed neither horror nor outrage at the crime.

He had to face the troubling realization that what he'd witnessed was characteristic of the new leadership and regime This went against every ideal he'd been taught about free societies. *That's wrong*, he thought. It went against what Willy had *learned*, not what he'd been taught. Willy had learned history as a chronological series of triumphant heroes, kings, generals, and presidents. These characters and the events surrounding them made for exciting stories and it wasn't necessary to read between the lines. He chided himself as an unsophisticated Pollyanna rejecting the history of man's inhumanity, his blind eyes shielded by rose-colored glasses.

When Willy returned to the question of uranium cross-sections, his uneasiness led inevitably to the prospects for a Nazi super weapon and he knew, with neither doubt nor qualification, that any decision to build and use that bomb would be made in the same detached fashion. *Humanity be damned!*

He pledged to himself to never aid such a project and he would not complete the calculations, regardless the Professor's commitments. Willy could convince himself that if the Professor were well, he too would reject it.

Professor Wagner's role was more than merely advisory, that he understood well. The Ministry of Education had agreed to accept his findings and recommendation. They felt it was the most credible available. But dozens of other capable men could be found in short order and the work would be completed with little delay. Willy would wait until the last possible moment to inform Heisenberg that the Professor would not be able to finish the work, which was due late in the summer, still three months away. There would be a delay, though only a short one. But Willy was in a quandary. An excuse would be needed and risk was that through Heisenberg or the Ministry, Professor Wagner's mental and physical condition would become known. If Willy simply sent a message saying that the report would be delayed, someone was likely to check up on them, even if it was just an innocent offer to help. If the unsympathetic Lieutenant Posen turned up again, the Professor would be in serious jeopardy. Willy had never forgotten what he'd heard in Berlin about Nazi euthanasia centers. Everything he'd seen and experienced told him that the story was true.

Was there a way to delay the project further? Both Heisenberg and the two army drones had said the Professor's input was crucial. Could Willy send a letter over the Professor's signature that he was having difficulties? That might buy several more months, though again such a letter was likely to draw questions and visitors. Even this idea would only work once and it did not represent any release from those promises. The question is, how could Willy set the Professor completely free from this obligation?

It occurred to Willy that if a report was presented that implied the absorption cross-sections were low, then the whole scheme would seem impractical and might be dropped. After all, the Professor had been asked to act as a final arbiter in the dispute between believers and non-believers. Would his calculations and conclusions be doubted or questioned? What would it mean to the Professor, to Lise, and to Willy, if a deception were exposed? Dishonor? Ridicule? Or something worse.

Would risks to the Wagners be greater than if no report were sent? No, not if Willy Petersen, village idiot, prepared and sent the false report, without the Professor's knowledge. Willy would be the one who'd hidden the Professor's temporary illness, Lise could swear. They'd ask, *didn't Herr Petersen contact you*? *No*, she could answer.

I could do it, he thought, unconcerned about his own punishment. *I know how*. But he couldn't ask the Wagners to risk anything more. The report must be completed, but it must not support the bomb builders. It was important that Lise understand all this. He had no right doing anything on his own. *Let her help me judge*.

"And I'm not sure I can explain the science and all its implications properly. Many things I don't understand completely. I guess I'm reacting more to how people are talking instead of what they're saying. Can you understand that?" Willy was embarrassed. He risked insulting Lise and he needed her patience. She was so intelligent and insightful. Willy had to organize things in his own mind first for her to understand how all the pieces fit together, and for Lise to come to a point where she could share his understanding and his fears. But he risked sounding condescending and making her feel like he thought she was stupid or ignorant. She was proud, like her father and sister, and just as quick to take offense.

They were seated side by side on the settee in the study in front of a smoldering fire the Professor insisted they maintain despite the mild weather. Willy had helped Lise move her father to his room upstairs and had waited for her to come down once the Professor had nodded off. Tonight, Professor Wagner had confused his daughters and despite their reassurance, expressed concern for *Lise's* absence. Such occasions were a relief of sorts, since these were times when the Professor had forgotten that Gabi was dead. Whenever he remembered, he'd sob uncontrollably until the shaking would become a convulsion and he'd have to be restrained in his bed.

"Willy, I'll try to understand as best I can. We've plenty of time. I want to help you. Tell me first about what you've heard people say."

"You've met some of them. When Professor Heisenberg visited your father before Christmas, I had a chance to talk to him about his work in a general way."

"Yes, I remember when you brought him to the house."

"That's right. When he spoke about how important his discoveries might be to future generations, he seemed troubled. Professor Heisenberg implied there was a remote possibility that because of his work those future generations would be born into a very different world, *if they were born at all.*"

"He's a very strange man who sometimes sounds more like a Bohemian poet than a physicist, at least any physicist I've ever met."

"I remember he played the piano so beautifully. His eyes were closed most of the time."

"A few weeks later two officers from Army Ordnance Research stopped by the lab to meet with your father. Their suggestion that Professor Heisenberg was somehow disloyal angered your father and he dismissed them like undergraduates." Willy had decided long ago not to alarm her concerning Posen's threat. "They left behind with me a long list of pertinent questions, but the thing that stood out was the army's interest in the purification of uranium, the separation of its various isotopes. They wanted to know what if would take in terms of planning, equipment, money, and manpower to build a separation and purification factory. Money was no object, they implied."

"I'm sorry Willy, but could you explain isotope? I've typed the word when I transcribed Vati's notes."

"An isotope is a special form of an element like uranium. Chemically it looks and behaves just like any other form of uranium, but it contains extra atomic particles called neutrons. Extra neutrons are critical if you want to get some sort of atomic chain reaction started. But let me return to that later.

"When I accompanied your father to Berlin, there was more talk about uranium. Several high ranking officers attended from the Army and Navy. One Colonel made a speech saying how important the conference was for the Fatherland and hinted at political and international complications. I saw the same two Army officers who'd come to see your father. I recall now that one man's name is Bose. Honestly, Lise, I could tell from some of the comments I overheard that Bose had traveled around and asked the same questions of many of other scientists who later attended the conference. The military's interest extends back at least two years. Someone else said it was ten years. The Army won't spend this much time, effort, and money on simple theories. And they aren't interested in civilian uses.

"Later Professor Hahn spoke about the tremendous energy and power that could be released by a chain reaction of uranium isotope, and while no one used the word, there's an implication that uranium could be used to build a bomb, one bigger and more deadly than any ever conceived. The men from the Army were writing everything down and whispering among themselves. Other attendees seemed to treat it all as a big joke, some paradoxical riddle like angels on the tip of a needle. But I think that Professor Heisenberg is very concerned, even frightened."

"But you said this was all just a theory that Professor Heisenberg has discovered?"

"I know. But his theories are tied to those of Einstein and Bohr and others, going back nearly thirty years. No one reported any real experimental results. 'We *think* we *might* be able to do this or that.' I didn't hear anything more concrete. But who knows what might be happening behind closed doors or in secret labs. There's logic and reason in the concepts. Men much smarter and more experienced than me appeared excited or anxious."

"But what makes you think research will result in bombs? Surely Professor Heisenberg wouldn't allow his ideas to be used to kill people. He seems so kind. All he could talk about was his little boys."

"I'm not sure he could stop, even if he wished to. The government now runs the Physics Institute and Professor Heisenberg works for the Institute. Same for many others. They still want to prove out their theories and need the resources of the Institute to set up their experiments. But some don't feel they have any responsibility for the applications of their own discoveries."

"Willy, I'm frightened," Lise said earnestly. "There's so much bitterness and hatred in Germany today. No one seems to care anymore about kindness. I've seen it myself. So have you. I loved Gabi very much and though she was always getting into trouble, she didn't deserve to die. She just wanted to have fun. The police didn't care and the men that killed her are still alive, protected by Party authority. In ten years they'll be free: maybe to kill again.

"Willy, you've seen how they treat Jewish people and other groups they don't like. Nazis are ruthless and all they know is hatred. I'm not smart enough to know whether there'll be another war, but I read newspapers and listen to radio broadcasts. I see how the Party is stirring up trouble now with Poland and France. Some of Vati's friends speak about revenge on the French and English for the last war. Perhaps the Nazis will attack to please these bitter old men. I don't know."

Willy nodded. "Until this spring I was able to read English and American newspapers at the university library. Now they're gone, but they're no longer necessary to judge the truth. It's simple enough to see that another war will come, if for no better reason than no one seems able to stop it. No one in Europe will stand up to Hitler and his threats," he said. His unconscious reflex was to lower his voice even though he knew no one could overhear them.

"The Army knows this too. They're always making plans and having maneuvers. They want new bombs for the war that's coming. To ensure victory. Victory at any cost. Isn't that how it always is?"

"But Lise, you must understand. This new bomb is not like any that you've ever read about from the Great War. I struggled through some of Professor Hahn's energy calculations. If it works, one bomb could obliterate an entire city: a single bomb, dropped from a single airplane.

Not massive armies attacking and advancing and retreating mile by mile. One, perhaps two men and one airplane. If the city were London or Paris, three million people would be killed in a single hour, as many as died in the four years of the Great War. And not just soldiers this time, but children and old people and women. Such a bomb won't be selective. If the Nazis had these bombs every country would have to surrender or die. Nazi Germany will conquer the entire world in a month. We agree what that will mean to the losers."

"But you say that it's all just Professor Heisenberg's theories. And they haven't been tested yet."

"Yes, but look how quickly things are accomplished when the Nazis get behind them. I've seen dramatic change in just the nine months I've been in Germany. I'm still in awe of the new buildings, hospitals, and factories going up everywhere. The Nazis do anything they set their minds to. No one gets in their way. When they say cost is no object, I believe them, literally. If this new bomb can be made, it will be."

"What could anyone do?"

"I don't know. You're the only person in Germany I trust. There's no one we can talk to, and even if there was, what could he do? If you oppose the Nazis you end up ruined, arrested, or you simply disappear."

"Can you talk to Professor Heisenberg? Tell him the same things you've told me. He can stop this research. He can refuse to continue. He could leave Germany, like many of his colleagues. Surely he doesn't want war nor would he want his discoveries used to harm innocent people. No one with his humanity and love of music would dream of it. Seems to me that the Professor is the key."

"I've considered that for months, but I don't think it will help. He knows all this and must have made up his mind. Lise, Professor Heisenberg's in America *right now*. He'll be warmly welcomed and could have any academic position he wants: respect, money, acclaim, anything. But frankly I have no doubt he will return at the end of his visit.

"In Berlin, he tried to distance himself from practical matters, but these men, these atomic physicists, are all very close to one another. They've worked together for years. Professor Heisenberg is their leader and whatever they're doing is happening at his direction or at least with his tacit blessings.

"Anyway, I'm just an assistant here. I have no title or position of responsibility. I'm not even a physicist and worst of all, I'm not a German citizen. At best he would think I'm a naïve meddler. Or he might turn me over to the Gestapo as an undesirable alien."

"I can't see him doing that."

"Perhaps not, but there are two other problems. First, I believe that if the authorities had realized who I was, I would have been tossed out of the Berlin conference on my ear. Because I'm your father's assistant, no one asked any questions. Besides Professor Heisenberg, I've met two or three other attendees here in Munich. I managed to avoid them at the conference, but that doesn't mean they didn't recognize me. Even a casual remark to someone in the government or army might have been disastrous. While I was drunk and tired at a student reception, I babbled for an hour with some German student on his way to Minnesota on a fellowship. I told him my life story and could have kicked myself the next morning. I didn't know who he was, whom he knows, or what his politics are. He could easily have been an agent of some sort. I've been lucky so far." Willy suddenly realized how Tellerman's nametag had said *fluorine*, a very toxic element. He *had* been warned, but like an idiot, hadn't listened. "Stupid, but lucky."

"Second, Lieutenant Bose implied Heisenberg wasn't trustworthy and he's probably watched by the Gestapo. A spotlight on him shines on anyone he talks to.

"Too many people in Germany know I'm an American, besides Heisenberg. I suppose the Gestapo could show up any day and haul me away." Willy sat thoughtfully. He'd realized that despite his intentions he'd put Lise in danger too. He had no right to do that. But she had read his expression.

"If they come, *we* will tell them nothing. You are Vati's assistant and you do only what he asks. You know nothing about German politics. You know nothing about this uranium research. After all, you're only an assistant and, as you said, not even a physicist.

"You attended the Berlin conference to watch over my father's health. *I insisted* you go. No one should suspect that you understand what this business is all about. Say you know nothing." Lise could see a pained and embarrassed look on Willy's face. She reached over and took his hand. His fingers were long and delicate.

"Willy, you must learn to be more cautious and less trusting. Act more like a modern German man!" They smiled together at the image

and their eyes met for a long moment. Lise looked away uneasily.
"I'm so sorry, Willy. You're much more than an assistant. My
father's getting worse every day and I know you've done all the work
coming out of the lab under his name alone. You deserve credit and I
hope someday it comes to you. But you must help me protect him, and
don't let *them* take him away. I'm afraid of what they will do to him."
She sat quietly for several minutes staring intently at the fireplace, anger
growing.

"In Munich nowadays, ignorance and thick-headedness are virtues.
Everyone is supposed to know their place and do their duty. I'm a new
German woman. I will stay home and obey my parents, remain chaste,
marry a new German man, and have a dozen new German children. My
duty does not include learning to read or to think. It doesn't include
having opinions or choices. I will never dare question my husband's
decisions.

"If you understand what's expected and play the role well, no one
will question your loyalty."

Willy sat stunned. Lise had expressed succinctly what was happening
in Germany under the Nazis. In public she's always been quiet and
restrained. He hadn't guessed the depth of her perception and her anger.
Her eyes burned.

"Willy, Vati has been sick since I was twelve years old. Gabi was
never much help and I've been taking care of him by myself, and just like
you, protecting him from himself, shielding him from any humiliation,
letting him maintain his dignity and the respect of his friends. It's all he
has left. Now you tell me the Nazis will kill him because he's a burden
on society. I will not allow that. Since I was a little girl I've been around
some of the smartest and most creative men in the world. No one ever
told me that I couldn't be one of them someday. I listened and remembered
everything I heard and read as much as I could to understand better. I
wanted to attend university so that someday I could work alongside these
men and others like them. When I was younger, Vati would not hear of
it. Tradition. But as I got older he began to share my aspirations. This
is not my expected role in the new Germany. Nothing changes for people
like me. You admire new buildings while the radio rants about Germany's
new place in the world. It offers nothing to me except new things to fear.

"So don't be so surprised. I see what's going on. Someday you'll
return to America with its freedoms. But my own future has changed,

without my permission, and I am angry. I hate these Nazis and everything they stand for. They are a plague that must be stopped. I want my dreams back.

"You and I will decide what to do and we'll work together to protect Vati. But we will not help them build this bomb."

"Do you believe anyone in America knows about these uranium bombs?"

It was later the same night and Willy and Lise were seated at Professor Wagner's giant desk, speculating, trying out new ideas, and gently criticizing bad ones. Willy had spent an hour explaining in more detail the physics behind the bomb, drawing diagrams on a piece of scrap writing paper from the Professor's desk. After midnight Lise had turned down the lights to avoid drawing the attention of suspicious neighbors or patrolling policemen. They both sensed that it was dangerous to draw attention to the house, especially now that they both shared an important secret. The fire had burned out long before. Since then they'd sat in the darkened study, talking quietly, the French doors cracked open to feel the cool June night.

"I don't know. So many of Professor Heisenberg's colleagues emigrated to the States and England that lots of people there have detailed understanding of the *implications* of his theories. Einstein is in Princeton. Last week I heard a rumor in the coffee shop at the Chemistry Institute. Professor Fermi from Italy, who won the Nobel Prize last year for his work on uranium chain reactions, went to Stockholm to pick up his medal and prize money but never returned to Italy. He took his wife and family directly to New York. Things are bad in Italy too, I guess. Fermi's wife is Jewish and evidently Jews are as bad off in Italy with Mussolini as in Germany with Herr Hitler.

"If these men are working together, or at least comparing notes, I'd hope that they'd unite and use their influence."

"How?"

Willy shrugged. "Good question. I'm not sure. They could warn President Roosevelt, but I don't know what might happen after that. They can warn the English and French but I can't see *them* taking definitive action. Hitler walks right over them every time. They've shown little moral courage over the last few years. Rearmament, the Spanish Civil War, the annexations of Austria and Czechoslovakia; none of these actions has been resisted.

"Frankly, things aren't much better in America. No state of war exists. Congress is strongly Isolationist and resists any effort by Roosevelt to get entangled with European...*politics*. It would have to be perceived as a direct threat to America. I think men like Einstein with his reputation and status could convince the President that there is a real threat. After that I don't know what will happen."

"Will they try to build the uranium bomb in America?"

"Yes, the War Department would, to counteract the Nazis and to maintain some sort of power balance. All the naval treaties after the last war were written for similar purposes though they obviously didn't hold up for long."

"You're implying that if both sides have these bombs, neither will use them. I disagree. If they have it they'll use it. I think that's the way military men think. Like mustard gas, that provides little advantage and kills your own soldiers."

"I'm afraid you're right."

"You said they were all friends. Do you think Professor Einstein will believe that Heisenberg and his associates *will* follow their consciences? Perhaps he will have few concerns about German efforts, if he thinks Professor Heisenberg won't participate."

"That's entirely possible and worrisome."

"Could you write to them and tell them what's happening? Would they get your letter, read it, and do something?"

"First, can we get a letter past the censors? Mail at the university is opened and read even from other German cities. If I put all the facts in a letter and it's discovered, I'll be considered a spy. You and your father would be implicated and arrested, too. I won't do anything that might cause that to happen.

"On the other hand, if I only *imply* things in a letter, the warning might not be discerned. I don't know many influential academics personally and some have secretaries to read their mail. And even if they grasp the message, they'd think I was a crank."

"Perhaps we can send a straight-forward letter through Switzerland or the American consulate."

"Let me think about that. If I cross the border, I probably won't be allowed to return. Your father needs my help. I won't leave on my own. If I visit a consulate, the local police or Gestapo will be alerted. It seems like my presence here has been overlooked somehow. We should leave it that way. In America we say, let sleeping dogs lie. Does that make sense?"

"No. And I think you should return to America. If war is coming you will be trapped here. In America you can talk to important men and tell them about the Nazis and their bomb. I know you can convince them and you'll be safe."

"But I have no evidence to show anyone back in the States. A list of questions from Bose. It's just bits and pieces. If I can't convince them, then I've left you and your father here alone for nothing.

"If I stay, there's a chance I might collect more evidence. You asked whether America would build an atomic bomb. I answered, yes, if they thought the Nazis were building one. But what if I was to return to America, manage to convince the War Department about this threat, they build their bomb, but in the meantime, the Nazis have given up. When the Nazis find out that America has an atomic bomb, they'll resurrect their project and the world ends up in the same horrible place. And I'll be responsible!"

"You're tired and we're going in circles, Willy. *You* aren't responsible for any of this. If we have any responsibility, it's to stop, or at least to delay the research. Professor Heisenberg came to ask for Vati's help. If Vati doesn't complete the calculations then that part of the project will not be completed."

"I've thought a lot about that. Heisenberg will just find another mathematician, someone with less credibility and stature, but the calculations will get done eventually. Heisenberg is returning in August. He'll get someone else and have the calculations submitted in a few months. The project will be delayed only by a six months at best. This would also publicize your father's condition." Nothing was said for several minutes. A clock somewhere in the old house chimed twice: two in the morning.

When the lights were first dimmed, Willy had the urge to reach out and touch Lise's face and hair, but was afraid it would become a clumsy grope, misinterpreted as something nasty and inappropriate. Now in the darkened room, he had only her voice and her mind, and he found himself bound to her tighter and more completely than with any other person in his life. Willy's spirit soared and his head felt strangely clear, even if his body was tired. Something clicked: a silly idea that made him smile again in the dark.

"Lise, I'd been thinking, what if the finished calculations were wrong; if they were inaccurate? What if the calculations said that a bomb wouldn't work?"

"How could we do that? Wouldn't someone find the mistakes?"

"I don't know. Professor Heisenberg asked your father to submit the completed calculations directly to someone at the Ministry of Education: a bureaucrat whom I gather is acting as a referee. Heisenberg specifically said that no one was supposed to see your father's work in advance. It must be completely independent and objective. A preliminary review is scheduled next month, while Professor Heisenberg is still in the States. Your father's results will be used to make important decisions on funding and staffing. If calculations show a bomb is impossible or impractical, the Ordnance Department might kill the whole thing and Heisenberg won't be around to defend it. As I told you, he just might be looking for an excuse to halt this work, but can't do it himself. Your father's opinion is beyond question, and even when Professor Heisenberg returns and figures out the results are wrong, he might see that as his way out. It's a stretch, I guess."

"Willy, this sounds like a good idea, but I don't believe the Professor would let it go that easily. His pride would be injured and he might feel his reputation was damaged if he left people with the idea that he was wrong."

"You might be right, *except that he'll know he was correct all along. So will his colleagues.* The Ministry demanded an outside review and they'd take the heat if the truth ever comes out. Privately, Heisenberg and his friends will laugh at the Ministry. He told me quite clearly that he considers them fools and interlopers. He won't care what *they* think about him professionally. Military efforts would halt, but basic research at the Physics Institute could continue."

Willy was elated. Once on the table, his plan seemed simpler. It provided a course with little additional risk to Lise and her father. If the truth got out, he'd be the sole suspect. And it was more college prank than an act of sabotage. It would show Lise that he was clever and funny. Right now he wanted nothing more in the world than to impress her and to make her smile. Was she smiling at him right now?

"Willy, can you do this? Can I help?" She spoke with excitement in her voice he hadn't heard before and he didn't want to lose.

"For energy to be released from a uranium atom, it has to be rendered unstable or unbalanced. That can happen when you added more mass to its core, the nucleus. If you add the right amount of extra mass, the unstable nucleus will split in half. When it splits, energy is liberated along with small packets of extra mass that can then be added to adjacent uranium nuclei, repeating the identical reaction sequence one step at a time: a chain reaction. If the chain reaction is sufficiently fast, the energy from millions of these steps is released almost instantly and you have an explosion."

It was several nights later, after their conspiracy had been formed and its ideas had taken root. Lise sat at her father's desk and Willy paced back and forth like a nervous graduate student before his thesis master. Lise's lean frame was almost lost in the high-backed chair and she leaned forward concentrating on Willy's every word, desperate to understand so she could contribute to the plan.

"What do you mean by fast?"

"Fast would be thousands or even millions of reactions in a single second. If the reaction and the release of energy are slow and controlled then the uranium could be used like a furnace or boiler to heat water and generate electricity. The amount of heat that could be released from a single gram of uranium is unbelievable, but many of the attendees in Berlin weren't convinced a chain reaction could be controlled. They worried that if one actually started such a reaction, once initiated, it might *always* result in an explosion. One senior man said he feared that even experiments were dangerous. He speculated that once the reaction began it might envelop the entire world within minutes and the earth would burn just like the sun." Lise look genuinely frightened. Willy smiled.

"Don't worry. No one took this idea very seriously. One basic presumption is that only uranium and a few other elements can be split and they are rare enough that there's no danger of a runaway reaction on that scale."

"So, how would you add this extra mass to the uranium atom's core?"

"I afraid I'm an American and the first analogy that comes to mind relates to an American sport called baseball.

"Say you have a tall, wide brick wall with a single glass window in the middle. If you stood back twenty meters and threw a baseball at the window, several different things might happen."

"Please stop for a moment. Is this ball soft or hard? Is it large or small? Please I just want to share the same image as you?"

"Sorry. A baseball is hard and about the size of a large apple."

"I understand."

"When you throw the ball at the window, first of all you might miss, especially if the window is small. If the window is very small, it's most likely that you'll miss. Maybe if you throw the ball at the small window one hundred times, you hit the window once. So the probability that you hit the window is one in one hundred times or one percent."

"I understand."

"Now if you do hit the window, two things can happen. If you throw the ball sufficiently hard you'll break the glass and the ball ends up inside the building. Let's describe that as the ball being caught or *captured*. You've added mass to the building equivalent to the weight of the ball.

"If the ball wasn't thrown hard enough, it might simply bounce off the window glass and the result is no different than striking brick. This means that there is some minimum energy or speed that the ball has to have in order to break the glass and fall inside the building. Actually this energy value ends up being pretty small, so the probability of striking the window is the crucial parameter."

"But if you make the window larger, then the chances of hitting the glass are greater are they not?"

"Exactly. In the simplest terms, the bigger the window the more likely you'll hit it, even if your toss is badly aimed or even random. The size of the window in proportion to the wall can be called the area or cross-section for capturing the ball. And that's what everyone is trying to calculate: How large is the effective capture cross-section of the nucleus of a uranium atom?

"If the capture or *absorption* cross-section is very high, then the reaction is easy to start and sustain. Random neutrons released from some source or from another uranium atom will be captured easily. If the cross-section's very small then the likelihood of initiating the sequence and then having the chain reaction continue is low. Nothing happens. No explosion. No large release of energy. Then the only way to make sure that the ball is captured is to put more small windows in the wall.

That's the practical equivalent of increasing the total number of uranium atoms in the starting material. If the cross-section is high you only need a small amount of uranium, a small number of large windows; if the capture cross-section is low, you'll need many times more uranium atoms to start with, a large number of small windows. If in one case you need ten kilos of uranium, in the other you might need one hundred times more, or one thousand kilos. That's already getting to be pretty impractical. They've designated this minimum quantity as a *critical mass*."

"Do you know what the correct value is? Does Professor Heisenberg know?"

"I believe the Professor thinks the answer is less than twenty-five kilos based on his calculations and some of Professor Hahn's early experiments. But even that would require the uranium be very pure: certain contaminants in the mass of uranium will stop the reaction by absorbing that extra mass without splitting. Like putting an impenetrable barrier in front of the windows. Not all the uranium isotopes have the same cross-section either. I don't know what the correct answer is yet. It probably can only be confirmed by large-scale experiments. I'd bet on Professor Heisenberg's calculations.

"But I don't have to be a genius to figure that if calculations show the cross-section is low enough so that the mass of uranium needed is too large to carry on an airplane, a bomb will never be built. I believe I can pick an impractical weight and manipulate the calculations so they give me that answer."

"How big a number will you choose?"

"Large enough that it's clearly impractical, but not so large that it's more than others have speculated. I'll try to find out more about airplanes and their bomb loads at the library, but if I had to guess, four thousand kilos should be enough. Perhaps a slow-moving Zeppelin can carry that much weight but I don't know of any modern airplanes that could. If we suggest a higher value, our calculations might be scrutinized."

"You're confident you can hide the intentional errors?"

"I'll introduce errors in the exponents. The most tedious part of any review of our report would be working back through logarithm tables. Anyone who doesn't use them every day will avoid that step.

"In some ways the calculations are simple enough, though tedious: a series of four equations with sixty steps each. This works to our advantage. I can't see anyone at the Ministry repeating the calculations to verify each step. Anyone with the time or interest would have already used the formula. We'll stick to the original equations so there'll be no logical inconsistencies.

"My plan is to incorporate a hundred-fold error in cross-sectional areas by *incorrectly* rounding off numbers throughout the middle of the paper. Just a little bit at each step. The helpful thing about exponents is that errors accumulate quickly. I think I can mask the errors sufficiently so someone would actually have to recalculate entire sections in order to find the problem. I won't do anything wrong in the first two steps or the last two. If someone does decide to recheck the work, they'll probably pick one of those pages and everything will look fine."

"But that means that you'll have to calculate the true values first, before you can make any changes."

"I know and that scares me. I may go insane if I knew the real value and that a uranium bomb was practical. But regardless, I have to set up the formula carefully. As I said, any error in the initial equations and everything else will lack credibility. Your father laid this all out in February, while he was still able to visit the lab."

"So you have the starting equations?"

"Yes, and the instructions that Professor Heisenberg left your father seem clear enough. I won't modify them. Otherwise it's likely someone would take a hard look at the entire presentation. Again, it really depends more than anything else, on the expectations of the reviewer. As I said the other night, there was some speculation in Berlin that the critical mass of uranium necessary to sustain the atomic reaction was many tons, more than could ever be collected and purified or transported by a bomber. Such a mass would be impossible to use as a weapon since it couldn't be moved to enemy territory. We will prove that those men were right. They'll be the last ones to doubt our work."

"So if a reviewer at the Ministry of Education shares that expectation, he'll be seeing results that support his view."

"Exactly. While there's an element of chance involved, I think two things are in our favor. First, there was a great deal of skepticism at the Berlin conference, especially from the bureaucratic types. It's part of their nature to be conservative and cautious. Second, the whole process has been politicized. I'm sure any review of work associated with Professor Heisenberg will be sent to someone with contrary opinions, someone who thinks it can't be done at all. Professor Heisenberg is a man who won't resist that type of challenge. He might even have insisted on such a person for the review. So there's a good chance that the reviewer will accept our calculations without looking beyond a summary page I'll place on top."

"But Willy, how long will this deception stand up? When Professor Heisenberg returns from America, he'll challenge the Ministry's review and your calculations."

"Oh, I strongly suspect that he'll be reluctant to do that, at least directly. Your father's reputation and integrity can't be attacked head-on. Professor Heisenberg has a very low opinion of Ministry bureaucrats and it's unlikely he'll condescend to argue with them. He'll probably try to ignore the report and their review and devise some new approach to advance his theories. On a reduced scale, he'll continue to build experimental evidence for his concepts. In any case, most of the Army men are engineers who want to see practical results from experiments, not theoretical calculations from thinkers. But without lots of money, these small-scale lab experiments might take years to complete. Perhaps by then the political situation in Germany will change for the better, before any large scale experimental apparatus is assembled."

"I wish I could share your optimism," Lise said gloomily.

"I can't see things any other way. We've both got to believe. And you have to believe in me. And trust me."

"Willy, I do. Understand that. There's just so much work for you to do that I can't help you with. I so wish I was a man and not an ignorant, uneducated girl."

"Don't talk like that. It isn't true anyway. I do need your help every step of the way. You're insightful. I won't feel confident unless I can fool you. You're twice as intelligent and clever as any of the Ministry men. When I finish the report, if you can't find the errors, they never will.

"I wish we had more help, but I'd rather have one more of you than anyone else. What we're doing is right and we'll beat them all, even Heisenberg himself if he's against us." Willy sat down, embarrassed by his outburst. He tried to change the subject.

"Frankly, again I wonder whether Professor Heisenberg might even be relieved if the report is unfavorable. It would take responsibility out of his hands and let him get back to theorizing. If the truth comes out later, everyone will blame the Ministry. The political equation again."

"How much time do we have?"

"We need to work quickly. Professor Heisenberg will be in America until August. We need to have our paper into the Ministry as soon as possible so that it will be acted on before he returns."

"Will it come back on Vati?"

"There's always a chance, but I doubt it very much. If someone later finds mathematical errors in the calculations then the Ministry should have picked them up. That was the sole purpose of their review. In the worst case, I'll tell the truth, sort of. I helped your father with the actual calculations and I'm a careless idiot, thank you very much."

"Then they'd know that you're an American. And they'll find out about Vati's condition."

"I think we're pretty safe. I'll be thrown out of the country for sure, but the government might be too embarrassed to take any action against your father and too many people will find out what happened. Nothing could be done secretly."

"I'm not as confident about that part of our plan, Willy. It seems to rely an awful lot on human nature instead of the mathematics and physics."

"There are scientists in America who say human nature will someday be just a predictable as physics. Somehow I doubt that very much. But even if our little deception slows plans for an atomic bomb by only six months, it could make all the difference in the world. Quite literally."

"Then we must go ahead. It's more important than Vati or you or me. I don't know whether I'm scared or excited."

"Oh, I know which I am! I'll start work tonight."

Books

Willy was dumbstruck. Four young men in party uniforms were rifling through Professor Wagner's bookshelves like depraved librarians, consulting printed lists, and when they found a cross reference, tossing books and bound journals into a small two-wheeled cart they'd managed somehow to wedge through the office door. The cart was already half full and there were gaps like missing teeth all along the tall bookshelves that covered three walls of the office.

"Please, what's going on?"

"Ah, Herr Petersen," said their leader, whom Willy recalled was a former chemistry student and current student committee member. "We were about to hunt for you. In the Professor's absence, we'll need you to receipt for these books." He waved his hand vaguely at the cart.

"I'm sorry, but I don't understand."

"The Student Committee has decided that books and other literature from certain authors should be...*centralized*, to control their distribution. We've been assigned this block of offices and laboratories. We're checking off each item as they're found. We wouldn't want to be accused of stealing or illegally seizing private property," the leader said. Willy easily read the acid sarcasm behind the banal legalities.

"Might I see the list?"

"Why, of course," the leader replied, handing Willy the copy he was using. The other three men had not paused in their efforts.

The list comprised nearly three hundred names with some sort of code following each. Willy instantly recognized dozens of names as some of the world's most important classic scientists and inventors: Einstein, Fermi, Rathenau, von Karman, Marie Curie, and Franck. At first glance, Willy was not tuned to the common themes of the list, however it was readily apparent that there were many Poles and Russians on the list. When he considered the abbreviations, it was easy to decipher that '*j*' stood for Jew, '*c*' for communist. The others were more obscure, but

Willy could imagine. He handed the list back.

"We apologize for disturbing your valuable work, Herr Petersen, however periodically the student committee has found it necessary to reexamine its collections in light of an expanded list of sensitive authors and topics." Willy started to say that this is a private collection that did not belong to the university, but that was obvious.

"What will you do with these books, sir? Some are important reference works for the Professor's research. I also know that some are first editions, signed by their authors, who were colleagues and acquaintances of Professor Wagner. I'm sure they're very valuable, at least to the Professor. I would prefer that you consult with him before you remove the books."

"Let me assure you that there'll be no problems," their leader said dismissively. "The Professor is known to be a loyal and trusted German. The committee is certain that he has no idea that some of these books are considered to be *sensitive*. After all, his personal collection is very large, and the professor is a very busy man. He, and his representatives, will have complete access to all these books at the central library. The committee and the Party have agreed that access must be restricted to protect impressionable people from degenerate and un-German ideas and teachings."

"We are also aware that Professor Wagner makes infrequent visits to his office these days and these books will be much more secure in our custody."

After the Professor had retired for the evening, Willy told Lise about what had happened that day. She was outraged. Those books had been her father's greatest treasures and part of his legacy.

She cursed herself. "We should have anticipated this and moved more of the books here to the house. How many are left?"

"Several hundred volumes I think. The committee took about half." Willy was embarrassed and was afraid that Lise was angry and disappointed that Willy had let the books be stolen so easily. But she didn't say anything like that.

"We should be careful not to draw their attention again. Would it be difficult for you to bring four or five book here from the University every time you come? Some afternoons, when I can get Frau Erna to sit with Vati, I'll come down and help."

"Lise, we need to be very careful. The last thing I want is for the committee to catch us and then decide that they want to look through the Professor's books here at the house."

"They wouldn't dare!"

"Maybe not right now, but I can see a time coming."

"Never. I don't care what you think."

"I hope you're right. What do we tell your father if he asks for any of these books?"

"I don't know. Maybe we can tell him the truth, as it's been told to us. The books have been moved to the main library for safe-keeping."

"Their leader told me that we would still have access to them but I must use most of them at the library under their thumbs. Other books I can borrow for the day but they need to be returned at night before closing."

"Like everything else nowadays, we'll have to adapt and make do. Is this going to interfere with the Ministry's report."

"No, I don't think so. But I've brought several more pages of calculation and notes for you to check, type, and proof. We're getting near the end now. We need to finish and send it to Berlin before Professor Heisenberg gets back from the states next month." He handed Lise several scribbled pages from his pocket.

"When you come tomorrow evening, I'll have these finished. Is there anything else I can help with?"

"Pray."

Rumor swept through the café that the committee was going to restage a ceremonial book burning on Friday evening in the plaza in front of the university's main library. Willy had heard stories about what happened throughout Germany in 1933 but was incredulous that book burning continued. He had assumed that the huge rallies of the past were manifestations of revolutionary fervor now held in check by the mature perspectives of an entrenched regime. He'd also heard about measures the young National Socialist government had taken to *save* books by authors who'd been inadvertently included on the lists by illiterate zealots. But the same story had it that the original list comprised some one hundred and sixty authors and writers. The list he had been shown was ten pages with thirty names on each page. Things weren't getting better after all.

Evidently the student party leadership considered book burning a passage rite and shared experience for its recruits, a dramatic way to reinforce the Party's ideas of what was un-German or injurious to the German spirit.

Willy had no intention of attending and had forgotten the date, but on Friday, after a long day typing bibliographies, he needed to return one of the 'sensitive' books to the library. He'd been told that if he didn't return these books every night he would lose his borrowing privileges.

The air lay heavy with humidity and it began to sprinkle. As he walked across the small square in front of the library, several workmen were using their wheelbarrows to cart in sand used to complete the base of a temporary pyre. A small pile of logs and scrap lumber lay nearby, which the workers arranged like a teepee. Willy paused to watch, reluctant to return the book he carried lest it end up later on the fire. Several other students, on their way into or out of the library, joined Willy and stood silently on the steps to the library door watching the preparations. No one spoke and everyone took care not to communicate their feelings or opinions about what they were witnessing and what it portended.

As the workmen were finishing laying the logs, Willy could hear the sound of a tinny brass band in the distance, coming closer. *Shit!* As soon as the parade entered the plaza, Willy realized that he and the other students were trapped. To walk away now might be interpreted as a statement of protest that someone was bound to report to the committee or to the political police, the SD. He could be absolutely positive there was an informer standing among them for that express purpose.

Lead by an honor guard carrying the national and state flags, the band was small, only six brass instruments and two drummers, all teenagers dressed in the uniforms of the Hitler Youth. Immediately behind the band followed a group of students, perhaps two dozen in all, each carrying a single book in both hands like some religious relic or solemn offering. Last in line came the leaders and members of the student corps, wearing colored caps that identified their individual sections. Many carried banners or torches that smoked and sputtered in the drizzling rain. As the corps began to fill the plaza, the press of the crowd forced Willy to move further up the steps towards the library door, but as a result he now had a grandstand view.

Everyone jockeyed for position around the bonfire and the bearers moved forward to add their torches to the pyre, which was soon blazing brightly. At a signal from someone, the band raggedly finished the march they were playing.

Cross Sections

Greeted by fitful applause, one of the student committee leaders stepped forward and began to address the crowd: "Friends, we're here today to consign to flames un-German books, books and their authors that continue to threaten the integrity and foundations of National Socialism. This is a task that will never be completed unless we all remain diligent and thorough in our efforts to identify and locate these books. If I may quote our esteemed leader, Reichsminister Goebbels, "the old goes up in flame, the new shall be fashioned from the flame in our hearts."

"While our present efforts might seem meager compared to those of the past, let me assure you all that we will be unrelenting. And this should also be a warning for those who would recklessly hoard and protect such trash: we will root you out in time and cauterize the wounds you inflict so thoughtlessly on your fellow countrymen."

He stepped back into the crowd and soon a young student stepped forward, book held at arms length and recited a rehearsed little speech: "Erich Maria Remarque – for degrading the German language and the highest patriotic ideal." As he finished, the young man tossed the book onto the pyre and stepped back. The crowd cheered and clapped. Willy was unsure what he should do. If he simply stood there passively, would he be singled out as a protestor? But as he glanced around he could see that most of the enthusiasm was centered among those closest to the fire. At the edges of the crowd, people seemed bored and impatient. It was apparent that they were all in the same boat. No one dared leave at this point, whether he or she had misgivings or simply something more urgent to do.

Another student, a young woman, approached the fire, struggling with a particularly thick volume. "Sigmund Freud – for falsifying our history and degrading its great figures!" She tried her best to throw the book onto the pile, but it was too heavy and she was too frightened to get up close to the flames. Her missile fell a meter short and someone had to retrieve the book by ducking low under the flames. His hair was singed to everyone's amusement, but his throw was strong and accurate, and he earned the only truly spontaneous applause of the evening.

More students came forward, one following another, each with a short speech outlining an author's sin against the German people. Willy did not recognize many of the names. He figured that most of the more obvious sinners had been turned up years ago. He continued to listen attentively to see whether any of Professor Wagner's books were destroyed. Nothing he could do, but he felt responsible somehow.

Willy considered how it must have taken a large measure of courage or foolishness for someone to hold back the copies of Marx and Lenin and he wondered at the fate of the person who'd so dared. But Willy cringed when he heard the names of familiar American authors, who did not appear to be immune, despite the Reich's continuing efforts to court American public opinion.

"Jack London......"

"Upton Sinclair...."

"Helen Keller...."

"Margaret Sanger....for her assault on the sanctity of the German family!"

At first the crowd had cheered and applauded each little speech, but some of the authors were obscure even to the German students and they would turn to one another and say, "Who?" and then clap politely. While Marx and Lenin drew big responses, by the end, after thirty books had been consigned, most people simply stood watching. The rain had intensified and umbrellas began to pop open. Willy stepped back under an overhang and pressed against the stone wall just out of the shower.

With the last book delivered to the fire, the leader stepped forward again, intending to make another address, but one look around at the impatient and restless crowd and he cut it short. He signaled to the band which started to play the *Horst Wessel Song*, but the young musicians couldn't maintain a fast tempo and the crowd finished singing well ahead of them and began to disperse even before the last note sounded.

Within five minutes the plaza was deserted except for the same workmen. The steady rain threatened to extinguish the bonfire and too few books had been provided as fuel. The workmen poked and stirred the pile trying to keep it going without success. They shrugged and went off to their homes for the night, leaving many of the last books scorched but not destroyed. Willy finally stirred from his spot, his arms actually stiff and sore from clutching his book close to his chest unconsciously all through the ceremony. *Well, I wanted to keep it dry didn't I?* He chided himself sarcastically. Inside the library he returned it to a disinterested clerk and made his way back to the hostel. As he lay on his bed, scanning an old newspaper he'd borrowed from the porter, he began to wish he had a Jack London novel to read and lose himself somewhere in the pristine and lonely north, away from Nazis and their inhumanity.

The following morning he returned to the library with a list of the Professor's books he needed to complete his bibliography, including the one he'd had to return for the night. The workmen were back with their wheelbarrows, shoveling the sand, ash and unburned logs and books, and hauling it off to somewhere.

When he presented his list to a clerk, the man returned after several minutes with just a single volume, the same Willy had returned the previous night. The clerk handed it over without comment.

"Excuse me, but what about the other three books?" Willy asked politely.

"They're gone," the clerk replied simply.

"Excuse me, what do you mean gone? Has someone else borrowed them?"

"They're gone. People from the student committee came by yesterday to collect all the restricted books. Those you've requested must have been among the ones they took."

"But these are technical books full of figures and tables; they aren't political in any way. There must be a mistake."

"You'll have to talk to the committee about that. Anything's possible. They took quite a few books, loaded them into crates, and took them off somewhere. It didn't look like they were keeping track."

"How many books did they take?" None of the Professor Wagner's books had been burned last night. Maybe he could get permission from the committee to sort through and rescue the Professor's reference books.

"I have no way of knowing, but they emptied about twenty meters of shelves in the storage room back there. Might have been three or four thousand volumes. From that section, that book is the only one left. Seems to be a matter of luck mostly."

Willy grabbed the remaining book and walked away from the counter. He made a decision and fighting his own dread, hurried over to the Committee office in the administration building.

He burst through the door determined to confront those responsible and to get the Professor's books back. This was a matter that could be addressed coldly and logically. If necessary he would go over each book, page by page with the Tribunal, to justify their rescue and show them how important and non-political they were. If pressed he could threaten to write the American Embassy or to American newspapers and stir up anti-Nazi sentiment. *Berlin won't like that,* I'll warn them. He was stirred to his core and emotions held back since Gabi's death were revived. He felt like he would burst at any moment. Tears, anger, a fit of some sort, he wasn't sure which.

But through the door, he was stymied. The office was very large with dozens of desks, file cabinets, and shelves, but only a few people were present, busy typing.

He approached the nearest desk where a young woman was sorting forms. "I...I need to talk to some about books that were taken from the library yesterday. It's very urgent that I speak to someone responsible."

"Certainly. If you'll follow me," she said pleasantly, perhaps a little startled by Willy's agitation. As she walked slowing towards the back, Willy was right on her heels, pressing her to hurry. "Sir, this is Party Secretary Kessel, perhaps he can help you," she offered, turning to retreat to her station.

"Yes, how can I help you?" Secretary Kessel was tall and athletic, a former footballer, obviously a reasonable and friendly man.

"Yes, thank you, sir," Willy began, fighting to stay composed and to keep his arguments ordered and rational. "My name is Petersen and I work as an assistant for Professor Ernst Wagner at the Chemistry Institute."

"Professor Wagner, yes, I know of him."

"Several weeks ago men from the committee collected some technical books from the Professor's office in order to store them safely at the main library. They gave me a receipt and list, which I still have at the laboratory. I'm sorry I don't have it with me right now.

"I've been coming to the library each day and borrowing individual volumes I need to help with our research, returning the books to storage every night as I'd been instructed. Today I was told that these books have been moved from the library. The clerks didn't know to where...

"I'm sure there's been some sort of mistake. Most of the books are strictly technical reference books full of data tables, sample calculations, and graphs. They have no political content at all. I was lucky to have this book at the lab yesterday," Willy said, offering the book to Kessel. "You can see what I mean. Just look it over. It's just a entire book of data tables about liquid solubility, boiling points, and so forth."

Kessel took the book without comment, examined the title, and leafed through the pages absently. He closed the book and sat it to the side. He stared at Willy curiously.

"You're William Petersen, the American, aren't you?"

"Yes. Yes, I am," Willy replied, surprised that he was recognized.

"I apologize if this has caused you any personal inconvenience."

"Personal? No, no, not at all. I'm just concerned about the Professor's books. They're crucial to the completion and documentation of his research, that's all."

"I understand. I understand completely. But you must understand that our procedures are very exacting. We maintain a large staff to make sure that we avoid mistakes. The Student Committee and the Reich Chamber of Literature in Berlin spends many hours revising and updating the criteria our examiners use in their decisions. We keep careful records of which books are collected and which are not.

"We have several avenues of appeal available for both authors and owners of these sensitive books. I'm afraid that it sounds like the Professor waited too long before contacting the committee."

"Yes, but I watched the ceremony last night and none of the Professor's books were destroyed. I listened very carefully."

"That doesn't surprise me. You must understand that it would be a waste to burn all these books, regardless how crucial it is to remind everyone that our task is important." Willy brightened. *There's a chance*.

"All these old books are sold to a paper mill. They're pulped and reconverted to new paper; I understand it's very high quality raw material. Nothing is wasted and the mill pays the party by weight. We use the money to pay the workmen, musicians, and for other legitimate Party expenses."

Willy felt faint and stood swaying and speechless.

"I'm so very sorry. But as you see there's nothing you or I can do about it now. I hope you understand."

Willy did understand. The whole thing was fantastical: its efficiency, accuracy, surgical precision, and irresistible momentum. It was another Nazi machine, an inhuman, uncaring device with the logic of a huge mechanical clock. There were workers who maintained the clock, kept it oiled and polished, but no one understood how the clock actually worked or whether it was giving the right time of day. He had nothing left except his anger and revulsion. He leaned forward and faced the Secretary directly.

Cross Sections

"No, I don't understand at all, Herr Kessel. Why was I not contacted before the final decision was made? You claim to be so highly organized and thorough, how could you fail to contact the Professor or me? That was your first mistake."

"As I said, there was no mistake," Kessel replied angrily, "and you have no business challenging our actions. The Party has no obligations to contact you about its decisions. If you had concerns, it's for you to come to us."

"That's shit. Those books were private property and that was acknowledged when I was given a receipt. Unless things have changed, property rights are still protected by German law." Kessel was now on his feet, his finger in Willy's face.

"Herr Petersen, German law and rights do not concern you. You are not a German citizen and are allowed to remain here at our pleasure. You are of course free to leave any time. If you're dissatisfied, I strongly suggest you return to your mongrel country with its Jews, its Blacks, and Irishmen. If you wish to stay, I suggest that you keep your mouth shut and stick to your research work, which I'll assume, might be valuable in some way to the Reich and German people.

"The committee has a long file on you and I'm aware of your outside interests and your friends here at the university, some of whom, I'm sorry to say, also don't know when to keep their mouths shut. I would have thought that Fräulein Wagner's death would have been sufficient warning for you. Your record has been clean for several months now and as a favor I will not make a record of this conversation. I'll accept that you are upset. But be aware that we are watching you.

"If you'll excuse me now, I have important matters at hand."

When Kessel mentioned Gabi, his words were body blows on Willy, and he stepped back from the desk stunned and off-balance. This man knew everything. Willy could be deported on this man's word alone, leaving Lise and her father unshielded. Kessel's impatient look told Willy that further protest was dangerous. How to bow out?

"Thank you for your time, Herr Kessel," Willy offered in a quavering monotone, "I understand much better now." He reached for the book lying on the desktop, but Kessel was faster, snatching it up, holding it gingerly with his fingers as if it were a moist turd.

"You know I've just recalled that the editor of *this* book is on our list somewhere. He's a Jew or a communist or something like that. I don't remember exactly. I'm confiscating this book. If you want to protest my decision again, feel free to write to the committee. That is the procedure. You'll get a hearing in a few months, if you're still here. You may leave now."

Empty-handed, Willy walked from the office and building. In the warm sunshine, he began to shake uncontrollably and sat on a bench beneath the trees. It was still humid and sticky after yesterday's rain.

He was such a fool and such a coward. Foolish to confront the authorities, stupid to lack the words, and a yellow coward for backing down at the end. He knew he was hiding behind Lise and her father. If he were expelled now, nothing would happen to them. The uranium report would remain unfinished and their attempted sabotage would end there and with it any danger for the Wagners. Without an assistant, Professor Wagner could not be expected to meet the deadlines. In any eventuality, it was not possible to hide the Professor's condition forever. Whatever reasons Willy had for staying were obviously selfish and maybe had more to do with lust than altruism.

Now, sitting here, it was all coming out with wave after wave of self-reproach. Willy felt an obligation to Professor Wagner because he'd betrayed his trust and was responsible for Gabi's murder. And worse, he could not control the lust he felt for Lise. It wasn't love or genuine affection or anything noble. *Who am I trying to fool? It's just like before...with Gabi.* Everything he did was part of a subtle ploy to bind Lise to him and eventually seduce her. He wasn't trustworthy or capable of anything more.

He stood suddenly and started to walk toward the river. He fought to clear his mind and every time an image popped up, he'd walk faster, almost running, until it went away. Four hours later found him well north of the city, where the paved sidewalks had given way to a disused, muddy towpath. The sun was high and Willy was soaked in sweat. His shins burned and there were blisters ballooning on the backs of his heels.

He turned around and looked down the path back towards the city, surprised how far he'd come. He sat on the stony bank staring across the wide river. A large group of men with shovels and pickaxes were leveling a broad area above the opposite bank. They were digging and hauling dirt from elevated areas to fill lower ones. Willy envied the simplicity of the work, aware that at the end of every day, workers could look back and measure what they'd completed. Each day provided its own sense of accomplishment, regardless how tedious the job might be. As he watched, the men, perhaps two hundred in all, were working strenuously even in the mid-day heat, literally running as they pushed wheelbarrows back and forth around the excavation. *Easy to be philosophical about manual labor when you're not the one doing it*, he mocked himself.

Angry shouting echoed from the opposite bank, something he couldn't make out repeated several times, each time more loudly. Watching more closely, Willy could now discern that the work party was comprised of prisoners wearing black and white striped uniforms, though they were so filthy that they appeared to be uniformly gray. Willy could only spot two brown-shirted guards, each carrying a rifle, standing at opposite ends of the site, though there did appear to be a few men, dressed like the rest of the prisoners, but with rods or truncheons, acting as foremen.

It was unlikely the laborers were convicts, that is, criminals. Willy guessed there'd be more armed guards. They probably came from the concentration camp at the old gunpowder factory in nearby Dachau. It was whispered that there were ten thousand people detained there, many held since it opened in 1933. He had never met anyone who had been there and no one was interested in visiting. There didn't seem to be any ex-inmates.

The shouting had started a new flurry of activity among the laborers, who were now sprinting from place to place or shoveling furiously.

He watched the armed guards for a few minutes. They hadn't moved, their postures bored and detached. How could so few men control so many? It would be so easy to sneak away from the work party, hide in the woods, and eventually make one's way into the city at night. Lots of places to hide there.

Or if the whole group were to revolt, the guards would never get off a single shot. But Willy had never heard of anyone escaping or revolts among the detainees, or about protests in the city in their favor. What kept them so placid and so easy to control? *Fear or hope?*

Willy started back towards the city, walking slowly now, acutely aware that it was going to take him hours to get back if the blisters got any worse. After about two miles he had to give up, stop, remove his shoes and socks, and continue barefoot.

He hopped along the path, wincing as he failed to avoid all the sharp shards of pottery and broken brick that lined the path. He smiled to himself. This is a pretty accurate metaphor for life in Germany, picking one's way with extreme care, but still tortured at random. He reminded himself that his perception wasn't unique. Many of his friends at the university bridled at the government's restrictions and were embarrassed by its actions. Lise complained all the time about how things had changed. He'd overheard shopkeepers grousing about this and that, some things trivial, others more fundamental. Even Professor Heisenberg voiced his concerns and frustrations, though only in private conversations with an outsider like Willy.

Perhaps Germany had become a nation of cowards like Willy, no one willing to stand up to the authorities or even to express openly their dissatisfaction and anger. Willy smiled ruefully to himself. *That's my problem. I've become just like them, fearful, self-centered, and timid. Kessel went after me and I let myself be intimidated, just like the Germans who'd stood silently watching the books burn and those who peeped from behind their curtains on Kristallnacht.*

Willy stopped for a moment, the tops of Munich's taller buildings and the spires of the churches now in view over the trees ahead.

Too late now for talk. It's probably been too late for several years now. The political regime was now a monolithic social system, one so precariously balanced that it could suffer no protest, no difference of opinion or viewpoint, and no wandering from its narrow path and destiny. The camps and the work parties were constant and visible reminders about what it would mean to challenge or stray from the system.

Willy had read *Mein Kampf* and as he walked back toward the city on this narrow path, he suddenly understood how *everything* Hitler promised in the book would come true regardless how obscure, how inane, how provocative, or how horrendous it might be. It was more than just words of political theory. Nothing and no one would be allowed to stand in the way. He and his Party would move to conquer Europe and dominate the rest of the world and would use everything at his command.

Heisenberg's plan to maintain control of his new uranium technology would fail. The idea that one man, outside the party, could influence events in Germany was obsolete and absurd. Willy's plan however might work. As he and Lise had discussed, their subversion would play the Party off its own momentum and rigid structure.

Kessel said that he knew that Willy had been a good boy for the last few months. Willy grinned mischievously. At least for now, all his fears were set aside. *Oh so sorry. There you're wrong, Herr Kessel. I've been a very naughty boy indeed.*

Early that evening with the sun setting behind the house, Lise answered the door and she found Willy Petersen standing at the threshold. His hair was dirty and matted with sweat. His pant legs were covered with splashes of mud. He was barefoot and looked like a beggar. And he was smiling ear to ear.

Bund

When Edward boarded through the front door of the bus for Symphony Hall, he was thrilled to see two tall, clean-cut teenagers sitting in the front row in full Nazi Party regalia, brown shirts starched stiff as boards, bold black armbands with prominent swastikas, and the red scarves and collar insignia of the Youth Corps. They wore short pants and long black socks with red garter tassels. Their leather belts and shoes were polished to a mirror finish.

Over the past few years groups of American party members had traveled to Germany for indoctrination and other training and the appearance of these boys epitomized the Hitler Youth back home. Though his father had imbued the son with both fear and hatred of communists and its Jewish intelligencia, Edward had been too old to participate in the years immediately prior to Czechoslovakia's annexation into the Reich, as Sudentenland strove for closer links with Germany. Before that, local Czech bureaucrats in his hometown had been intolerant of Party recruiting activities. To take part or to espouse National Socialist causes was to expose oneself to abuse and ridicule by other children and adults. So as a teenager, Edward was confined to reading everything he could about the Party and its promises for German peoples. Now again, here in the United States, Edward found himself isolated and frustrated.

During these first three months, Edward had kept his political views very much to himself. His fellow research assistants, in their never-ending quest to waste time, theirs and his, asked Edward if he'd read this or that newspaper article, or had he heard some speech on the radio. He would deny having spare time or interest for such matters. But he overheard enough banter between the other students to appreciate their opinions which, though naïve, seemed totally committed to internationalism. They constantly complained about the isolationist views of their elders and heaped scorn on the fascist policies of Germany, Italy, and Spain.

But Edward's passion continued to grow from within. German language newspapers in St. Paul reprinted the *Führer's* speeches in full. He lingered on every word and phrase. Photographs and accounts in *Life* magazine and *The Saturday Evening Post* accented the great contrasts between Germany and America. In Germany, unity of spirit and purpose prevailed, massive rallies in Nürnberg and Berlin demonstrating patriotic fervor and commitment. The contemporary American story told of labor riots, tent camps, soup kitchens, racial unrest, and polarization between different groups and separate sections of the country.

America was a great country if it weren't for some of the people. Its society was mongrelized, its riches wasted. Hedonism was rampant. His fellow students thrived on a diet of jazz music, sex, alcohol, and Hollywood films. With little respect for authority and institutions, everything was open for debate. People argued for the sake of argument; no political or social function was free of acrimony and dissent. There was no civility in America: no one knew their place. The basest worker assumed he had a right to show disrespect whenever it suited him. The government at every level was corrupt. Gangsters and murderers were folk heroes in a culture with little history or pride.

But these young men, his fellow passengers, could be a wave of the future. If only the thick-skulled, self-centered Americans would grasp how the salvation of their culture and nation could be found in the discipline and unity of the Nazi Party.

From outside, the movement appeared small: the papers said there were hundreds of thousands of members spread all over the country. But the Party had many more sympathizers. A rally in February had drawn over twenty thousand people to Madison Square Garden in New York. Enraptured, Edward had watched a newsreel report. Unfortunately communists, Jews, and their friends had gained admittance and tried to disrupt the rally. Fistfights erupted and local police emptied the giant hall. But only after the opening ceremony and several stirring speeches had broadcast the Party's message with great impact.

On a Sunday morning, outside the German bakery near campus, Edward was handed a leaflet announcing a Party rally in St. Paul's Symphony Hall. Speakers were to include the national party leader, Commander Fritz Kuhn, as well as Reverend Coughlin, the head of the American Union Party, a vocal enemy of the international Jewish conspiracy and ally to the American Nazi Party.

Edward couldn't resist, though with sentiments running hot against Germany and other national socialist movements, he did not share his plans with anyone in the lab or dormitory. He studied the bus route maps carefully and was on his way early Saturday morning to assure a good seat in the crowded hall.

As the bus stopped at the corner opposite Symphony Hall, Edward could see several hundred people milling around whom he assumed were waiting to get in. But as he left the bus and trailed the two uniformed youths across the street, a chorus of boos and jeers rained down on them, or at least on the two boys. Edward had a choice to close ranks with them or move away. He fell back and as the crowd grew louder, they ignored him. Dozens of police officers lined a narrow path up the walkway facing the noisy crowd, but as the youths started up the walk, the police couldn't prevent a barrage of abuse and ridicule. At a bottleneck, just before the stairs leading to the door, a bearded man forced his way through the crowd and before police could react, he spat at the youths, striking one on the side of his head, phlegm dripping down on his shoulder. Several officers waded into the crowd to grab the assailant and while the crowd was distracted, Edward and two other people dashed up the stairs and through the glass doors.

A large group of uniformed party members stood in the lobby watching the crowd through the windows. Edward drew near to them.

"Communists and Bolsheviks!" one declared.

"Jews and homosexuals!"

"We should go out and take care of them ourselves. The police are cowards."

"Leave it to the police, comrades," an older officer ordered. His brown uniform was decorated with gold buttons and insignia. "The Party stands for order and discipline, and as much as I agree we should rid the streets of such vermin, we need to retain our dignity. Let everyone witness the strengths of our characters. That's what will draw true Americans to our cause. These people are all half-breeds and non-Aryans. They aren't worth a single drop of Aryan sweat or blood. Soon the time will come when these animals can be dealt with systematically, as in the Fatherland."

Edward saw placards outside from many groups including the Socialist Workers' Party, the American Legion, and Irish War Veterans: probably all communist front organizations. American cities were rife with them.

The leader was speaking again to his fellow party officers: "Comrades, did you read this morning's paper? The American Civil Liberties organization announced *support* for our rally. Even a local rabbi told the paper we should be allowed to meet." They all chuckled at the irony, but the leader continued more seriously. "But understand what's going on: just as I said, these people pray we will respond violently to the taunts of the crowd. Then Jews and their lackeys will try to claim the high moral ground. We cannot allow that to happen. Keep your men under control."

More police had arrived, some on horses, and they began to force the crowd back so that people arriving for the rally in increasing numbers could enter without interference. As Edward watched, a few rocks were thrown, but the police reacted quickly. And first dozens, then hundreds, of men and women began to pour in.

The group of Party officials broke up and began to work their way through the crowd towards the auditorium, shaking hands with many of the people they met, exchanging straight-armed salutes with uniformed comrades: "Sieg Heil!"

A dozen gray-haired ladies were selling tickets from a long line of tables in the lobby. Others were passing out party brochures or hawking books and memorabilia. Edward bought his ticket for one dollar. He joined a crush of people trying to enter the auditorium but until near the door he didn't realize that Party security men were searching everyone. City police officers were monitoring the process. No one was complaining; but neither did they underestimate the animosity the party generated among certain elements. But everyone was anxious that they'd miss part of the ceremonial. Past the door Edward could feel excitement building as the hall filled. A military-style brass band was warming up on the floor of the hall immediately in front of the stage.

Teenage girls acted as ushers, wearing modest black skirts and socks along with their brown shirts and red scarves. As Edward and a half dozen others followed one of the girls to an empty section of seats, Edward gazed up and around the hall. Banners hung from balcony rails: *'Wake Up America – Smash Jewish Communism!' 'Stop Jewish Domination of Christian America!' '1,000,000 Members by 1940!'* A huge picture of the *Führer*, flanked by two giant swastikas, formed a backdrop for the stage. Along the sides of the hall were large portraits of party leaders, both Germans and German-Americans. Edward recognized

Reichsmarshal Goering and several others.

Officials were gathering on stage, still exchanging salutes and shaking hands. The band began to play a march and the audience settled in their seats. Many of the crowd surrounding Edward were older men and women who appeared awestruck. As band music displaced the babble in the hall it was difficult to carry on conversations, but everyone nearby acknowledged one another with handshakes, nods, and sincere smiles. Edward hoped no one would question why Edward wasn't standing among the other young men in uniform, but if challenged he was prepared to proclaim his identity as a German citizen and true Nazi who didn't need trappings to show his patriotism. He daydreamed about how they would honor him as a visiting dignitary. Perhaps they'd beseech him to stand before the whole audience or even to join the important men on the stage. He yearned for it to happen on one level and he feared that it might happen on another. What if he wasn't equal to the attention? Best just to sit anonymously. But if these people only knew.

As the opening march ended, a Party officer strode to the podium, adjusted the microphone and began:

"Welcome, Comrades!" he paused as the crowd cheered. "Welcome, Christian Patriots!" More cheers and applause. "I am Gruppenführer Browning, chairman of the Minnesota district. For you who've arrived from out of town, welcome to St. Paul!

"As is our tradition, let us begin with the National Anthem. Everyone please join in. Make sure those animals outside can hear us!"

As the band stood and began to introduce the tune, from the rear an honor guard started down the center aisle carrying flags. "Oooh, say can you see...."

Taking his cue from the Americans around him, Edward placed his right hand over his heart. He didn't know the words to the song, but moved his lips pretending. He watched as the flags passed. State flags accompanied the American national flag, but most prominent was the German national flag, held perfectly erect and level with the Stars and Stripes. Edward felt a sob sticking in his throat and his eyes misted. As the anthem ended, the flags were borne onto the stage and mounted in holders behind the podium. Another speaker stood at the microphone.

"My fellow Christian Americans, remain standing and please allow me to lead you in the Pledge of Allegiance. *I pledge allegiance....*"

Again Edward was caught off guard as everyone around him slowly recited. He could not, of course, pledge to the United States. His silence was easy to defend. He prayed someone would challenge him about this. Then the whole audience would know.

A benediction followed intoned by a Lutheran bishop and Gruppenführer Browning returned to the microphone gesturing broadly for every one to be seated.

"I'd like to introduce the dignitaries on stage with me this afternoon, but first I have a sad announcement. We had hoped that our esteemed leader, Fritz Kuhn, would be with us today. Those of you who've met him or who've heard his radio broadcasts, all know what a dynamic speaker he is." There was a murmur of anticipation and comment in the hall. "But unfortunately, I was informed only moments ago, that Herr Kuhn has been *arrested* in Pennsylvania on trumped-up charges and is being held in a jail in New York City." The audience let out a collective moan. "He is a prisoner of conscience persecuted by the communist government in Washington lead by President Franklin Rosenfeld."

There were angry shouts from around the hall: "Shame! Shame! Free Kuhn!"

"Comrades! This has happened before and will happen again. We must stick together. Let me assure you that the Party will do everything in its power to win Fritz's freedom. Later this afternoon, when our youngsters pass among you asking for donations, please be generous. We promise to forward a substantial portion for Fritz's legal fees. Thank you all."

At this point Herr Browning began his introductions and a series of speeches followed. Some speakers were dynamic and the crowd responded loudly, booing when Roosevelt was mentioned (it was always Rosenfeld) and, for some reason Edward didn't understand, cheering when former President Hoover was mentioned. Likewise the crowd responded loudly and exuberantly to the names of other American politicians and businessmen, Senator Burton Wheeler, Henry Ford, and Charles Lindbergh among them.

Among other themes, the fear was repeatedly evinced that America was becoming a Bolshevik paradise. Less captivating speakers delivered dry lessons on dogma. A very shy young man reported on the activities and growth of Party youth groups and training camps established all around the country.

Everyone referred respectfully in their talks to the upcoming keynote address from Reverend Coughlin. Doctor Coughlin was the man who'd single-handedly exposed the international Jewish conspiracy of bankers and bureaucrats and their bid to control the world's wealth and property. This was the story everyone had come to hear: an explanation for every hardship and failure in their lives.

But as Coughlin was introduced and made to join the others from backstage, the lights suddenly went dark. There was no panic and everyone sat still waiting for the lights to come back on, whispering to their neighbors in the dark, speculating on whether protestors outside were responsible. Then from somewhere several rows behind Edward, he heard a *pop* like a champagne cork followed by a slow hiss. An instant later a loud *whoomp* shook the hall, accompanied by a flash of light, not an explosion like a bomb but more like the sound of a gas oven igniting late. A few people had ducked low in their seats after the first pop and were cringing expecting an explosion. It didn't sound like a bomb to Edward, but before he had time to consider alternatives, he was assaulted by a wave of foul-smelling gas so overpowering that he thought he might faint.

He tried to hold his breath but was already so excited from the blackout that he didn't last for more than a brief moment. A poison gas attack? Was he dying even as he crouched under his seat? He wasn't going to wait to find out, and along with two thousand other people, he elbowed and shoved his way to the aisle. He could hear people screaming from fear and pain as those who didn't move fast enough were trampled by their comrades. Edward tripped and stumbled as his feet tangled in the arms and legs sprawled on the floor beneath. People were retching and the smell of vomit was mixed with the sulfurous gas that seemed to penetrate everywhere and everything. Bedlam!

By Monday morning Edward had already laundered his clothes twice and taken three shower baths, to no avail. The sour sewer smell seemed to cling to everything, contaminating clothing he wasn't even wearing on Saturday. He suspected the odor had actually impregnated his nose and lungs. Though maybe only he could still smell the aftereffects, he couldn't take any chances, nor did he trust anyone enough to ask. Defeated at last, he bundled up his good suit and best shirt and tossed them in a trashcan along the way to the lab. During the morning, he kept his distance from the other technicians and assistants and whenever he interacted with someone, he searched for any sign that they detected anything unusual.

At lunchtime he claimed a lonely table in the back corner of the cafeteria, but several of his co-workers spotted him and came to sit down. Joey had a copy of the morning paper. "Did any of you read this? About the Nazis at Symphony Hall? Somebody planted a stink bomb and emptied the place out!"

"Read it out loud," asked someone.

He began: "Headline reads 'Someone makes big stink about Nazis…Saturday afternoon's Bund meeting at St. Paul's Symphony Hall was interrupted when some sort of device was activated filling the Hall with sulfurous gas. While the gas was essentially harmless, the foul odor drove everyone choking and gagging from the Hall. Several dozen audience members were treated for minor injuries after they were knocked to the floor and trampled in the panic that ensued. As of Sunday night a disgusting odor, described variously as smelling like a sewer or mortuary, lingered, causing cancellation of Sunday evening's scheduled piano recital.' "

"How ironic," somebody said.

"Hey, I heard a rumor this morning that someone in the chemistry department did it."

"You're joking."

"Nope. Nobody's talking much. City cops are pretty pissed. Marty said some detective called Dean Andersen on Sunday to ask if he knew anything. Emmett told me he got a call last night, too. Seems the bomb was pretty sophisticated. First thing they thought was, 'college students'."

"Who do *you* think was in on it?"

"Hey, my first thought was *you*, Joey, maybe you and Linda. I remember a few months ago how you two were ripping the Nazis. And it's just your style!"

"Well, it wasn't me, I'll tell you that. I wish I *had* thought of it. Linda's been sneaking around a lot, in the lab 'til late at night. What's she been up to?"

"I figured she was hanging around with Tellerman," Fred said, looking across the table at Edward with a sly grin. "He's usually the only guy around after six." The whole group erupted with a roar of laughter. Edward was mortified. He sat rigid with both hands flat on the tabletop afraid to look up, to meet their eyes. He was sure that everyone in the cafeteria was staring at him. He hated them all.

"Speaking of bestiality, listen to this," Joey said calling for attention. "There's an article about this guy Kuhn, the head of the Nazis, the guy who was supposed to give a speech on Saturday. He was arrested in Pennsylvania for embezzling donations to blow on his girlfriends. Feds say they've got him dead to rights. Wanna know how? One of his girlfriends is a FBI informer! I guess *he's* the one who got fucked!"

"They're all pond scum."

"Oh, I'm a little surprised. I thought they were all homos."

"Listen to this," Joey continued. "The FBI is also checking to see whether any bills Kuhn spent on his lady friends came from the Lindbergh baby kidnapping."

Edward sat fuming in his chair even though the teasing had been dropped. But as he listened, the insults and gibes kept coming. Lie after lie. Don't these people realize who owns the newspapers? Who controls the radio and the cinema? They're so naïve, so ignorant and hopeless.

Gathering himself and without looking at anyone he collected his dishes and silverware and skulked away from the table. It was difficult to walk without stumbling; he had to concentrate on what he was doing afraid to forfeit whatever pride he had left.

"Freddie, I think you hit a nerve there," Joey said under his voice as Edward disappeared out the door. "Tellerman's a really weird guy. I'll bet he's been thinking hard about a romp with Linda the Loveless. You just caught him with his fly open and his dick in his hand. He keeps thing bottled up tight. Were you watching him? I thought he'd explode like that stink bomb."

"Fuck him. Tellerman's a stiff. He needs to learn to loosen up. He's lucky to be here and not back in Czechoslovakia, wearing a blindfold, with his back against some wall. The Nazis are shooting college students in Prague like it was duck season. He has more reasons to hate the Nazis than any of us."

"Maybe he's just pissed 'cause he didn't get in on the bomb making."

"He's too big a sissy. I can't see it; just can't see it."

"Okay, but now the truth. Give it to us. Who built the bomb?"

"My lips are sealed," Fred smiled.

"Asshole!"

Munich, Germany – September 1939

"It's war, fucking, bloody war," Walther cursed, throwing the folded newspaper on the café table, splashing coffee everywhere. No one was close enough to overhear. Rudi picked it up, scanned the headlines, and passed it over to Willy. "This is the end of everything. The fucking politicians finally pushed too hard; the French and Brits have to respond. Rudi, you and I are dead men, we just don't know it yet. Our exemptions will be revoked. We'll be in uniform within a fortnight." He slumped heavily into an empty chair. The sweltering late summer heat was oppressive and everyone was short-tempered. Walther had apparently been drinking already that morning. His long blond hair was dirty and matted, his blue eyes blood-shot, and his eyelids puffy and dark.

"Don't you think it will all blow over? It's only *Poland* for God's sake," Rudi said hopefully. "Twenty years ago Poland didn't even exist."

"Listen to me, you fool," Walther snarled, his voice quivering. "I'm the historian, remember. Armies shoot at each other across borders all the time; it's sort of a game, part of training. But when politicians get involved and declare war, escalation is inevitable, because, unlike soldiers, politicians have no concept or personal stake about what happens afterwards. Soldiers will push things only so far, and every soldier on each side understands those limits. It's part of their common language and culture. That culture includes elements of honor unknown to politicians regardless their party. Modern warfare is ultimately dishonorable and *soldiers* avoid it at any cost."

"You're nuts. Soldiers love to fight, especially German soldiers," Rudi interrupted.

"No, you're mistaken. Conventional thinking is wrong. Fools like you imagine there's all this wrangling back and forth between ambassadors and when diplomacy fails the soldiers take over. That's backwards. Diplomacy is an inherently honorable effort, quite compatible with military thinking and virtues. When diplomacy fails, it's the partisan politicians that take over and commit the country to war and all the horrors that follow. It's their big chance to consolidate power and negate any influence their citizens, soldiers, or statesmen might try to retain. Then soldiers will fight desperately to end the horror and restore honor.

"The only soldiers you'll see begging for a fight are those that have never seen one, like all these idiots who've enlisted in the last few years. And we both know dozens who volunteered, our friends, for Christ's sake. But they've joined less for true German nationalism than for National Socialism, a political entity."

"Is there a difference?" Willy asked.

"The Party would like you to think it's the same. They want it to become the same. Old-timers know the difference. Most of us can't see it."

"Walther," Willy interrupted, "I've watched the parades and rallies. I read the editorials. Hitler appears to have tremendous support, regardless his methods."

"I challenge you to find any event, any social or political decision, in any society, country, or recorded time, that commanded a consensus as overwhelming as claimed by Berlin. It's against human nature. Your perception's being manipulated. It's that simple."

Rudi persisted. "But you're saying that the war must escalate. I don't see that as inevitable. No one wants another Great War. It wrecked all the countries involved, except Willy's, which managed to stay out until near the end. Millions of soldiers died. Herr Hitler was there: you've read his military record. He saw the worst of it and came out with honor. He knows what war means."

"Then he's forgotten or else he left some part of his brain or soul on the battlefield twenty years ago. Somewhere in his evolution from soldier to politician, he left honor behind."

"Walther, keep your voice down," Rudi whispered desperately, his flushed face nearly as red as his hair.

"Sorry," Walther apologized, glancing nervously around the hall before he continued under more control. "I'm telling you that we're in for the very worst that you can imagine and horrors you can't conjure even in your most vivid nightmares."

While the debate continued between his two friends, Willy sat quietly, staring at his coffee cup. He had skimmed through the newspaper story as Walther talked and there was no mention of any response by the United

States. Unless things had changed dramatically in the twelve months since he left Wisconsin, America would maintain its isolation for the meantime. There would be outrage among the Poles back home, especially in Wisconsin, where they live side by side with German-Americans. Half the kids in Willy's high school were Polish and he counted them as his friends and peers. It was hard for Willy to envision a source of conflict between Germans and Poles deep enough to engender open war.

Chances are folks back home, except for Polish immigrants, would view things the same way, assume this is a teapot tempest, and ignore the whole thing. There were certainly enough apologists for the Nazis in America: the *Bund* had actively recruited on campus and posters announcing rallies often appeared on telephone poles around his tiny hometown. The United States will stay out of the war unless directly attacked, and neither side in the war would be that stupid.

But Willy knew about things that his friends did not. Terrible things that scared him more than any story he'd ever read, picture he'd ever seen, or experience he'd heard recounted. This war would be worse than Walther, the historian, could predict. But Walther *had* described the exact reason why the most powerful weapons would be developed and then used. Politics. It would be used as much to retain hold over the German people as to destroy and defeat Germany's enemies. Professor Heisenberg was absolutely wrong. Perhaps if there were peace, he and his coworkers could have controlled the information and technology to their own ends. No longer.

He began to shiver and sweat coldly, despite the heat.

Walther noted his discomfort. "Willy, don't *you* get depressed. We need an island of calm in this sea of calamity. Without your naïve American perspective, or at least your nonchalant American manners, we'll expire from paralytic seriousness long before we face bullets. You're the one who also sees good in bad, light in dark, and humor in dour and tedious things. Don't give up on us now; otherwise we'll lose all hope."

Willy forced a smile for his friends, but knew it looked wooden and insincere.

"Don't try to dump that load on me, thank you very much. Rudi, what are you going to do?"

"My father's active in the Party back home. He suggested that if war comes, I should volunteer for the SD cadet corps rather than wait for conscription into the army. He says there'll be better chances for promotion. He'll nominate me for the Party later and I can switch to the SS. Personally, I think the army would be more honorable," he sighed, studying his friend Walther, "but my mother insists I follow father's advice since it keep's me out of combat."

Walther snickered, "So I have Hitler to contend with and you have your mother. The world is full of dictators. Someday when you're torturing me, Rudi, as a favor, friend to friend, keep the voltage low. Okay? Remember, I still owe you money!"

Willy wanted to help cheer his friends. "Gentlemen, if the Nazis really want to win the war, the last thing they need is either of you two fighting on their side. Now if they paid you with beer, gave brandy in lieu of promotions, and awarded schnapps instead of medals…"

More than anything, he needed to talk to Lise Wagner.

"Will you have to leave and return to America?" Lise asked, obviously agitated.

"The newspaper suggests just the opposite. The Gestapo is arresting visitors and businessmen from England, France, and the other countries, and sending them to concentration camps. Even as we were sitting in the café Saturday morning, the SD showed up looking for a couple of French assistants working over in the Engineering Institute. It was all very efficient. Obviously this was planned out in advance and it suggests that the so-called counterattack on Poland was also staged, just as the BBC suggested."

"But what about you?"

"Oh, everyone was especially nice to me today. I suspect the SD and Gestapo have orders to keep their paws off Americans and other important neutrals. And since Monday's news about the sinking of the *Athenia* and the Americans that died, everyone's going out of their way to say how sorry they are. They're equally adamant that it could not have been a German U-boat. Some are sincere, others are not. But after waiting for two months, a clerk from the bursar's office showed up at the lab Tuesday morning with all the stipend monies they owed me, going back to last March. He was very gracious and apologetic. Some clerical error was uncovered."

One evening in mid-September, two weeks after Britain and France declared war, Willy and Lise sat beside the big short-wave radio in the

Professor's study. News from the front was upbeat and confident. Nothing on the streets of Munich hinted how battles still raged only five hundred kilometers to the northeast.

Rudi had visited the lab several days before to say good-bye. His cadet training was to begin immediately at a camp south of Munich. They shared their concerns and hopes for Walther who had vanished a few days after the war declarations by France and Britain. Rudi reported how all Walther's possessions had disappeared from his tiny apartment near the university. At least the Gestapo hadn't arrested him in the middle of the night. As often as they'd tried to get him to curb his tongue, it wouldn't have surprised them if he had finally popped off in front of the wrong person.

The conquest of Poland was nearly complete after only two weeks and tonight Adolph Hitler was speaking to the German people and the world from the former free port of Danzig in newly occupied Poland. The speech had been initially conciliatory and as they listened, hope for an armistice grew. The *Führer* had said: " I have no war aims against Britain and France." And he urged that all sides to reflect "on the blessings of peace." He spoke about the historic links between Britain and Germany and suggested that they were natural allies.

But near the end, the *Führer* offered vinegar if the sugar wasn't tempting enough. His voice reverted to a sarcastic pitch Willy had heard many times before. Despite his prayers for peace, Hitler declared that Germany would suffer no resistance to its aspirations. Then he promised that the Reich was ready to fight if resisted, and "*Germany would employ a weapon against which no defense would avail.*"

In early August, Willy and Lise had finished their two hundred-page fabrication, forwarded directly to the Ministry of Education. A polite and formulated note had been returned acknowledging the receipt, but nothing since then. So far it seemed like a big waste of time.

Now the two friends looked at each other. No words were needed. They could delay no longer. The world needed to know what was going on and about the dangers that lurked beyond the guns, cannons, battleships, and airplanes pointed at them.

America

It was Professor Emmett's habit to sit down with his senior and graduate students on Friday afternoons. "A little touch of Ralphie in the night," as one of his more literate students gibed. But it provided an opportunity to hear and share the gossip that fuels the politics of academia. With the beginning of the fall term, there was a backlog of tales, tall and otherwise, to be spun.

Emmett held court: "In July, I stopped in Ann Arbor on the way back from the Warm Springs Symposium. Damnedest thing. Physics Chairman tossed me a casual invitation to a bash at his faculty club. Had my doubts, you gotta know. I've been there before, a really stuffy bunch, bow ties, tweed jackets, if you know what I mean. Sherry by the teaspoon. No beer in sight." Everyone tittered.

"Hard to believe that anyone at the University of Michigan would be so pretentious. It's a long haul from Harvard." Several of the assistants nodded insincerely. Michigan had been their first choice over Minnesota. Fact was that in the academic pecking order, anything between Chicago and the California State line was considered gauche and second-rate. "But was I surprised," Emmett continued, absently trying to relight his briar pipe. "Twenty men were present, almost all foreigners of one sort or another. A regular League of Nations, or rather a League of Former Nations. No offense, Ed…." Tellerman could only shrug and smile weakly. Since Germany had invaded Poland three weeks before, Edward's urge to crow his pride in the swift advance of his Fatherland's panzers had been beaten down by an avalanche of scorn and abuse for anything European.

"So here's all these top scientists milling around, hailing each other in God-only-knows what language, back-slapping, and drinking keg beer and the club's brandy like men dying of thirst.

"The old UM dons must have been apoplectic." Emmett paused to dig wattle from his pipe, ashes dropping in his lap.

"Who was there?" someone prompted.

"You name it. Enough Nobel medals to decorate a Christmas tree. Enrico Fermi from Rome showed up with his wife. Told the craziest story about how he got permission from Mussolini to attend the Nobel ceremony in Stockholm in '38 and never went back. Left Italy with fifty dollars in their pockets and all the gold watches they could wear. Somebody whispered that Fermi's buried his Nobel Prize money in a coffee can under his new house in Jersey. Doesn't trust banks.

"Teller and Szilard, the two Hungarians were there, Leo wheelin' and dealin' as usual. Robert Oppenheimer showed up from Cal Tech and Arthur Compton from Chicago. I gotta tell you, air was getting pretty rare. But that's not the half of it...

"Turns out the shindig was arranged to welcome Werner Heisenberg from Germany. First time I've met him. Seems like a good man. Very pleasant and unpretentious. He's making some sort of grand tour of the states over the summer. I guess he could have timed it better. He said he was scheduled to return to Germany mid-August. Heisenberg was joking that he needed to get back for his annual ten-day stint in the German army reserves. Can't see him in a Nazi uniform, traipsing through Poland. Bit too old for it if you ask me. A few more weeks and he could have been comfortably interned here for the duration. Could have had any faculty job he wanted. Bad timing and bad luck, I guess.

"Anyway, Heisenberg had already been to Columbia, Harvard, and Princeton, where he had an audience with Einstein himself. Everyone asked, but he wouldn't say how that went; though you could guess that they didn't talk about baseball scores or china patterns.

"Gossip runs that Otto Hahn and Fritz Strassmann in Berlin have successfully confirmed nuclear fission in their lab, though it took Lise Meitner in Sweden and her nephew in England to put all the pieces together. Szilard's bragging that he already has an application patent filed and is willing to sign the rights over to the U.S. Navy for free. You had to see it to believe, all these guys, fresh off the boat, accents as thick as tar, acting as American as apple pie and root beer.

"Behind Heisenberg's back, a lot of folks are pretty worried. There's Werner Heisenberg, all smiles and reassurance, but if there's a chance that Hahn's discovery could lead to some sort of military weapon, no one doubts that the Nazis would press ahead regardless Heisenberg's scruples.

"Now we've got a war and Heisenberg's back in Berlin. That doesn't bode well as far as I'm concerned. He says he's not working on a bomb and I can't see him lying to all his old friends at the party, but...other than Einstein himself or maybe Oppie, Werner's probably the smartest man on earth. If he's decided to help with weapons development, the Brits are screwed and we're not far behind...sorry, Linda. Forgive my French."

As Edward sat listening to Emmett's mindless ramblings, he was flush with new pride and patriotism. So, despite Germany's increasing isolation over the past five years, the most important and momentous discoveries still belong to the Reich. Heisenberg had been correct to deny German weapons-related research, but Edward had himself attended the *Uranium Club* conference the previous April and knew something of the truth, at least more than Professor Emmett and his naïve and foolish colleagues. This knowledge made Edward feel even more superior, if that was possible.

But if the Americans did come to know about ongoing research in the Reich, they might initiate a parallel program of their own. After six months in the United States, Edward harbored few illusions about the extensive capabilities and resources available in America, a country rich in everything except honor and moral courage. He considered everything Professor Emmett had reported, sifting through it all, word by word, looking for every fragment and clue about what was going on back in his homeland. It took Linda some effort to get his attention.

"Eddie, I hope I'm not being too forward, but if you're free this evening, I'd like to invite you to have dinner with me and my parents. Will you come?"

Edward looked up, distracted from his own thoughts. The group had broken up, and he realized he was alone in the student lounge with Linda.

"Excuse me?" He said, trying to take in what she'd asked.

"If nothing else, you'll get a home-cooked meal for a change instead of cafeteria crap."

His mind still five thousand miles away, Edward wasn't nimble enough to invent another excuse. Linda took his silence for affirmation and charged ahead.

"It's all very casual. Come just as you are," she said with some emphasis. Linda neither wanted to give him a chance to beg off nor an opportunity to change into that ridiculous formal suit he'd worn to

Professor Emmett's reception, the one long since consigned to the trash. "I'll meet you in front of the building at five." She darted off and avoided him for the rest of the afternoon, lest he have an opening to communicate a change of mind.

At breakfast that morning, she'd forewarned her parents about a possible dinner guest.

"I don't know if he'll come. Eddie is very quiet and thoughtful. But he's been so forlorn since the war started, I really feel sorry for him. Here he is, a refugee, his country annexed by the Nazis, and now with even less chance that he can ever return home or even hear from his family again."

Linda's mother was heartened that her daughter was showing interest in a young man, especially someone with apparent ambition and brains. A medical doctor might be better but Mrs. Trout had few illusions about her daughter's chubby looks, bad complexion, demanding disposition, and faint prospects.

"Make sure that he comes, Linda dear. We'll do everything we can to make him feel at home...won't we Nathan? You say he's from Czechoslovakia?"

"Please, mother, you know how you can be. Please don't ask any personal questions about him or his family. It'll just make him more depressed. Just be yourselves," she pleaded with her father and mother.

From behind his morning paper, her father was still doubtful. "Princess, tonight begins the *Sabbath*. It will only be proper if he joins in. If he's not a practicing Jew, he might be embarrassed. That makes me ask...he is Jewish isn't he?"

His wife chimed in. "Nathan, what a silly question? Of course he is. Aren't they all?"

Balance

"Willy, I don't know what to say. I shake with anger whenever I see them walking around, joking and singing."

"Whom are you talking about, Rudi?"

"The cadets who killed Fräulein Wagner. Look, you've worked with Professor Wagner for a long time. I don't know him well. I only took one undergraduate lecture from him three years ago. He wouldn't remember me from Adam. But I had to tell someone before I burst."

"Just relax," Willy suggested, choking back a scream. Memories he'd submerged for months instantly and vividly resurfaced. Rudi sat quietly for a few moments, reluctant to begin again. He had appeared in the laboratory that afternoon, nervous and agitated, unwilling to meet Willy's eyes.

"I also have this fear that if I went directly to the Professor, he'd look at my uniform and think that I'm one of them. Willy, I volunteered for the SD so I could stay far away from the front. What I've seen has frightened me badly, but it's too late to leave now.

"I was stunned when I heard what happened to Fräulein Wagner in April. But when the trial was over, like everyone one else, I could accept the sentences passed down by the judges. Later, after I joined the cadet corps, it was difficult to believe those comrades, men from my own regiment, could have done such a thing.."

"I'm not sure the Professor and his other daughter would agree, Rudi."

"I understand. I understand. But what I suspect you don't know is that a week after the verdict, the camp commandant reduced the sentences to *six months special duty*. The six of them are restricted to the camp itself and live together in their own barracks. But within the fence, they come and go as they please. They wear their infamy like a badge of honor to impress other cadets with how tough and ferocious they are. Many of the younger cadets look up to them like war heroes and follow them around like puppies. And in a few weeks, even these restrictions will be dropped. It isn't right. It just isn't right."

"Why do you come to me?"

"You're my friend, Willy; I trust you completely. I had to tell someone. This kind of thing is not discussed at camp, openly or otherwise. I'm breaking the honor code by talking to you about it. But you work with the Professor and might have an idea how to let him know about what's happened. Professor Wagner is famous and influential. If he were to register protest with the civil authorities, perhaps the pressure would force the commandant reinstitute the original sentences."

"Do you honestly think that's likely to happen?"

"I don't know, but it could. Isn't it worth trying?"

"The Professor was hurt badly by Fräulein Gabrielle's murder and has been very ill every since. I'm not sure that this news might not break him completely."

"Then what can be done? Isn't there anyone who could help?"

Rudy looked at the floor, abject and lost. Willy was silent for some minutes. While he'd fought to remain calm while Rudi told his story, he felt flushed and dizzy. He turned away and looked around the lab so Rudi would not read anything in his eyes. Insanity. Madness. Willy was comfortable within the quiet and well-ordered confines of the laboratory. In here he understood how things worked, how chemical and mathematical equations were written and balanced. But outside, beyond the walls and windows, things were happening that continued to defy logic and reason. Again it seemed nothing he knew and understood and believed was applicable...out there.

For the last year he'd been a passive witness, a spectator detached from events, at best a clownish trickster. But Gabi's death had cut him to the core. While he would never be sure now how he felt about her in his heart, she was a part of him. He could clearly recollect how she smelled and how she felt. And for every time she had humiliated and embarrassed him, he could recall the thrill of her in bed. This would always remain his secret, but that didn't stop him from continuing to ache when he thought about her. And now this.

News four months ago that the cadets had been sentenced harshly, however unsatisfactory it might be intellectually, had helped Willy emotionally to put her death outside of the realm of obsession where he'd been living. And while Lise was still angry, Willy had returned to the lab burying himself in his work and then in the conspiracy he and Lise had forged.

He couldn't possibly tell Lise about what Rudi had recounted. She might precipitate something with her father's important friends. If a new investigation began, the SS might try to impugn Gabi this time. Willy's relationship with Gabi might surface. If the Professor were confronted with this horror again, he would be driven even further from reality. It would kill him.

But what could Willy do? He looked around the lab again, running his eyes along the familiar shelves packed with bottles, vials, and flasks of chemicals.

"Rudi," Willy asked quietly, "tell me about your training camp. If I wanted to see these men, to confirm the story with my own eyes, could you help me get in and out of the camp?"

"Yes, Willy, that would be simple. There is no need for guards. When we're not on duty or in training classes, we come and go as we like. We're volunteers after all," Rudi said bitterly. "But you don't believe my story? It's true, you must believe me. My barracks is near theirs. I see them everyday."

"I believe you, Rudi. Completely. Don't worry about that. But if I'm going to go to the Professor or his friends, I must see this for myself. And I don't want to involve you or have to give your name."

"No. No. You're right, of course. Thank you, Willy."

"Would I need to wear a uniform of some sort to move around inside?"

Fraternization

Tellerman stood under a steaming hot shower, reluctant to step out. He let the near-scalding water play on the back and top of his head. In his dorm room, he had kept reaching back, touching the spot where it felt as if the *yarmulke* was still pinned in place. He was gripped by an irrational fear that this sensation might never go away and somehow, once back in the Fatherland, he might be marked for life in a way that would leave him outcast among his countrymen.

"Hey, Tellerman, you're using up all the hot water, you fuckin' Bohunk! Give me a break," some yelled into the stall.

Arriving for dinner, everyone had been quite charming. Linda had driven him the short distance to the house in her old car; odd enough to sit stone-faced as a *woman* drove him around. She said something about getting to the house before sundown and how she would walk him home after dinner. Edward shrugged. A brisk walk after dinner was a very German habit and he was secretly glad that she would not drive him home after dark. Linda's father was gracious, offering sweet red wine. Her mother was solicitous, asking if he was comfortable enough, cool enough, and so forth. The two women went off to the kitchen to finish preparing dinner and set the table.

Alone with Linda's father, Edward was questioned pleasantly about his course of study and his impressions about American universities. Edward had learned it was best to remain positive in his comments. Americans were highly sensitive to the slightest criticism, implied, or otherwise.

"I find your American universities to be quite different from those in Germany. Neither better nor worse, only different."

At one point Mr. Trout tried to emphasize a point by saying something in German or some crude German dialect. But Edward could barely understand a word and from his blank expression, Mr. Trout knew better than to try that again. Mr. Trout had little enough occasion to speak Yiddish over the twenty years since he'd moved to St. Paul from Chicago. Perhaps he could only fault himself for not keeping up with his studies and making more effort to form a congregation, however small, with the few other Jewish families living in the city. *Whatever!*

Edward reciprocated politely by asking Mr. Trout about his business, which turned out to be *shoes*. He owned a small store on Main Street and, once prompted, volunteered an endless stream of anecdotes and minutia about the shoe business under the Roosevelt administration, which according to Mr. Trout were closely intertwined. Through it all, Edward couldn't divine Mr. Trout's basic or true opinion about Roosevelt, whom Edward still thought of as *Rosenfelt*. After twenty minutes of conversation, Edward concluded that Mr. Trout had many opinions but no beliefs, like almost all the Americans he'd met. But they all had a common passion for money and materialist things money would buy.

At one point Linda sat next to her father on the large stuffed sofa, but she quickly became enraged at some of the things her father was saying about Democrat politics, and after several sharp exchanges, she left in a huff. Edward was shocked and thought she was very disrespectful. Most German girls would never dare contradict their fathers publicly, at least in his family, another weakness he noted among these Americans.

Called to the table by Mrs. Trout, as they entered the small dining room, Mr. Trout handed Edward a small round piece of embroidered cloth. As Edward stood there, totally at a loss, Mr. Trout unfolded an identical piece and placed it on his head, fastening it in place with a pin. Edward's mouth dropped and he suddenly felt dizzy. He knew so little about Jews that he'd reached this point in the evening before realizing where he was. Now it was too late to escape and he was too stunned to protest or resist. He looked down at the yarmulke in his hand as if it were some creature from the darkest sea bottom.

Linda saw him hesitate and jumped in to help. "Daddy, Eddie doesn't have a pin." Finding one on the side table, Linda proceeded to attach the skullcap to Edward's head with motherly care then pushed the catatonic young German to his chair.

As the pre-meal ritual began with the *Kiddush* cup, wine and *Hallah* bread, Mr. Trout looked several times for Edward to participate, to take up the responses, as was his responsibility as the other adult male present. The man seemed nonplussed, so Mr. Trout finished the prayers and blessings as he did most Friday nights in the absence of another male: "Blessed are you, God, You are He, Who has sanctified the Sabbath." With a mumbled prayer, portions of bread were passed down the table.

Jews! Edward felt like he'd gone to sleep to wake up in a madhouse, feet nailed to the floor and arms clamped to the chair. The ritual was over before he knew it and his plate and bowl were quickly filled with food. He peered at it like it was poison, but suddenly overwhelmed with a fatalistic sense that his death was near, he submitted to Mrs. Trout's persistent urgings and raised a spoon of steaming soup to his lips. In Symphony Hall he'd clawed and fought like a wildman to escape through the crowd. But the will to fight was gone. It was all so clear. Best to die now, himself a victim of the Jewish menace. The broth was tasteless, with a pale lump of dough floating in the middle. Edward sipped slowly and waited for the poison to take effect. But evidently the torture was to be drawn out.

Dish after dish was shoved his way and he managed to get by with only a fork or spoonful of each. A lump was indeed forming in Edward's gullet and stomach that he was convinced would swell until it consumed and killed him.

His finicky eating aroused great concern in Mrs. Trout. What a shame the young man is so effected. Perhaps this was a mistake. Obviously we've only managed to increase his heartache. Why else would a healthy young man refuse to eat? But such passionate feelings in a man. Such love for his family.

The evening ended swiftly as Mr. Trout rushed through the closing psalm and grace. Mr. Trout needed to open his shop early on Saturday morning, despite the Sabbath, and was glad to be rid of this gloomy, morbid presence. Linda thought the evening had gone fairly well. She was, of course, inured to Edward's stoicism. Her father granted her dispensation to drive Edward back to his dormitory, and they left at eight, Edward stuttering out his thanks automatically.

"He's a fine young man," Mrs. Trout proffered, firing off the opening volley in what she knew would be a contentious dissection of their guest.

"He's an idiot, Mildred, and must be the son of another idiot. Either he wasn't instructed properly by his father and rabbi, or he's utterly forgotten basic ritual."

"But Linda says that Edward is depressed, especially now that war was declared. He's just a sensitive boy."

"Horse manure. He's just one of those artistic types, self-centered and always thinking how tough his own life is. Other people have troubles too, you know."

"Well you'd better prepare to change your opinion. Your daughter, twenty-four and unmarried, is quite smitten by this *artist*. She tells me that he's a brilliant scientist with a great career ahead of him. She could do much worse."

"Brilliant scientist, you say. Just like your silly, spinster daughter, studying moo-la-crews and a-tums and other nonsense. Could he manage a shoe store? Deal with customers and vendors? Stock shelves? Keep the books? That's the important question, I tell you. There's not a practical bone in his body. Hers either!"

"Well, unless you want to be staring at her across the dinner table ten years from now, you'd better get on board. Don't you dare criticize that young man in front of her. If you can't say anything good, then keep your trap shut."

"Bah!"

In the car, parked in the dark lot behind Edward's dorm block, Linda was all hands. With the radio tuned to Tommy Dorsey's Band with Frank Sinatra playing *Be Careful It's My Heart*, she was purring like a giant house cat. Without warning, or at least without any sign Edward discerned, she slid over to the passenger side, crowding Edward against his door.

"My mother really likes you, Eddie. And she's pretty particular," she said, stretching the truth just short of its breaking point. She reached over in the dark and took his left hand in both of hers, kneading it like dough.

"Don't worry about my father. He's always a difficult case. He'll come around."

She lifted his hand to her chest, then rubbed it against her cheek, inching closer and twisting to face him. Edward was paralyzed, looking straight ahead with glazed eyes. He didn't seem to have control of his limbs again. *Maybe that's how the poison works.* He glanced right, towards the door handle, knew it was the sole avenue of escape, but was incapable of lifting his free hand.

"I can't begin to tell you how much I like you, Eddie…dearest. It's so difficult to talk around the lab. The other guys are all such loud-mouths and they think you're a stiff." She giggled at her own *double-entendre*.

"Anyway, now we're here alone and it doesn't matter what anyone else thinks or what they might say." Linda continued to squeeze and caress his cold, limp hand, first clutching it to her ample bosom, and then stroking the back of his hand against the swollen nipples protruding through her brassiere and thin cashmere sweater.

The street lamps high above, shining through the windshield, left their faces in the dark, but their torsos bathed in pale light, otherwise she might have seen the abject terror in his eyes. Linda twisted on her back, stretched along the bench seat, so that her head rested face up in Edward's lap. It made him jump, this face appearing so suddenly in such an unexpected place.

"Eddie, what are you thinking right now?" she cooed, her eyes half shut.

Without thinking, Edward mumbled in German: "*Ich kann es nicht begreifen.*"

Well, Linda thought, *I'd rather he speak French. Maybe for a Czech, German is romantic. It'll have to do for now. Perhaps if I give him something...French."*

She smoothly rolled over and got up with her knees on the car seat. Linda groped for his flybuttons and quickly had them open and Edward's belt loosened. A little disappointed that there was no signpost to guide her, she hunted through his underwear until she found his flaccid manhood.

Poor guy is shy, she told herself, eyes closed, trying to concentrate on the task at hand. While Linda had had few steady boyfriends over the years, it wasn't for want of trying and on several occasions boys had let her get this far and a bit beyond. She knew what to do with her hands and mouth, the expected responses, and ultimate result.

Edward, on the other hand, had never been more intimate with a girl than a limp... handshake. Paralyzed, the only parts of his body operating were his heart, which produced a pronounced pounding in his chest, ears, and behind his eyes, his sweat glands working overtime despite the cool autumn night, and his eyes which now stared unblinking at the back of her head. Edward's penis was not on the list.

As Linda squeezed and tugged, she was aware of two things. Despite her best effort and enthusiasm (and she'd been told she was *the best*),

Eddie wasn't responding. She'd heard of such things, every girl's nightmare. This might be a problem if it wasn't temporary. But further, as she manipulated his soft member, it somehow felt different. She raised her head slightly and opened her eyes. Now it was her turn to be startled and she sat up, her hand still gripping tightly.

"You…you…you haven't been cut," she babbled, somehow unable to come up with the right word.

"You…you need to be cut, to have this thing cut," she stuttered, pulling on his penis to emphasize her point. "*Circumcise*, that's it! You need to be circumcised," she demanded, the correct term rolling off her tongue at last. "I can't do this if you're not circumcised. At least I don't think so."

Edward's English had improved remarkably since he arrived in America, but circumcise was an unfamiliar term, *beschneiden* in German. But her demand to cut his part finally broke his stupor. All the whispered tales about Jewish women flashed through his mind, how they would emasculate Gentile men or give them horrendous diseases that would make one's private parts rot and wither away. His whole body convulsed in panic and he crashed his head into the car's ceiling and his knees into the bottom of the dashboard.

Somehow he located the door handle and shoved the door open so hard that it rebounded on its springy hinges and smashed him hard on his shoulder and hip as he tried to roll out of the seat onto the pavement.

Linda, afraid now that another prospect, however odd and unsuited, was about to run off, crawled over to the open passenger door. She had embarrassed him.

"Eddie, please, please, don't go. It doesn't matter. Don't go. I was just surprised. That's all. And…and if it makes a difference to you, any doctor can do it. It's never too late, I've heard. Please come back."

Outside Edward jumped to his feet and was able to take two steps before his unbuckled pants slid down his legs and sent him head first over a short row of scrubs and on to the lawn in front of the dormitory. In his struggle to regain his feet he managed somehow to extricate one leg, foot, and shoe from a trouser leg and started to run toward the front door.

The elderly porter at his table just inside the door looked up from his *Life* magazine as the door slammed open and that foreign fella, whatever his name was, hobbled past with one bare leg and his cock dangling free. Their eyes met for a moment. Edward's looked like a deer caught in on-coming headlights. The porter grinned back and as Edward rushed past headed for the stairs, the porter shrugged and went back to his magazine. Its new photos showed German soldiers smiling and mugging for the cameras, as they ranged unchallenged across Poland. Well, in twenty years at the university he'd seen worse. *Damn students. And damn them foreign students specially, always starting something they can't finish properly.*

Bavarian Alps – November 1939

"Are they all dead, Captain?"

"No, Herr General. Three were dead when the corporal came to check on them this morning when they didn't muster for role call. Another died at the hospital. According to the doctors, the last two will live, but have suffered irreparable brain damage."

"I'll speak to the doctors later today. It would probably be best if neither man ever left the hospital alive. Bad for morale. And someone might mistake them for war heroes and we can't have that. "

"No sir, we can't. I'll take care of it, if you wish."

"This doesn't seem to bother you, Captain. You are camp commandant. These were your men."

"Yes, sir, and I do feel sympathy for their families. But you must understand that these men were an embarrassment, a stain on the reputation of my section."

"Because they raped that girl in Munich?"

"Yes, but also because they were careless. They chose the wrong girl, someone well-connected. We had a very difficult time keeping the incident quiet. Secondly, they failed to silence the sole witness to their act, some old half-Jew who'd managed to escape our citywide efforts to move them all out. The dead ringleader, Cadet Captain Wunsch, ordered two of his comrades to silence the tavern owner. But the two proved to be cowards and disobeyed his orders, thinking mere threats would suffice. But the frightened man went directly to the civil authorities at town hall. Too many people had heard his story by the time an officer from the SS arrived to take charge and try to put the genie back into the bottle."

"My office in Munich was inundated with calls from the *Rathaus*."

"Yes, General, and when the girl was identified, we had hell to pay. We received calls and telegrams from half the ministries and foreign embassies in Berlin. In the normal course of events, we would have rumored that the girl was a prostitute, even a Jew, and no one would dare say a word. The Wagner girl was known to the local police as a troublemaker, a rich tart with no respect for authority and many suspicious friends.

"We were barely able to keep the trial under SS oversight. As it was, the cadets were sentenced to ten years hard labor under the premise that they did not intend to kill the girl and they believed she was a Jewess. Once the tumult died away, we reduced the sentences to six months confinement to barracks. As an object lesson, I've had them rebuilding stone walls along the camp's northern boundary. Their sentence would have been up in thirty days. My plan was to break up the group and distribute them around the country. The two cowards were to be assigned to concentration camp guard units, but the others had potential and might have redeemed themselves completely in time."

"But as I said, you don't seem bothered."

"Yes, sir. I was raised in the church at the insistence of my devout mother, and while I've managed to purge all its ridiculous mythology, somewhere in the back of my mind I see God or someone balancing the ledger on this."

"So, you're convinced this event was divinely ordered and executed?" the General smiled ironically.

"Of course not. It was just an accident. Carbon monoxide poisoning, the doctors say. Some malfunction in the barracks's heater. What else could it be?"

Christmas 1939

On Knocking Night, the Thursday before Christmas, Lise and Willy sat in front of the fireplace, but instead of the playful rattling of cans outside, the distant booms of antiaircraft cannons punctuated the evening, test-fired an hour after sunset. While air raid sirens sounded almost daily, so far the British had only bombed Munich with propaganda leaflets, accusing the Gestapo of murdering Poles, as if that might still shock somebody here.

They huddled self-consciously to share warmth. For the first time in her life, no candles had been placed in the windows and curtains were drawn all along the street, obeying strict blackout regulations. Lise had found a small Christmas tree, lugged it home, and decorated it by herself. For now only the three Advent candles were burning. She wanted to save the tree lights for Christmas Eve like when she was little. The tree and lights reminded her of Gabi and frequently, when Willy was gone, she would cry forlornly.

BBC Radio was playing Brahms, but with the bad weather the signal faded in and out, to their frustration and disappointment. German radio stations were broadcasting their usual heavy and depressing Wagner cycles, but at least tonight, both sides avoided war news and political speeches. The Führer was with his troops in the west to celebrate Christmas.

Lise and Willy had checked the Professor several times in his room to make certain that he was well-covered with his blankets and feather comforter, and had gingerly carried a relay of old-fashioned warm bricks from the fireplace to place near the Professor's feet. The gas supply was unreliable, shut off during every alert. The man who for years had supplied the house with firewood had disappeared and they were trying to make a limited store last. With the freezing weather Lise endeavored to keep her father in his bed as much as possible. The Professor, now feeble and shrunken, lacked the energy to protest.

Since the cold spell began several weeks earlier, Willy spent most nights on the sofa at the house; often falling asleep nestled next to Lise. Gabi's room was at the top of the house but Willy would not have slept there even if it weren't for the cold. While he was testing the dye they would use for the letters, Willy trudged back to the lab, but since he'd completed the experiments, he'd given up the struggle with the snowdrifts and icy streets. The university was completed deserted in any case, the boilers and furnaces unattended. The letters and envelopes for America could be prepared at the Professor's study desk.

Between experiments and preparations, during the day they would read books and discuss what they'd read. Willy chose authors from the study shelves he knew to be proscribed by the Party, like Thomas Mann. It might be a trifling rebellion, but it was a means of confronting and challenging fears they shared. It had been years since he'd taken time to carefully read a novel and he found comfortable distraction in immersion. Lise was rereading Remarque. Sometimes Willy would catch her misty-eyed and somber.

Lise had stated her determination to attend Midnight Mass at the Frauenkirche on Christmas Eve, though there was no sign that the weather would cooperate and relent. So this night, Willy entertained Lise with anecdotes about fierce winters in northern Wisconsin where deep snow and sub-zero temperatures were routine. But regardless how nonchalant he tried to be, his shivering evidenced his discomfort.

He told stories about childhood Christmas celebrations, and recounted tales of ice fishing on the Great Lakes, and deer hunting expeditions on snowshoes when he was a teenager. Lise's questions about America were quite different from Gabi's. She asked about his family and neighbors. What carols did they sing? How do people live? Do children attend school when the weather is so cold? How do American parents punish children when they misbehave?

Willy read to her from a letter he'd just received from his parents. The letter was postmarked the past September and the envelope had been neatly slit opened when it was delivered at the laboratory. While there was no specific mention of the war news from Germany, only general questions about his health and comfort, Willy explained how its very tone implied concern on the part of his parents. Earlier letters had been merely a terse journal of events back home. His father and mother were normally unexpressive and phlegmatic. This most recent letter was chatty and several pages long with sections written by both parents. They were worried and though they would never suggest or even hint that he should consider returning to America, he sensed their intent to tempt him to return with reminders about familiar objects, close friends, family pets, and cozy gatherings.

"Do you want to go back to America, Willy?" Lise asked, her voice controlled and even.

"Of course. It's home. My family is there."

"Your home can be where you live. If it weren't for the Nazi, could you settle in Munich? Could your home be here?"

"Honestly? I don't know. In many ways, everything here is familiar and comfortable. The rolling hills and farms in the countryside. The people look the same, dress the same, and do the same jobs."

"But…"

"But the differences hit me hard everyday. Fear is palpable. Fear of men in uniforms. Fear of informants. Fear of your neighbors. Streets are crowded and busy, but everyone looks straight ahead as if they're wearing horse blinders. Here people are frightened by memories of the past, the aftermath of the war and depression. Americans have much the same fear. But most Germans seem to have fear of the future coupled with dark fatalism unlike anything I've ever seen in America."

"Fatalism?"

"Fatalism is accepting that there's nothing you can do to change what's happening around you. Am I making sense?"

"I guess I understand."

"And I guess as long as the Nazis promise great things, the ball will keep rolling along, unchecked and unquestioned."

"But I question."

Willy smiled at her. "Relentlessly. You're unique. Your father taught you to ask questions until you understand things. It's part of scientific method. You've grown up independent and confident with your own decisions. I admire you."

"Me? But you said Germans are fatalistic and self-absorbed. If you accept a single exception, you must concede there might be millions. Do you really think we're all so hopeless?"

"If you were Chancellor, maybe not. For whatever reason, German voters haven't elected you yet. Unfortunately, many bad things will happen before then."

Lise folded her arms in front of her chest and glared at him. "Can't you take anything seriously? You say Germans are all too serious, but if you're really a prime example, America is full of comedians and tall, goofy clowns."

"Well, you'll have to go there and find out for yourself, won't you?"

Last year Willy had reveled in Munich's weeklong Christmas Fair, hundreds of temporary stalls selling seasonal food, sweets, and drinks. Other vendors had offered clever, handmade toys and intricate tree ornaments for which the region was famous. Stalls had filled the *Marienplatz* in front of the city hall. Bands played Christmas music every afternoon and long into crisp, clear nights.

This year the winter weather was horrendous, supposedly the worst in a hundred years. Heavy snowfalls paralyzed the country and temperatures held below freezing for weeks on end. With the war economy, sugar and other staples were already tightly rationed and the few food vendors who put up stalls ran out of enthusiasm the first day and out of their meager stocks the second.

Old men and women continued to sell toys and ornaments, but foul weather, travel restrictions, and fuel rationing limited their numbers, too. Few people were in a mood to exchange gifts. Not a few of these craftsmen, once retired from the factories and shops, had been recalled, and the old women who remained behind grumbled endlessly about the war and the cold.

Many stalls now offered military toys, cast metal soldiers, tanks, airplanes, and ships, and children, especially the boys, flocked around these displays. They played games, testing each other's knowledge about the real military equipment sold in replica, sharing dreams of future glory in the service of the Reich. *Maybe it's always been like this*, Willy thought as he had watched one small group of boys. But this season, in this place, the children's passionate interest was disturbing. In seven or eight years, these ten-year olds might be enthusiastic volunteers sustaining the Nazi war effort for an entire decade.

Willy managed to find a tiny, intricately carved figure of the Virgin Mary as a present for Lise. He had hoped for some hothouse flowers, but they couldn't be had at any price. Though raised a Lutheran, Willy was not devout, but somehow with the backdrop of the war and dismal Christmas weather, the other gifts Willy had considered seemed somehow hollow or superfluous. Maybe the carving was too serious, but…

Their relationship was odd but somehow comfortable. Lise and Willy were coconspirators and confidants, but they were not yet lovers. Both were lonely and isolated, kept apart by their separate memories of Gabi. Willy promised himself never to tell her about his visit to the SD camp. He had sought vengeance, but felt somehow fouled and empty afterwards. *What would Lise think if she knew? I want her to know I'm different from these people. If she knew what I did, she'll see me as no different.*

On weekend leave several weeks ago, Rudi had sought Willy out again at the laboratory. He told Willy all he knew about what had happened to Gabi's killers but refrained from asking the critical question. *How?* Rudi guessed everything, of course, but his friendly manner and the sincerity of his long handshake left Willy assured that his secret was safe. Rudi expressed respect Willy did not feel for himself. He saw himself as a coward and sneak, and the real danger was to his own state of mind.

Willy continued to worry he would be responsible for Lise's arrest when someone discovered the tinkering with the Ministry's calculations or if the censors deciphered hidden messages they planned to mail to America. In turn, Lise was haunted by an expectation that Willy would be compelled to return to America and she'd endure yet another painful loss. For now they only had each other, common fears, and a shared duty to Professor Wagner.

Besides Rudi, most of Willy's friends at the university had been conscripted or had taken war industry jobs to maintain their exemptions. Those that remained had kept their distance since an American arms embargo had been lifted the previous month. Despite Nazi promises and threats, the United States was now selling weapons and other strategic materials to the British and French, and the unexpected warmth in September had cooled just as quickly in November. At first Willy was simply ignored and shunned. But a few days after a bomb exploded in the beer hall where Hitler himself had just given a speech, some people had grown openly hostile. He knew the Party's Student Committee was watching him more closely now, and he walked a narrow line as he tried to avoid them without appearing he was hiding something. When he was experimenting with the letters, he carefully hid his test materials when he was out of the lab, certain someone rifled through his papers and desk drawers whenever he left.

Late on the Knocking Night, the streets outside quiet as a museum, Lise excused herself to check again on her father and retire to bed. "Will you be all right here, Willy? Add another log to the fire if you need. We have plenty of extra blankets. Would you like another?" "I'll be fine, thank you. Is there anything I can help you with?" "I don't think so. Vati's been sleeping very quietly for the last week. That's a good sign, I think. Good night, Willy." "Good night, Lise." He listened as she climbed the stairs and could hear the floor creaking above as she made her way to her father's bedroom. Moments later he heard her steps as she walked to her own room. Then all was quiet except for the soft cracking and snapping of the small fire.

Willy lay back on the sofa. He tried to imagine a future where Lise returned with him to America. How would he introduce her to his parents and friends? He could show her the places he'd tried so hard to describe and explain. Everyone would try to make her laugh.

What would it be like if he stayed here with her? This is her home after all and all arguments he made about his ties to America were equally valid. He didn't want to think about it, but when he closed his eyes and tried to sleep, images of *Kristallnacht*, Berlin, Gabi, the trial, the Jewish baker and his wife, slave laborers along the river, and the book burning all churned in his mind. The dead faces and eyes of Gabi's murderers haunted him, too.

He rose from the comfortable sofa and wrapping a blanket around his shoulders he added another small log on the fire, checked to make sure the drapes were fully closed, and turned up the gas lamp over the Professor's desk. He took out the letters he was preparing to send to America and started to type more copies: carbons wouldn't work.

How many will be enough?

Letters Home

Lise and Willy had typed and tested four identical samples of the draft letter, with four possible dye formulations. Two seemed like they might be successful, and in a third case, only when the letter was held up to the light was the faint blue dye apparent. That wasn't going to work. The blue color in the fourth version started to appear after a single day. Willy considered that dangerous. He could readily imagine an opened, unfolded letter sitting on a censor's table for two days.

When it worked well, the blue dye took three days before it magically appeared, highlighting specific words and letters. Who could hope that one of his letters might lie out in the sunlight that long? Willy knew it was most likely each letter would be read immediately then discarded or filed away. He smiled ruefully at a thought that the planet's fate might be predicated on the habitual disorganization of a professor's desk.

But little time remained for further trials. After Hitler's speech in Poland, Lise and Willy had worked for weeks using different dyes, papers, and inks. The trick was to get a dye to change from clear to pale blue after three or four days in the light. The dye couldn't run; otherwise details of the message would blur. The quality of the paper turned out to be important. Sometimes the dye performed well, but the ink underneath faded. Each factor had to be considered, tested, and used in a simulated letter. Lise ran sunlight and lamplight exposure tests in her bedroom at home, avoiding the prying eyes around the Institute.

Willy explained his theory to Lise. Since war had been declared his letters to home sometimes took nearly two months to reach Wisconsin. If a steamship took ten days in passage and the U. S. Post Office took another ten days to deliver the letter, that meant that the letter lingered in Germany for more than a month before a censor passed it through. They had to make sure the transparent dye didn't begin to turn blue while the letter lingered somewhere before it left Germany. From the time they started in late September, they only managed two complete series of tests and after Lise pointed out that the letters would arrive in mid-winter when days are shorter, Willy had to modify his procedures. By Christmas Willy was satisfied, though plagued by an uneasy feeling that there were other important factors they hadn't weighed properly.

Finally, they had to draft text that provided an excuse to send identical letters to ten different addressees. Willy drafted a letter to Dr. Lawrence Frankel at the University of Chicago for whom Willy had once helped host a graduate seminar. When this test letter was left in the sun for two winter days on Lise's windowsill blue dye appeared behind individual words and it read as follows:

January 2, 1940
Munich, Germany

Dear Dr. Frankel,

My thesis advisor, Professor Ernst Wagner, suggested I write you in the way of introducing myself. When my studies are completed here, I am hoping that you might consider my application to work with you in Chicago. Professor Wagner has given me a **warning** that you can be a tough grader, but that **warning** comes with his assurance that you are also the very best teacher around.

Though my studies here in **Germany** are rewarding and Professor Wagner **is working on** some interesting problems in zirconium, hafnium and **uranium** salts, I have come a**cross sections** that relate closely to things I have read in your publications. I am not sure I understand them all, but **Professor Wagner is helping** me **with the calculations**. I will never be as good as the researchers *for the Kaiser Wilhelm Institute* but I am **near success**.

Otherwise things here are very pleasant. I listen to the **radio**, and am **active** socially. I read in the newspapers that the European political situation is **explosive**, but nothing in Munich suggests anything other than continued peace **is probable**.

If you **please**, Professor Wagner asks that you **please forward** his **message** of best wishes **to Dr. Einstein in**

Princeton. Thank you for your consideration. I will write again before I complete my work here.

Sincerely yours,

William Petersen, MSc. (Marquette, '37)
Chemistry Institute
Munich University
Munich, Germany

"What do you think?" Willy asked anxiously.

"I don't know Willy. I *know* there's a message, so of course I see it right away. Can we increase the chance someone will see it more easily?"

In the end, the only way they could figure to boost their chances was to send more letters.

Willy carefully typed out ten versions of the letter; each addressed to a different person. He didn't dare write Professor Einstein directly. His name was too well known throughout Europe and Willy had included a reference to Einstein in each letter with reluctance. But atomic physics was not Willy's field and he admitted to Lise that he didn't know who else would readily comprehend the significance of his hidden message and then get someone to act decisively. Dr. Frankel at the University of Chicago, Dr. Emmett at Minnesota, Dr. Schmidt at Marquette, and Professor Manson at DePaul were men he knew would at least read his letter personally. The others, all eminent in their fields, probably receive a stack of similar letters seeking fellowships everyday and have secretaries or undergraduate assistants who preview their correspondence, just like Willy did for Professor Wagner.

Each letter had a different addressee and Willy was careful to use different dates. He planned to send them over the period of a week with the idea that no two of the letters would come across the desk of a single censor on the same day. Some he planned to mail from post boxes near the *Bahnhof*, others from the university, or from boxes near Lise's house, again so that no one person would see he was sending multiple letters.

On New Year's Eve, with the Professor asleep upstairs, in the dim gas light with curtains drawn, Lise and Willy sat at the study desk carefully overwriting the hidden message with the blue dye that Willy had brought over from the lab. As they worked, the radio broadcast Joseph Goebbels' New Year's message in which he invoked God, the Almighty, as Protector of the Reich. Goebbels reviewed the events of the year and railed against the English plutocrats who had started it.

Willy was astounded to hear Goebbels say that 1939 "was a year burned into the book of history." How morbidly ironic, since so many history books had been burned. Willy had decided on six more names and addresses at the last moment and the task took almost ten hours. They folded each letter carefully then wrapped each with an extra sheet of heavy, blank paper. Willy took the first four; he would mail two on January 2nd and two more the following day. The others Lise hid in a drawer in her room careful to avoid any premature exposure to light. She would post four letters each on Wednesday, Thursday, and Friday at different postal substations around the city.

After the letters were mailed, Lise and Willy still could not breathe easily. For the first few weeks, they lived with the nightmare that the Gestapo would pound on the door and haul them off under arrest. German newspapers and the BBC were full of reports about U-boat attacks or air attacks on neutral ships. They were forced to consider the possibility that all the letters might go down on the same ship. Willy cursed himself for not spreading the letters out over more time. More dangerous was the possibility that the whole process was delayed by the shipping crisis and the letters were still somewhere in Germany, unopened and uncensored, the clock ticking for the sensitive blue dye.

Later they accepted that they didn't know what to expect even if the secret messages were read, understood, and forwarded. Perhaps there was nothing Dr. Einstein or the American government could do, for that matter. They might even contact the German government and Lise's and Willy's roles would be exposed. They would never be safe. Their one faint hope was a return letter that might contain some sort of acknowledgement that their hidden message was received.

Eight weeks later Willy received a letter at the university from Dr. Manson. The envelope was already opened, as was the case for every letter he or Professor Wagner received. Party operatives at the university were reading everyone's mail ferreting out sedition.

Willy ran to the Wagner's house, the letter unread, when he realized where it was from. Lise and Willy read it together, Willy translating the

Cross Sections

terse English.

February 27, 1940
DePaul University
Chicago, Illinois

Dear Mr. Petersen,
    Thank you for your letter of January 2. As you must understand, our program receives many applications for fellowships and assistantships each year. Our selection process begins in May for the upcoming fall semester and you are welcome to make a formal application.
    At that time your work with Professor Wagner will doubtless play no small role in our considerations.
    We thank you for your interest and look forward to hearing from you soon.

Yours truly,

Roger Manson, Ph.D.
Associate Professor of Chemistry

    Willy's first reaction was disappointment. He set the letter down and he and Lise looked at each other at a loss for something to say.
    "Willy, is it possible Professor Manson understood our message and has written back to us in the same manner?" Lise mused.
    Willy was suddenly ecstatic. "Of course, he would."

    For the rest of the afternoon, Lise and Willy did everything they could to detect a response hidden in the letter from America. They heated the letter over the radiator and later in the kitchen oven. They laid it out in the afternoon sun and held it up to the light. Long into the evening and night Willy struggled with the letters and words which like Poe's *Purloined Letter* might contain an encrypted message or anagram. Tired and depressed, by midnight Willy accepted that Manson's letter was only what it seemed: an innocuous response to his solicitation. He had little

190

hope for any of the other letters by this time.

Lise, wrapped in a blanket on the sofa by the dying fireplace, was thoughtful. "Perhaps a response to your letter will come to my father. You must read his letters very carefully, Willy, especially those from America. Even the simplest letter might include a response. It might not even come from someone you know. Professor Einstein would surely not write to you himself. You can't give up. We must have hope" Willy joined her on the sofa and sitting closely, holding hands under the blanket, they both fell asleep.

During the coming weeks, Willy watched and waited for more replies but none arrived. He carefully examined every letter Professor Wagner received from America, Canada, and England. He couldn't be sure anyone would answer and was equally unsure that he would be able to recognize a cleverly disguised response. Nothing else was possible for now. Lise would not leave her father, who was rapidly deteriorating and becoming helpless. Willy wouldn't desert them to return to America, though Lise continually urged that course on Willy.

"Vati and I will be fine here, Willy. We have a home and money. And his reputation will help shield us from danger. I've been thinking that we can write to the university over Vati's signature and inform them how he's taking a sabbatical...to write a book. No one will question his plans and motives. With so few students left to teach, we'll be left alone."

"I won't leave you. It won't be possible to keep these secrets if I go back to America. Too many people will get involved. Word will get back here. You and your father will be in danger. And how long will it take before the authorities find out about your father's condition. They'll find out that we've been writing his letters and sending out inaccurate calculations. This will be traced back to you. We need to maintain pretenses, especially if it's the only thing slowing down the radiation bomb's progress."

One day Lise asked, "How long should we wait before we try and write to someone in America again?"

"I don't know. Censorship is getting tighter every day. Several faculty members in other departments at the university have been summoned to the Student Tribunal to answer questions about their correspondence. At least two have lost their positions in the past month. Rumor says the Tribunal has turned records from the hearings over to the Gestapo.

"Who knows whether mail from abroad is even being delivered and not impounded?"

"At least we know the first series of letters got through," reassured Lise.

"But I think we'd be wasting our time and taking unreasonable risks with a second batch."

"But we *must* do something."

Inside the Third Reich

Lise huddled shivering on the sofa in front of her fireplace, wrapped head to toe with fluffy eiderdown bedcovers, propped up with pillows from her bedroom upstairs. She watched Willy's back and shoulders as he kneeled setting a new log on the roaring blaze. The city had shut down the gas mains in her neighborhood and others around Munich in order to maintain system-wide pressure in the face of shortages. Though the icy weather that blanketed Europe had relented over the previous week, tonight the freeze was back with vengeance. Snow fell outside; promising to add to the drifts that had covered the city and countryside since mid-November.

She had avoided his eyes all evening, embarrassed about what had happened today, though many details still eluded her. She *did* remember that Willy had undressed her and touched her in private places. Regardless his motives and the outcome, this one thing stuck in her mind. All the danger and mortal fear had fallen away, but now she was obsessing on one silly and momentary event. Willy reassured her how it was the drugs she'd been given and that the effects might last for days. "Hallucinations and paranoia," he suggested sympathetically. He had held her hands and warned Lise that she'd probably begin to remember other, horrible things as the drugs wore off, but for now she seemed incapable of thinking about anything except how he had touched her and how those places still tingled. She understood these sensations and this deepened her embarrassment. Petulantly, she found herself beginning to resent Willy's solicitation and presence.

How stupid can I be? He saved my life. I was there and now I'm home. She accepted that much. Lise wanted to ask how, but…

His back was still turned. Even after all these months, Lise didn't understand a great deal about this man. Outwardly so friendly and good-natured, Willy was taciturn and reserved about himself and his deepest thoughts. They could debate for hours about philosophy, but she wasn't sure about his true beliefs. Willy was easy to spend time with, asks for little, and was always generous and sincere. Despite his height and intellectual maturity, Lise had thought of him as gangly and clumsy, lacking grace in a disarming, rustic way. How often had she and her friends, and even Gabi, made fun of him behind his back?

Both recognized the risks and dangers they'd shared over the last months, though to Lise it all remained something abstract, something happening at a safe distance. They created the bogus report for the Ministry in this very room and at the quiet laboratory at the university. Letters mailed to America in the New Year were typed with the ancient machine on the table by the window. Willy and Lise had anguished about discovery by the Gestapo and had peeked fearfully from behind these very curtains whenever they heard automobiles in the street outside. Her fears then had been intense, or at least she thought so. But sitting here now, she realized how, deep inside, she never expected those terrors would actually reach into this room, into her house, invading her familiar world. From now on, the door, the drapes, the warmth, and the order of the house would not be sufficient to provide any respite.

Though he'd never volunteered details, Lise was aware of Willy's past run-ins with the police and Gestapo on the streets, and once with Gabi at some nightclub. He had witnessed attacks on Jews and students that disturbed him profoundly. And he had attended the trial of the men who'd murdered Gabi, returning every evening near tears, never able to fully recount all he'd seen and heard. But she never thought of Willy as a man of action, a physical person, an individual with arms and legs and muscles, someone who might do something courageous, perhaps something from the fairy tales about modest and heroic knights her mother had read to her when she was little.

Lise caught herself admiring Willy's broad shoulders as he crouched and stoked the fire. The tingling returned suddenly and, fighting the sensation, she closed her eyes and seeking distraction, tried to remember more of what had occurred. One moment Lise and Annamarie had been laughing and in the next instant the Gestapo smashed open the doors of the university café.

Annamarie liked to sit, sipping tea, and watching the handsome, older boys pass by, as scared that one might speak to her, as she was that none of them would. Annamarie would whisper the most outrageous things, things Lise would never repeat and was even embarrassed to think about. But Annamarie was fun and the terrible weather had kept Lise trapped at home for nearly two months. Yesterday, when the sun had broken through again, Willy offered to stay with Professor Wagner if Lise wished to break away for the day. It had felt so good to laugh and forget the world's troubles for a few hours.

Willy stirred and changed positions, still staring thoughtfully into the flames. Lise closed her eyes and began to doze. *He saved me. How? I was there and now I'm here.*

Sitting much too close to the fire, its heat nearly singing his face and hands, Willy's emotions were returning to normal levels of terror. He remembered every detail of the last two days, but unlike Lise, was struggling to erase them from his memory. Every time he let his mind drift back, or when Lise plied him with questions, he started to sweat coldly and then to shake, despite the heat. Therein lay his uneasiness. In hindsight he recognized that if he had wavered for the merest second over the last thirty-six hours, he would have crumbled and failed. If he'd had a second thought or had heeded his inner voices, Lise would be on her way to the camp at Dachau, or even worse if the Gestapo's threats were realized. Willy could have been arrested as a spy. In wartime, everybody shoot spies.

They'd been lucky, very lucky. Willy's Lutheran upbringing had planted within the lingering sense that God doesn't play favorites and always evens the score someday. Next time or sometime, he wouldn't be so fortunate.

Hopefully Lise wouldn't remember much about what happened and would remain so vague that he could sidestep her questions, at least until enough time had passed to take the edge off the horrors. Then he would tell her about how easy it had been, how foolish and lax the Gestapo was, and how he hadn't the least concern. Willy could always find some way to make the story funny and they would laugh together.

Exhausted, Frau Erna had finally returned home. Willy had helped her put Professor Wagner into bed, but in Willy's absence, the sprightly old woman had earned a year's wages and Willy's undying thanks. The house was now quiet as a tomb except for the crackling fire and an occasional clink of Lise's teacup and saucer.

Lise was still suffering the aftereffects of her adventure and each time he peeked at her, so frail and childlike, wrapped in blankets and surrounded by stuffed pillows, the battle for his own sanity would begin again.

Annamarie had been gushing over one particularly tall but seedy looking student and together, watching him from the corners of their eyes, they'd been inventing ridiculous and steamy stories about him as he sat nearby reading a newspaper.

"Too much tea," Annamarie giggled as she went off to find the lavatory. Alone now, Lise was a little self-conscious, afraid people nearby had overheard their silly chatter. How pleasant it might be to sit here with Willy, talking philosophy or religion. Lise had grown up believing that some day she would attend university, but now, in these days, options for young women were narrowing. The Reich trumpeted its tenet that the primary responsibility of German women was to give birth to German workers and soldiers.

From the first instant the brown-shirts burst in, Lise thought about her sister. It flashed in her mind that she was to suffer the same fate, but that fear was quickly replaced by the black anger and bitterness she'd kept to herself since Gabi's murder and the subsequent, farcical trial. To her these were the very same men: nameless, with collective identities, brown-shirted, and belligerent.

Arms crossed and red-faced with anger, she continued to sit at her table, assuming that the raid had nothing to do with her and she was blind-sided when rapped sharply on the upper arm and shoulder by a truncheon.

"I said *get up*," the SD private yelled at her now that he had her complete attention. Lise stood rubbing her arm and started to respond almost apologetically, but was pushed and shoved across the room, stumbling several times, into a group of students herded into one corner of the large room. When she regained her voice and started to protest, her words went unheeded in the cacophony of confused pleadings and shouted orders.

Several Gestapo and police officers appeared, accompanied by student committee leaders, and they stood at ease, chatting as if they were in an art gallery or museum.

"Well, Herr Kessel," the senior man asked pleasantly. "Can you help us sort through this lot? I understand you've compiled cases against some of these people. If you give us a hand, many can be transported directly to Dachau and save us a world of paperwork. Ringleaders, of course, will stand trial, but we have only a limited amount of space left at Gestapo headquarters. So please make your picks."

"Thank you, Captain, I'll do what I can." Kessel was quite pleased with himself. This raid was going to be a tall feather in his cap. He saw how the student committee's work was complete: first prohibited books, then disloyal faculty members, and now troublesome and recalcitrant students. But in war, important honors were had by those men nearest the front, if not actually in combat itself. He had to think about his career and the prospects for advancement and party membership. This mess needed to be cleaned up for good. Kessel would then apply directly to the SS.

Among the young men now pinned behind the line of truncheons and helmeted guards were doubtless students clinging quietly to ideals and beliefs contrary to Party teachings. But honestly, the serious instigators and protestors, quiet and otherwise, had left the university years before. Almost all the young men and women who remained were simply serious students with neither politics nor opinions, some at university only because medical or physical conditions kept them out of the army.

Kessel really didn't have a shred of evidence or proof about anti-party activity at the university, but he could assure himself that, at the very least, this raid would convey a message to everyone that no one was safe from committee scrutiny and summary action by the student tribunal. Some inconvenience for a few of his fellow students would be a small price to pay for an effective reminder and for the boost to Kessel's career. Those with family connections or those for whom some prominent faculty member would vouch, would be freed soon enough, all the wiser for their experience. Others didn't matter in the least.

About thirty students had been rounded up in the café. Kessel recognized several of the faces and checked carefully to make sure none his own friends had been swept up inadvertently. A veiled warning at last night's committee meeting had steered them away from the café this morning, but there was a chance that some dunderhead didn't get the message.

Kessel recognized Erik Dahmel with whom he'd once competed for a spot on the senior football squad. Dahmel was a crude country boy with little finesse on the football pitch, but some sort of head for esoteric mathematics. But Kessel knew that the abrasive Dahmel had no family and few friends.

"That man there, Herr Dahmel, is one of the ringleaders. No, the one further back with the long hair and blue jacket," Kessel directed the guards who like sheep dogs were dividing and cutting the crowd. As Dahmel was brought forward he had a bewildered expression. Kessel turned away to avoid his eyes.

"The man in the gray shirt with spectacles, on the left, in front. His name is Geller. He's another." Geller, hearing his name, started to fight his way to the back of the crowd and as the guards closed in on him, he began to scream. When guards reached him, he turned to attack, scratching and biting, still screaming and hissing like a cat, until one of the guards was able to deliver a solid *thwack* to Geller's head with his cosh. Two men, one at each ankle, dragged Geller from the room, leaving a weaving trail of bright red blood across the floor.

The room was suddenly quiet and the gory sight shocked even Kessel. Perhaps he'd done enough for one day.

"Those are the two leaders, Captain. The rest are mostly mislead souls who do not yet understand the concept of loyalty. Others I do not recognize and are probably not students here at all. They might be outside agitators, but I'm afraid that falls beyond my jurisdiction and responsibility."

"Of course you are correct, Herr Kessel. And I greatly appreciate your help. My report will highlight your contributions and obvious efficiency. And let me say personally, if there is any way in which I can be of assistance, please feel free to call on me."

"Thank you very much, Captain Fleger. Thank you, sir," Kessel said beaming.

The Gestapo captain gestured one of sergeants over and quietly gave his orders: "Manfred, take the whole lot out to the trucks one at a time. Make a neat list of names and dates of birth. Also hair and eye color, that sort of thing. Anyone who doesn't cooperate fully should be taken to headquarters for interrogation. The rest can be transported to the admissions center at Dachau. We'll sort them out there."

Lise, pressed tightly against the wall in the rear, had heard but not witnessed the vicious attack on Geller, but when they finally came to her, after peeling off people one at a time, she found herself staring down the bloody trail leading hypnotically to some fate beyond the doors. In many places the blood was smeared and tracked by shoes and boots.

She'd had time to make some decisions. Regardless what the Gestapo might say or threaten, she'd done nothing. If she could find the courage and fortitude, eventually they'd have to give up and let her go. If she surrendered, it was inevitable that her father and Willy would be drawn in and all three of them would be in danger. *Willy*. Willy was her other hope. It appeared as if Annamarie had escaped the Gestapo's dragnet. Annamarie would know to go to Willy, and he would know how to approach the authorities, shielding her father as always.

Dignity, she told herself as she was brought forward to a café table where the sergeant was making his lists. He didn't look up.

"Name?" he demanded. She said nothing.

"Name?" he repeated, glancing up from his notes. "Ah, Fräulein. How pleasant. What is your name, *Liebchen?*"

"You have no right," she said, summoning as much icy dignity as she could, standing straight and twisting out of the grasp of the two soldiers who'd held her arms loosely.

"I'm sorry, I didn't catch that," the sergeant offered with a friendly smile meant to convey how he was willing to give her every chance to be helpful. "What was your name again?"

"That's my business and not yours," she said weakly, caught off guard by his smile.

"Unfortunately, my chief tells me that it is my business and I'm afraid that I have to insist. You wouldn't want to get me in trouble with my officer now, do you?"

"No…Yes…No, you have no right," she stammered.

"Innocent people have nothing to fear. One last chance, *Liebchen*," the sergeant said, impatient this time.

"No," she said softly.

"Private, take the Fräulein out to truck number three." The two guards grabbed her by the arms, tightly this time. "And, Lauff, you two better search her carefully. Make sure she's not concealing any secrets." He went back to his notes.

"Yes, Sergeant," he grinned and the two privates led her away.

The Professor had been quiet all day. Willy had witnessed many of the Professor's recent spells and they were frightening enough. Sometimes the mindless shouting and cursing would be followed by a series of violent convulsions that would leave the Professor and anyone nearby bruised and exhausted. Willy had noticed purple and yellow marks on Lise's arms. He'd been there to help on many occasions, but suspected that Lise had suffered through much worse, many times. He had little right to complain.

Lise had left about ten o'clock to meet with Annamarie. To keep the Professor's schedule as structured as possible, she'd made sure he was awake and dressed. Willy sat at the dining table as the Professor ate a meager breakfast, providing an update and commentary about progress at the lab, though after only a few minutes it was apparent Professor Wagner wasn't absorbing much of what he'd been told. He asked a few simple questions, the same he'd asked every day for several months, and Willy patiently repeated the answers. As always, the Professor asked after several of his colleagues and Willy passed on their regards, though in truth many of them had disappeared from the university. Indeed one had recently committed suicide with cyanide from his own laboratory stores.

Later, seated in the study, Willy read aloud journal articles and letters for the Professor until, inevitably, he fell asleep in his chair, snoring peacefully. Willy brought out some reading of his own and sat studying and making notations, nearby if he was needed.

Though constantly plagued by guilt that he was accomplishing nothing in regards to his scientific work, Willy's mind always returned to the issue of the uranium project. As far as he could tell, nothing had come of the mathematical game they'd played with the report on absorption cross-sections for the Ministry of Education. While no one had challenged their 'findings,' nothing hinted that the obstacles he and Lise tried to erect had had the slightest effect. Indeed veiled talk around the university suggested there had been no slowing of the uranium project. Two graduate assistants from Munich's Physics Department had been tapped to move to the *Kaiser Wilhelm-Institut* and would eventually be reassigned to the new facility in the Berlin suburb of Dahlem, now named for the famous physicist, Max Planck.

Two more innocuous responses had arrived from American academics and by now the entire business of the secret writing seemed very juvenile and silly. Lise and Willy had promised each other to consider some other action, to "do something," but with time they only came to feel increasingly isolated and helpless.

If America entered the war, Willy would be arrested and jailed as an enemy alien. Somehow he continued to elude the bureaucracy and the direct interest of the Gestapo, but German efficiency would take care of that the moment it was an important issue. The thought of internment didn't concern Willy as much as his inability to continue to help the Wagners. And honestly, the idea of being separated from Lise was heartrending.

He'd allow the thought to evolve slowly in his mind that he was in love with her and that his motives were honest and sincere. It was more difficult to tell how she felt. Lise was as phlegmatic as ever, keeping everything bottled up, never really showing emotions except for intimidating flares of anger and her continuing and absolute devotion to her father.

Once a thin young girl, in the last eighteen months she'd changed in many dimensions: taller, leaner, wiser, and more determined, if that was conceivable. Willy wondered how Lise had seemingly leapfrogged past him from unapproachable girl to an unattainable woman, at seventeen, nearly eighteen now.

While they often sat together, holding hands sometimes when alone, neither had tried to change their relationship from how it had stood since they'd joined forces after Gabi's death. They had certainly never discussed their feelings about one another and infrequently spoke about the future more than a few weeks ahead. Perhaps wartime was not a good time for romance, but in his heart, in his loneliest moments, Willy knew that he could never say anything or give any sign of his feelings until memories of Gabi faded. The deaths of her murderers had been an incautious act of retribution but if he'd harbored any faint hope that there might be absolution, he was wrong to have thought that the ledger could be balanced so easily.

Willy had an image in his mind, part drawn from traditional upbringing and part from a steady diet of Hollywood movies as a teenager in Wisconsin. It was his responsibility as a man to woo his love, to take the lead in their relationship, to be charming, strong, and manly. Looking back and forward, Willy had little confidence that he'd ever reach a point of grace and suavity to match these European men who seemed to have this stuff down pat. Half the time around German women, regardless their age, he felt like the coarsest farmer, muddy from the field. The rest of the time, even with Lise, he felt like a circus clown with a red rubber

ss Sections

nose and giant feet.

Every hour the housekeeper, Frau Erna, would poke her head into the study and had brought Willy some thick soup and a hunk of hard bread for his lunch. Lise would return at three when they would wake Professor Wagner for his early dinner. It was just after one o'clock when the housekeeper, very agitated, returned to the study.

"Herr Petersen, can you please come?" she whispered, trying hard not to wake the Professor. "I'll sit here until you return. Fräulein Annamarie is in the kitchen. She's very upset."

Without comment but already worried, Willy hurried from the study back down the long hallway to the kitchen. Annamarie was sitting in a stiff back chair, her arms crossed tightly and shivering as if she were still out in the snow instead of inside the stiflingly hot kitchen. A cup of steaming tea sat on the table nearby.

"Herr Petersen! Oh, thank God, I'm so glad you're here," she exploded. Her eyes were wide. Tears were flowing down her face and she sniffled repeatedly between her sentences. "You've got to do something. You must help her. They took her. I don't know where, but I saw it myself."

"Please, Annamarie. Please slow down. Take a deep breath and start again." He reached out and pried her hands loose rubbing them between his. "Someone took Lise? Who? When?" He realized that now he was rushing ahead, took his own advice, and started again.

"Tell me what happened. Slowly from the beginning. Here," he handed her the teacup, "take a sip. Careful, it's very hot."

"Thank you, Herr Petersen. Thank you. I was so scared. I feel better now. Lise always says that you know how to make her feel better too. Thank you."

"Tell me what happened, if you're ready."

"Lise and I went shopping this morning along *Theatinerstrasse* and then decided to stop at the university on the way home. It's always so much fun to sit around the café and pretend we're already grown up to be students ourselves. It's been so long since we last played our games.

"I went to the lavatory and while I was inside, I heard this loud commotion outside, shouting and screaming, and I was too scared to come back out. In a few minutes it was quiet again and when I peeked out there were police and soldiers everywhere. A big crowd of students was gathering behind a line of police officers but all the people in the café had been arrested. I watched soldiers drag one man out by his feet. I think he was dead. His body was limp and there was blood everywhere. I almost fainted." Willy gestured for her to take more tea and she sipped with her eyes closed.

"The police ordered us to disperse and go about our business, but I was worried about Lise and managed to hang back as the people from the café were lead out one at a time. At last two men brought Lise out, holding her arms twisted behind her. Her clothes were all mussed and she was crying. I followed them outdoors and they shoved her into an army truck. I heard her cry out when she fell down in the back of the truck.

"I had to tell someone that there must be a mistake. Lise and I are just girls. There's no reason to arrest her. We were just drinking tea.

"I don't know what came over me. I was still scared. But I walked up to this officer and told him about the mistake. 'You've arrested my friend by mistake. We were just drinking tea and making jokes.' I asked if he would help us.

"But he just stared at me and then asked whether I'd been in the café. I realized that he might arrest me, too, and I turned and ran away. I don't know whether someone followed me or not but I didn't stop until I got back to the English Gardens. I was still scared that they might be after me, so I sneaked around behind this house, and climbed through a hole in the fence Lise and I used when we were little. I knocked and knocked but it took forever for Frau Erna to open the back door.

"They might be here any minute," she said, her terror returning as she recounted her escape. "Herr Petersen, you have to help me and you have to help Lise. Please help Lise."

"Annamarie, try to remember. Were the soldiers from the SD or city police? Were they wearing brown uniforms or gray?"

"Some were in brown, but others were wearing black coats and hats."

Gestapo, he thought.

"Did you see which way the truck went?"

"No, I'm sorry. I ran before they drove away. I'm sorry. I'm so sorry. I shouldn't have left my friend. But I was so scared." Annamarie began to cry hard now, sobbing violently. Willy took her hands again.

"Don't worry, Annamarie. There's nothing to worry about. The police don't know who you are and if they'd followed you, they'd be here already. You're safe and can stay as long as you like. Later I'll walk you home. Just sit here and keep warm. I'm just going to talk to Frau Erna for a moment and will be right back." She sniffed loudly and nodded her understanding.

Outside the study he tried to explain to Frau Erna without alarming her too much.

"Some minor problem at the university and Fräulein Elise has volunteered to help the police with their inquiries. All the uniforms and noise frightened Fräulein Annamarie but I'm convinced there's nothing to be concerned about. If you can stay with the Professor, I need to go down to the university and bring Fräulein Elise back. Annamarie is still in the kitchen. I told her to stay here and later I'll escort her home. Perhaps you can get her to help you when the Professor wakes up, but make sure Annamarie understands she should mention nothing about Lise and the police to Professor Wagner or to her parents.

Frau Erna was a wise and wary lady who guessed more than she'd been told and she was already choked up.

"I understand, Herr Petersen, I understand. Please help my little Elise. The Professor will be all right. I will stay here. Annamarie can run and fetch my husband when he comes home from the factory. Just help little Elise. I've lost my dear Gabrielle already," she croaked, holding back her own tears. "Please bring her back to us."

Willy ranged around the university grounds, chatting up any acquaintance he'd run across, casually mentioning the raid to see whether anyone had witnessed the round up. He tried to treat it all lightly, as a bit of a joke, in order to avoid showing serious interest. Informers were everywhere. But no one knew anything and the café remained closed so he couldn't question the waiters and servers. He peaked through a window from the courtyard and could see all the chairs and tables upset and piled to one side and a long dark-brown stain on the floor he suspected might be blood.

He walked to his laboratory where he could sit and think. Lise was only seventeen and was not a student at the university. So regardless who or what the Gestapo was looking for, it wasn't her. In the normal course of events, once her identity was known, she'd be dumped at her own front door with nasty threats and a dark warning about the company she was keeping. Given the publicity surrounding Gabi's death, it was likely that the Gestapo would go out of its way to avoid similar complications. They'd treat Lise with kid gloves.

If they *didn't* return her unharmed, then they *didn't* know who she was. Annamarie said she was conscious when tossed in the truck so that suggested that she wasn't talking. Willy knew Lise's temperament and guessed she'd do anything to keep the Gestapo far away from her father. He could be sure that Lise would not be as scared of the Gestapo as she should be. He'd seen many things over the last year that he'd not told her about. Now he wished he had, to put the real fear of God, and the Gestapo, in her. He'd been a fool to make light of these things.

Nazis have an obsession with precision. No one would be sent to a camp or prison until he or she was fully documented, measured, and pigeonholed. Annamarie had said that the black-shirts were in charge of the raid, and it was likely, almost certain, that they would take Lise to their huge headquarters adjacent the *Rathaus* in the *Marienplatz*. That's where he needed to be. He grabbed his coat and scarf and ran out the door.

Too impatient to wait for the right sequence of streetcars, Willy rushed to the *Marienplatz* on foot. Late in the cold afternoon, the wide square was filled with shoppers and workers heading home. No sign marked Gestapo headquarters, but Willy doubted any resident of the city was unaware of its location. Trying to blend with the commuters, he made his way all the way around the building that took up an entire city block. Every side had at least two entrances, two guards with Mauser rifles at each. Like any busy government or commercial building, a constant stream of people flowed in and out of every door. Most of the traffic consisted of Gestapo and SD officers and soldiers, but late in the day, dozens of secretaries and clerks were leaving, headed home to dinner.

Willy bought a bag of roasted hazelnuts from a vendor and found a vacant bench near the main entrance where he could watch everyone come and go without arousing suspicion. Right at six o'clock the floodgates opened and hundreds of men and women spilled out from all the doors, shaking hands and waving goodnight to their coworkers and comrades.

A familiar uniform caught his attention when a small group of SD cadets trooped out, laughing and shouting to one another, heading off towards the *Hofbrauhaus*. As the crowd began to thin and Willy finished his nuts, he decided to move along. The hostel was closest, so he made his way there first. He had the germ of an idea. What he needed was hidden behind heavy drawers in the laboratory. Why he hadn't burned or destroyed the evidence he didn't know, but was now glad he hadn't. He laid on his cot staring at the ceiling for several hours trying to organize his jumbled thoughts into the semblance of a plan.

At eight o'clock he gathered his things and headed back to the laboratory and then on to the Wagner's house.

The initial interrogation had been very polite and businesslike, almost as if it were *de rigueur* for suspects to refuse cooperation, something expected, comprehended, and patiently accepted. Her interviewer, a young, dapper Gestapo lieutenant, had inquired after her health and had expressed concern that she might have been treated roughly.

"Fräulein, I'm sure there is some sort of mix-up. If you help us clear up this matter, you'll be home before dark. We have a list of suspected criminal and anti-social elements. Your name is certainly not on that list, but how can *we* be sure if you won't help us."

"I'm sorry but you have no right…" she started again.

"Yes, Fräulein, you've said that before, but it's not my job to address legal details. I'm just a junior functionary with a very simple job, comparing lists. If you're not on the list, you shouldn't be here, plain and simple. Please show me that you're not on the list." He waved a sheet of paper at her.

Despite a bad bruise on her shoulder, Lise had worked her way back through fear and anxiety to anger and frustration. It was all so transparent to her. Nothing she would hear would be true or honest. Everything was lies, deceit, and show.

"Please, Fräulein, will you help me, as a personal favor?" She stood silent and defiant, aware that this smooth and persuasive man would turn anything she said against her.

"Well, I'm sorry, very sorry. I'm allowed only ten minutes for my work and you'll now be passed up the line. I'll apologize ahead of time for my comrades. Many of the men you'll meet next are not very cultured or patient.

"Are you quite certain you can't help me?

"*Well*," he said, standing and reaching for the door handle, "best of luck to you, Fräulein. Please remain here," he said unnecessarily. The room was bare and poorly heated. Lise's winter coat was somewhere among the wreckage at the café.

It was nearly an hour before anyone came to retrieve her. Intellectually she guessed that this was part of their tactics, but understanding didn't make her any warmer. And with discomfort and isolation came both old and new fears. She wanted to get up and walk around but something told her that she was watched every second and was determined not to show weakness.

Two bulky matrons came for her with shackles for her ankles and wrists. Once chained, Lise was searched again, this time with a thoroughness and coldness worse even than the two lecherous soldiers at the university. Her clothes were loosened and underclothes yanked down. Every inch of her body was felt and probed and when she tensed up as they spread her knees, she was slapped across the face without warning.

Afterwards, still without a single word, Lise, hobbled and disheveled, was led out of the room, along a long corridor, and then down several sets of narrow steps. Since she didn't recall climbing any stairs when she was first brought in, they could only be taking her to the basement. The matrons stopped in front of a barred cell, one of a long line extending as far as she could see in the dim light, opened the door with a noisy set of large keys, and stood patiently as Lise shuffled in on her own. The door clanged shut behind her and the matrons disappeared back up the steps. The only light came from a few bare bulbs outside along the corridor. The cell smelled like a country outhouse and the only object inside was an old gasoline can cut in half, obviously to be used as a toilet. *Too much tea*, she shrugged. It was difficult to use the bucket even with her back braced against the clammy concrete wall. And for the third time today, Lise felt violated and humiliated. But she carried on calmly. If they thought she was susceptible, her weaknesses would be used against her.

As Lise sat on the floor she realized she could discern sounds and voices from the other cells. Someone was sobbing: a man or a woman, she couldn't tell. Somewhere else, she could hear an angry man asking questions over and over, a deep, insistent voice rising until it rolled down the corridor. Then there was silence, broken only by the same sad sobbing as before. Despite the cold, Lise was exhausted, and sitting on the cold floor, her back to the far wall, she found herself dozing. *Probably a good way to make time pass*, she thought to herself. *What's Willy doing? If Vati suspects something's wrong, he'll be impossible to handle.*

Without a clock Lise had no way of telling time when something woke her. She was very stiff and had to pee again. At first the noises were far away, but as she listened she recognized the sound of boots marching in unison down the corridor. *What does it mean? Are they coming to get me?* But as she watched a half dozen soldiers with machine guns tramped right past her cell, a single man half walking, half dragged between two of the soldiers. She could not see his face but the prisoner was dressed in stripped pajamas and was barefoot.

An officer with an incongruous riding crop trailed behind and paused to peer into Lise's cell. He was a short, gaunt man, bald under his tall black hat. He was perfectly dressed, his trousers and shirt pressed to knife-edges, his medals and insignia polished and shining. The death's head symbols on his lapels and cap flashed in the harsh light and mirrored the man's own skull-like head and face. Their eyes met for just a flash and for Lise it was like looking into a cat's eyes. Magnified by his thick spectacles, they were inhuman and coldly calculating. She cringed despite herself and the man passed on without comment or expression.

Lise edged to the front of the cell and could hear the group as they passed through a door at the near end of the corridor. She shut her eyes and tried hard to clear her head of waking nightmares. Lise breathed deeply and had begun to regain control when the basement cell block was filled with the rattles and echoes of gunfire, several dozen rapid shots, followed ten seconds later by a single loud bang whose slowly fading reverberation lasted an eternity. Hearing the same door open again, Lise crouched in the rear corner of her cell with her eyes squeezed shut, terrified now that she might look again into the executioner's eyes. She kept them closed long after the squad's boot steps passed by.

Lise wanted to believe that no one had died, that this was just another theatrical trick to intimidate her. But that was infantile and self-centered, she reasoned. Quite the contrary, Lise meant absolutely nothing to these people. No one was going to waste any time on her. Reality was horrible enough. Lise's fate would take one of two paths: she'd be disposed or forgotten. And at this moment, after only twelve hours in custody, she already felt totally abandoned. *Why hasn't someone come to find me? How can they leave me here like this? No one cares about me.*

Despite her hardest determination, Lise began to cry, adding her quiet sobs to those of the two hundred other lost souls locked in the cells beneath Gestapo headquarters.

"Excuse me sir, I'm looking for this address. Could you point me in the right direction?" Willy smiled cheerfully, contrasting the dour and suspicious stare of the desk sergeant at the front entrance. He took the slip of paper Willy offered.

"Back out the front door, turn left and follow the signs for the *Gartnerplatz*. You'll see this building opposite the *U-Bahn* station." He tossed the note back to Willy who was effusive in his thanks despite the man's terse rudeness.

"Thanks very much. They say that if you're lost, you should always stop at a police station."

"Move along, please."

Outside, Willy wadded the note and tossed it in a nearby waste can. He had scribbled it only minutes before to have an excuse to test the building's security procedures. Everyone entering Gestapo headquarters was required to stop and state his business and a notation was made about whom he was visiting. Willy could see that regular staff members were nodded through, but everyone else was scrutinized, recognized, or questioned.

Walking around the building again, it was apparent that every entrance had its own desk sergeant and Willy had no reason to believe procedures were lax at the side or back entrances. The morning was cold and crisp, the sun shining brightly at a low angle. Willy hadn't slept a single moment all night and the bite of the north wind blowing through the *Marienplatz* helped clear his head. Unlike yesterday when everything shimmered dreamlike, today the sky, the people, the buildings, everything all seemed sharply detailed.

Lise was somewhere inside that building. *How many rooms are there? Hundreds. Locked in a cell? Most likely. Where?* The exterior walls had wide windows, including the uppermost floor, and as he had walked around the building, Willy could see no signs of bars or other reinforcement on any windows. So the cells must be in the basement.

Think, Petersen, think. It was too cold and blustery to linger long in the open square especially in view of the stone-faced guards stationed outside. When he stood up, frigid air leaked inside his coat and he shivered. He needed to eat and have a hot drink otherwise he'd be weak and distracted later. Willy recalled a bakery shop on a side street nearby. A long line of early morning patrons extended along the sidewalk, some people reading their papers as they waited, others stomping their feet impatiently, but most chattering brightly with friends and neighbors. The queue moved quickly but as Willy neared the door, a stout woman in a tent-like gray uniform greatcoat, walked directly to the front of the line and squeezed through the door ignoring the hisses and glares of the other folks in line.

"Fat bitch," someone whisper behind Willy.

"Quiet, you fool," another voice advised.

Moments later the same women left the shop with a large box tied with string and Willy watched her pass around the corner back towards the *Rathaus*. Once inside Willy purchased a mug of tea and a small pastry that he ate standing at the bar shelf against the shop window. Simultaneously he discovered that the pastry was quite good and how he could get inside Gestapo headquarters.

"My name is Henkle, Fräulein," the fat man said, politely enough. He continued to study a thin file, the only object on the top of his large, ornate desk. Lise had been bundled upstairs, though until she saw the morning sunlight streaming through the office window, she'd lost track of time and still believed it was late the first night. Though her feet and hands were numb from the cold except where the shackles had chaffed her raw, the warm room was a relief. She decided she should try to stall as long as possible to delay a return to the icy basement cell.

"Good morning, Herr Henkle," she offered.

"Thank you, Fräulein, but you have me now at a disadvantage. You know my name but I don't have yours. That will make our conversation very clumsy and short."

"I'm sorry," she said meekly, trying to keep her protest less combative than before.

Herr Henkle studied the file again. "Young lady, I can't tell whether you're being rude or merely stupid." He looked up hoping for some response, then continued.

"Let me tell you what it says here. You were arrested in the company of traitorous conspirators, perhaps friends or associates of yours. Those whom we've identified have already been dealt with…summarily. But many of the people arrested have been released with clean records, as it seems they were merely taking tea in the café.

"You, on the other hand, refuse to say anything at all. We've questioned the others and no one admits knowing you. We find that suspicious in itself. Why, despite careful interrogation, would they continue to protect you? You see our problem.

"On the other hand, it says here that your clothing and jewelry were expensive and tasteful. Your teeth are straight and well maintained. You are still a virgin, which suggests you're not whoring for these filthy traitors."

"How dare you?" she demanded angrily, reminded of how she'd been violated.

"...And you have a snippy, condescending air that suggests that you should know better." Now Major Henkle was angry. He leaped to his feet and leaned across the desk ready to slap her with the back of his hand. But he held back at the last second.

"I know your type. High in the clouds, lost in your own little world of wealth and privilege. Above all the mundane and dirty tasks that fall to us peasants. Oblivious to the fact that things have changed; how the world's turned upside down.

"Let me describe what will happen next, unless you cooperate. It's all written down, step by step, in our rules and procedures. No one will have to make any decisions regarding your case. It's all spelled out.

"You'll go before an administrative magistrate as Fräulein X. Since we don't know who you are, no one will be called to testify or speak for you. Your failure to cooperate is categorized as disloyalty, and those with a pattern of disloyalty are considered traitors. Traitors are executed, simple as that. We don't waste bed and board on traitors.

"Some traitors are shot and I understand you might have sampled something of that last night." Henkle consulted his notes. "Herr...Herr Dahmel was one of the lucky ones by the way. When we wish to set an example, traitors are hung alive, suspended on meathooks. It's a spectacle I try to avoid, but when we parade lesser miscreants past, the effects on future behavior are wondrous.

"On other occasions, when there's little time for formality, the traitor is simply garroted in his or her cell. Some of our men a quite efficient, but I'm afraid to say that others are very clumsy or perhaps take a bit too much pleasure in the assignment."

Major Henkle had leaned back in his comfortable chair, reveling in his own words. He had discussed this case with his colonel before Lise was brought upstairs. She posed something of a dilemma. While she was obviously hiding something, her age, clothes, and virginity hinted that she might just be a rich girl with a bad attitude. Rich girl meant rich, influential parents, and though no one had called to claim her during the night, the colonel was reluctant to risk any physical damage.

Still they couldn't just release her, nor could they ship her off to detention. The bureaucrats at Dachau wouldn't accept an unidentified prisoner. If her arrest had been less public, she might simply disappear. The municipal police were frequently called upon to drag the rivers and lakes for suspected suicides, when the Gestapo knew very well that the search was fruitless. Henkle still had another card to play.

"Alternatively, the magistrate might decide that you could still provide the Reich with valuable service. You're young and very pretty and evidently disease-free. The army and SS have opened special facilities around the country and in occupied Poland. They have two purposes, first to serve the sexual needs of our fighting men, and second, to produce good Aryan children to be reared by the Reich. I can see you ending up at such a place, though I'm afraid that with your dark hair, it's likely you'd be sterilized and consigned permanently to the brothel. It's entirely possible that you'd prefer the garrote to a brothel, but I'm trying to explain to you, for the last time, that you will have no say in the matter.

"For the final time. Will you tell me your name?"

Lise wanted to cry out, to scream for her Vati. When she was little, he was always there to protect her and would magically appear whenever she was hurt or scared. He'd lift her up and hug her tightly and carry her back to the house for cookies and cocoa. When her mother died, he grew even closer to Lise and Gabi, always supportive, though stern, never arbitrary or cruelly distant like her friends' fathers.

She was willing to die to protect him, not despite his illness, but rather because of it. She would never desert him when he was scared and hurt. When Henkle mentioned SS facilities, Lise remembered what Willy had recounted about the euthanasia centers. She was absolutely certain that if her father's condition became known, he would be taken from her and would die alone and frightened in such a place.

And Willy. *Love* and *adore* were words that she and Annamarie used freely in their girlish games. But on another level, Lise thought that she loved Willy. She felt a certain way when he was around, especially when they were close and alone together. His feelings were difficult to read. Sometimes he acted like any suitor in her fairy tale books, gallant, charming, and solicitous. But then he'd hesitate, he'd be thoughtful for a while, and then distant and almost unapproachable. Even if it were her place to say something, Lise was very prideful and would not risk being rejected outright or off-handedly.

So they just carried on, closer than brother and sister, yet far from lovers. They'd grown comfortable with each other, their mutual trust unquestioned. She could accept that Willy might suffer if she never returned, but their fates were linked together now, with her father at the center. But if she could only see Willy one more time, and ask him boldly...

"So be it," Henkle said several seconds later after watching as her thoughts moved across her face and eyes. Finally he'd read the return of determination and defiance on her brow. After twenty years in the police and now the Gestapo, Major Henkle could recognize a suspect who did not yet understand her jeopardy, whether from stupidity or misdirected confidence. Pain would normally be the next step: intermittent, sharp pain ministered by experts. But...

"Matrons," he shouted to the closed door and when the women entered he said, "Take Fräulein X here upstairs to Ward Number Three. Handcuff her to a bed. Tell the staff that their orders will be forwarded in due course. Good day, Fräulein."

The SS major stared out his office window and tapped his pencil thoughtfully. Henkle and his colonel had settled on one last option: *drugs*. There was still a considerable range of risks including permanent brain damage or death, but it was worth trying before resorting to traditional methods of close interrogation. The two Gestapo officers had absolutely no doubt that the girl would break down and talk under torture. The Gestapo had settled years ago on six preferred methods and had developed them to the level of sophistication that could be passed along to new generations of interrogators. *Beating, hanging, burning, shocking, and immersion in cold water* could be used separately or as stages of a program geared to recalcitrant prisoners. The sixth method, *crushing*, was reserved for male prisoners.

One thing had been demonstrated over the years. Once an interrogation began, two results were inevitable: the prisoner *would talk*, if he or she actually knew something, and the prisoner *would die*. Survival was considered to be something miraculous and skilled interrogators kept score and bragged about the number of sentient prisoners they were actually able to pass along to the camps or execution squads.

If, under the drugs, Fräulein X finally talked, but the information was of little value, she could be cleaned up and released, recalling little of her experience. If the drugs didn't work, then the doctors would continue to increase dosage until it did or until she died. Her corpse would be none the worse for wear and if some angry father turned up, one with friends in some ministry or at the *Rathaus*, he would have to accept the doctor's standard explanation regardless his suspicions. The unfortunate death would be attributed to suicide or an accidental overdose of pharmaceuticals used to treat her inexplicable psychotic behavior. Everyone at headquarters would be suitably upset and sympathetic, a performance repeated every week by specialists chosen to deal with outsiders.

Who could gainsay them? After all, Gestapo pathologists would perform any autopsy. In Nazi Germany, independent opinion or appeal to a higher authority no longer existed.

And if no one claimed the body, the Gestapo had lost a promising candidate for the officers' brothel, nothing more.

The colonel had taken some interest in this case and Henkle would have to follow through, though it would be much more pleasant to spend a rare day outside in the sunshine, despite the cold. The sooner the doctors began the better. He pushed his substantial bulk away from this desk and followed the matrons upstairs to the medical ward.

While Lise couldn't guess how long she'd slept, light leaked through the heavy curtains hiding the windows at the end of the long ward. It had a grayness suggesting twilight, but whether it was the same day or the next morning she didn't know. But the room was spinning around and about some point on the ceiling above her and she had to close her eyes to suppress the nausea welling in her stomach. The rest of her body felt like it was made of lead, not the hopeless sensations accompanying paralysis, but rather the heaviness that accompanies fatigue. With an effort she lifted her right arm and found it still cuffed to the iron bedframe.

She could remember bits and pieces from the morning, her interview with Major Henkle, and a routine, unobtrusive examination by a doctor where her blood pressure and pulse were checked. An injection…she'd been given an injection and she'd gone right to sleep, welcoming that oblivion as never before in her life.

Her dreams were confused. She was being chased. Willy and Annamarie were there. And Professor Heisenberg and his little boys. Strange men and women were shouting at her. Others kept passing her sheets of blue paper, but the printing was appearing, then disappearing before she could read it. But in her dreams she felt somehow protected and detached. When she ran, she could easily outpace them all. When they yelled she could turn away and their voices would fade. But when she tried to talk, no one seemed to listen. The dreams were actually more vivid than her current wakefulness, and made it all the more difficult to tell for sure if she was awake or still asleep.

Her stomach was upset and her mouth as dry as old paper and she was lying still, dozing, when she heard voices talking over her.

"Nothing unusual here, Major Henkle. It's actually rare for the first injection to yield results. Pentobarbital works effectively only within a very narrow range of dosage. Too much and the subject will sleep like a baby for six or eight hours; too little and they'll just get drowsy. We weigh the subjects and use textbook tables to calculate an initial dose but everyone's metabolism is different. As a matter of fact, we have insufficient data regarding female subjects."

"Fine, *Herr Doktor*. I'll accept the explanation for your initial failure. What's the next step?"

"We'll give her a second injection in a few minutes, a little smaller this time. Come back in four hours and try again with your questions."

Drugs are tools used by the Gestapo's doctors instead of the usual cadre of interrogators and bullies. While these doctors did not suffer from conscience any more than the crudest Gestapo bone-breaker, they did display a fastidiousness that sometimes frustrated investigating officers under pressure from their superiors to close cases quickly. Henkle *was* frustrated. His day was wasted and evidently far from over. He looked at his wristwatch.

"It's five o'clock now, so you're saying she'll be ready by nine tonight."

"Yes, Major. There are no guarantees of course..."

"Don't quibble with me, *Herr Doktor*. Just get it right this time." Lise heard steps as someone walked away. It was quiet in the ward and she must have dozed again because she jumped when pricked by the needle. She opened her eyes and recognized the same doctor as before, now spinning with the room. Just as suddenly it was done and he was a gone, sliding the curtain closed all around her bed.

It wasn't clear to her what they were doing, but she could feel herself relax. The dreams began again even while she was partly conscious. Vati and Gabi were there and so was her mother. Frau Erna was busy in the cozy kitchen and she must be baking apricot strudel, little Elise's special favorite, because she could smell it *perfectly* even here in this terrible place.

The first part was so easy that he had to smile, however grimly, though nothing would have focused unwanted attention on him faster, surrounded by an army of humorless, self-important bureaucrats walking the corridors, each on his own little mission.

At the hostel, Willy donned the cadet uniform shirt and accessories Rudi acquired for him last year. That morning, at F.W. Woolworth, he managed to find black trousers and sweaters that closely matched the style worn by cadets in the winter. The thrifty services provided a single set of uniforms to cadets and trainees. If you needed something extra or a replacement item, they were available in department and surplus stores all over the city. He lacked the proper overcoat but hoped to use that to his advantage, paying a steep price later on. It only mattered if his plan succeeded, in which case cost was irrelevant.

Wearing his own ragged greatcoat with a cadet's hat hidden under his arm he made his way to the *Marienplatz* in front of Gestapo headquarters. The giant mechanical clock on the tower of the *Rathaus* chimed four o'clock.

Adjacent the northwest corner of Gestapo headquarters was a narrow alley where trash containers were stored. Willy passed down its length to make sure no one was around and then returned to the end closest to the headquarters building. Here he removed his greatcoat and jammed it behind an old crate, settled his cap on his head, straightened his tie, and hurried out of the alley, around the corner of the headquarters building, hustling up to a secondary entrance on the north side. He was already shivering from the cold when he nodded to the sentry outside the door and ducked inside. Willy went straight to the security desk and was met by an odd look from the sergeant.

"Sorry to bother you, Sergeant," Willy began innocently, "the colonel's secretary asked me to run over to Sotzer's Bakery to pick up pastries for his meeting with the general. I've only been here a few days, and I'm afraid I've gotten turned around somehow. She said the shop was left out the main door, then right at the corner. But I guess I heard it wrong."

"You got it right, you big idiot, but you haven't gone far enough. Keep going to your right another hundred meters. Sotzer's is on the opposite side of the street. Where's your coat, man? Haven't you any sense at all?"

"The lady said it was urgent and that the shop was nearby…"

"Yes. It's near *this* door, you fool. You came out the wrong side of the building."

"Thanks, Sergeant, thanks," Willy said smiling and rushed back out the door.

The sergeant started to shout after him, "Your coat…" But Willy didn't stop and the man could only shake his head in dismay. *Where do they find these farmers?*

Ten minutes later, Willy, still coatless but gingerly carrying a large, string-bound pastry box in both hands, returned to the same north entrance, hurrying inside. As he breezed past the same sergeant, Willy held up his box in triumph, shook off the cold like a wet dog, and shouted, "thanks again" over his shoulder. The sergeant shrugged dismissively and went back to his paperwork.

He was now in the bowels of the Gestapo. Despite everyone's apparent distraction, he knew he couldn't simply wander the hallways, peering into rooms, until he found Lise. Someone would eventually ask his business, certainly after six o'clock when the building began to empty. At the same time, he couldn't very well ask for *Elise Wagner*: if she was here, it was likely she still refused to provide her name. He positioned himself in the wide lobby so that it might seem that he was waiting for someone to come in by the main entrance.

A wistful hope that there might be signage posted along the walls was only that, but sitting in the dark last night in Professor Wagner's study, he had tried to imagine this scene. The cells had to be down. And where there were prisoners, they would be either heading to the cells or away from the cells. In the short time Willy had watched from the street the previous day, a half dozen cars and trucks had driven up to the front entrance with prisoners and suspects escorted inside. He only had to wait.

Willy was ready when three men, already clad in striped prison garb, were led in from the street. The soldiers signed them over to building guards and they were hustled along several long hallways, with Willy trailing at a discrete distance. A nondescript door was opened and Willy ambled by in time to see the party head down a flight of narrow steps before the last escort closed the door behind. Evidently the guard expected to return momentarily and did not latch the door behind him.

Willy only had a few seconds. He hurried back to another security station at the front entrance. Several men were arguing with the man behind the desk. "Sergeant, I'm to leave these here and someone from upstairs will come and get them in a few minutes." The sergeant waved him away impatiently, and Willy left the distinctive box on the end of the counter.

Quickly, Willy was down the stairs towards the cells, passing the same set of building guards returning from below. He squeezed past them without comment. At the foot of the stairs was another door propped open with a brick. Reaching under his sweater and into his shirt pocket Willy pulled out a small paper pad and a fountain pen. With a deep breath, he passed through the door.

A dozen meters along the dingy hallway a grizzled, old corporal sat reading his newspaper. Mustering as much authority as possible, Willy stepped up to the table.

"Excuse me, Corporal, you have a young woman in custody. Tall. Dark hair. Refuses to give her name. I've been ordered to collect a handwriting sample from her. To help with the identification." He held up his pen and notepad as evidence.

"Sure thing, son, but she's not here anymore. Matrons took her up to Ward Three this morning. Haven't brought her back yet. Don't know if they will. Usually don't."

"No problem for me," Willy shrugged. "Ward Three's on the third floor, north end?"

"Second floor, south end. Numbers over the doors. Hey, what's your hurry? Stay and visit for a while. It's pretty lonely down here. I'm not supposed to talk to the guests."

"Sorry, I have my orders. Next time maybe."

"That's what everybody says, but nobody likes to come down here."

"Sorry."

Back on the main floor, Willy pretended to pass casually by the front desk. He caught the sergeant's eye and stepped over.

"Are these still here?" he asked rhetorically, gesturing at the pastry box. "No one's come to pick them up?"

"Not yet. Five more minutes and I'm going to untie the string and check for contraband," the sergeant threatened gruffly. Willy could feel the hair rise on the back of his neck. "Just in case the contents are poisoned, it's my responsibility to sample everything in the box... Well, maybe it's more privilege than responsibility," the security man now grinned. "Better remove the temptation, cadet, before some fat officer misses his snack."

"Thank you, Sergeant," Willy said as he snatched up the box protectively and hurried off to the elevators. On the second floor Willy reoriented himself and wandered casually toward the south end of the building. Wards opened off the broad main corridor, Number One on the left, Number Six on the right. Double doors with two-way hinges opened in to each ward. It was half-past five and the main corridor was deserted, though Willy could hear animated voices somewhere ahead. Without looking, afraid to meet anyone's eyes, he dove through the swinging doors into Ward Three.

Fifteen iron-framed beds lined each side of the room and most appeared occupied. The lighting here was dimmer than the corridor and it took a few seconds for Willy's eyes to adjust. No nurses or doctors were around, but that wasn't likely to last for long, even though sick inmates were unlikely to be lent the same attention as patients in other wards. Willy passed along the beds on the right side first, taking care to look carefully at each woman's face, particularly when their heads were covered or bandaged. Two of the woman were awake and met his eyes hopefully. Others were asleep, unconscious, or comatose. The rest lay still, eyes open but dull and glazed.

Starting back down the other side of the room, all the beds were shrouded off by thin curtains hanging from a ceiling framework. In the first lay a dead woman, dead for some time, her mouth overflowing with bloody vomit, her eyes rolled back into her head. It was hard for Willy to peer into that face to make sure that it wasn't Lise.

The next two beds were empty. Lise was lying behind the fourth set of curtains, her dark hair spread on her pillow, her eyes half closed, a dreamy, relaxed expression on her face. Stepping inside and closing the curtain behind him, Willy sat the box down on the side table, walked up beside her, and leaned over to whisper in her ear.

"Lise…Lise," he said quietly. She opened her eyes a bit more, but there was no sign that she recognized him. *Drugs!* He took her face in both his hands and shook it gently. She moaned faintly. He lifted her upright by the shoulders. Her body was like unbaked dough. When he let go, she didn't fall back on her pillow, but rather remained partially upright, molded by his movement.

Willy quickly untied the string on his pastry box, and lifted out the first layer of paperboard and the pastries on top. He pushed them under the bed out of the way. In the bottom of the box were a variety of items, a large knife, a long piece of light rope, a roll of sticky tape, several feet of rubber-coated electrical cord, heavy wire cutters, a wad of putty, and several other tools like screwdrivers and an awl. Willy couldn't recall all the scenarios he'd imagined that prompted him to include individual items, but fortunately he had brought the one he really needed. The handcuffs were made from high quality steel, but squeezing and twisting with all his might he managed to cut a link attaching the two bracelets, one left dangling from the bed frame, the other from Lise's right wrist. He took Lise by the shoulders and pulled her upright again, twisting her around so that her bare feet hung over the side of the bed.

Willy stripped off his sweater. He was wearing another underneath. Last night he had tried to fit into one of Lise's own sweaters with little luck, so he'd purchased a new one at Woolworth's that, while still tight on him, might not appear too large on Lise. He pulled the new sweater over his head and put his own back on.

Wrapped in paper in the box were shoes, socks, and a light, summery skirt. None of Lise's winter skirts would fit in the box, so Willy had done the best he could. There had been no space to include a blouse, so the high neck pullover would have to make do. Without thinking, Willy reached over Lise's shoulders and pulled her gray prison smock over her head. Matrons had taken her underclothes and Willy didn't have anything to replace them with. In slow motion, she raised her arms to cover her breasts. Good, he thought, at least she's aware of some of what was happening. After all, Willy wasn't going to be able to carry her out bodily.

He hesitated, unsure whether a skirt was best put on over her head or legs, a technical problem in indirect measurement. *Over the legs.* He had to lower her head back on the bed in order to raise her hips, but somehow managed to draw the skirt up to her waist and button it closed.

He froze when he heard the double doors bang open and listened as several people entered and made their way towards Lise's bed. Willy reached over and quietly retrieved the heavy wire cutters and a knife from the box, the only weapons at hand. The steps went past to another patient's bed. After a short muffled discussion, more footsteps took them back out.

Brown ankle socks came next, and her shoes. Taking her hands he gently raised her back up. He tried putting the sweater over Lise's neck first, but her arms seemed to have minds of their own and after a few moments he started over by pulling each wrist through the sweater arms and then lowering the collar over her head. He pulled her long hair out from beneath the collar and brushed it back with his fingers. Under his own hat, he had crammed one of Lise's French berets, folded flat. On it went.

He paused to examine his work. The bracelet from the handcuffs continued to dangle at her wrist. Willy pulled up her sleeve and used sticky tape, wrapped around her lower arm several times, to hold the bracelet up and to keep it from making any noise. When the sweater's sleeve was pulled down, the bracelet was invisible.

His watch showed five forty-five.

"Lise...Lise...Lise," Willy repeated, raising his voice as loud as he dared. He squeezed her hands tightly, rubbed her cheeks and temples, and finally tried pinching her earlobes.

"Ow," she whined childishly. "That hurts..." Her eyes were still glassy and unfocused, but they were open.

"You've got to stand up and walk. Can you stand?"

"I don't want to. Just let me sleep. Tired, I'm very tired."

"You can sleep later." Willy lifted her up on her feet and though she swayed like a drunkard, she didn't topple over immediately.

"Don't move. Just stand there." He peeked out through the curtain. No one was in sight and he couldn't hear anyone talking outside near the door.

Back by the bed, Lise was still standing, facing exactly as Willy had left her.

"We've got to go. We're going home now. Do you understand home? Lise, just do as I say. You have to keep walking whatever happens, no matter how tired you are. Do you understand?" She might have nodded or her head might have sagged involuntarily, but Willy knew that he wasn't going to get any more right now. She might get better or worse, but time had run out. He pulled back the curtain and pushed her out into the room. She managed a few steps on her own and then stopped. At the last second, Willy turned back, dumped his tools and other items onto the bed, covered them with the sheet. He replaced the pastries in the empty box, considered retying the string, but gave up the idea just as quickly.

"Let's go. Walk to the doors." Balancing the box in one hand he took her arm with the other and steered her to the door. He cracked it open and peered out. No one in sight. Without a word he pulled Lise through the doors and started down the empty corridor toward the elevators. They made it about ten paces.

"Hey, you two. What are you doing here?" The female voice was harsh and grating. "Stop where you are." Willy turned around to face the nurse, but left Lise standing alone still aimed down the corridor.

"What are you two doing here?"

"Good evening, Matron. Some pastries were left over from the conference downstairs. We thought we might bring them up to share with the sick patients. They shouldn't go to waste."

"Let me see," she growled. Willy backtracked up the corridor and met her halfway. He opened the box and showed her what was left.

"You've come to the wrong part of medical, boy. Patients here are all prisoners. I doubt they'd appreciate your gesture. Staff and family members are treated upstairs. Are those apricot? Tell you what, I'm heading that way in a few minutes myself. If you like, I'll take them up for you. Save you two wandering around and getting lost again."

"Thank you, Matron. Thank you very much. That's very kind. If it's no trouble?"

"Not at all. It's very thoughtful of you children. Anytime." Her mouth watered.

Willy turned and walked back to where Lise swayed like a tree on a breezy day. He took her arm and pushed her along. The elevator came within a minute and they move to the back after Willy signaled for the ground floor. The elevator stopped on the first floor and three people got on, but they absently turned to face the front, ignoring Willy and Lise.

The main corridor was now crowded with staff and visitors all leaving at the end of the day. Willy merged into a large group and moved with them towards the northern exit. It wasn't easy. Lise wouldn't walk fast enough to keep up with the flow toward the door. And she kept tripping over her own feet or the slightest imaginary irregularity in the limestone floor. Several times Willy found himself holding her up, bearing all her weight as she tried to regain her feet.

But all at once they were outside on the street. Somehow no one had taken notice as they left. They were just a part of the crowd, everyone intent on home and dinner. It was freezing cold. The sun had set and streetlights had been lit, at least until the next blackout was ordered. Willy had considered taking Lise to the hostel or the lab, but a wave of exhaustion, mental and physical, swept over him and he could only think of home. The Wagner house was home now. He wanted to get there as fast as possible, build the fire as large as he dared, close all the curtains and shut out the rest of the world for days, if not forever.

The cold didn't shock Lise to consciousness like Willy hoped. His difficulties continued for another miserable hour, but at the end Frau Erna was hugging Lise in the front hall, wailing like a banshee, and Willy closed the door behind him before the neighbors could hear anything.

When Lise awoke, Willy was still there, quietly contemplating the fire. This time she felt much better, indeed Lise realized that she was very hungry and could not remember having anything to eat in two days. "Willy?" she croaked, then cleared her throat as he turned smiling at the sound of her voice. "Willy, I'm hungry. Do you think Frau Erna might have left any apricot strudel in the pantry? I don't know why, but I have this craving…"

Minneapolis, Minnesota

"Hey Ed, didn't you tell me that you met Bill Petersen in Berlin?" Emmett shouted through his open office door into the lab. It took Edward a moment to connect Bill Petersen to Willy Petersen. He climbed off the lab stool and poked his head into Emmett's office.

"Yes, Professor. At a Berlin technical symposium last year, just before I came here."

"Well there's a letter here from him mailed from Munich. Took two friggin' months to get here. Sounds like he's having a good time. Look, I've got to drive down to Madison for a conference with my editor. If you don't mind, could you send him back a note? Give him my regards. Tell him a little about what we're working on and what's planned for next year. Let him know he's always welcome if he wants to come. We'll make room for him if we need to. Bill's a smart kid and my wife thinks he's adorable. Salt of the earth, if you know what I mean." He waved the letter at Edward.

Edward didn't know what he meant. These Americans would never learn how to speak clearly. Their English was just one idiomatic expression after another. He rapidly read over the letter Willy and Lise had so carefully prepared. Nothing out of the ordinary. He walked back to his desk and added the letter to one of the neat stacks of correspondence, articles, and notes that awaited action. A response could wait. Edward had no use for Herr Petersen and his politics and felt very uncomfortable with the idea of Willy joining the research group at the university here. If he thought it through carefully, perhaps he could craft a response that wouldn't sound quite so promising as Professor Emmett's off-hand invitation.

The following Monday, with Professor Emmett away for several days, Edward sat down at the Professor's typewriter to prepare an abstract for a technical paper to be submitted to the *Journal of Chemistry*. Edward was not a skilled typist and it took him several hours before he was satisfied with the results.

Now was a good time to respond to Willy Petersen since he didn't have the Emmett looking over his shoulder, dictating a totally positive reply. He stood up and walked back to his desk and picked the letter off the top of a pile of documents on the windowsill. Without looking at it, he went back to the typewriter and rolled in fresh paper and carbons. *Does Petersen's letter have a return address?* Edward asked himself. He looked at the letter again.

At first Edward thought the letter had gotten wet and the ink had run for the page was covered in light blue smudges. His second thought was that some clumsy ass in the lab had spilled a chemical on the letter, since black ink in the letter wouldn't bleed blue. Oddly the smudges seemed like they were arranged in symmetrically lines. At arms length he held the letter up to the sunlight coming through the window. He examined at letter more carefully and read the unstained areas:

"Professor Wagner has given me a….. that you can be a tough grader…"

What nonsense, Edward thought. Emmett was a fool and his tests unchallenging. When he lowered the letter to the desktop, the blue smudges leapt out at him along with the words they highlighted:

"..warning …. warning … Germany … is working on … uranium … cross … sections … Professor Wagner is helping … with the calculations … for the Kaiser Wilhelm Institute … and … near success … radio … active … explosive … is probable … please forward … message … to Dr. Einstein in Princeton…"

Edward paused, took a breath, and read the hidden message again slowly. His heart was racing. He stood up and walked outside the office and slumped in his own chair. This must be a joke or some freak coincidence. With the letter in the other room it was easier to think clearly. He must be wrong. Some one here must be playing an elaborate practical joke: maybe Petersen himself. Perhaps the same people responsible for disrupting the Bund meeting. But to what end? Edward got up again and hurried down the hallway to the lavatory. He relieved himself and carefully washed his hands, splashing cold water on his face. As he toweled off, he suddenly remembered that he'd left the letter sitting by the typewriter in Emmett's office where anyone might pick it up, read the message, unaware it was a prank. He rushed back to the office, recovered the letter, and nervously folded it and slipped it in his lab coat pocket. He sat at his desk staring out the window, not daring to reread the message, deeply afraid that it might be real.

But Edward didn't need to read the letter again. He knew it was genuine. His suspicions were true: *Petersen is a spy.* How could he have guessed that back in Berlin? How could he have let the idea pass so nonchalantly? It had been his duty to report his suspicions whatever their basis, no matter how silly the idea might sound. His first chance to serve the Fatherland was wasted. He would have to make it right again.

Only now did he begin to consider the contents of the message. Making sure no one else was around, he took out the letter and carefully reread the message. He thought for a moment about writing it out but decided that any copy would be even more dangerous to have around.

The message was meant to alert Einstein and the Americans that Germany was developing a uranium bomb. Edward remembered speculation about such possibilities at the very Berlin symposium where he met Petersen. Now he understood why Petersen had been present. Some traitor had arranged Petersen's invitation.

Edward felt a surge of pride that Germany might accomplish such a scientific and engineering feat so quickly, from such rudimentary beginnings. "… Near success …" the message read. So what if the world came to know what Germany had achieved? Perhaps England would now sue for peace, and the Fatherland could consolidate its new territories and protectorates.

So what was the message meant to do? Petersen must believe that Einstein and his friends might somehow halt the German project or perhaps begin their own. While America was not actively involved in the fighting, public sentiment, as Edward had discovered, was decidedly pro-British. Einstein and his Jew friends were very vocal about America's international responsibilities. Maybe Einstein would use this message to influence his cronies in the American government to unite with the English and attack the Fatherland before this new weapon could be completed.

He considered what he should do. He must contact the German authorities in person. There was no one in America or Germany he could call or write who knew him or would believe him. No one to trust locally: he cringed and flushed with embarrassment about his experience with the local Bund, doubtless infiltrated by the FBI.

The nearest German Consulate was in Chicago. Take the train to Chicago immediately. Someone there would know how to send word secretly back to the Fatherland: *William Petersen's a spy and knows details about the uranium project. He must be arrested and questioned. Must have accomplices. Stop him.*

The *SS Granada*

Tellerman shivered in the damp, penetrating cold. He had crammed himself, sitting upright, into the corner of his berth, his back to the icy steel bulkhead, dressed in all his clothes and wrapped in a half dozen clammy blankets he'd collected from adjacent, empty cabins. He was wet through. His life-vest was a sponge and whenever he's shift position, freezing water would be squeezed out, running down his neck inside his shirt. Edward was hungry, nauseous, and groggy from lack of sleep. The bare bulb overhead somehow made the room feel even colder and it kept Edward focused on a reality he'd rather escape. He'd suffered several crying jags and even now was only barely in control of his emotions.

For three consecutive nights, alarms had sounded almost hourly as a terrified Spanish crew raced again and again to lifeboat stations prepared to abandon ship quickly if they were attacked. Everyone slept in lifejackets. Despite the driving rain, off-duty seamen dozed fitfully in the uncovered lifeboats, unwilling to go below decks to their bunks, expecting a torpedo to hit at any moment. Edward had wanted to appear a stoic in front of the cowardly Spaniards, but each time the bells rang, he too found himself on deck, pushing himself to the front of the mob clamoring into the nearest lifeboat. In desperation, time and time again, lifeboats had been left free and swung out, ready to be lowered instantly. Three of them had been smashed against the ship's side when the ship rolled and now everyone knew there weren't enough places for everyone aboard the remaining boats.

The captain was zigzagging his ship constantly, doubling the actually length of the trip, and now that they'd entered the English Channel, the added risks of shoals, rocks, and minefields made the crew's fears palpable. In the open Atlantic, German U-boats were the danger. Now the Spaniards were frightened about air attacks from England, France, and Germany. The captain spat on Edward's shoes when he came to tell him that his German friends had just invaded Denmark and that the dangers to them all had just multiplied ten-fold.

The *Granada's* superstructure had been recently and sloppily painted white and every vertical post, mast, and wire carried a battered Spanish flag. All the deck floodlights burned brightly even in daytime. But the Spaniards knew how all sides despised neutrals. No one would care if they were sunk inadvertently or used for target practice.

The *Granada* had been overflown three times since they passed Lizard Point at dawn. Each time, the English and French planes had executed mock attacks. Everyone cringed and cowered on deck unsure until the very last second that the attack wouldn't be carried through.

One more day would take them to Hamburg and the relative safety of the harbor batteries. The "Phony War" over the channel was quiet, but who knew when the British or French would decide to escalate and bomb German ports in retaliation for the attacks in the north. Four days after its arrival, the *Granada* would go out again, retracing its course down the Channel on its way to Gibraltar and Barcelona. The captain questioned how he could prevent his crew from jumping ship and trying to make their way home by land. He knew it was possible: the captain was considering it himself.

Edward had boarded the ship in Baltimore and found himself the only passenger on the small tramp. The Captain told him that on the in-bound trip from Barcelona to Baltimore, he'd carried two hundred passengers, twice the ship's legal capacity. People, refugees from all parts of central Europe, had eaten and slept in unheated spaces and on the bare decks in the saloon and dining room. That trip had been very profitable, but the captain did not think there would be another, even if he managed to sail his ship back to Spain unscathed. When no passengers booked passage on the scheduled sailing to Hamburg, the Captain stranded most of his men on shore in America and had kept only a skeleton crew. Edward had to eat cold food with the crew, sleep in a filthy, unheated cabin, and spend most of his time alone and scared.

Edward had expected to be welcomed warmly by the Spaniards. After all, the Reich had been instrumental in bringing Franco to power. Many Germans had died in their cause. The Spanish should be grateful. Spain and Germany were friendly, if not allies yet in the war with France and England.

But the crew openly and loudly damned Edward because he was German, and the second mate had suggested to his watch during dinner the first night, that if the English stopped the *Granada* to inspect cargo, he would order Edward dropped overboard with the other contraband.

"I do it myself. Little man make no splash."

The hatred ran strong and deep.

"You Germans have deserted us. Your Hitler has deceived the *Caudillo*."

"Our families are hungry. At home there is no rain and English stop ships that bring food. English are angry when U-boats hide in Spanish ports. English take revenge on us."

"Maybe we choose wrong side. Maybe we do English a favor by killing Germans. We start with you."

Edward did not consider it an idle threat.

He feared arrest by the English, too. He had made a small parcel containing Petersen's letter and hidden message, weighting it down with a glass ashtray from his cabin. If he were about to be captured or searched he would throw it overboard so that message would remain undelivered.

The ship's departure had been delayed by two days when the local stevedores refused to load supplies and general cargo. America was aflame with anger over the sinking of an American navy destroyer assigned to convoy American and neutral supply ships to mid-ocean where English escorts would take over.

In Baltimore, the hostile atmosphere at the customs house had resulted in seizure of Edward's personal notebooks. Since his notes were in German and the Customs agents didn't have anyone handy who could determine what they were, the agents decided to confiscate them. Edward could file an appeal with the American consulate in Germany, if he cared to. In retrospect, Edward felt fortunate that he hadn't been detained himself. The questioning had been impolite and very personal: typically American.

All the time, Petersen's letter was folded inside a waxpaper envelope under Edward's shirt. While he had to empty his pockets and allow the agents to examine the contents of his wallet and small valise, he was not physically searched. He was still shaking with both rage and anxiety when he finally reached the top of the ship's gangplank.

He'd used the last of his American money to book passage and had to haggle the price down to just the amount left in his wallet. The nights before the ship departed he'd had to convince the captain to let him sleep aboard. He had no money for a hotel or hostel. His clothes were dirty and he hadn't properly bathed for almost a week.

Willy reread the invitation:

March 25, 1940

My Dear Petersen,

I am glad you can finally visit the new experimental facility in Dahlem. There are many things I want you to see, though unfortunately I can't be there to conduct the tour myself. I have sent a telegram to Von Weizsächer and Hahn to make sure your visit goes smoothly. If you can send them the details of your trip, they will have someone meet you at the station. We will arrange for you to stay at the Institute's guesthouse on April tenth, so please don't concern yourself with arrangements for lodging.

As you'll see for yourself, we are making good progress with our experimental uranium reactor, and we are only weeks from initial operation.

I am sure you will have many questions and I have asked my associates to answer them all. In any case, after you have returned to Munich, please send me a note with your comments and observations. It is critical that people outside Germany understand what we are trying to accomplish here, and your eyewitness account will be very important.

Best regards,

Werner Heisenberg
University of Leipzig

As his train clicked along the high-speed tracks from Munich to Berlin, Willy wondered how much Heisenberg had told his colleagues about their visitor. Did they even know that Willy was an American? It was obvious that Heisenberg wanted someone from outside Germany to visit and eventually carry a message outside, that the new facility in

Cross Sections

Dahlem was focused on basic research unrelated to weapons development. Everything Professor Heisenberg had said about Karl von Weizsächer and Otto Hahn suggested that they passionately shared his views, but this was Nazi Germany in 1940, and who could really know what anyone thought or believed. He had hoped that this would afford him an opportunity to gain more insight into Heisenberg's true feelings. Despite their talks over the past fifteen months, Willy wasn't sure exactly where Heisenberg stood. When Lise had suggested they confide in him, Willy had been vehemently opposed. Even if Heisenberg's moral stand was consistent, his concern for his family would give the Gestapo maximum leverage if they became suspicious. Heisenberg squandered his own opportunity to escape and stay in the States during his visit in '39. In those days it would have been relatively easy to sneak his family over the border to Switzerland and they'd all be safe and free. Without Heisenberg, the German uranium projects would be effectively blocked. But he returned as equivocal and abstruse as ever. The Ordnance Department and Gestapo surely know how important he is. If they allowed him to travel so freely abroad, they must trust him thoroughly. Why? In Willy's worst imagining, Heisenberg had traveled to the States as a Nazi spy, to bring back information about American research, not to explain away the German projects. Whom could Willy trust?

As Willy's train arrived at the *Bahnhof* in Dahlem, it became apparent immediately that he was not going to get his answers. A young, bored graduate student from Professor Hahn's group met Willy and walked with him to the Institute. The young man, who introduced himself as Robert Abele, handed Willy a note of apology from Hahn and von Weizsächer. They were tied up in meetings and assured Willy that Herr Abele would be an excellent guide. Even on the short walk, Herr Abele proved to be more phlegmatic than guarded. He seemed to consider guide duty as demeaning.

So despite Heisenberg's assurances and courtesies, no one wanted to be directly linked with Willy's visit. If questioned by the Gestapo, they could say that they were acting as a courtesy to Professor Heisenberg, they didn't know who Willy was, and they did not meet or talk with him personally. And if that meant that Hahn and others were aware that Willy Petersen was an American, it could only mean that the Gestapo would know sooner rather than later. Willy's time was nearly up. The slightest hint from any of these great men, purposeful or inadvertent, would put Willy in a concentration camp for the rest of the war…if they didn't quietly shoot him in his cell.

Perhaps this would work out for the best, Willy thought. He could linger longer without worrying so much about being polite and getting tied up with meetings and inane conversations. He had to stay focused. Over the last month Lise and Willy had considered dozens of options, some simple and elegant, others impossibly complex and silly. Their goal was simple: delay or slow the experiments on self-sustaining nuclear reactions. At one end of the spectrum was outright sabotage and arson. Burn the facility to the ground, destroying equipment and records. They understood well how this would be a very daunting task. From the descriptions he'd overheard at the Berlin conference, he knew that the experimental work would be spread over several existing buildings, substantial old stone and masonry structures that would be very difficult to set ablaze, even if Willy had the skills.

His first look at Max Planck-Institute confirmed their doubts. Installed in an old estate, the Institute took up two large and a whole series of smaller buildings and cottages, all constructed of native stone. But Willy was heartened. A tall stone wall surrounded the old estate, but the front gate, formed from ornamental iron, was open and unguarded. Workmen and other tradesmen were coming and going freely and while he watched, a large covered truck pulled slowly through the gate and drove up the road toward the main building.

Leaving Willy's bag with a receptionist, Abele took Willy through several large laboratories on the ground floor of the main building. The first few rooms were dedicated to radiation measurement and chemical analyses. The third large room was already filled with a complex series of glass tubes, condensers, heaters, and vacuum pumps.

"Herr Petersen, this apparatus will test several new theories concerning uranium purification. I understand from Professor Hahn that this is your primary interest. I'm sorry none of the researchers in this group is here to meet you today, but as you can see, they're just now getting started here. They're still transferring equipment to Dahlem from Berlin and Leipzig."

"I'm very sorry to miss meeting them. What can you tell me about their work?"

Herr Abele seemed pleased to be consulted outside his area, which involved the pile itself.

"I'll tell you what I know, though as you already understand, this work is very tedious and exacting. The idea behind this work is to exploit the very slight difference in boiling point between the fluoride salts of specific uranium isotopes. The lighter the isotope, like uranium 235, the lower the salt's boiling point compared to the dominant isotope, uranium 238. But the differences are minute and in order to extract and concentrate the salts of the lighter, fissionable isotope, distillation and fractionation must be performed again and again, perhaps as many as a thousand times in sequence. Even then we expect a yield of only gram quantities of active, fissionable isotope. I also understand that the uranium compounds used are highly corrosive and toxic. That obviously complicates this laboratory's work.

"Personally, I find this kind of research boring and frustrating," Herr Abele offered but then recalled that his visitor was a specialist in this area. "But of course all such work is equally important. I just meant to say that it's not for me." Willy, hoping to keep his guide off-balance, simply nodded. "Please, Herr Petersen, if you care to look around here, take your time."

Willy spent twenty minutes examining the equipment and apparatus. All the glassware was hand-made and the equipment was brand new and of the very best quality, nothing like the salvaged, cannibalized, and obsolete equipment Willy was using in Munich. He had no doubt that with this set-up, Willy or any competent technician should be able to produce purified samples of uranium isotope 235. But it was only glassware, easily replaced, despite the cost. Given unlimited funds and two technicians, Willy could assemble an identical apparatus in two weeks. If, as Hahn had speculated in Berlin the year before, the key to unlimited application of uranium fission lay in significant quantities of purified ^{235}U, it would take this laboratory twenty years to produce a single kilogram. Full-scale purification would require an industrial-sized facility that would cost millions of Reichmarks and take years to erect. Any mischief Willy and Lise planned would need to be directed elsewhere. To avoid raising any suspicion, Willy didn't take notes during his tour, but he took his time and carefully memorized as many details as possible. He would jot them all down later.

"Thank you, Herr Abele. This is all very impressive. My regards to the men who put this together. I don't think Professor Wagner or I would have anything valuable to add to its design. I will commend them to Professor Wagner. Really excellent work."

Abele was impressed with the praise given his coworkers and was now anxious to show Willy his own area.

"I thank you for them, Herr Petersen, and will pass along your generous comments. I've heard them mention Professor Wagner many times. Nothing short of worship. Your praise will mean a great deal to them. If you'll follow me, we can quickly finish the tour of the main building and get along to the really good things."

The rest of the main building comprised offices, reading and meeting rooms, and the library. Many of the offices were occupied, but Herr Abele made no effort to introduce Willy to any of the senior men. Eventually they found themselves back in the lobby.

"Perhaps you'd like to have some lunch before we visit the experimental pile. There's a pleasant tavern right just down the road from the gate." The short walk gave Willy an opportunity to look over the area around the Institute: mostly small houses and a few tiny shops spaced well apart. Willy speculated that the neighborhood would be quiet and dark at night.

Lunch was pleasant enough and true to the social atmosphere pervasive in Nazi Germany, conversation was very general and shallow. Neither man asked any personal questions, discussed politics, or exchanged gossip. Sports seemed to be a safe subject and Willy could remember just enough from the radio broadcasts and newspaper reports to hold up his half. Herr Abele was a great football fan.

Back at Max Planck, Abele lead Willy through the ornate gardens to the estate's pavilion, its elaborate and substantial greenhouse. Trucks had torn up some of the brown and dry scrubs and flowerbeds, and it was unlikely the gardens would ever be the same again, though there were signs of early blooms. The stone building was twenty feet tall at its peak, with long, high windows all along the southern, eastern, and western sides. Large dormers along the roof were designed to let in even more light on short winter days in Germany. The windows along the roof were controlled by chains, the lower windows, still two meters off the ground, were latched from the inside. Willy noted that despite the chill, several of the lower windows were propped open for fresh air and ventilation.

Inside, still mounted on a heavy wooden pallet, a large metal tank had been squeezed through the doors and lay tilted on its side.

"This tank will form the bottom and sides of our containment vessel,"

Abele beamed. "You wouldn't believe the fuss raised by the Navy. They lay claim to all stainless steel production in the Reich. Colonel Diebner threatened to take our case directly to the Führer. It only arrived last Friday and will take us a few more days to install. Much of the other equipment is already on site. Let me show you."

Willy only had to smile and nod. The young engineer was obviously proud of his group's design work and was willing to expound on any item or issue where Willy showed interest.

"We have this whole bank of neutron counters from *Herr Doktor* Geiger in Berlin. We've tested their lower detection limits with samples of polonium, but until we begin to generate neutrons from the uranium pile itself next week, we won't be sure about saturation levels for the detectors. This equipment is quite unique in the world."

Willy wondered if this was true and if so, was this more valuable information that needed to find its way to America? *Keep focused!*

"On this bench, we've set up our temperature measurement gear. We'll place thermocouples all through the pile itself," Herr Able smiled. "As you've probably heard, some of the old men at the Physics Institute are afraid that once the chain reaction begins it can never be halted. The planet will be consumed and start to burn like the sun."

"And what is your opinion?"

"I've seen the calculations. As long as we control the shape and size of the uranium pile and the flow and level of the heavy water, nothing like that will happen.

"Despite their foolishness, I've reviewed the overall energy calculations and if this pile were to explode, it would only destroy this town and an area extending out a few kilometers." Herr Abele had an eerie gleam in his eyes. "But what a wondrous thing that would be. Everything in sight vaporized in a millisecond. Can you imagine such a thing, Herr Petersen? Nothing like that has ever occurred in the entire history of the universe. To be part of such an event would be a profound, almost religious experience."

Especially for the people in town, Willy thought, but said, "Your enthusiasm is infectious, Herr Abele. But hopefully this is not your plan, is it? It would be a premature end to a promising career for you," Willy mugged, then continued more seriously.

"Professor Heisenberg tells me that his primary goal is to develop a power engine based on the uranium reaction. Did I misinterpret the

Professor's plans?"

"Oh, the Professor has his own plans. But many of us, particularly younger men like you and I, strongly believe this technology will have even more important applications, important for the war effort and eventual victory for the Reich."

"Yes, I understand," Willy said, trying hard to keep his feelings off his face.

On his way to his room at the Institute's guesthouse that night, many of the other visitors had gathered together in the lobby and were talking animatedly. As Willy passed by, he eyes were drawn to the headlines on a discarded newspaper: German troops had invaded Denmark and Norway that very morning. The commanding generals assured success.

Norway meant more to Willy than the expansion of the war. The conquest of Norway would give Germany an unlimited source of heavy water and the remaining material obstacle to the development of a German uranium bomb would disappear.

Tellerman's journey from Minnesota to Baltimore had been a series of crushing disappointments.

In a discarded Chicago newspaper, he read about the U-boat attack on the *USS Henricks*. While the paper's editors ranted about this violation of neutrality, Edward was equally angry about America's duplicity: claiming the rights of a neutral while providing aid and support to the English. He still couldn't comprehend why America wouldn't wake up and realize how the Jew bankers in London and New York were manipulating the American government to their own ends. Germany was well within its rights to attack belligerents. If the American government had sent spies like Petersen to Germany, they had already chosen their side. Lessons Americans should have learned in the Great War obviously must be taught them again.

An elderly woman at Traveler's Aid in Chicago Union Station had given him the address of the German consulate. After walking halfway across town, he found the Consulate closed and guarded by the Chicago Police. He nervously approached one of the officers and was told how the consular staff had been recalled to Germany several days ago after the newspapers announced the sinking of the *Henricks*. Angry crowds had gathered several times outside the consulate and the police were here to keep someone from burning it down. The fire might spread and damage some other building after all. Otherwise....

When the officer began to question Edward about his business, Edward quickly excused himself and hurried off, certain that the officers would follow him. He made his way back to the station and used his dwindling cash to purchase a second class ticket to Washington. He had to wait for several hours for his train to arrive and every moment he was convinced he was watched and followed. The trip took two days and two nights, Edward sleeping in a corner of the car with his arms tightly wrapped around his bag, protecting the packet inside his shirt. He spent the hours going over in his mind how he would present his story to German authorities in Washington. How he would convince them and how they would recognize instantly the importance of the message he carried. They would relieve Edward of responsibility. He would be considered a hero and they would arrange safe passage back to Germany. His family and townsmen in Sudetenland would be so very proud. It would be an important contribution from the *new Germans*.

But other *new Germans* spoiled his plans. A map at Washington's Union Station directed Edward to the German embassy on Massachusetts Avenue. He heard the noisy crowd even before he turned the closest corner. Men and women carrying placards filled the street all along the block in front of the Embassy. They were chanting at the windows of the embassy, some in English, others in German or Czech.

"Murderers! Killers!"

Somewhere in the raggedy crowd, a few people were singing, and as he worked his way along the fringe of the crowd, he realized they were mangling the old Czech national anthem. A line of police officers with batons had taken up position, their backs to the main gate. Edward circled the whole block to see whether he could find an alternative entrance: there was none.

Back in front of the Embassy gates, he knew he'd have to wait until the demonstration was over and he crossed to the other side of the broad avenue to watch and wait for his chance. From a distance Edward studied the placards and listened to the shouts and jeers. The Czechs proclaimed that Germans were responsible for the massacre of their university students. But Edward had grown up dealing with these people. Many had worked for his late father in the mines. From his father he inherited little respect for Czechs. He had told his son that all Czechs were lazy and liars. Most were Communists who could not be trusted. He was outraged that the ordinary Americans, witnessing this display, would not recognize the fabrications. He could see the locals watching from the park across from the Embassy and from nearby office windows. *How can I make them understand?*

Two older men in gray overcoats were standing nearby calmly watching the demonstrations. They were both tall and clean-cut, with closely cropped hair. Edward was close enough to overhear them speaking German to one another. He edged closer and tried to make out what they were saying. There's a good chance these men were connected with the Embassy and were also waiting to get back inside.

Edward was desperate and there was no indication that the demonstration was waning. The longer he watched them the more he convinced himself that these men are connected with the Embassy and could help him.

"Excuse me, *meine Herren*," he said softly in German. "Do you gentlemen work at the German Embassy?" The two men looked at one another.

"Yes," one replied.

"It is very important that I speak immediately with someone in authority. I have…I have information important for the war."

"You are a German citizen?" the other asked.

"Yes, mein Herr."

"May I see your passport, please?"

"Yes, of course," Edward pulled his papers from his jacket pocket, and without thinking, presented his newer Reich passport first. Before he'd left Germany for America, there hadn't been time to obtain an American visa in his new German passport. His student visa had been granted in Prague prior to annexation. The first man leafed through the pages and handed it to the other man who began to examine it closely, looking back and forth several times comparing Edward's photograph to his person.

Across the avenue, the demonstration was becoming more frenzied. Edward turned for a moment to watch. Clumps of soil mixed with dirty snow were hurled over the fence aimed at the swastika flag flying on a pole within the driveway circle. The crowd was beginning to boil as the city police officers half-heartedly began to push them away from the gate and nearby fence.

"Swine," he said half to himself, sure that his fellow Germans shared his opinion. He turned back expectantly to the two men.

In English the taller man said accusingly, "You have no visa or entry stamps in your passport, *mein Herr*. We're with the FBI. You'll have to come with us down to headquarters to sort this out." The second of the two men had pocketed Edward's German passport and was maneuvering to get behind him to cut off any avenue of escape. But Edward's senses were heightened and his adrenaline flowing. Before the agents could react, Edward bolted and ran back across the street dodging the slow moving cars.

"Stop! Federal agents! Stop!" he could hear the agents shout. Just as he reached the furthest curb he heard a gunshot as one of the agents fired his pistol in the air. Edward didn't hesitate or turn around. As he jostled his way into the crowd, panic broke loose. Some people dropped to the ground, some were frozen in place like statures, and others fled screaming down the sidewalk to the left and right of the front entrance. The agents had followed but lost sight of Edward almost immediately in the melee. Edward paused when he neared the Embassy gate. For an instant he had hope he might have a chance to force his way through the policemen at the gate. But when he got to the rear of the crowd, now faced toward the street, he could see that the iron gate was closed and bolted. In the excitement the city cops had started to beat the nearest protesters with their batons, driving them in the direction of the gunshot. Embassy security men, guns drawn, were incuriously watching the crowd outside through the vertical bars. Edward thought perhaps he could yell to one of them through the fence but knew he would never be heard over the noise of the screaming and terrified crowd and that the FBI men would see him as the crowd dispersed. Just behind him he could sense people reacting as someone was pushing their way through: the FBI men.

"Get back! Get down!" they shouted.

Edward spun to his right and quickly overtook the fleeing crowd as it ran east on the avenue. As he reached the corner, moving parallel to the fence, he found himself suddenly free, as the protestors scattered widely. He took his bearings and headed back toward the train station, looking over his shoulder ever few seconds to see if he was being pursued. At the station, the big board overhead announced that the next train scheduled to depart was headed north for Baltimore, Philadelphia, and New York: *now boarding*. He bought a ticket for Baltimore and ran downstairs to the platform, jumping aboard train just as it began to move. He didn't think he'd been followed to the station, but he knew that federal agents and the police would soon be searching for him.

He was gasping for breath and was soaked in sweat even on this cold late winter day. Finally able to relax, he felt a little pride at having eluded the agents. When he returned home this would become another part of the legend that would impress his townsmen. He started to review the whole thing in that light until the part where he remembered that the FBI agent had his German passport. Now they knew Edward's name and had his photograph, too. Then a new complication occurred to him: he needed his passport to get out of the country and back into Germany. He pulled out his notecase. Sorting through his papers and monies, he found that he still had his old Czech passport with its American visa granted prior to the Nazi takeover. This could be used to get out of the country and surely once he was back on German soil he could convince authorities of his nationality. Once they heard his story, he could have his Reich passport replaced immediately. Right now, he needed to get out of the United States as quickly as possible.

In Baltimore, he wandered the Inner Harbor, examining postings in the windows of shipping offices facing the waterfront. Here he found the agent for the *SS Granada*, neutral Spanish flag, destination Hamburg. He had to bargain for passage, finally agreeing to pay with all his remaining dollars. He felt humiliated and suspected that the shipping agent was a Jew who enjoyed taking all his money.

"I don't know why anyone would want to go there. Young man, you must be insane. Ten to one, you end up in either the jail or the army. Probably never make it to Hamburg anyway. U-boats are attacking everybody. Without warning. No refunds on this ticket! The ship is scheduled to arrive in Hamburg on April the tenth: no guarantees. Give my regards to *Der Führer* when you see him."

Edward half expected Customs and Immigration agents at dockside to be on the lookout for him. An inspector examined his Czech passport and looked at him curiously but shrugged, rubber-stamped a page, and passed him down the line, where the customs agents gave him such a difficult time. Edward found himself finally aboard the *Granada* and entering a whole new hell. But for now he was glad to be free of America and its Jews and Blacks, Italians and Irishmen, its sunshine Germans and its whining intellectuals.

Now, he was still twenty-four hours from safety. Edward wanted to sleep and then awake only when the ship had made port. But he couldn't escape the alarms and the fearful shouting of the crew. Every clatter of chain, creak of deck, and groan of the rusty old hull was magnified by his frayed nerves. He would close his eyes tight, think of home, and try to imagine the honors ahead. But when he opened his eyes and checked his watch, only few minutes had passed.

The alarms sounded again. *Damn the traitor Petersen! Damn all Americans!* He began to sob again uncontrollably from fear, anger, and frustration. *I don't want to move. I don't care what happens anymore. Let me die.* But if he hesitated, he wouldn't have a place in one of the remaining lifeboats, so he jumped unsteadily to his feet and ran out on the deck.

Late the same night, alone in his Spartan room at the Institute's guest house, Willy sat at a small table, making notes, trying to remember everything he'd seen and heard. Willy had hoped that some option, the germ of some plan would leap out at him as he finished his tour through the former garden pavilion. He knew that heavy water was in short supply. But Willy noted only three drums stored in the pavilion. Someone had enough foresight not to keep them all together in case of an accident, though they were essentially unguarded.

Days before, back in front of the fireplace in Munich with Lise, one option had involved broaching the heavy water storage drums or tanks, but Willy admitted to her that besides the difficulty of doing the job quickly and completely, the heavy water would be replaced eventually.

Now he knew that this first option was out. Their second idea had been to find some way of contaminating the heavy water, but now that option could be abandoned for the same reason. Once the contamination was discovered, extra drums would be brought in. Any delay would span only a few weeks at most.

Willy flipped back in his notes to examine the maps he made of the grounds and building interiors. Tomorrow after breakfast, he would beg off any offer from Herr Abele to accompany him to the rail station. If he left the guesthouse early, he'd have time to wander around the Institute's perimeter wall and through the town.

He sat back in his chair and peered out the open window trying to make out the lights from nearby houses. He wondered to himself whether blackout rules were in place or if the neighborhood was always this dark. A cold, dank wind was blowing across northern Germany from the Atlantic and the North Sea.

What he needed was a way to contaminate the project's *data,* not just its equipment. The conflict between the believers and non-believers was apparent even here. If something could be done favoring the opinions of the non-believers, funding and staffing would be slashed, maybe even stopped. The Institute was at loggerheads with the military about critical materials. The political balance here is very tenuous.

To contaminate the data, he would have to do something to the meters and measuring equipment, most of which was routinely calibrated. There were metering stations for temperature, radiation, and conductance. Unfortunately Willy did not understand the workings of Dr. Geiger's radiation detection gear, and anyway, if radiation increases, so will the temperature, so one reading correlates continually with the other.

But the conductance meter was something he understood very well. Indeed it was identical to one in Professor Wagner's lab in Munich. Same model and everything. The meter was used to constantly assay the purity of the heavy water. Any impurity in the water would interfere with the nuclear reactions, absorbing stray neutrons and inhibiting increases in the reaction rates. Some specific compounds like carbon and boron were known to kill the reaction entirely. Their absorption cross-sections were very high so boron and carbon effectively block nuclear processes.

Is there a way to contaminate the heavy water with a strong absorber without anyone knowing? Maybe.

Willy spent the rest of the night calculating solubilities and electrical conductances, the stuff of freshmen chemistry. *And with all the makings of another freshman prank*, he grimaced.

Hamburg

Edward's left eye was swollen shut and all his front teeth felt like they would fall out with the merest push of his tongue. If he lay perfectly still on the soggy, bare earth inside the tiny fenced pen, he found that most of the pain receded. Though his right eye was uninjured, the stars and moon above him were hazy and indistinct. Fear began to grow that he'd been permanently blinded by the blows that had rained down on his head. Without sight he would be helpless.

But blindness wasn't the only terror that possessed him. At one point the Gestapo men had pulled his trousers and undershorts down to his knees and examined his penis with the end of a sharp rod. The fact that Edward was not circumcised and therefore probably not a Jew didn't seem to satisfy them in the least. Just the contrary: if Edward was a Jew, procedures were well defined.

He overheard one man asked his superior whether he should retrieve electrodes and batteries from inside. "No. Not yet, at least," was the reply.

Throughout the beating the Gestapo men had demanded Edward tell them the truth, but very soon the pain and fear were so overwhelming that he no longer could think clearly enough to invent a lie that might stop the pummeling. He was left only with a truth that these angry men were unwilling to accept. *Truth* was that after the first few moments the guards weren't listening to anything Edward was trying to say. The pleasure they took from their job was engaging and endless.

At first Edward's surprise and confusion had disarmed him and made him vulnerable. His attitude when first questioned after leaving the ship was forceful and insistent. *He* had an important message to convey to the authorities, critical to the future of the Reich. After suffering the Spaniards for eleven days, he wanted to cut through this petty bureaucracy quickly. He had presented himself to a Gestapo sergeant, and demanded to see an officer. But when he produced his Czech passport, no explanation, however loud, clear, rational, or pleading, was going to save him from arrest and abuse. The beating was part of the process, a means to passivate suspects and witnesses alike, a way of clearly establishing in everyone's mind who was in charge.

As another round of questioning began, his interrogators wanted yes or no answers to their impossible questions: any attempt to elaborate was met with another blow from a fist or from the sand-filled cosh one of the Gestapo men seemed to favor.

"Are you a spy?"

"Are you a communist?"

"Are you a Jew?"

"You say you're a loyal German, but all I see is some filthy Czech."

"Who are you working with? Tell us where they are?"

The two interrogators circled him continuously. One was always behind him, and as each man in turn passed in front of his chair, he'd lean down and shout questions within inches of Edward's face. Each of the two Gestapo agents had his own series of questions and as the beating and abuse continued, Edward lost track of which man was which, which was the last question, and what his last answer had been. Even when they'd ask more open questions, they'd quickly become impatient with anything more than the simplest response:

"Why were you in America?"

"I was studying Chemistry."

"Why would you go to America to do that? What were you running away from?"

"I wasn't running away from anything. I thought I'd learn about things the Americans specialize in." Edward was struck from behind on the top of his shoulder with the heavy cosh.

"That wasn't my question. What were you running from? Are you a deserter?"

After several hours the two Gestapo men seemed to get bored and their frustration peaked. Since they were just fishing for a confession or admission about something, the intellectual challenge of coming up with probing questions was too much for them. One of them pulled the chair from under Edward, pitching him forward on his face in the mud. The second man kicked Edward in the kidneys with the point of his shoe. Edward gasped and panted like a fish out of water. They left him on the ground and went back inside the guard shack.

Later in the evening, their officer passed by their desks on his way home for the evening.

"Anything to report on our newest guest?"

"Nothing much, sir. But he is no longer belligerent and insulting."

"Well, gentlemen, did you find out anything?"

"No, sir, but we've reached some conclusions we'd like you to consider," said the first, consulting some rough notes. "The man claims his Reich passport was taken by the American FBI in Washington when he was trying to enter our embassy there."

"Why would the FBI be interested in this creature?"

"He says he had secrets important to the Reich that he needed to pass along to someone, anyone, at the embassy, sir."

"He insists that the FBI shot at him and tried to kill him. It all sounds fantastical to me, sir," offered the second interrogator.

"Is he claiming to be a German intelligence officer?"

"No, sir. Just a student who somehow learned about an American spy loose in Germany. Someone who's sending secret messages to American scientists using disappearing ink or something like that."

"What horseshit!"

The agent reached over and opened an envelope, producing Willy's letter to Professor Emmett. "Sir, he was carrying this letter in a waxpaper envelope under his shirt. Note the words highlighted in blue color."

The officer took a few minutes to read it over.

"He claims, sir, that soon after he took possession of the letter, blue color around some of the words magically appeared. He discovered a hidden message and decide to inform German authorities."

"Why didn't he telephone someone or go to a consulate somewhere? German citizens may travel freely in America."

"He ranted about phones being tapped, consulates closed, and the German embassy besieged by angry Jews and Czechs. He's totally paranoid and delusional."

"But what about this letter? Could it be true, regardless the instability of the man carrying it?"

"We don't think so, sir," he said, a little uneasily. "We ran a little experiment ourselves. We chose a newspaper article about Sunday's football match between Essen and Frankfurt and started to pick out individual words. Let me show you what we did. Here's the original article from the paper."

'*Essen and Frankfurt clashed last Sunday in Berlin's Sports Stadium for the all-German championship semifinals. The Führer was an enthusiastic spectator who personally awarded a silver trophy to the eventual winner. The outcome was decided when Luti Fuchs, center forward for Essen, moved downfield and made the winning shot, outrunning all ten men for the Frankfurt side. Frankfurt captain, Johannes Nesher, was seen complaining to the umpire that Fuchs was offside, but regulations don't provide grounds disallowing umpire's decisions. Essen will next travel to Wiesbaden to face the reigning all-German champs.*'

"Sir, we picked words in sequence from the article and circled them to see if we could create secret messages ourselves. Here's another copy of the same item with some words circled: read just the words we circled, sir."

The Gestapo captain read aloud slowly:

"*Last Sunday...in Berlin...the Führer...personally ...shot...ten men...for...complaining...about...regulations ...allowing...travels...to Wiesbaden.*"

"Sir, the hidden message we *found* doesn't make much sense, but it took us only minutes to pick it out of a random newspaper article. Bruner and I agree this man is obsessed and paranoid. He picked up a trivial and harmless letter addressed to someone else and went over it again and again until he *found* his secret message. He then marked the words he wanted with blue ink. This letter is the result."

The captain looked back and forth from the original newspaper article in one hand to the marked version in the other. He set them down and picked up Willy's letter.

"What's this nonsense about *radio...active...explosives*? Have you ever heard of such a thing?"

Bruner chuckled, "Captain Braun, at one point last night the man was babbling about some sort of *Stink Bombe* he claims almost suffocated him at a Party meeting in America. I think he's as mad as a hatter."

The captain decided. "An excellent piece of work, men," he said graciously. "What are you going to do with him now?"

The two Gestapo sergeants were relieved and elated at the praise from their chief. After all, they never knew how their bosses would react and they feared no one else in Germany. "Sir, we still need to confirm his identity. We cabled Gestapo headquarters in Prague last night to check the validity of this Czech passport. A message this morning says that all the Czech passport records were burned as our troops entered Prague last March. They don't have anything. When they have a chance, they'll check with officials in Gottwaldov, the birthplace listed on the passport, to see if anyone there has ever heard of him. The man claims to be an ethnic German, but Prague says the village Gottwaldov is not in Sudentenland. They also warned us not to expect much cooperation from the Czechs: they've destroyed other records to aid dissidents and communists in their escapes.

"We'll forward our report to Berlin this afternoon with a request to examine Foreign Office records to see whether the man really holds a German passport. I suspect this will take several weeks to get squared away. Until then we'll keep him locked up here."

"What about this American fellow Petersen who this man claims wrote the original letter?"

Bruner consulted his notes. "We called Berlin, sir. First thing we did when we found the letter. Foreign Office says Petersen has a perfectly valid visa. Entered Germany in September '38. According to their records he's working with some famous professor in Munich on coloring agents. Completely innocuous work. Nothing to do with weapons or military research. The only Gestapo file they have at headquarters concerning this Petersen fellow is a student party committee report from Munich twelve months ago. They reported that Petersen is dull, unsophisticated, technically backwards, possibly stupid, and probably a drunkard. But apolitical.

"Then some stuffed shirt at the F.O. came on the phone line and warned us to treat the American with kid gloves. Their policy is to go out of the way to be friendly to Americans. Some shit about keeping them neutral. In any case, we'll put this all in the report for *Prinz Albrecht Strasse.*

"Don't send the report out quite yet. Continue with your inquiries. Gather all your information together and leave it on my desk when you go home tonight. I'll review it myself in the morning. Will you two continue to question this Czech fellow?" Braun asked.

"Of course, sir, more *formally* this time. The man smells bad and we think it's time he had a cold bath!" Bruner nodded enthusiastically.

Berlin - April 19, 1940

The broad east-west avenue was bordered with long vertical red banners suspended from tall poles spaced every twenty feet for as far as Willy could see. In the brisk breeze the banners shimmered, resembling a row of flames consuming the roadway and lapping the buildings at its edge with cold fire. Lise and Willy were standing underneath the Brandenberg Gate, *der Brandenbergertor*, looking east back down *Unter den Linden*, Berlin's most famous street. The approaching sound of a military band had drawn everyone to the sides of the street, tourists, vendors, shoppers, and businessmen alike.

Until you experienced the crowds, it was easy to forget that Berlin was the fourth largest city in the world after New York, London, and Tokyo, six million souls spread over more than four hundred square kilometers. Except along *Unter den Linden* where the famous plane trees had been cut down when the *U-Bahn* subway was built, the city was filled with beautiful trees and parks, it's beauty rivaling any capital in the world.

Roaring cheers from crowds out of sight back along the parade route mixed with the brassy music to reinforce the physical sensation that the crest of an ocean wave was approaching. Traffic on cross streets was halted and passengers on the top of Berlin's double-decker buses craned out the windows to watch. As the first troops came into view, led by an honor guard carrying Nazi and regimental flags, it appeared they were marching miraculously out of the fire. The effect was very dramatic and stirring. Stark, modern buildings were mixed among traditional government buildings all along Berlin's broad boulevard, forming here a steep canyon where the massed gray troops disgorged from the flames as they entered the wide square before the victory arch. The high-stepping troops sounded like a train as they approached.

Like a wave, as the flags passed even with the crowd, men, women, and children, with a single voice, raised their right arms in salute shouting again and again, *"Seig Heil! Seig Heil! Seig Heil!"* then broke into unrestrained applause for the soldiers themselves.

The entire city was alive. Every day troops like these were moved west from Poland toward France and Holland where everyone expected the *phony war* would soon become real. Without warning, ten days before, on April ninth, Germany had suddenly invaded Denmark and Norway. The peaceful Danes had been overwhelmed within hours but a bloody battle for Norway was underway pitting German forces directly against British soldiers for the first time in twenty years. While the BBC reported the Germans were being repulsed up and down Norway, Willy could not find a German man or woman who wasn't utterly confident victory was only days ahead. Willy harbored no hope that the Germans wouldn't prevail in Norway as they had in Czechoslovakia, Poland, and Denmark.

How many men in England or America understood the source of Willy's special dread? If the Norwegian heavy water plant was captured in tact, the German uranium bomb project would lose it last serious obstacle. Inside Germany it was probably too late for anyone else to do anything, even if the Nazis' interests were appreciated. But *someone* had to stop them and the very idea that something so momentous fell to Willy and Lise was so bizarre as to seem impossible. As he watched the last goose-stepping storm troopers pass by, he felt the weight of the entire German army on his back. Willy doubted he could deal with any single one of these soldiers in a physical contest. And there were millions of soldiers…and tens of thousands of Gestapo agents and policemen. And informers…literally every person in this crush of humanity would turn them over to the Gestapo at the slightest hint of their intentions: be it a whisper, a side-long glance, a thought read on one's face. He could see no way that they could avoid the merest slip and that it wouldn't be marked and reported by a million pairs of probing eyes. A hot, constricting sensation swept over him. He couldn't breath and he felt a panic rising in his throat.

Just as suddenly the crowd began to disperse until only Lise was left at his side. Berlin's infamous traffic resumed noisily. Willy forced himself to take a long, deep breath. Lise watched him curiously. She reached up and touched his cheek. It was clammy and ashen. He smiled back at her nervously.

Saturday was the *Führer's* fifty-first birthday, and though no formal ceremonies were planned, spontaneous demonstrations were breaking out every hour as groups of workers, merchants, and civil servants gathered on the streets to cheer and salute Hitler's picture, framed in gilded laurel wreaths, displayed in every shop. Nazi flags hung from every window, whether a residence or business office. Inspired by the tone and demeanor of the marchers, everyone moved through the streets with soldier-like determination, a nation on a common mission.

Like everyone else it seemed, Lise and Willy had business of their own, and holding hands, they set off.

The Gestapo agents made no attempt to disguise themselves or to blend with the American staff or with the milling crowd of visa applicants. If the sole idea was to identify and detain Germans trying to emigrate, it would have been simple to snatch them up as they left the consulate. But other purposes were effectively served by the high visibility, including the intimidation of American residents, businessmen, clergymen, and other travelers who might cling to the obsolete and ridiculous notion that the embassy and consulate could somehow shield them from the omniscient Gestapo. If foreigners, even nominal allies, were allowed to move about or conduct business unchallenged, the Gestapo's stranglehold, and the fear it engendered, would not seem unassailable.

Allied spies would never employ a neutral embassy as an operations base, but continuing threats to the Reich from disenchanted Germans and their foreign sympathizers could not be ignored.

As Willy took his time filling out several forms, cleaning his eyeglasses, sharpening his pencil, and so forth, he reckoned he'd spotted four Nazi agents. These men never seemed to complete their own forms and were never called to the counters from chairs in the waiting room. All the legitimate visitors were nervous and in a rush to finish their business and leave unobtrusively, but these four men all appeared patient, maybe bored.

If Willy could spot these four so easily there'd be others less obvious. Since the invasion of Poland the staff in the consular section had been reduced as families and non-essential workers and diplomats were repatriated to the states. The men and women behind the counters and desks were almost all Germans: they might *all* be Gestapo agents for that matter. They were all informers, in any case. It was only a matter of a scale from reluctance to enthusiasm. No one, however loyal to his nominal employer, would dare hold secrets back from the Gestapo. *Treat everyone like he's a Nazi, even the Americans*, Willy reminded himself, recalling Lise's whispered warning.

"Can I be of assistance, sir?"

"Yes, thank you," Willy replied in German, handing over his paperwork. "My U.S. passport disappeared during the overnight train trip from Munich and I didn't notice the loss until after I'd arrived in Berlin this morning."

"Did you report the loss to the police?"

"No, I came directly here. I'm confused as to how I should report the loss and I've no reason to believe it was stolen. If a police report is necessary perhaps you can help me with that also. I only have a few days in Berlin and I must present my passport in order to register at my hotel…" Willy let it all spill out, trying to appear as helpless and inept as possible. The clerk read his name from the top of the form.

"Please, Herr Petersen, it is not a problem and happens all the time. That's why we're here," the clerk was reassuring. "We will file a police report for you. Actually it's most likely your passport was stolen or has ended in the hands of some criminal who's already on his way out of the country. Once a police report is circulated, every border and customs station will be on alert. A stolen passport is useful for only a short time, but is very valuable nonetheless.

"If you'll have a seat, we'll review your papers. In a few minutes someone will come and take you to the photo lab. It will be necessary for you to have an interview with the consul, but I don't anticipate any delays. If you have any questions, please feel free to ask. We're only here to help." Willy took a chair in the waiting area next to one of the more obvious Gestapo agents.

"Herr Petersen, if you'll come with me," the short man said in English with a faint smile. "My name is Hister. The vice-consul asked me to personally escort you through our procedures." Herr Hister was another German staff member. He led Willy through a set of locked doors and down a long hallway.

"I'm sorry for your inconvenience. I'm sure we can resolve this matter quickly so you can enjoy your visit."

"Thank you, Herr Hister. It's me who should apologize. I feel quite the fool for losing my passport of all things."

"Don't criticize yourself needlessly. We can be quite sure that it was stolen. Such documents are unbelievably valuable on today's black market, worth perhaps fifty thousand Reichmarks." Hister was looking over at Willy most intently and it took Willy a few moments to realize that Hister was trying to read Willy's expression. Hister suspected Willy might have sold the passport himself.

"That seems a great deal of money for something so easily replaced," Willy offered with a shrug.

"I can assure you that men have been murdered for these papers."

"I can't believe that!"

"Oh, yes indeed. You need to be more careful in the future. We're suggesting to all our American residents that they turn their passports over to the local police where you reside. For safekeeping, you understand. A voluntary measure: at least for now."

"I understand. Thank you for the advice. I'll certainly do that when I return to Munich." Then the police and Gestapo would know instantly when and where Willy was traveling. His options were closing quickly.

"It's the safest thing. We'll go to the photography laboratory first for new passport pictures and then I'll introduce you to the vice-consul, Herr Gardner. Just through here please."

The photographer took ten different poses, though only two were required for the replacement passport. The photographer was a German and Willy had no doubt the extras were for the Gestapo's convenience. When finished, Hister led Willy to the first floor office of the vice-consul. Herr Gardner turned out to be a young man, perhaps no older than Willy. He was tall and clean-cut, but appeared tired.

"Herr Petersen, this is Vice-consul Gardner. Herr Gardner, this is William Petersen from Wisconsin."

"Thanks, Herr Hister," Gardner said offering Willy his hand. Gardner had tried to be dismissive, but apparently Hister had no intention of leaving the two Americans alone. He simply stepped back several paces and stood with his back to the wall, hands behind his back, like a soldier *at-ease*.

"It's nice to meet you, *Mister* Petersen. First trip to Berlin?"

"I was here a year ago, but didn't have a chance to see the sights. But the weather's been so wonderful after the horrible winter that I had to make another trip. Been here long?"

"Only six months actually. What with the weather and the war, it's been pretty hectic and I haven't had time to travel far outside Berlin." It occurred to Willy that Gardner might even be an intelligence agent for the War Department. Nothing could be more fortuitous.

"I see you've been in Germany since '38. Lots of changes since then, I guess. What are your plans?"

"Our research keeps us busy at the university. Most of the German students have joined the military or left for work at munitions plants."

Willy saw Gardner look past Willy's shoulder at Hister, perhaps acknowledging some sort of signal or gesture. "What's the nature of your research?" Willy was stunned by the idea the German would prompt Gardner, if he'd read things right. But he answered casually.

"Pigments and dye-stuff. Red and yellow colors for fabrics, paint, and so forth. Not *exactly* important for the German war effort. Our research won't make planes and tanks more deadly, though it might make them prettier." Gardner laughed along with Willy, who didn't turn to see Hister's reaction. Willy had tried to send a subtle message to Gardner that while his work wasn't *exactly* important, it might be important nonetheless. Gardner gave no sign he'd gotten the message. But Willy didn't want to give Herr Hister an opportunity to think about what he'd said.

"Sorry," he said. "I'm just a little giddy. This is my longest conversation in English for twelve months."

"I understand. I understand. How much longer will you stay in Germany?"

"Lots of work ahead of us; at least two years, I'd guess. German research in this field is the best in the world. I'm learning a lot." There was no need to aggravate Hister further, but he hoped that he'd formed a bond with Gardner. *Them and us*.

"How long will you be in Berlin?"

"Only for the weekend. I'll take the train back on Sunday afternoon. Can you recommend some things to do and places to eat? Maybe someplace familiar where American residents congregate. It's great to hear English again."

"I often go to the Black Pig, the *Schwarzes Ferkel*, near the university. Forgive my high school German. Am I pronouncing that correctly, Herr Hister?"

"Yes, Consul, better every day."

"You're just being polite, but I appreciate it nonetheless," Gardner smiled and turned back to Willy. "Despite the name, order the veal. Any plans for your evenings?"

"No."

"You must attend one of Berlin's cabarets. It'll be a unique experience, I can assure you, not what you'd imagine. Try the *Kadeko*. On Fridays and Saturdays all the bigwigs will be there. Tell the maitre d'hôtel that you're an American tourist and he'll get you a table *mach schnell*. Very accommodating."

"How about you?"

"I don't know yet. It depends on how the rest of my day goes. Perhaps I'll see you there and you can buy me a drink: German champagne, of course. The French stuff's rare as pearls nowadays.

"Herr Hister, please show Mr. Petersen to the conference room. Have one of the secretaries bring him a cup of coffee. I'm sure he's tired of the *ersatz* stuff you Germans drink. He can wait there in comfort until his new passport is ready. Keep him company if you insist." Gardner signed off on Willy's application with a flourish.

"It's been a pleasure, Mr. Petersen. I hope to see you again. In any event, good luck to you."

Lise was seated on a park bench with the late afternoon sun behind her. Willy strolled right past without acknowledgement as he made his way across the *Tiergarten* towards a memorial column honoring dead soldiers from the Great War. He wandered around the column reading the inscriptions and then returned, passing Lise a second time. Early that morning, they'd chosen a narrow and winding path that would require anyone following Willy to stay close. He paused just inside the park's ornate gate until Lise joined him and with a nod they walked together quickly down the street in the direction of the *Kurfurstendamm* and their hotel. The exercise was futile to the extent that the Gestapo knew the name of Willy's hotel: it was in his passport application. There were still thousands of foreigners in Berlin and it was fair to assume that they couldn't be followed all the time. So if Willy had not piqued the Gestapo's interest at the consulate, the two might be left alone for the next few days. That was all the time they needed.

As they hurried along without speaking, Willy was thinking about time. Though they would never speak about it, their time together was nearly over. Willy could no longer imagine that America would stay out of this war. Regardless how desperately Americans might wish to remain neutral, Nazi Germany was not going to allow that to happen. Nazis only knew loyal allies and deadly enemies with no room in their universe for equivocators or fence sitters.

If nothing else happened, Willy would soon become an enemy alien. If lucky he might be expelled; more likely he'd be interned in a concentration camp. War was going to spread around the world and last years into the future.

In Munich, world war was a distant rumor. Other than an occasional truckload of draftees or the humorous sight of ancient and overweight reservists parading in city parks, there was little sign that battles were raging in Poland and Norway, in the air over the English Channel, and on the North Sea. Newsreels in the theaters originated in some Reich Ministry or other and were difficult to differentiate from fictionalized accounts of the Great War screened to inspire patriotism and reawaken anti-French sentiment.

But here in Berlin, the streets, restaurants, cabarets, museums, and hotels were filled with soldiers. The troops they'd reviewed that morning were not polished and silvery ceremonial regiments, rather grizzled and dusty veterans from Poland. There was no mistaking their efficiency, purpose, pride, and grim determination.

"Any problem at the embassy?" Lise asked at last, breaking their long silence.

Willy glanced over his shoulder to make certain no one was trailing close behind.

"No. The embassy was full of Gestapo, but no one seemed to pay special attention. I guess they're mostly interested in other Germans and their business."

"Two hours…I was worried. Did you get a new passport or will you have to go back again?"

"It's in my pocket. New photograph and all. German efficiency coupled with easy-going American bureaucracy. I had to file a report for the local police, but I don't think they're likely to follow up until Monday. By then we'll be gone, though they'll probably forward a copy to the authorities in Munich. While they might *suspect* that I sold my passport or gave it to a German friend, until it turns up at a border crossing, they've got better things to do. Least I hope so."

"Don't underestimate them, Willy. I don't any more. Were you able speak with any American officials?"

"Yes and no. I had a brief interview with the assistant consul, but there was an embassy employee, a German, standing right behind me all the time: obviously an informer or Gestapo agent. If I'd asked to speak to the consul alone, we'd have an entire squad of leather coats on our tails right now. But the consul, his name is Gardner, seems like a good guy and I think I managed to convey that I'd like to meet him somewhere away from his office. He specifically recommended a restaurant near Berlin University where American residents go for dinner. Some place named the *Schwarzes Ferkel*, the Black Pig. Eats there frequently himself.

"We should go tonight. If we *accidentally* run into Gardner I might be able to get him alone for a few seconds or set another meeting in a park somewhere."

"Can we truly trust him? Look at Lord Haw-Haw on the radio. He's an English aristocrat, but he's working for the Nazis. We've got to be careful, Willy. Somewhere the Gestapo has our descriptions on file and must be looking for us. Apart we look like anybody else, but together we make a pretty unique couple that people in Munich will have remembered and reported. Perhaps we shouldn't go to the restaurant together."

"I'm not letting you out of my sight. This afternoon was bad enough. The last time, you ended up in jail, goofy on drugs. We'll take our chances together."

"Well, crouch down more so that you won't look like such a big freak."

"Why don't we dye your hair blond? I have just the right chemicals in my valise. You'd be the perfect German *Mädchen*."

"And I'd end up with white hair or bald as a doorknob. If it came to bleaching my hair, I wouldn't trust my own father, and he's the world's greatest chemist. *You*...don't even think about it." They both laughed out loud at their parries and some of the tension melted away.

"Anyway, if I got the message right, if Gardner isn't at the restaurant, he might be at the *Kadeko* Cabaret tonight. He insisted it was something I needed to see."

"A fellow pervert?"

"Oh, I understand the clubs in Berlin that remain open are *officially* sanctioned."

"And you consider the Nazis to be champions of good taste?"

"Do you want to go with me or not?" He stopped in his tracks and smiled at her back as she continued to walk along.

"I'm not letting you out of my sight," she said without looking back.

Willy waited in the hotel lobby while Lise finished dressing upstairs. Despite the fact they would share the room and its twin beds this night, they continued to be considerate about their privacy. While people came down from their rooms and left for the restaurants around the city, the big radio in the lobby blared marshal music and occasional news headlines from the fronts. To hear it, everything was going better than planned, though for some reason a great deal of German heroism and inventiveness was still needed to conquer the hapless Poles. News from Norway included even fewer specifics.

An announcer promising an important message from Herr Goebbels, Reichsminister of Information, interrupted a Wagner overture and with a trumpet fanfare, in a smooth, silky voice, Joseph Goebbels began his annual speech honoring the *Führer* on his birthday. Other hotel guests and employees paused to listen intently.

Launching an attack on the British plutocracy, still blaming them for the present war, Goebbels drew parallels with South Africa and the Boers, attributing the invention of concentration camps to the English. He stressed the strong bond between Hitler and the German nation. That relationship is "the strongest weapon that the German nation has in its battle for existence" and this connection "is incomprehensible to the so-called democratic peoples." He chided that no "English merchant's soul" could ever "understand."

Goebbels reported how the *Führer* was careworn and "weighed down by his thoughts" and by the isolation of command and responsibility.

He asked that all Germans honor the *Führer* with hard work, sacrifice, and their loyal and unquestioning support of German soldiers in Norway and Denmark…

"The entire people have one thought: Long live the *Führer!*" While Willy listened, the lobby filled with guests and pedestrians who'd come in off the street. As the Reichsminister finished, everyone broke into applause; modest at first then louder and louder as everyone competed to demonstrate their enthusiasm. Reluctantly, Willy stood and joined in the clapping.

As the crowd broke up, Lise came down the stairs and pushed her way though.

"What was that all about? Were you dancing on the table and acting the fool again?"

"Someone was."

The restaurant was packed though few students were in evidence despite its reputation as a favorite among the university crowd. Willy had no doubt that Berlin's universities and institutes had been emptied in the same fashion as in Munich. Willy gave his name and they waited in the anteroom for a table. Willy saw no sign of Gardner waiting outside. With a nod the two split up, pretending to look at the various pictures and yellowing posters lining the walls, but eavesdropping on conversations listening for one in English. After circling the large room in opposite direction, the came together and exchanged shrugs.

It was tempting to initiate their own conversation in English, but it was obvious to both that this was the wrong audience: too many government types.

After they were shown to their table, they placed their order, veal cutlets and beer, and took turns visiting the toilets, watching and listening along the way. Nothing. Still no sign of Gardner and no English-speaking patrons. Hope faded.

Outside the cabaret, Willy felt self-conscious and conspicuous. He'd brought a jacket and tie on the trip, but many patrons queuing under the neon marquee and streaming through the wide doors wore tuxedos or full-dress uniforms. When Willy and Lise finally reached the entrance, the managers greeting guests were already turning away couples without reservations. Hesitant at first to call attention to himself, Willy didn't want to miss a chance to see Gardner again, and took the consul's advice.

"Excuse me, sir," he began nervously. "I overheard you tell the last gentleman that the club was full." The doorman looked unsympathetic.

"I'm an American visiting Berlin. I've heard good reviews for your show. Perhaps you can find some small spot for us, even if we have to stand. We wouldn't mind."

But the big man had already brightened. For a moment Willy was sure he anticipated a bribe, something Willy was unable to pay, but...

"Americans! Americans! There's always room for visitors from

America. Would you please follow me?"

The maitre d' led them right through the milling crowds, making a path for Willy and Lise like a Panzer tank through the forest. Stopping just in front of the stage apron, he whistled loudly and magically two chairs and a small table appeared, carried overhead by white-jacketed waiters. With terse excuses and no little body English, enough space was opened for the table to be set down. In a wink of an eye, napkins, silver, a stem vase, glasses, and a bottle of chilled champagne materialized, complements of the proprietors.

Their waiter, Udo, was introduced and informed that their care was his special responsibility. The club was indeed full. Here in front, the patrons were literally shoulder to shoulder. Private conversation was impossible, even if one could be heard over the din. Willy and Lise could only smile helplessly at each other. There might be a hundred Americans at the *Kadeko* that night, but unless Gardner found Willy, it was doubtful Willy would spot him among the teeming and noisy crowd. They were very fortunate to be seated prominently up front. As long as the house lights were up, Willy was visible to anyone in the theater.

As Udo filled their glasses, he pointed to a large table on a platform raised above stage level to Willy's far right.

"Reichsminister Goebbels himself," Udo whispered in Willy's ear. Willy looked up at the man whose voice he'd heard only hours before on the radio. From this angle he appeared a small man. He was seated with an attractive woman, his wife Willy assumed, and was joined by other well-dressed and elegant friends. Champagne was being poured and Willy considered his own bottle wondering if the Reichsminister's patriotism demanded that he too, suffer domestic product.

Willy leaned over to yell in Lise's ear: "The waiter says the little man up there in the…"

"I recognize him from newsreels," Lise yelled back dismissively and sat back staring hatefully. Willy gave her a warning look and she turned away.

Willy leafed through the program booklet that teased patrons with its cryptic descriptions of the skits, tableaus, and special musical numbers to be performed…

Cross Sections

Overture: Kadeko Orchestra

'Perfect Formations' by The Berliner Girls

A Living Sculpture: 'The Rhein Maidens!'

A Bavarian Flower Song.

Comedy Skit: 'The University Professors,
* the Way They Shouldn't Be!'*

Juggling Acrobats from Vienna

Finale: The Berliner Girls, Honoring
Our Men at the Front.

Between each act, the house orchestra promised lively arrangements from its own conductor. Willy watched the musicians finding their seats in the shallow pit beyond the rail just in front of their table. As they began to tune their instruments a wave of applause swept across the theater. The stage was empty and Willy first looked up towards Goebbels' table assuming the crowd was acknowledging his presence. But the Reichsminister himself was clapping politely and staring passively toward the opposite side of the stage, over Willy's shoulder. Lise caught his eye and nodded for him to turn around.

On a platform at the left side of the stage, equal in height and prominence was another table. Standing in front, bowing with a ridiculous flourish, was Reichsmarshal Goering. He was accompanied by a group of high military officers dressed in formal blue, white, or black uniforms.

As Goering moved ponderously back to his chair, the applause subsided and as if on cue, the orchestra began its overture and the house lights dimmed.

A merry marching tune began as the curtain opened. A kickline of pale, young, blond girls, dressed in skimpy versions of Wehrmacht uniforms, paraded on to the stage from both wings, forming and reforming double lines and pinwheels, each new set-piece greeted by enthusiastic clapping and shouts from the audience. Near the end of the number, the girls formed a single line stretching the entire width of the stage and began to kick higher and higher, alternating legs, in perfect precision.

And as the music finished, a long deep drum roll started and an honor guard of girls carrying German flags marched to center stage. They stopped, clicked their heels, and the orchestra began to play the national anthem. Everyone leaped to their feet and began to sing, some saluting, some rigidly at attention, and others with hands over their hearts. The packed theater literally shook from the raised voices, drowning out the instruments.

Everyone's attention was focused on the stage, the girls, and the flags, but Willy, mouthing his words, stole a glance first to the right and then the left, curious about how the two famous men were responding. Would they sing louder, stand taller, or somehow glow in this patriotic fervor? Both stood rigidly, arms raised in salute, but Willy could see that the two men were staring over the audience at each other. In Willy's imagination he sensed hostility or at least, mutual disdain. As the anthem ended on a crescendo, the audience broke into applause and the lights came up. Now the two dignitaries were all smiles, bowing to the audience and to each other.

As Willy sat in his chair amidst the loud babbling of five hundred voices, he needed time to consider what he'd witnessed. For the first time since Willy arrived, Nazi Germany had a face, or rather two faces. Clear thinking wasn't possible though, as the music started again. Lise hadn't seen the same thing and Willy wanted to share his observation, but too many strangers were too close to risk anything but the most innocuous conversation.

After a duet by a young couple dressed in lederhosen in front of a poorly painted backdrop of the Bavarian Alps, the orchestra began to play a more modern piece. The arrangement sounded symphonic but Willy suddenly recognized the melody as one by an American Negro, Fats Waller, probably arranged to escape Goebbel's orders banning jazz and Africanized music. The Reichsminister was ignoring the music, chatting amiably with his lady companion, showing no sign that he either approved or disapproved of this version.

Willy wondered whether this rendition of "Ain't Misbehavin" was some sort of quiet, subtle protest in favor of artistic freedom by the musicians or the club owners themselves. But this was wartime Nazi Germany in the spring of 1940. The Nazis were at the peak of power and support by the German people. Willy couldn't imagine that anyone would dare challenge or mock a Reichsminister and a Reichsmarshal to their faces, even in decadent and irreverent Berlin. But if Willy could find a way to believe there existed some germ of resistance left in this country, he might feel more hopeful.

If Germany's armies couldn't be defeated in the field or its airplanes in the skies, what good would it do for Willy and Lise to try to disrupt work at the Institute. Delay, waiting for what? He started to sense his own fear rising again from somewhere in the back of his consciousness. Everything was against them, this entire, unified nation, its scientists and industry, and time, most of all time. If the war lasted four years, the Nazis would have an atomic bomb. Even Willy, the amateur physicist, could see what was possible. Heisenberg's reluctance meant less than nothing, even if it did exist.

Willy began to consider how he would tell Lise that he now believed they were on a fool's errand and that they should return to Munich and keep out of sight, leaving history to history makers.

But Willy's mind changed again during the skit that followed. Entitled, *University Professors, the Way They Shouldn't Be*, it was acted by comedians in frizzy wigs, starched collars, and frock coats so saturated in chalk dust that they threw up great clouds at the slightest movement. One professor had all the bad ideas which he offered with a lisp and painfully convoluted logic. The other professor just babbled incoherently, his voice rising and falling as he made statements and asked questions speaking in some fake language called *Manganese*. The ministry official from whom they were seeking support was calm, patient, and totally rational, pointing out the flaws in their ideas and trying to steer them towards research that would serve the war effort more directly.

Among a half dozen bizarre proposals, one professor wanted to enhance the libido of worms so they'd produce more silk for parachutes and ladies' stockings. He also wanted to produce rubber bullets that bounce back to be used again. On the surface it seemed clear that in the skit the ministry man represented the new Germany, rational, clear thinking, cultivated, and focused. The eccentric academics were part of the old German, wasteful, undirected, quaint, and useless, heads full of theories and impractical conjecture.

But as proposals continued to fly, Willy came to appreciate that the friendliest audience response was reserved for the old professors. The audience on the whole seemed sympathetic and comfortable with the funny old men, who in a deeper truth, also represented some former time. As the ministry man gently chided the old gentlemen, Willy could actually hear quiet booing from several places in the room.

Willy stole another look at Goebbels. Though the lights were dim, he certainly wasn't laughing with the audience. He was staring bullets at the actors, who were so close that they couldn't have been unaware of Goebbels' reaction.

The skit rolled to an uneven end, but as the actors stood and faced the audience and took their bows, it was apparent that the ministry man was a distinctly unpopular character, with the heartiest cheers for the actors portraying the professors.

It was such a little thing. Maybe nothing. Not much of a seed for hope, but perhaps in laughter there was an opportunity for people, even this cross-section of Berlin's elite, to express discontent or at least discomfort with the inhumanity of the party's *rational man*. It mirrored Willy's own discomfort with cold scientific logic as it contrasted inevitably with the harmonious beauty of nature.

Now as he watched the remainder of the revue, he was seeing it quite differently. He watched the faces of the dancers, beyond their identical costumes and makeup. Some were small, others tall, some smiled sincerely, while others looked bored or just plain lost. Some of the girls were unstylishly skinny and others almost plump. But every one of them was different, just like the people in the audience. And if they were different from each other, then they were different from their leaders, like the two who sat swilling champagne at opposite ends of the stage, while their soldiers were fighting and dying in Poland and Norway. The two leaders had given Willy the hint and the small hope that they weren't perfectly in step, anymore than *The Berliner Girls*.

For an hour, Lise had watched over Willy's shoulder as he worked on his original American passport, using a powerful magnifying glass clamped to the electric table lamp. The work was delicate and tedious. Willy had no pretensions that he could produce a true forgery; he lacked the artistic skills and fine-pointed tools needed to form entire letters. He was working with chemicals they'd brought from the lab in small vials. Solvent to raise the original ink, permanganate to oxidize its residues, and hypochlorite to bleach the paper back to the proper shade.

Willy and Lise had returned to the *Schwarzes Ferkel* for a second evening, with no sign of Gardner or anyone else from the embassy. But the restaurant was again filled with government and military officials from the War Ministry just down the street. They ate quickly and took the *U-Bahn* back to their hotel. Tomorrow they would take a local train to Dahlem. A discrete telephone call from the *Bahnhof* had reserved a room at a *Gasthaus* in a nearby village, under the name *Beters*.

An air raid blackout was in effect and the curtains were drawn, but Willy had opened the windows to disperse the chemical smells from his work.

Willy had practiced back in Munich but hadn't dared to make a test on the passport's lettering, lest some casual challenge on the train alert a sharp-eyed policeman. Confident he could restore the paper's original appearance, he didn't trust himself to experiment with any lettering. He knew he'd have just one chance to do it right. Willy realized that any expert using a simple ultraviolet light source would detect his modifications instantly, but it wasn't their intent to fool the police or Gestapo. Hopefully the passport would only have to pass muster at the *Gasthaus* near the Institute in Dahlem, where in compliance with German regulations, foreign passports were held by the hotel or inn for the duration of the visit.

While waiting for chemicals and inks to dry, Willy stood to stretch and walked to the bedside where Lise was lying awake in near darkness. She reached out with her hand to draw him down next to her and their fingers twisted and laced together. Willy knelt on the floor next to the bed, staring into her eyes. In the dim light his eyes were tired and sad.

"Almost finished?" she asked quietly.

"Another hour, I think."

"Is it working well?"

"Better than I had thought, but I have to be very careful. My hands are not as steady as I'd like. I guess I haven't slept very well for the last few nights."

"Take your time. Perhaps you should rest for awhile. Is there anything I can do?"

"No…thank you." They were silent for several minutes. Willy kept glancing away and then back as if he was unsure whether she'd still be there when he looked again.

"Willy, what are you thinking? Are you worried?"

"Of course. Even scared. But not about tomorrow. I'm not sure my imagination is vivid enough to worry about what will happen tomorrow night. It's after that. Somehow as I sit over there defacing my old passport, I sense an end is near. Lise, with everything else that's happened, we were always able to duck back into our own private world and if we kept our heads low, nothing happened to remind us about the chances we'd taken and how scared we were. At least how scared I was!" he smiled ruefully. "You're a lot braver than me."

"Don't joke…"

"Oh, I know the truth. But now I'm doing something that represents evidence of a sort, something irrefutable and undeniable. Whether the Gestapo has the passport or whether it's in my pocket, it's proof that I'm a state enemy. And everyone around me is an enemy by implication, including you and your father, Frau Erna, Rudi, Walther, and on and on. When I lifted the very first letter on my passport, it's almost as if a narrow, dark tunnel has opened in front of me. There's no going back, there's no way to stop, and no where to turn aside."

"It's fate. It's always fate."

"I don't know. I always connected fate to some ultimate end late in life. When you're young it's luck, not fate. At least that's the way I've always looked at it…until now."

"Perhaps luck is something always considered in hindsight. Fate is in front of us, never behind."

"But I refuse to believe that everything that's happened has been fated, each event foretold and contingent on the one before." Willy began to chuckle. "Maybe I'm finally starting to understand Professor Heisenberg's *Uncertainty Principle*. There has to be an allowance for coincidence and accident."

"I understand what you're saying, but maybe fate and inevitability come from inside us. It's not events or other people who shape what happens, but what's in our minds and hearts. And that's shaped by how we're raised from babies, by our parents, and the things we experience as children.

"Willy, what you've done was inevitable because of the kind of person you are. Good people do good things. Strong people take strong action. Caring people attack inhumanity. Capable people get things done. Brave people act courageously." Lise reached up and touched his face.

"You are the best and bravest man in the world. I would feel safe going anywhere with you, any time."

"You have to say that right now," Willy laughed. "Look where I've brought you."

"You always joke about serious things. It's so difficult to talk to you about personal things," she said, with rising frustration.

"I'm sorry, Lise. It's just my way to avoid scary things."

"And what's so scary about me?" she sat up abruptly.

"It's what you might say."

"You don't want me to say that I love you?" she challenged.

"Too late now."

"What?"

"You just said it."

"What?"

"That you love me."

"Well, I guess I did, didn't I. I can always take it back, you know."

"No you can't."

"You're teasing me."

"Yes, I am."

"Well, you're a bastard, too."

"I love you, Lise."

"So there it is at last. But you're still a bastard." She wrapped both arms around his neck and wrestled him down on her bed.

Max Planck Institute – Dahlem

It didn't begin well. Instead of a sleepy porter, Willy counted two armed guards who appeared to be quite alert. The ornamental gates were swung wide but a wooden vehicle barrier had been erected. Its gate was down. Beyond the new guard shack, the Institute's buildings were dark and vacant but the grounds in front were brightly lit with floods mounted on tall poles. Much had changed in two weeks.

Willy and Lise worked their way around the wall out of sight of the front gate. When he chinned himself up and peered over the top of the wall, he could see that a metal link fence, topped with razor wire, was being installed all long the inside parameter of the grounds, invisible from the road outside. Reels of wire and fencing, shovels, and other tools were spread all over the grounds and luckily there were still gaps in the fence. Willy noted insulators mounted along the fence top. It would soon be electrified. He dropped back down to the ground. Though he couldn't see Lise in the darkness, he could feel her questions. This was not what he'd described to her.

During the long hike from the village of Ullem, they had kept to the shadows and had not spoken more than a few words. Fortunately blackout rules had doused the streetlights and gasoline rationing was keeping most people close to home. Lise and Willy were both anxious about their mission and self-conscious about the previous night. The darkness only accentuated these feelings.

And now as he crouched at the foot of the wall, his mind was in turmoil. Suddenly his *prank* had become very dangerous. At the same time, it was obvious that the German Army must now consider the Institute's work to be very important if the new experimental pile was to be closely guarded. Any hope he had of being branded a curious interloper if caught evaporated. If they went through with this and were captured, he'd be executed as a spy and Lise as a traitor.

Willy was prepared to accept the risk but there was Lise to think about. She'd helped him arrange everything from the beginning. Willy didn't believe he could withstand any sort of beating of the kind he'd witnessed in the streets of Munich; nor could he resist the truth drugs the Gestapo had shown they would use. He would confess inevitably and it would all spill out. Professor Wagner could no longer protect his daughter and he would die if Lise weren't there to care for him. The image of Lise, tortured like her sister, made Willy tremble. His eyes misted, and for the first time he knew mortal fear, the kind not balanced or overcome by exhilaration.

"It looks okay," he whispered. "Wait here. Give me one hour. After that, you must start for the station in Grunewald. Just go. If I'm delayed, I'll catch up with you there or in Potsdam. Remember the plan. Stick to the plan. Promise me."

"I'll be right here." She squeaked nervously. He could barely hear her voice.

"Lise, please follow the plan. One hour and then go. Don't wait a minute longer. Promise."

"Just hurry. Don't waste time. Please be careful. I love you, Willy. Hurry." Her hands groped in the darkness, feeling for his face. She took it in both hands, pulled him down, and kissed him clumsily on the cheeks and lips. "Go!"

Willy was so tense and excited that he nearly threw himself up and over the wall and rather than drop stealthily, he crashed noisily to the ground on the other side. He fought with himself to remain still for a moment, then raising himself he looked around the grounds. He could see the rear of the guard shack and the lights over the front gate, but he couldn't discern any movement there. *Quiet*, he ordered himself. On hands and knees he scrambled along a cobbled path leading to the garden pavilion. He tried to keep low using the spring flowers as cover and banged his kneecaps repeatedly on the uneven stones. Willy headed towards the back of the pavilion where he hoped to find an open window out of view from the gate. He was lucky.

The window was high above the ground, but for once Willy's height was an advantage. He was able to stretch up and try the window. It was unlocked and tilted up easily and quietly. He waited for several minutes listening for any sounds coming from inside. But outside noises from insects and the night breeze masked them completely. Even Willy wasn't tall enough to see in through the window, but the room appeared to be unlit. He vaguely recalled long rows of old potting tables inside beneath these windows.

With his arms above his head he grasped the sill and jumped, hauling himself up so that he was balanced half way in with the sill against his stomach. The room was completely dark. Again he listened for warning sounds, but this time couldn't hear anything over the sound of this own panting.

He freed one hand and reached down, feeling to see whether there was anything below the window. Willy found what seemed to be a bench top and as he felt around, his hand touched tools, stray pieces of electrical wire, and loose papers.

Reaching to the far edge of the table, he grabbed it with one hand and as slowly as possible he started to pull the trunk of his body through the window. He was successful to the point where he had to draw in his long legs and almost curl up on the bench top. The bench top was cluttered with equipment and tools and he was startled when the first item fell off the bench on to the concrete floor with a clang. Willy was sure that the guards at the front gate could hear the racket and he froze lest the first noise be followed by a second. Sharp items on the bench top were poking into his ribs, forearms, and thighs.

He tried counting the seconds afraid he'd lose track of how long he was waiting but was distracted by the pain and the need to concentrate on keeping perfectly still. When he couldn't stand it any longer, he slowly began to rotate himself around so that he could drop his legs over the edge of the bench top. He reached down with his hand to try and find objects his legs might sweep off onto the floor. As he located items he reached over and placed them carefully behind his legs. But he didn't find them all and twice more something fell to the floor, luckily with more thump than crash.

At last Willy found himself sitting upright on the edge of the bench top looking around at the unlit room. The only light seemed to come from the high windows and skylights. The contrast of light and dark was so dramatic, it seemed impossible that no one had spotted him as he had sneaked across the garden from the trees near the wall.

Quiet. Hurry.

First the electrical conductance meter. He'd marked the type and model when Herr Abele had given the tour. Professor Wagner's lab had the identical equipment and Willy had practiced for days until he could disassemble the device in the dark. Willy looked around and decided he could light his small candle. Against the bright lights outside, no one would see its glow through the high windows. Carefully shielding the flare, he stuck a match and touched the wick. He looked around the room and was reassured that the shadows cast were diffuse and would be blocked by his body as he worked on the meter box. A green indicator light showed that the meter was on and Willy noted the dial reading and checked its settings before he switched it off.

He had replacement components in his pocket and with the aid of a screwdriver, in five minutes he had removed the meter's cover and substituted resistors he'd cannibalized from the meter in Munich. When the cover was back in place, the meter would no longer properly measure the conductance of the heavy water. Until it was recalibrated, any contamination Willy spiked into the heavy water supply would go undetected.

On his tour the previous week he'd noticed a series of three calibration solutions in five-liter glass bottles neatly arranged on a nearby shelf. Each was labeled with its specific concentration of carefully prepared solutions. Small quantities would be poured out into a beaker whenever the conductance meter required calibration. When the meter probe was dunked into the beaker, the dials would be recalibrated to match the solution's known conductance. The three bottles contained solutions with standard conductances differing ten-fold, one low, one medium, and one with high conductance. During the routine calibration procedure, the meter's settings would be adjusted to match each of these three levels to make sure its response was linear.

Willy took the first bottle, the one with the lowest concentration and lowest conductance and dumped it in a nearby slop sink. Then he transferred the solution from the second bottle into the first, and the third into the second. Into the third he shook a small vial of crystals from his pocket and then carefully refilled this last bottle to the top with distilled water from a nearby carboy, shaking the last bottle to help dissolve the salt crystals.

When the meter was recalibrated, each adjustment point would be off by a factor of ten, the same range of modification he'd introduced to the meter's wiring. Now any contamination of the pile's heavy water supply would go unnoticed, at least until the calibration solutions were routinely replace. Hopefully the bottles would last for several months.

The giant containment tank had been fully assembled and Willy walked completely around it in the faint candlelight. He could hear a small pump running somewhere inside, probably circulating and filtering cooling water. It appeared that the tank and pile were already active. They hadn't wasted any time. He had planned to add boron salts to contaminate the heavy water storage drums but the active pile was more important. *Hurry!*

It took all his strength to lift the heavy metal cover atop the tank just a crack. Centered inside was an inner cylinder that appeared to be aluminum. Between the inner and outer walls was a pool of water nearly two feet deep, filling the tank halfway. A frame had been built over the tank for a chain hoist that would attach to four eyebolts positioned around the circumference of the lid. Willy needed only to lift the lid far enough to sprinkle finely ground boron powder widely across surface of the heavy water contained within the inner cylinder. The water was cold and if he dumped the crystals all at one point they might not dissolve completely by the time the tank was reopened. If there was obvious contamination, then someone would immediately check the conductance meter and nothing would have been achieved.

There wasn't time to attach and operate the hoist and, in any case, Willy was sure it would make too much noise. Standing on a brick step that ran all around the tank, Willy could get some purchase on the rolled edge of the lid. He found a two foot-long, solid wooden plank underneath a nearby work bench and set it beside his point of attack. He was just tall enough to stand on the step, reach down, and have sufficient leverage to lift the lid about eight inches. With another effort, he raised the lid several more inches and propping the lid with his knee, he reached down and shoved the plank in the gap. The round lid was balanced very precariously over an eighteen inch opening. He pulled a small glassine packet from his pocket and bent down with his head and right arm extended far inside the tank. Teetering precariously over the pool of water across the gap between the inner and outer cylinders, Willy stretched out and carefully distributed the dusty powder on the surface of the heavy water inside. Very little light shown in the tank from the windows or candle and Willy could only imagine the uranium oxide bricks piled in the center just under the surface of the heavy water and the neutron source inside its core.

He listened for the fall of the crystals on the water, for the fizzy effervescence he knew was a sign the crystals were dissolving, but with his head inside the tank, the throb of the circulation pump was more distinct. When he finished he pulled his trunk and head back out and was stepping down when a key rattled in the metal door latch. It was like a church bell.

Trapped. Cornered. Lise would be caught and hurt. He had only seconds before the door would swing open. From the door, even in the dim light, anyone would be able to see the open tank lid. If he tried to close it too quickly, the lid would clang an alarm. He grabbed the candle, extinguishing the flame in the palm of his hand and with no forethought, except to hide, he turned around and squeezed himself through the tight gap, into the tank. To lower the lid noiselessly, Willy twisted around and slipped backwards. The water was up to his knees and felt very cold. Completely inside the tank, he braced his bent back against the lid, pushed it up slightly to free the wooded prop, and slowly bent his back and knees to close the lid over himself and the tank. The wooden plank fell into the water with a faint splash.

With the lid shut, there was no light at all, and the pump roared like an automobile engine. But over the pump noise, he could feel the reverberations as someone opened the heavy door, entered, and slammed the door shut behind him. Willy couldn't hear anything else. He assumed a guard was in the pile room but could hear neither voices nor footsteps. He could only wait until he heard the door open and shut again. *What if the guard came in to sleep?* he asked himself.

Willy was bowed almost double in the tank, with his knees slightly bent. The water had quickly soaked his shoes and he could feel cold water wicking up his trousers toward his crotch. He felt with his fingers for some edge to grasp, to take some load off his lower back, but the inside wall of the tank was smooth as glass. He considered for a moment about twisting around and kneeling down. Then only his shoulders and head would be above the water. It was frigid but he didn't know how much longer he could stand bent over like this. How long did he dare wait?

Only then did the significance of the tank and its contents strike him. If the uranium pile and its neutron source were installed, the tank was radioactive and Willy was exposed every second he remained. He'd read horror stories about the slow, agonizing deaths of old-time radium researchers. As this new realization and fear built, Willy almost raised up in panic, throwing off the metal cover. But he had to wait. If the tank and its contents were dangerous, it was only to Willy. If he gave himself up to the guards, they would arrest Lise. His fears for her were greater than any he had for himself. As he slowly turned to kneel down, he trembled and almost screamed out loud. Willy could actually see a dark blue light faintly emanating from the center of the tank, *a light no other human had ever seen*.

As suddenly as before, he thought he heard the door open and then clang shut. The guard had left. Willy wouldn't allow himself to consider any other possibility. Desperate to escape the radiation, Willy turned back around, and plunged his hand into the water, fishing and splashing for the fallen plank. He knew it must be his imagination but the water now felt warm on his hands and arms. Totally disoriented, the plank might be anywhere in the tank. When he finally found it floating near the center, Willy felt an hour had passed.

He moved to an edge and pressing his back and shoulder against the lid, stood up. When the lid was high enough he replaced the prop and slithered out of the tank falling headfirst over the edge of the retaining wall and onto the brick step. There he lay on his back for several minutes, his heart pounding, gasping for air like a man nearly drowned. Any moment he expected the guard to return and he could not resist or escape a second time. Willy closed his eyes and let a few more minutes pass, his heartbeat finally slowing. He sat up with a start. *How long in the tank?* It was too dark to read his watch. His candle stub was in his pocket, but he knew his matches were soaked and useless. Willy stood and moved to the nearest window on the front side of the pavilion. He closed his eyes for a moment to adjust faster to the low light. *Shit*. It had been almost an hour since he'd climbed over the wall. He had to finish and get out before Lise started off on her own. As much as he had insisted she adhere to their plan and head for Grunewald, he hoped in his heart that she would give him some extra time. Willy didn't want to be on his own. He wanted her close, forever.

He went back to the front of the tank, removed the wooden prop and returned it to the bench shelf where he'd found it. He could only hope it would be dry enough in the morning that no one would notice. With that prompting, he realized that he'd been dripping water all over the floor in front of the tank and over towards the front window. In the dark, he felt the floor with his hands and located several separate puddles. Feeling along the bench tops, Willy tried to find rags or towels. Perhaps he could use his shirt, which was at least partly dry. But he needed to wait until just when he was leaving and then try to clean up the wet footprints he'd leave on his way to the open window. *Okay, that will work.*

He paused to check the conductance meter one last time. He switched it back on, the green indicator lit and he waited for a minute while the dial reading settled down. *Fuck.* The dial reading was perfect. Anyone comparing data points would not be alerted by a variation from the previous notation. It would have to be enough. He had more boron crystals in his pockets but they were certainly now wet and partially dissolved. The storage drums were safe from him.

The second time, the sound of the latchkey seemed even louder and before he could react, the door cracked open letting in a long shaft of bright light. All Willy could do was to duck down behind and under the rim of the tank, crawling desperately around to the side opposite the door. As he crouched, holding his breath, the overhead lamps were switched on and the room was flooded with light. He blinked and tried to look away. The light seemed to hurt physically. Though he knew better, it felt hot.

He could hear footsteps advancing from the electrical panel near the door and as they reached the tank area, Willy realized that someone was humming a tune, in a low tone, like a man. As he listened, the steps seemed to move from table to table along the wall and Willy scuttled further around the round tank trying to keep it between him and the footsteps. The man must now be near the conductance meter. *He's checking the readings*, Willy thought. *When he's done, he'll leave.*

"*Scheisse*," the man moaned. "The damn tank's leaking," he mumbled to himself. He'd seen the water on the floor. Steps started around the tank, and in a panic Willy knew the man was following the trail of water from his wet pants and shoes. He was cornered like a rat.

Willy leapt forward with his hands extending towards the man's throat. Defensively, the man tried to push him away and then began to punch Willy's chest and stomach. To avoid the punches Willy twisted the man's neck with his hand and the man's body followed until Willy could reposition himself behind. The man was trying to swing back around and was wildly throwing his elbows. Releasing one hand for just an instant Willy was able to get the man's throat into the crook of his elbow. He could then move his other hand to the man's forehead twisting it to counteract the man's attempts to swing back around.

Willy squeezed and squeezed, consciously not wanting to kill him but desperate to keep him quiet. Gradually the man's struggle began to wane, but Willy continued to crush him tightly in case he was faking. Willy's arm ached and at last he began to slowly relax his hold, alert every second for any attempt by the man to run or renew an attack. The man was still. And as he began to relax Willy realized that he was bearing all the man's bulk. He released his hold around the man's throat and lowered him slowly to the floor.

Is he dead? He tried to check for breathing and for a pulse but his own rasping was so loud and heartbeat so fast that he couldn't concentrate. Willy slumped against the tank wall staring at the man lying in a heap next to him.

What should he do now? If alive, the man had surely seen Willy's face. Willy should get out as quickly as possible and get far away from the Institute. In their naïve scheme, Lise and Willy hadn't allowed for the necessity to hide or escape: anonymity was all they'd sought. Whether this man was dead or alive, they were now fugitives and when the man's body was found, the police and Gestapo would spare no effort to apprehend the intruder and any accomplices. Every choice he made from this point on meant life and death for himself, for Lise, and for her father. But at this moment he couldn't seem to catch his breath, he was panting so hard he was beginning to get dizzy. He closed his eyes and concentrated on slowing his breathing.

When he opened his eyes, the pavilion room seemed much more distinct. He was regaining some control. Staring again at the man lying next to him, he couldn't clearly recall their struggle. It was almost as if Willy had gone to sleep and was now reawakening hours after the fight. He panicked for a moment at the thought that perhaps he *had* passed out, but a glance at his wristwatch told him that only ten minutes had passed since he first prepared to leave.

His attention went back to the man and as Willy watched, he thought he could see the man's chest rising and falling slowing. He struggled to his hands and knees and crawled over to the man's side. He put his hand on the man's shirtfront and within a few moments was convinced the man was breathing and was still alive. If he revived their struggle would start again and Willy couldn't fight anymore. He needed to immobilize the man before he came to. He hadn't brought any rope. It was difficult to think. Wire! There were pieces of electrical wire on the bench and he'd knocked some of them on to the floor when he first climbed in the window.

Still on his hands and knees he crept back to the bench area. Standing, he searched around the bench top and quickly located several pieces of wire. Willy discarded several pieces aside that were too short to be useful, but after several tries Willy had collected three wire sections each about a meter long. Two were small diameter, but the third was thicker and stronger.

He made his way back across the large room to the tank. Now Willy could absorb more detail. The man was not very big and had sparse gray hair and a prominent moustache and bushy eyebrows. He was wearing a dark blue work jacket and work boots. Not a guard or policeman. Probably not a scientist. Most likely a lab technician or mechanic. Willy was certain he did not recognized the man from his visit two weeks before.

The man must be working the graveyard shift monitoring experiments and equipment. He was probably working alone and had come to take hourly measurements: to read the conductance meter and check coolant temperatures. If someone else was also on duty tonight, Willy might not have much time before this man was missed and someone came looking for him.

Willy bent down and rolled the man over on to his stomach, intending to tie his hands behind his back with the heavy wire like in the movies. But when he rolled him over, the man's right arm got trapped underneath him and Willy had to lift him bodily to free the arm. He began to twist the wire tightly around one of the man's wrists, then paused, realizing that he would completely cut off blood circulation to his hands and fingers. So Willy more carefully tied a slipknot forming a bracelet which was smaller than the man's hand but relatively loose on his wrist. He then looped it several times around the other wrist and anchored it with a crude knot around the strands between the wrists. When finished he stood looking dully at the bindings trying to imagine whether the man would be able to free himself. At the last moment Willy bent down again and used a length of smaller wire to bind the man's ankles together.

Willy knew he couldn't leave the man lying in the middle of the floor. If a guard returned on his rounds, there'd be no doubt that something serious was afoot and a general alarm would be sounded. So he grabbed the man's boots and dragged him around in back of the tank. Bumping into furniture and equipment, Willy managed to haul the lab technician to a point behind the tank where he couldn't be seen from the outside door or any of the windows.

If the man awoke, Willy thought, he can still cry out. Willy took his own handkerchief from his pocket and stuffed it into the man's mouth.

Willy returned and carefully and quietly locked the door to the outside. He switched off the lights and hurried back to the open window.

Local

When he dropped back over the wall, Willy was disoriented, his vision blurred and tunneling from exertion and fear. He'd clung to the hope that Lise would be waiting for him on the far side of the wall, but when he hit the ground he was alone in the dark. He listened to see if she was calling quietly from somewhere nearby – she surely could have seen him silhouetted at the top of the wall by the floodlights shining within the enclosed grounds – but he was gasping so loudly that he could neither hear nor concentrate.

He slumped down with his back against the wall. With fits and starts he finally began to breath more regularly and could focus long enough to look up at the stars and then towards the road. As he adjusted again to the darkness, he could begin to discern shadows and outlines of buildings and houses opposite the institute. Despite the blackout, he could see faint streams of light filtering through shutters and curtains: the homes of local people, farmers and the like, who rise early every morning.

Willy had climbed back over the wrong wall, one facing the main road rather than the alley along the left side. Fortunately no one was driving along the road or putting out the cat at the instant he'd hesitated at the top of the wall, else an alarm would have been given before he managed to find Lise and flee. It wouldn't be long before some of these people began to stir around outside: sunrise was only an hour away.

The alley where she might still be waiting was to the north, his right, so he crept along the wall, crouching and staying in the deepest shadow at its base. At the corner he peered down the alleyway. Darkness was total, except for the upper branches of trees standing tall along and above the wall, illuminated eerily by lights inside the compound.

Willy hurried down the center of the gravel track, aware of the crunching noise he made, but anxious to find Lise, if she was still there, and be far from the Institute before the sun rose. When he reached a point near where he thought he'd first scaled the wall, he slowed and turned toward the shrubs where he had told Lise to wait. He stopped once to listen and was about to whisper her name when something struck him hard and high in the middle of his back, knocking him to his knees. He only had time to think, *guard*, before someone grabbed him roughly around the neck and began to throttle him with a forearm across his throat. His attacker was like a wolf, shaking his prey, trying to break its neck, not satisfied with strangulation. Willy tried to twist around to face the attacker, but the hold tightened even more. He felt his breath running out and in desperation he pitched forward on his hands and knees, bringing the attacker's weight full on his back. Then he pushed with his feet and rolled heels over head, trapping the attacker between his back and the ground. When his weight came down on the attacker, Willy heard a grunt as the wind was knocked out of the attacker's lungs. The stranglehold was loosened just enough for Willy to twist around. And when he faced the attacker at last, he pushed away violently with his hands and groped for the attacker's throat. It was kill or be killed. The attacker was pushing and punching with his hands, his fingers trying to find Willy's face and eyes.

He found the neck but as his fingers squeezed, the neck was very thin; his hand went around it easily, unlike the technician's stout neck. It had to be Lise struggling and fighting underneath him. He moved his hands to her shoulders and held them down to restrain her flaying arms and fingernails.

"Lise! It's me! It's me! Stop it! Please, stop it!" he croaked. She was still fighting and trying now to kick him in the groin with her knee, but even when she relented, it wasn't sudden, but almost reluctantly.

"Get off me. Get off me," she whispered harshly. Willy rolled on to his back next to her, for the third time in ten minutes, breathless. But she wasn't done. Lise rolled over and straddled his hips and without warning started to pound on his chest with her closed fists.

"You ass! Pig! Are you crazy? Why did you sneak up on me like that?" she demanded angrily, but the pounding stopped. Then like a switch, anger was concern.

"Are you all right? Did I hurt you?" she fell on his chest, cradled his head, and began to search for his lips with hers. She kissed him again and again, losing his lips and finding them again. "I'm sorry. I'm sorry.

I was so scared. You'd been in there too long. I was watching the top of the wall and heard someone coming. I thought it must be a watchman. I only had a broken tree limb but I didn't want him to see you climb back over. He might have had a whistle or bell." Now she was sobbing and Willy felt the first tears dripping onto his face.

"Quiet. It's all right. It's all right. But you must keep it down. Someone will hear you." She stopped talking but her hard breathing and intermittent sobs sounded like a roaring crowd so close to his ear. He held her still with his arms and kissed her cheek. She was trembling, or rather they were both trembling violently together. As they lay quietly, both began to calm down. Willy could listen and there were no signs that anyone had heard them or was stirring nearby. He closed his eyes to help clear his head. He could hear Lise's breathing, almost regular now. And he could hear birds begin to chirp and sing. This was an alarm for Willy and with a start, he was reminded where they were and the danger so near. The sky above the eastern horizon was starting to brighten.

"Lise. Lise. We've got to get going. It will be light soon. We need to get as far away from here as possible."

"Yes, I'm sorry, you're right," she said rolling off to the side and sitting up. Willy could just start to make out her outline against the darkness under the trees beyond. Willy got to his shakily to his feet, and searched out with his hand to help her up. They embraced and kissed again.

"Where's our bag?"

"Under the tree. I'll get it."

"Let's go. It's ten kilometers to the station at Grunewald; the local train to Potsdam leaves at eight o'clock." Willy took the rucksack from Lise and slung it over his shoulder. They passed down the alley, paused for a moment to check for road traffic and began to walk quickly down the road to the north, sticking to the far shoulder under the overhanging trees. After five minutes they were able to cut down a lonely side road and could walk more openly breaking into a trot where the road was open or when their nervousness took control.

Willy wondered how long it might be before the technician's body was discovered. The original plan to poison the uranium pile would not have been uncovered for weeks, perhaps for months. They could have strolled away calmly and with little fear of being challenged. But things didn't go as planned. He had decided not to tell Lise about the technician or his own radiation exposure.

They had never talked frankly about what they would do once they were back on the train, though both had considered the options, many unhappy ones. But a decision point was coming, Willy knew, and now they must rush towards it. There was going to be little time for discussion or explanation. As he walked, his wet pants legs were cold despite the exertion. Willy tried to put it out of his mind. He didn't feel fear, but he understood clearly that if the radiation poisoning was at lethal levels, there was only one option open to him: get word out of Germany about the uranium project. No time for more secret letters, no time to try to find a contact in Germany he could trust and who would sneak word out.

He knew that people like Pierre and Marie Curie had lived for years after exposures to radiation from radium, but this was something new. The radiation had been intense enough to glow near his feet. *Don't think about it. Just walk. We've got to catch that train.*

When it was light enough to see, she asked, "Why are your pants and shoes wet?"

"I stepped in a fish pond in the garden." Willy's pants legs dried on the long walk, but his shoes were still squishy and when he let himself think about it, he imagined irrationally that somehow the water in his shoes was radioactive and that he was carrying that poison with him. He knew that it didn't work that way, but nonetheless, every step he took reminded him again of the steel tank, the blue light, and the decisions to come.

The local train to Potsdam from Grunewald was crowded with commuters and people on their way to the city for shopping and other errands. Jumping on the train at just the last moment, Willy and Lise had to stand most of the way. Willy knew that when he stood, people took notice of his height, but there wasn't much he could do about it. But there was a certain anonymity in the tight crowd that helped his state of mind. And Lise and Willy could stand close without necessarily appearing to be travelling together. Everyone was minding their own business and no one was so impolite as to stare in these close quarters.

During the fast hike to Grunewald station, Lise had asked Willy about what happened inside the Institute. He gave her all the details up to the point where he had to hide inside the tank, and of course, omitted the part about throttling the technician. He finished the story by saying that it had taken longer than he'd thought to rewire the resistors in the conductance meter and he had lost his way outside the garden laboratory and climbed back over the wrong wall. He hadn't seen or heard anyone, and had completed the job without leaving any traces behind.

"The closest I came to danger was when a crazed maniac, recently escaped from a Munich mental hospital, jumped me in the dark and nearly strangled me before I beat her off." Lise didn't smile, but turned her head and looked at him blankly.

"If the limb hadn't broken after the first swing, I would have beat you to death, before you could say a thing." Then she smiled faintly. "What would I have told Vati? Where's Willy Petersen, he'd ask? Oh so sorry, Vati. He was acting like an ass so I killed him. So you shut-up about it or it might still happen."

"Don't worry, I've learned my lesson. I'll wear a cowbell now whenever you're around, so you won't ever be surprised. I'm glad you didn't have a knife."

"You should be."

At Grunewald's tiny depot, they stepped up separately to the single ticket window, Lise bought two tickets for Berlin to the east and Willy two for Potsdam to the south and west, and they waited on the eastbound platform until just before the westbound train arrived. Though Willy sometimes acted on his urge to pace, Lise was quick to yank him back down to his seat, so fewer people might remember a nervous, tall, blond idiot.

After they arrived in Potsdam, they spent over an hour carefully covering their tracks by purchasing single tickets, all round-trips, to six different destinations: Berlin, Rostock, Frankfurt, Leipzig, Dresden and points between. Consulting the schedule, they had already agreed to head for Hamburg on the express train, which they could pick up further down the line. It would carry them away from Dahlem further and faster than any other train and it departed sooner than any others heading west or south. Still they had an hour before the connecting train would begin to board and were reluctant to hang around the station or platforms. It was mid-morning and with the early crowds thinned, it was much more difficult to avoid the ever-curious eyes of railroad policemen and even their fellow travelers.

They left the station and choosing a dusty road running parallel to the tracks, wandered along looking for some shady and deserted place to sit and wait until departure time. Half a mile up the road they found a small cluster of trees and a sad patch of grass beneath. Across the road was a row of vacant warehouses and beside the trees was chain link fence, topped with razor wire, to keep people out of the extensive marshaling yard beyond.

Lise tore up one of the remaining hard rolls and they took turns sipping warm water from the hiker's flask she pulled from the bag. The yard was busy. Shunting engines were pushing or pulling individual cars this way and that, breaking down arriving trains and assembling new ones. Besides passenger cars there were hundreds of boxcars, tankers, and flatbeds, many loaded with brand-new, gray-painted trucks, probably destined for the western front.

As Willy and Lise ate their meager lunch, an engine approached running very slowly along the rail spur closest to the fence, pulling three cattle cars, the type with slatted, ventilated sides and wide doors Willy knew from back home in Wisconsin. So his attention was drawn to the cars as they rolled slowly to a stop ten meters away. The engineers dropped the cars and sped off on another task. The first thing Willy noticed was the smell, a fetid and carrion odor, not the sweet perfume he associated with cows. Nor was it the less attractive smell of pigs or sheep, rather more like a backed-up sewer or an ancient *pissoir*. Lise was memorizing the railroad schedules, paying little attention to the train movements and noise beyond the fence, but she couldn't help noticing the smell.

"Whew! What's that?"

"I don't know. But it looks like these railcars are going to sit here for awhile. We'd best move. Anyway, it's almost time to get back to the station. If we take our time, we won't reach the platform too early." Willy rose as Lise leaned over to repack their bag. He stood with his back to the fence with his hands in his pockets, lingering in the shade for as long as he could stand the smell. He was surprised to hear a voice from right behind him.

"Hey, you! Excuse me, *mein Herr*! Please! Excuse me!" Willy turned and looked all around. No one was in sight. When the voice called again, it came from the middle of the three cattle cars.

"Excuse me, sir, excuse me," the voice repeated plaintively.

"Yes," Willy replied. Lise had picked up the bag and was standing next to him.

"Could you please tell me what place this is?" While the man's voice was polite, there was stress behind it. Willy could now see the man's face peeking out from between two broken slats near the middle of the car. Willy and Lise looked at each other equally mystified.

"This is Potsdam *Bahnhof*," Willy said. He turned to Lise and whispered, "Must be a deserter or someone running from conscription and hiding on the train." Then he noticed the heavy chain and lock on the sliding door.

"Potsdam? Potsdam. Potsdam. Yes, thank-you. And what is the day?"

"Today is Monday," Willy replied.

"I'm sorry. Excuse me. What is the *date*?"

"Monday, April the twenty-third."

"Monday the twenty-third. Yes, thank you."

"Who are you?" Lise shouted.

"Only a thirsty and hungry man," was the reply. "That's all that matters anymore...."

"We have a little food," she said quickly, looking up and down along the fence, "and would be glad to share, but there's no opening in the fence." She too had seen the padlock and chain.

"Yes, I can see. I'm afraid I'm locked in this car and can't come up to the fence," the man said sadly, "but I thank you for the generous offer."

"I'm sorry, too," Lise spoke softly, "Where are you going?"

"I don't know that either, I'm afraid. Eastward, it seems."

"Where are you from?" Willy asked trying to see the man's eyes. It was hard to read true feelings in just his voice.

"From Düsseldorf...of that I am sure," he answer with painful irony.

"How did you come to be in that car?" Willy questioned, genuinely wanting to understand.

"I suppose you could say I was born to end up in this car," he laughed enigmatically and then choked on a sob.

"Willy, we need to get to the station," Lise prompted quietly.

"Yes, I know," he said. He spoke to the car, "I'm sorry again that we can't help you, but we have to be going. We only stopped here for a moment."

"I understand. But if I might call on your kindness for one small thing," he plead.

"Yes, we will try."

"Could you contact my wife for me? Send her a little note. Her name is *Golda Weinstein*. My house is at number 25, *Gabelstrasse* in Düsseldorf. Just tell her that you saw me. And tell her that I love her."

"Yes, Golda Weinstein. *Gabelstrasse* 25 in Düsseldorf. Yes, I will remember."

"Thank you, sir, and you, Fräulein. It would mean so much to her. Sir, I wish I could shake your hand, but this is as close as I can get. Please accept the gesture." He squeezed his hand between the slats, but could only get his fingers and half his palm through the narrow crack. Without thinking, Willy extended his fingers as far as he could through the metal links of the chain fence.

But then miraculously, two, then a dozen, then a hundred fingers and hands began to squeeze between the slats. Some were the hands of children who managed to get their whole arm through, others like the first man, could only manage a few fingers. Fingers and hands appeared between the slats all along the sides of the other cars, too. Then another man's voice called out a name and address, *Lilith Koch, Frankfurterstrasse 61*. Then another and another, until there was a continuous murmur of names and addresses. Then as each competed to have Willy and Lise hear their name, the murmur became a rumble and then a roar.

Willy and Lise were overwhelmed and horrified at the same time, and backed away from the fence, stumbling over roots and broken paving stones, until they reached the road. Lise pressed her hands to her ears and moaned. Without looking back or speaking they began to hurry toward the *Bahnhof*, running most of the way.

In the bustle of the station and the crowded train, there were few chances to talk privately for several hours. They sat across and cattycorner from each other on facing seats. But it was obvious what they were both thinking about. Tears had come to Willy's eyes several times. He'd wipe them away, hoping Lise wouldn't notice. He'd be all right for a while, until suddenly they'd start to flow again. Several times he would catch Lise sobbing, trying to hold it back and not attract the attention of the other passengers.

"Who were those people, Willy?" She whispered when they were alone for a moment as other passengers disembarked.

"Jews."

"Where are they going?"

"The newspaper says displaced Jews are to be resettled peacefully in Poland."

"You don't believe that?"

"No, I don't. Your *Führer* wrote fifteen years ago how all Jews should be eradicated, wiped from the earth. I think that this is just the beginning. It's more than taking their jobs and stealing their property."

"Do you think Doctor Blum and Herr Rosenzweig, the jeweler, were taken and treated like that? They disappeared months ago. Both were wealthy and respected men, friends of my father since he was a boy. Do you think they'll be killed?"

"I don't know, Lise, I only fear." She was quiet for several minutes.

"Willy, please don't ever say again that he's *my Führer*. Please." She was very serious.

Dahlem

"Herr Major, local police have located a *Gasthaus* in the village of Ullem, ten kilometers from here. The owner says an American man booked a room by telephone two days ago. When he arrived Sunday morning, he was accompanied by a young woman. The owner believes she's German. The local police searched their room and found nothing suspicious, however the American paid for two nights and it appears that no one used the room last night. Their luggage is also gone. I asked the police to bring the owner here at once. Should arrive in ten minutes."

"Good. Send Sergeants Müller and Schmidt to the *Gasthaus*. I don't trust locals to conduct a proper search."

"Yes, Herr Major," Lieutenant Ziegler replied and hurried off with his orders.

An American, thought Major Frick. He knew that several thousand Americans remained in Germany after the war began, businessmen, diplomats, scholars, and students. While some might be harmless, the Gestapo believed they were all potential spies if not already active agents or provocateurs. Most were closely monitored by wiretaps and postal censors. Within the Gestapo's limited resources, high profile Americans were followed constantly. But with new demands in Czechoslovakia, Poland, Denmark, and now Norway, the Gestapo was spread thin. In many cases they were forced to rely on ineffective local policemen and untrained party members.

Perhaps he's just another sheepish American, taking in the countryside with some dancehall tart. But the timing was unlikely to be a coincidence. Gestapo Major Wolfgang Frick paced up and down the Institute's boardroom, which he'd commandeered. When a patrolling guard had discovered the unconscious technician, Gestapo headquarters in Berlin had been notified immediately. Before he'd been dispatched early this morning from Berlin, Reichsmarshal Himmler confronted Frick to personally reinforce the seriousness of the situation. Frick had jumped to his feet as the bespectacled little man appeared at the door to his office without warning.

"Major, I cannot emphasize how important it is that we find out who broke into the Physics Institute's laboratory. Who and why. I *will* tell you that this laboratory is engaged in weapons research of immeasurable value to the Reich. You are to apprehend the intruder, alive if possible. In the Führer's name, you have access to all the resources of the government. If they manage to elude you and escape the country, my advice is to return home and gather your family for prayer. Then shoot your wife and two children: young boys, aren't they? It will much less painful for them than piano wire. You understand your orders and the price of failure?"

"Yes, Herr Reichsmarshal," Frick replied, saluting stiff-armed as Himmler turned and strode out of the office.

During the car ride from Berlin to the Institute in Berlin-Dahlem, Frick fought to contain his emotions. Cold-blooded focus was required. If he rushed the investigation, some key clue might be missed. He had authority to stop the trains and close the borders. He could turn out the entire Army and SS if needed. But most important was to be clever and thoughtful. Files concerning the Institute he'd snatched up as he hurried from Gestapo Headquarters were incomplete but hinted about the many minefields that lay ahead.

By the time his investigative team arrived, they found the technician awake but still groggy and incoherent. Frick ordered two of his sergeants to interrogate the man thoroughly, and of course they understood precisely what that might involve. After thirty minutes, they reported back how the technician recalled little except how he'd been attacked by someone hiding in the pavilion laboratory. The man was tall and tried to strangle him. The intruder was a stranger as far as the technician could recall.

All the guards on duty that night had been arrested and sent by truck to Berlin for more *formal* questioning. Given that the technician was not discovered until nearly seven o'clock in the morning, three hours after he left his desk in the administration building to check meters in the pile room, the guards had been remiss or criminally negligent. It didn't matter which. The penalty was the same.

One of Frick's scientific officers came up and saluted. "Herr Major, we've been able to lift several sets of fresh fingerprints from a window jamb where the intruder entered. I've had a runner carry them to Berlin headquarters for comparison."

"Call Berlin and mention that the fingerprints might belong to an American. That should speed up their search."

"Yes, sir. Sir, we allowed scientists and technicians from the Institute back into the laboratory building. They've examined their equipment and supplies. Apparently nothing was taken or disturbed. The most important part of the apparatus is inside the large water tank protected by a heavy metal cover. Headman says all the real secrets are inside that tank. I watched him check some of their meters and instruments. He appears unconcerned."

"He is a fool. Berlin says the very existence of this equipment is a state secret of inestimable value," Major Frick said angrily. "Tell Lieutenant Meier that I want the entire staff of the Institute kept isolated in the main building until I say otherwise. Don't let them talk to each other or to anyone on the outside."

"They will protest, Herr Major," the scientific officer said with a smile.

"Good for them. At last perhaps, they will understand that Germany is at war."

Lieutenant Ziegler returned with an obese burgher trailing nervously behind, hat in hand. "Major, this is Herr Schwimmer, owner of the Gasthaus in Ullem. He's brought along his hotel register. Herr Schwimmer, this is Major Frick."

"Relax, Herr Schwimmer. I just have a few questions."

"Thank you, Major," the burgher said doubtfully.

"You told the police that an American man checked into your hotel yesterday. Describe him please."

"Very tall, Herr Major, maybe two hundred centimeters. Very thin and pale. Blond hair. Poorly dressed. Young, Herr Major. Perhaps twenty-five years old. Good German."

"His companion?"

"Young, Herr Major. Maybe eighteen. Very pretty. Clean, well dressed. Dark hair. When she spoke: a Bavarian accent, definitely southern in any case."

"Their deportment?"

"Nervous, Herr Major. But honestly, they appeared to be young people sneaking off for romance. Perhaps it was their first time together," the innkeeper shrugged and grinned lecherously. "But a dangerous look on Frick's face wiped it away.

"Did she have a name? Did the American call her by name?"

"No, Herr Major. Not that I heard."

"The American's name?"

Schwimmer referred to his register. "William Beters, Herr Major."

"Where's his passport?"

"I don't have it, Herr Major. He said he was going to visit the foreign ministry in Berlin today, leaving early, so I returned it to him last night. It is allowed, Herr Major," Herr Schwimmer offered, frightened he'd run afoul of some new regulation. "I did copy the passport number and other details for my records. They're here in the register." He passed it over to Frick and pointed with a fat finger.

"And last night, Herr Schwimmer? No one saw them leave last night or early this morning?" Ziegler prompted.

"No sir. And when I checked this morning, the room was apparently not used last night. Herr Betters paid for two nights in advance."

"Thank you, Herr Schwimmer," Frick said courteously returning the thick bound book. Herr Schwimmer bowed his way out the door mumbling, "Yes, Herr Major. Thank you, Herr Major."

"One more thing, Herr Schwimmer," the Major stopped him cold. "Did the American have a car? Bicycles?"

"No, Herr Major, I didn't see a car. Yesterday I saw them arrive at the hotel on foot probably from the rail station." Frick nodded dismissively and turned to his aide.

"Ziegler, send these details to Berlin. If this is our man, the passport information is probably false. Write up a description of the American and the woman and have headquarters send it out to all SS and police units in the Berlin district. Concentrate on the rail stations and on the highway to Berlin."

"Yes, Major. Sir, one of the Institute's directors, Professor Heisenberg, asks if he could speak with you a moment." Frick had expected this. He sat back and took a few deep breaths to refocus himself.

"Show him in, then get that information to Berlin."

Ziegler paused at the door, "If you please, Professor, the Major will see you now." Heisenberg sauntered into the boardroom, broad-shouldered, handsome and impeccably dressed, with a broad, friendly smile.

"Major, it is a pleasure to meet you. I must say, this is the most excitement we've had for years."

Frick stood up and his face went red.

"Professor, you don't seem to be taking this very seriously. I have been told by Berlin that this facility is engaged in important weapons research. Such a breach of security surely endangers that research. It also reflects badly on the management of the institution." Heisenberg stiffened and his smile was gone.

"The management of this institution is not a matter for your concern. We are under the direct supervision of Education Minister Rust and the Army Ordnance Department. I answer only to them.

"This institute is only involved in research on fundamental science. The application of our discoveries is a political matter, out of my hands. I will be happy to refer you to the appropriate people in Berlin, if you have any more such questions or comments."

Frick knew there was little to be gained by bearding this puffed-up martinet. He sat back down. "I apologize Professor, but my orders are quite specific. An intruder has entered your laboratory, and it is my assignment to find out why."

"Why? A likely explanation is that some local boys sneaked in to look at the dragon..."

"The dragon?" Frick was taken aback.

"Yes, Major. Most of the staff and laborers at the Institute are small-town people with little education. After work they meet in the tavern and trade stories about what we're working on here. The latest version insists we've a fire-breathing dragon living in a tank of water in the garden building. An amusing metaphor, I must say. But it does keep superstitious adults away. But on several occasions guards have had to chase away local boys who'll stand for hours peeking through the fence for a glimpse of the dragon."

"But Professor, I am told that your researches are top secret."

"I suppose the Army would say so, but frankly the work we do here is highly theoretical. No ordinary intruder would know what to look for, nor would he comprehend what he sees. There aren't ten men in Germany who fully understand the implications and substance of our work."

"Then I'm sorry if we interfere in any way with your work, Professor, but I must assume the worst and hope for the best. I have asked that all your people remain within the Institute until our physical investigation is completed. Hopefully that will not last more than a few hours."

Heisenberg could only shrug, in response. "Professor, I understand that you've had a chance to examine all your equipment. Did you find any signs of tampering? Was anything disturbed or missing?"

"Aside from Heinz, my frightened technician, none whatsoever, Major. With the exception of some monitoring equipment and spare drums of heavy water, our secrets, as you call them, are all stored under water inside the tank. There's no sign that the hoist was used to lift the tank's cover. We recalibrated our meters and checked the conductance in the reactor tank as well as a sample from each of the spare drums, and everything is fine. Your aide told me that Heinz was not seriously harmed. When can we have him back?"

Frick refrained from asking about heavy water. "Herr Professor, have you had any Americans visit the institute recently? Even before the guards were posted?"

"I don't think so, Major. I'd have to check my appointment book to make sure. No one from the States has visited for several years, certainly not since we assembled the pile."

"Professor Heisenberg, we have a clue suggesting the intruder was an American named Beters. Young man, very tall and thin, blond hair. Does this remind you of anyone?"

Heisenberg thought for a moment. "Not that I recall."

"Think about it and in any case, please check your records and get back to me or one of my officers if you find something relevant. Thank you for your time and help, Professor." Frick stood and offered his hand. Heisenberg's was clammy. The Professor wasn't quite as nonchalant as he pretended, thought Frick, as he watched the Professor leave. He turned and stared out the window. Flowers were blooming in a garden plot outside.

"Ziegler!" shouted Frick through the door.

"Yes, Major."

"Is the Professor gone? Yes? I want you to make sure that all calls and correspondence from the Institute are monitored day and night. And tap the wires of any of the senior staff that have telephones at home."

"Yes, Herr Major."

"Ziegler, the Professor thinks young boys broke in to the laboratory building to satisfy their curiosity. Would you agree with that possibility?"

"No, Major, I would not. Clumsy boys would have disturbed something and probably stolen items to impress their friends. Our intruder was careful to leave no signs. It was not local boys."

"I agree. I'm returning to Berlin. Keep the scientific team here. Have them go over the building one more time. Then send them to the hotel. Turn it inside out. Dust for fingerprints. Arrest that fat innkeeper if he makes a peep.

"On the way to Berlin we'll stop at the station and pick up schedules for the local trains. Send Schmidt to the offices of local bus companies. Question ticket sellers. Give them copies of the descriptions. Someone has seen this tall, skinny American. It's unlikely he's gone far. Make certain the bus and railroad people understand how important this is to the Gestapo. Go."

Frick was thoughtful during the drive back to Gestapo Headquarters on *Prinz Albrecht Strasse*. He read the Gestapo's file on the Institute's staff and its content was disquieting. The Physics Institute was under the control of the Army and Ministry of Education. The Gestapo could claim priority over either group. But two of the institute's staff were untouchable: Heisenberg's dossier included a letter of support from Reichsmarshal Himmler himself; Von Weizsächer's father held ministerial rank in the Foreign Office. But five minutes of conversation with Heisenberg cast serious doubt in Frick's mind about Heisenberg's loyalty and forthrightness. These intellectuals were all from the same cloth: aristocrats and snobs, egotistical and arrogant. Frick would have to tread carefully, culpability for the lax security meted out surgically. Dramatic and violent enough to send a strong message to these fools, but without threatening them directly.

While the file did little to explain the purpose of the Institute's current work, there were enough hints to suggest it was important to men close to the *Führer*. Frick repeated the Reichsmarshal's threat over and over in his mind, trying to determine whether it contained any suggestion regarding Himmler's preferred outcome. There was nothing. What kind of minefield was he in?

Arriving at his office, he called his staff together and briskly issued orders to each.

"Hartz, go down to Records right now. Examine recent reports about *American* intelligence activity in Germany. Go back two years. The laboratory at the Institute wasn't built until last year: that gives us a starting point. Look over everything: completed reports, raw data, signal intelligence, everything. If you find anything, bring it here immediately. Borrow the originals: steal them if you have to. We haven't time for paper-pushers to make copies.

"When he returns from Ullem, you and Müller review everything item by item. Anything related to American interest in physics or chemistry should be collected for me to review personally. Müller has a copy of the description of this American named Beters. References to anyone even vaguely resembling Beters should be brought to me immediately. Understood?"

"Yes, Herr Major!"

"Captain Weiter," Frick said, turning to his chief of staff. "Ziegler has train schedules from the Dahlem station. Review them and come up with a plan for concentrating our searches and surveillance. But first, send out an order under my name for all local centers in the Berlin region: recall all their staffs, ready for deployment. Get them your plans within the hour and start them moving."

"Immediately, Herr Major!" Weiter clicked his heels and dashed out.

Other men were dispatched to increase surveillance on the American Embassy and other neutral legations. Quickly the whole attention of the Gestapo in northern Germany turned to William Beters and his unidentified woman friend.

By late that evening little had turned up that represented a valuable lead. Men had rushed off in all directions investigating messages and telephone calls from station managers all around Berlin. None proved to be significant, and as each false report was resolved, Frick grew angrier, and his men more frantic in reaction. It was difficult for Frick to sit in his office when he sensed that his quarry was getting more distant from him every passing moment.

The Professor was wrong, Frick knew. The intruder, probably this man Beters, had seen what he needed to see at the Institute and now had to report to his bosses. Beters had made little attempt to cover his tracks at the inn and this told Frick that Beters' mission was complete. He was now racing toward the border. The question was which one. Only two options made sense: Sweden through German or Danish ports and south to Switzerland. The southern border was well guarded by both the Germans and Swiss, who were as reluctant to allow such people into their country as Germany was to let them leave. The northern border, to the contrary, was full of holes. There was still a great deal of commerce between Sweden and Germany and ferries sailed daily from at least six Baltic ports. Two weeks after its *conquest*, Denmark was like a sieve. The Foreign Ministry had convinced Hitler that the Danes and their monarch needed to be treated delicately and it was well known within the Gestapo that many prominent Danes had actively helped Jews and German deserters escape to Sweden. Eventually Berlin would see the light and seize total control of the Danish government, but for now Denmark was categorized as a *protectorate* and the Gestapo could do no more than watch and wait and keep lists.

Did Beters still have the girl with him? No experienced agent would allow himself to be encumbered. But if she is still accompanying him, will that slow him down? Who is she? Does she know about Beters' mission or is she just another blind?

After the first two hours the clerks were convinced that Beters' passport was false. But nearly six thousand Americans had been granted visas since 1937 and even using thirty men, it would take until Tuesday morning to examine all the visa applications comparing descriptions. Thousands of Americans had scrambled to leave Germany in the wake of the intervention in Poland and the war declaration by France and England eight months before. His men phoned in to complain how Customs and the Foreign Office had lost track of hundreds of Americans in the ensuing chaos. There was no accurate, up-to-date list of which Americans were still in the Fatherland. Frick was convinced that many of those who remained behind were unfriendly agents whether in the guise of businessmen or journalists. Beters would be one of them.

That evening, headquarters had grown quiet. Everyone was still on duty, but fresh reports had petered out. Frick sat at his desk, rereading the file on the physics work at the Institute, trying to get a feel for the importance of the intelligence Beters had walked away with. Who would benefit? He made careful notes to himself in the margins. First, what was the intruder after? Could there be some piece of equipment Beters could describe, some sample of chemicals or materials he could deliver? As time passed, did the things Beters saw become more or less important? There must have been something, but neither Frick nor his officers could come up with it. Was it the very existence of the laboratory that was of interest? Perhaps, but Frick did not believe the secret was well kept.

297

Everyone at the institute had spoken very freely, without any threats or inducements. How could he believe that hundreds of people around Dahlem didn't know about the construction and research there? Beters could get these answers at the local tavern for the price of a single liter of beer.

Only someone well versed in science could appreciate the true secrets of the work at the Institute. The director said only ten people in Germany understood the full significance of his work. Assuming Beters had entered Germany legally, was the so-called Beters one of these elite: a university professor or researcher himself? He made a note: another item to crosscheck in Records.

Frick heard the phone ring in the outer office and the muffled voice of Sergeant Müller. A few seconds later, Müller rapped on Frick's door and entered without waiting for an acknowledgement.

"Major, I believe we have information on the American. The district commander in Lauenburg, sixty kilometers west of Potsdam, showed initiative and sent men to roust railway agents who had already gone home for the day when our requests and descriptions first came through. He's been questioning a ticket seller who says he sold tickets today to a tall man accompanied by a pretty young woman with dark hair."

"What time?"

"He recalls it was just before 11:00 a.m., when he normally takes his lunch."

"Go on," Frick demanded excitedly.

"Sir, the ticket agent thinks that the two arrived at the station on foot. At least he didn't see any vehicles. They carried only one small bag each."

"I don't need to guess that they bought tickets to Hamburg."

"Exactly, sir. You're right. The district chief already alerted Gestapo headquarters in the city, the Hamburg police, and the railroad people in Hamburg. Unfortunately the train from Lauenburg is an express and was scheduled to arrive at *Bahnhof* Hamburg before six p.m. Hamburg wasn't on alert until seven o'clock." Both men looked at their watches.

"Müller, get the car ready immediately. Call Ziegler and Schmidt over at Records and tell them to bring everything they have right now. We'll leave as soon as they return. They can continue their work in the car. If we leave now, we can be in Hamburg in four hours, faster than we can requisition a plane or special train.

"Sergeant, after that, connect me with Gestapo headquarters in Hamburg. I want the city shut down. No one leaves until I say so."

The *Autobahn* was busy even this late in the evening. Leaning on his horn and flashing his headlights, Frick's driver whizzed past a dozen convoys of army trucks and trailered Panzer tanks headed west to reinforce formations at the Dutch border. Frick knew from Army friends in Berlin that the 'phony' war was to end within a few days. Everyone was confident German shock troops would be in Amsterdam, Brussels, and Paris within thirty days.

Four men sat in the back of the car trying to concentrate on several stacks of files they'd carried from Berlin, using flashlights to augment the dim lights in the back of the big car.

"I owe the Records chief a bottle of *Schnapps*, sir," Ziegler had reported. "He didn't want to let any of these files out of his sight. They're all originals."

Frick snorted his disdain.

Despite a blackout, the lights of the great city were glowing ahead in the distance, reflected by low clouds. If a single man went to ground there, it might take months to find him. *No…Beters has information he wants to get back to his masters in Washington or London. How?*

Nothing. We have less than nothing. We must get ahead of the spy. As long as he's in front of us, the chance we'll catch him is slim.

Frick leaned forward and shouted, "Faster, driver, go faster."

"Yes, Herr Major!" replied the driver and the speedometer inched past one hundred eighty kilometers per hour.

Express

It was safer, they agreed, to sit apart, though in the same train car. If the Gestapo had descriptions from the *Gasthaus*, they would be searching for a couple, not two solitary travelers. Willy saw everyone as a possible agent of the Gestapo: any soldier, railroad employee, newspaper seller, or child might expose them.

Lise was less concerned about dangers from ordinary Germans, but she too was careful and cautious. They took turns watching and listening so the other person could sleep. Willy could never have pulled this off without her. He owed her everything.

But Willy lied to Lise. He didn't tell her about the technician at the Physics Institute. That man should be able to provide the Gestapo with Willy's description. On this basis the authorities could very well be looking for Willy alone, especially if they hadn't checked with all the hotels and inns around Dahlem. And he didn't tell her about the pile and its lethal blue light.

In any case Willy didn't know what to think or what to say about it. Best to keep quiet for now. If he developed serious symptoms, his secret plan was to leave her for her own safety. If the radiation poisoning was debilitating, it would slow them down and he would be caught, if not on the road then when they returned to Munich and Lise called in a doctor. As far as he knew there were neither treatments nor cures for radiation poisoning. There *was* an odd itching sensation in his legs but that might just be nerves and paranoia. Perhaps chemicals in the tank had caused some minor irritation. No sense telling Lise: if it was serious, there was nothing she could do that didn't risk her freedom and life. If it were nothing, she would have worried needlessly.

At each rail station they'd be as discrete as possible, buying unreserved tickets separately. In the waiting rooms they sat far apart ignoring one another.

Monday afternoon, finally aboard the express to Hamburg, Willy awoke to find Lise in the adjacent seat. There were few sounds besides the hypnotic clacking of wheels on rails and an occasional staccato as the train raced across a set of switching points. He was glad she was near. He wouldn't have risked it on his own. It was amazing to Willy how Lise seemed to fill so many gaps in his life. She was bold where he was overly cautious, righteous when he equivocated, and funny or amorous when he got too serious.

It was hard to bury old images, easy to see Lise again as the serious teenager he'd met nearly two years before. And while he had deceived himself about her, misjudging her maturity and intelligence from the very beginning, this was a young woman next to him, though Willy couldn't be sure that she was taller or fuller or stronger now. She was becoming part of him and he saw her less with his eyes than with his heart.

Lise had curled her arm under his and laid her head against his shoulder. Willy could smell her hair and was instantly aroused. *Idiot*, he chided himself. *We're in mortal danger with a secret police force after us, and I get excited when we hold hands. I should think about how to save us both. I should consider everything that might happen and have plans ready. Lise's my responsibility; that's what comes with love. She loves me and I have to take care of her now. Nothing else matters.*

But it *was* funny, if precarious, Willy smiled to himself. Even as he fought to get *those* thoughts out of his head, the train sped around a tight bend and Lise's pressed even harder against him. Now he was really out of control, and it was only the prospect of his embarrassment, if she discovered him that brought relief. Willy stared out the window, but everything was gray in the approaching twilight. From the newspapers Willy knew Hamburg was well within range of British and French bombers. Blackouts had been ordered months ago. Closer to Berlin there had been few restrictions and if it weren't for all the soldiers in the stations and troop trains along the way, he saw few indications that war raging to the east and north.

Willy squirmed in his seat trying hard not to wake Lise. Or maybe he wasn't trying so very hard after all.

The train was passing through a small town and as Willy peered out the window he could see a dim light in the distance, probably some poorly shuttered building or shed. In an instant it all came back to him: the suffocating darkness of the heavy water tank and the blue glow of the radioactive pile. So much more had already been risked than they had planned. Discovery would mean death for them both. Willy might already be dying from radiation poisoning. Or he might be crippled and emasculated. He just didn't know which yet. He began to sweat despite the late night chill. He was thinking in circles.

Plan, he must plan.

They had managed to get aboard the express in Lauenburg. Whenever the train stopped over the next several hours, Willy and Lise took turns running to buy new tickets to different destinations on trains leaving all evening and even the following morning. Anyone trying to trace them would have to consider that they'd left the express along the way.

They were careful to never go to the same window or agent twice. They bought individual roundtrip tickets to Berlin, Nürnburg, Leipzig, Rostock, Frankfurt, and Hamburg. From Hamburg, they would make their way back to Munich. The expense was phenomenal, but when Lise had opened her bag in a depot's café, Willy could see that she had literally thousands of Reichmarks with her.

"Who do you think you are, Bonnie Parker?" he whispered amazed.

Her eyes gleamed: "So you think I robbed a bank? I've been handling Vati's money since I was fifteen years old. He was not to be trusted. He would overpay the housekeepers and gardeners and forget to pay bills for coal and electricity. Vati would give everything he had in his pocket to any stranger that asked and would waste money on research assistants who ought to know how to fend for themselves.

"Vati has plenty of money and since the war began, I've been withdrawing small amounts from the bank, and hiding it at home. Until a few months ago, I had been buying small amounts of gold from Herr Rosenzweig, the jeweler on Leopoldstrasse. But since his store was looted and burned in November, there was no one else I could trust.

"I wasn't born when the last war ended but I remember hearing how desperate things were when a cartload of Weimar currency wouldn't buy a turnip. Vati and I will be better prepared this time.

"I brought along as much cash as I could carry in case we needed to bribe anyone along the way. Despite all that's said about the new Germany, some things never change."

"Lise, I never thought about these things," Willy said embarrassed.

"We're partners aren't we: you do some things and I do others.

The whole is greater than the sum of the parts."

"I love you, Lise," Willy said.

"Oh, but now you love me only for my money, like all the American men I see in the movies...a gigolo!"

"No, not me!" Willy protested. "I'm the guy in the cowboy movie: the righteous man in a white hat who believes in justice."

"Yes, the cowboy who loves only his horse," Lise teased. "Does this mean you think of me like your horse?" This discussion was getting too erotic for the circumstances.

"Shut-up and keep the cash out of sight. If someone steals it from you, we can hardly go to the police."

During a stop for gasoline, Ziegler had phoned headquarters in Berlin. Back on the *Autobahn*, he briefed Major Frick.

"Hamburg reports that everyone has been recalled to duty. Beters' description had been circulated all around the city and some railway employees are already being questioned about possible sightings. We'll arrive in Hamburg in two hours and they promise a report by then."

"Any other leads?"

"No, sir. Beters evidently boarded a train in Potsdam, but reports from ticket agents are very confused. It seems he may have purchased tickets to several destinations at different ticket windows over a period of several hours. Two ticket agents think they may have sold tickets to the girl, also to different cities, but that's less certain. Interrogations will continue until everyone's memory is clear.

"The Lauenburg lead continues to be the best. It's a small station one stop past Potsdam with a single ticket window. Beters and the girl could not have bought extra tickets without attracting attention.

"A second bit of good news: we have two plainclothesmen travelling aboard the express as a routine matter. They were supposed to receive the descriptions at an intermediate stop before the train reaches Hamburg. Berlin can't confirm that this was done, but we could get lucky."

"You're convinced Beters is heading for Hamburg?"

"Yes, Herr Major, I am."

"So am I." But he knew he was still one step behind the spy.

Nearing Hamburg, they were also closer to the front and at each stop more and more soldiers boarded, some in full battle kit and others still in civilian clothing, all hurrying to catch up with their units after being left behind because of illness or other circumstances. All were excited and full of themselves. When Willy returned from the restroom, he found Lise surrounded by a noisy group.

"Fräulein, these other men may *say* they want to marry you, however I am their natural leader and the only choice for you." The young soldier, hardly more than a teenager, reached for Lise's hand and bowing his head, kissed its back. She smiled at the gallantry; best not to make a scene. Willy, sure that she was playing along, felt a sharp pang of jealously nonetheless. He stood in the aisle feeling stupid and immature.

"And Fräulein, who is this giant?"

"This is my brother Thomas and you've taken his seat. Gentlemen, please let him sit back down." Soldiers had crammed into seats and crowded the aisles all around Lise and all vied for her attention, for a smile or other recognition. Willy squeezed through and reclaimed a seat next to the window facing Lise. The soldiers ignored him and continued an artillery barrage of questions and suggestions. Most were shy, others emboldened by their own image of how real soldiers would behave. But none made any blatantly rude comments or propositions; even the boldest were new to the game of playing soldier and hero.

Willy tried to catch her eye, looking for some reassurance, but Lise continued to answer the soldiers' questions, all be it with the calm dignity of an older, experienced woman. Willy was peeved and a little wounded.

"Please, what is your name Fräulein?"

"Where are you from?"

"Can I have your address so I can write you a letter?"

"Where are you going?"

"That is near where I'll be billeted. Perhaps we'll see one another in town."

Suddenly Lise snatched a field cap from one of the soldiers and jammed it on Willy's head as he sat across from her listening to the banter.

"What do you gentlemen think? Won't Thomas make a handsome soldier?"

There was a wide difference of opinion, all offered loudly and at the same time:

"Thomas is too old; he'll never keep up."

"He's too tall. He's too big a target. Even the Frenchies can't miss."

"He can enlist in the signal corps and be a radio antenna!"

"I'm still more handsome!"

As they teased him somebody scrunched the cap down over his ears and eyes. Everyone thought this was hilarious except for Willy, troubled that Lise would do something to focus attention and to embarrass him. *Why is she mocking me?* When its owner grabbed the cap back off his head, Willy turned to stare at Lise flushed and angry. Her eyes were gleaming and with a flicker she gestured for him to look towards her left. Moving slowly down the aisle were two men in long leather coats and slouch hats, obviously policemen or Gestapo. During the commotion the two had passed through the boisterous group and continued down the car pausing a moment at each row to look carefully at each passenger. He met Lise's eyes and they were on fire with excitement. She had seen the two agents when they entered the car behind Willy. Her quick action had made it appear like Willy was just another soldier hassling a pretty, unattached girl. Lise smiled at Willy and all his anger and embarrassment and fatigue and fear vaporized in an instant. For a brief moment there were only the two of them on the train.

"Fräulein, please give me something of yours to keep for luck!"

"Fräulein, Fräulein! My name is Walter Meyer. Just wait and you'll soon see my name in the newspapers."

But one by one the young soldiers began to settle back into their own seats, grateful of the distraction but now quietly thoughtful or nervously talkative about what lay ahead. But when any soldier passed by in the aisle, he would always try to catch her eye, somehow sensing and somehow aware that this was a final glimpse of an ordinary life.

Two of the young soldiers kept their seats next to them, so Lise and Willy could not speak except about innocuous things, but several times while jostling with their possessions and books they managed to touch one another, and both were exhilarated.

When the conductor passed through the car announcing that Hamburg was the last stop, the two soldiers, now serious, shook Lise and Willy's hands, apologized for the behavior of their comrades, and wished them a safe journey. Lise gave each a smile.

"Please take care of yourselves, gentlemen. I'll pray for your safe return."

Lise and Willy collected their bag and joined the crowd alighting from the cars and moving down the platform towards the main station floor.

"Wait for a moment," she said setting her bag down on a bench half way along the platform.

"We need to stay with the crowd."

"Here, put this on." Lise produced a purloined army field cap from her bag. "I should have cut your hair the other evening instead of wasting time on other things," she teased. "You don't look very soldierly, but it can't hurt."

"I love you Lise."

"Let's keep moving."

There were policemen at the turnstile gate as they left the platform but no one paid them any attention. They left the station building and found a quiet little park where they could sit and make plans.

They sat close together on a stone bench. The evening was damp and cool. Around the little park, other couples sat close together talking or kissing. So near the station, it was a place of waiting and parting.

"We haven't much time. I just have this sense that the Gestapo is out there right now looking for us and is getting closer every minute.

"Willy, we should return to Munich tonight. By tomorrow afternoon we can be safe at my father's house. If the Gestapo comes looking for you, I can hide you in the attic or the basement."

"Lise, I can't hide in the house. The war might last years. The Nazi might win. You and your father would be in danger forever. And if they found me they would know that you'd been helping me. Right now, I'm just your father's research assistant. As far as you know, I just vanished one day, abandoning my work at the lab. Your father honestly knows nothing about my activities: he's been very ill, you can explain. His reputation will protect you both and you can contact Professor Heisenberg for his help if you're in trouble. I'll be the American spy who tricked you as well as Heisenberg and the authorities at the university and Education Ministry.

"It's best that I leave the country. Lise, we don't know whether our messages reached Professor Einstein. I do know that it will not take the Institute more than a few weeks or a month at best to discover the contamination and the rewired meter. I have information I must get back to America. No one else knows what's happening here and how much danger we're all in if the Nazis succeed with this research. No one understands the importance of the heavy water plant in Norway."

"Then I will come with you. You'll need my help. As we get closer to the border there'll be more guards and soldiers and Gestapo. I can help."

"You must get back to your father, Lise," Willy said.

"Then you must come back with me. I can hide you until we find a way to get you to Switzerland."

"No, if the Gestapo believes that I'm still in Germany, they'll investigate deeper and the whole story will eventually come out. Someone will report that I'm headed the other way and that's where they'll follow. I just need to stay a step ahead for the next few days."

"But I can help. You'll need my help," she pleaded.

"I know I do, but we have different responsibilities. Your father can't make it on his own for long. You must keep him away from the authorities or else they'll surely take him away and kill him.

"I have to get news to my country. And I have to make sure you're safe. You must agree with my decision."

"Willy, you need me to help," she was crying now.

"I know. But I'll make it, I promise. Once I get to Copenhagen, I might be able to find help through Professor Bohr at the Carlsberg Institute. Professor Heisenberg told me that Bohr has helped other people escape to Sweden."

"What will I do without you? I'll never see you again and I'll never know what happened to you. You're leaving to save Vati and me. I don't think I can live with that. I love you, Willy. I want to be with you. Please don't leave me like this."

"You have to live, Lise. So your father can live, too. The war can't last forever. I'll find you again, I promise. Somehow I'll get word to you that I'm safe. And we'll be together again, together forever. I promise. I promise."

"Willy, I want to spend my life with you, but now I can't have even another hour. What is wrong with the world? How did things ever get this way? I want them the way they were. It isn't fair." Lise was collecting herself now, her despair turning to anger.

"We have to get back to the station."

Willy bought tickets for Frankfurt and Cologne, Lise for Neumünster and Kiel, which they exchanged. Lise's train south was scheduled to depart at half past seven and Willy's at eight. They walked down the platform where Lise's train was waiting and stood kissing clumsily, holding one another until the last possible second. A large group of Hitler Youth came racing down the platform and in the crush, bumped and jostled by the happy crowd, Lise and Willy became separated. She was swept away in the river of children, brown shirts, red scarves, and swastika armbands. Willy was left standing alone.

When the conductor closed the door, Willy was suddenly desperate for one last look, and he rushed down the platform as the train began to pull out, looking for Lise in the windows. He couldn't find her face anywhere among the hundreds of others. When he reached the platform's end, he could only stop and watch the train merge into the confusion of tracks and overhead wires just outside the huge *Bahnhof*.

Willy's whole body was clinched tight. He wanted to lie down and curl into a ball. Another train entering the busy station blocked his view of the end of Lise's train and the connection was broken.

He continued to stand at the end of the platform for ten minutes until with a start, he realized how visible and vulnerable he was out here alone. He quickly returned to the main floor to hide within the churning crowds of commuters and other travelers.

At eleven o'clock, Frick's car pulled up in front of the Hamburg *Bahnhof* and his team ran off to the phones and to find the local Gestapo commanders. Alone for a moment, Frick walked through the glass doors and into the station. A sea of travelers, businessmen, students, factory workers, and soldiers still covered every square meter of floor. The café was packed and men swarmed around the newsstand and ticket windows, though, as always, a circle of space magically opened in front of Frick as he strode through the crowd.

As he advanced he could now hear the bells and whistles of departing trains. His orders had been ignored.

"Stop the trains. Stop all the trains!" he wanted to shout, to command with all the power within him. Beters was here. He knew it in his soul. But he had to stop these trains. *Where is the stationmaster's office?*

On a train headed south toward Frankfurt and Munich, Lise sat sobbing, tears running down her face. She knew that she was stupid calling attention to herself like this, but she couldn't stop.

Two elderly conductors came upon her and hesitated for a moment watching helplessly. They'd passed through ten cars already and Lise was one of a dozen women crying alone on the train, mothers, daughters, wives, perhaps girlfriends. They both remembered how it had been during the Great War and their hearts went out. They looked at one another, shrugged, and continued towards the rear of the train, knowing from sad experience how much crying was yet to come.

Conjunction

"Major Frick, it's a coincidence that strains credulity, but I think we have some information that might prove critical." Captain Braun was agitated. Five minutes into Frick's briefing in the stationmaster's commandeered office, Braun knew he had crucial details Frick didn't. While he was confident his news was important, Frick had a reputation for impatience and ruthlessness within the Gestapo. Indeed the section-head who'd ignored orders to shut down the *Bahnhof* had been arrested when Frick arrived and might already be dead.

Braun could think of several reasons his own section could be criticized. He'd been sitting on the Tellerman file for two weeks. Prison doctors had told him that Tellerman might die and Braun didn't want to forward the file to Berlin until that was resolved. No word had yet come from Prague confirming Tellerman's mad tales and Braun personally thought the whole thing was rubbish. Now, though….

"Show me what you have. Talk as I read," growled Frick, opening the large envelope and dumping its contents on the tabletop.

"Sir, this is the original case file for a man we arrested trying to enter Germany off a Spanish ship in Hamburg Port two weeks ago. He insists his name was Edward Tellerman and he carried an out-dated Czech Republic passport in that name. We've made inquiries through the Gestapo office in Prague, but they complain the Czechs are stonewalling about older passport files in an attempt to protect Jews and Communists still traveling in unoccupied countries on the old documents. Many of the records have been purposely destroyed or mislocated.

"In any case, Tellerman claims to have been in America as a university research assistant when the war began: in the state of Minnesota.

"About six weeks ago now, he says he stumbled on a plot to pass secrets about German weapons research from an American student living in Germany to contacts in America using special inks to convey messages buried within the text of longer, innocuous letters. He had one such letter in his possession when we arrested him," Braun leaned forward to rifle through the stack and found Willy's letter to Emmett.

"Tellerman, or whomever he is, says that at first there was no hidden message but after sitting on his desk for a week the faint blue color, highlighting individual, specific words, miraculously appeared. We thought it likely that this madman had stared at the letter so hard he hallucinated. Then Tellerman added the color himself." Frick was as red as a beet; his eyes were bulging as if he were being slowly strangled. *Tread carefully*, Braun warned himself.

"When he discovered the alleged plot, he tried to get to the German Consul in Chicago and later to our embassy in Washington. As he tells it, the American Federal Bureau of Investigation was after him every step of the way and tried to kill him outside the embassy. All very paranoid. The man insisted that the Fatherland was in great jeopardy and managed to book passage on a neutral Spanish ship to Hamburg.

"He says the American student's name was Wilhelm Petersen and that he actually met the man at a scientific conference in Berlin in 1938."

Frick jumped to his feet, dropping the Czech passport he'd been examining: "Keep talking."

"Well, it all seemed quite preposterous. The man Tellerman was delusional. He babbled other stories about stink bombs at *Bund* meetings and about some Jewish woman who tried to bite off his penis. He was raving about a plot by crewmen on the Spanish cargo ship to tie him up and rape him. *Alles verruckt!* Totally crazy!

"My interrogators were convinced he was feigning madness and intensified the questioning. Unfortunately they underestimated the man's condition and he's still unconscious in our prison hospital. I was awaiting an opportunity to question him myself before I forwarded my report."

"Who else knows about this man?"

"Just my staff and prison hospital personnel. Everything we have is in front of you now. No copies have been made." Frick spent five more minutes examining everything in the envelope. He studied the secret message to Professor Emmett closely. *Radioactivity*. A word Frick had heard at the Physics Institute. When they'd been poking around the laboratory the technicians kept insisting that the apparatus was radioactive and somehow dangerous. *I thought they were talking shit*. He picked up a torn and dirty photograph.

"What is this?"

"Tellerman claimed it was a group photograph of the attendees at the Berlin conference where he met the American Petersen. According to Tellerman, Petersen is the fourth man from the left in the back-most row. The tall one." Frick stared hard for several moments and handed the photograph to Müller standing nearby. Schmidt studied it over Müller's shoulder. Braun could tell by Frick's stony expression that he was in serious, perhaps deadly trouble.

Lieutenant Ziegler was also scanning the notes and letter as Braun talked and he suddenly interrupted.

"Major Frick! Petersen, the name William Petersen. Look how simple it would be to change letters in a passport to give Beters. Erase the final 'en' and add a short ink stroke to 'P' and you have William *Beters*. Any child could do it well enough to fool a fat innkeeper. This has to be right, sir."

"I agree." The pieces were coming together. Now they had a description, a picture, and solid identification.

"Captain Braun, consider yourself under arrest." Braun flinched. "If this information helps us catch this...Petersen, then I'll see that you're rewarded. If Petersen escapes, I assure you that you'll share my failure and fate. Beyond the fact that we now know the spy has breached our security for two years, during the two weeks you've known about it, he has penetrated a top secret weapons research facility outside Berlin and is doubtless trying to escape the country right now with new, detailed information.

"Braun, get more men over to the prison. Keep the man Tellerman under close guard indefinitely. Instruct your doctors that this man is to live. Make sure they understand the consequences. When he's conscious again, he is to talk to no one. He already knows more about the secret research than anyone outside the project. He himself constitutes a serious security risk. No one at the prison or hospital should know why he's being held. When this affair is over, *I'll* decide what to do with Tellerman and with you."

With a loud rap, a young Gestapo lieutenant entered and saluted with a click of his heels.

"Sir," he said, addressing Frick as the senior man. "We have completed a search of the station building. We found no one matching the description you provided. However, no one has been allowed to leave yet. We can conduct an examination of everyone's travel documents if you desire. However, sir, we detained approximately two hundred men and women and it might take several more hours to screen everyone.

"Let everyone go, but all through one exit. Müller, Schmidt: take the photograph with you. You know what to do. After all the passengers are through, go back to all the ticket agents, conductors, porters, and railway guards. Show them the picture; give them the description again. Someone has seen this man and knows which way he went. Do anything or say anything needed to make certain they understand how important this is. Go now. Everyone out of the room." Frick sat at the table. He laid out each individual item from Braun's envelope and his own notes from Dahlem. Not much to go on. Nothing to suggest what direction Petersen might take. Counting the local Hamburg trains and regional schedule, twenty trains had departed between six and when the station was finally sealed at eleven. He stood and studied the wall maps.

There was always a chance Petersen would board a neutral ship in the port, but Frick dismissed the idea. He didn't believe Petersen had set out with a specific destination in mind and had no appointed escape route. Knowing that a certain ship would be in port at a certain date required planning and a support network of some sort. Petersen had been trying to throw them off track every step of the way and had taken less direct and slower stages. If he'd had a plan, tickets could have been purchased weeks before and Petersen wouldn't have had to worry about his description and all these ticket agents.

After two hours the two sergeants returned to report negative results. The station was still closed and Müller had ordered the railway police to search all the storage, luggage, and other spaces before they reopened the *Bahnhof*. Müller left in search of some cold food for the Major. It was two in the morning.

Twenty minutes later Sergeant Schmidt knocked on the door before he entered escorting a bugged-eyed ticket agent and an ancient white-haired porter nervously twisting his red felt cap first one way and then the other.

"You first," Schmidt told the ticket agent. "Tell the Major what you told me."

"Herr Major, sir, your man showed me a photograph and asked about one face. I didn't recognize him at first. The picture is very poor and my eyesight is not the best," he said fingering his spectacles. "But then he said that the man in the photograph is very tall. Then I remembered. I've seen this man. This afternoon or earlier this evening. Not a regular customer. Very tall: he had to bend down to speak through the slot in my little window. He wanted to know the schedules for northbound trains to Kiel on the Baltic Sea. He spoke like a southerner, Bavarian maybe. Two trains were leaving an hour apart and he bought a round-trip, unreserved ticket for the later one."

"What were the departures?" prompted Schmidt.

"Sorry, sir. First one left at 7:45 p.m. The second left the station at 8:50 p.m."

"You said he bought a round-trip ticket?" Frick asked. "You're sure of that."

"Yes, Herr Major." Frick and Schmidt exchanged glances: *One misdirection…were there others?*

"Thank you. You may go." It took some seconds before the agent realized that he would live, wouldn't be conscripted, or suffer one of the dozen other possible outcomes of contact with the secret police. He backed out of the room bowing like a toady to the king.

"Now you, grandfather. Tell the Major what you saw. About the tall man."

"Excellency, I take my meal on a bench out near the end of platform number six. Everyday. Twenty years now. Since I came back from the siege at Tannenburg, grace be to God, devil take all Russians!"

"Please grandfather, the Major is very busy."

"Beg your pardon, Excellency," the old porter bowed deeply. "The two of thems were sitting close up on the last bench at the end of the platform. All lovey-dovey. Holding hands and what not. Well, I kind of kept an eye out, case things got really interesting. No luck there, I guess. As I was getting ready to get back to my post, thems two stood up and started to head back towards the main platform. Then I saw how tall the gent was and he was nearly twice the girl's height. Real pretty girl. Tall, too. Prettiest I've seen in a long time. Well, I was kind of thinking about how they get around to doing it, when they walked right past."

"Did you show him the photo?" Frick asked Schmidt. Schmidt nodded.

"I'm sorry, Excellency, it could be the man, but I didn't want to take my eyes off the girl."

"What time did you take your dinner?" Frick asked patiently.

Schmidt responded, "I checked sir, with his supervisor: seven to seven-thirty." Frick nodded thoughtfully.

"Go home now, grandfather," Schmidt said, but the old porter hesitated, hat in hand, hinting about a tip.

"I hope I've been some small help," he tried one last time, but gave up at last and walked away shaking his head: *pretty girl, very pretty girl.*

"Have you worked through the connecting schedules?" Frick asked Schmidt. When the porter had confirmed that Petersen was still in the station at seven, it limited the possibilities.

"The train to Kiel takes five hours: the 7:55 departure is an express. It should have arrived there an hour ago. It made only four stops: Norderstedt, Kaltenkirche, Neumünster, and Kielsüd. Local trains connect at each of these stops, but Neumünster is a major railhead, with connections east to Lubeck, west to the coast and north to Flensberg. If Petersen is trying to leave the country, there are ferries from each of these ports to Sweden. Major, I assume you agree that the round-trip ticket to Kiel was probably a trick. Petersen made a big deal out of it, questioning the ticket agent, so he'd be remembered."

"Of course. But it also suggests he now has some sort of plan. He's heading somewhere specifically and wants us to go in the opposite direction. Perhaps he has a contact somewhere who's going to help hide him or get him out of the country."

"Your orders, sir?"

"Phone all the ferry ports up and down the coast. None are to leave tonight or tomorrow morning until we have enough men at each to make sure Petersen doesn't get past. Orders come from the authority of Reichsmarshal Himmler in Berlin. No exceptions, this time. They are to post guards to prevent anyone from sneaking aboard ahead of time. Alert all the district offices between here, both coasts, and the Danish border. Double manpower at every checkpoint, every border crossing, every railway station, bus station, and airfield. And add this: an attempt should be made to capture Petersen alive, but he must not be allowed to escape. Kill him to prevent that."

"The girl?"

"We must assume they're still together, but don't let this confuse anyone. '*Pretty's* not enough description to go on. Concentrate on the man. He's unique."

"Yes, Herr Major," Schmidt, Müller, and Ziegler moved to leave.

"Someone get me a cot and blanket and bring it here. I don't want to get caught out on the road again. We'll wait here until we have some sort of solid lead."

"Yes, Herr Major," they all said at once.

Major Frick was lying on a canvas cot, his boots at attention on the floor nearby and his uniform coat over the back of the stationmaster's chair. He had been rereading Petersen's letter to Emmett. *If the secret letter was real, Petersen had been in communication with a scientist in America; Petersen met Tellerman at a scientific meeting; both were research assistants. All academics. Always banded together in effete little cliques, oblivious to the rest of the world. Like that man Heisenberg in Dahlem.*

Wearily he got up and returned to the desk. It took four phone calls to Berlin waking sleepy functionaries. *Who's in charge of these foolish scientists? What's his phone number at home?*

One man recalled a list and another found it among his files: a list handwritten by the great Heisenberg himself. Within an hour Frick had a name and a likely destination: *the name was Professor Niels Bohr.*

It was five a.m. Tuesday morning.

"Müller! Schmidt!" he shouted, certain that his faithful hunting dogs would be just outside the door. The door flew open before Frick located his left boot.

"Schmidt, find Ziegler. We need a car to the airport and as large a plane as possible, crewed, fueled, and ready to go. Müller, gather up all the papers, maps, and notes from the table and put it in my attaché. Then find me some coffee."

"Destination, sir, for the pilot?" Schmidt asked. *How could Frick know?*

"Copenhagen."

Copenhagen

Near the end of the long night, as Willy's train rumbled through the northern most parts of Germany, pain in his legs grew progressively more distracting. They felt as if they were burning deep inside but neither massage nor cold towel from the train's lavatory provided relief. Though the pain was like the worst imaginable sunburn, when he lifted his pants' legs in the train's lavatory, he could detect only a slight reddening that might have come from his own constant rubbing. As he sat quietly, trying as best he could to remain unobtrusive, sudden, sharp pains would shoot up his legs to his groin and his whole body would want to go rigid. These episodes would leave him shaking and sweaty despite the cool night. He wanted to put it out of his mind. Each time he let himself contemplate what might be happening to his body, his heart would begin to pound and he felt panicked. Irrationally, he was convinced that a relentless and corrosive acid was eating him away from the inside out. It was just twenty-four hours since he'd been exposed.

Rationally he told himself there was nothing he could do. The damage was done. It would run its course with no way to know where that might lead. Many researchers and technicians had died from radiation poisoning in the early days and others suffered longer-term health problems after constant exposures. How much exposure had he received? Willy had never read of any therapy or treatment. People in Copenhagen would know and tell him, but it still would make no difference in terms of his ultimate fate. Only an hour to go before the border. It was nearly five in the morning: a Tuesday, Willy was sure.

Willy had managed a close connection in Neumünster, sixty kilometers north of Hamburg, and then continued north, away from Kiel, towards Flensburg and the Danish border. He'd claimed a seat in the last car and at each stop he would get up, leaving his bag on his seat, and go to the rear most door. He would mention to the conductor that he was going to stretch his legs for a moment while the train was stopped.

"No problem, just don't wander away and listen for my whistle."

Looking out an open window Willy could peer ahead at the platform. Any sign of policemen or the Gestapo and he was ready to jump off the rear of the train before they would begin their car-to-car search. Until now he had seen no evidence of pursuit or ambush.

Overnight the train had been nearly deserted with only two or three sleepy passengers sharing Willy's car. Then early in the morning as the train stopped in small stations, the passenger cars began to fill with farmers and merchants heading for market towns up the tracks. It was a friendly and noisy country crowd with old friends sharing gossip and war news: high politics and low.

"I hear that the Norwegians are secretly negotiating surrender..."

"Who'd have thought they'd hold out this long?"

"My nephew in Berlin told his mother that the *Führer* will make the Frenchies sign any armistice papers in the same railcar as the Kaiser did."

"Mathias told me he's already seen Danish butter on store shelves in Düsseldorf. Mark my words, Dieter, it's going to make prices crash, and we'll all go broke. I don't care how many commissary contracts you think you have."

"I overheard someone at the *Biergarten* in Schleswig saying that Von Ribbentrop's been talking secretly to President Roosevelt. America's going to join the Axis any day now."

"An army agent came by to look at my horses, but his offer was ridiculous. I'm as patriotic as the next man, but my family has to eat."

The train was to cross the Danish border at the small town of Kupfermühle just after sunrise. Willy planned to leave the train on the German side, before any customs men boarded. He could then try to locate a secluded spot to sneak across the border the next night or if he was lucky, he might be able to find a northbound freight train or truck where he could stow-away. With the Nazis controlling both sides of the border now security was likely to be more lax. He hoped.

As the train began to slow, the conductor walked back from car to car, "Kupfermühle, Kupfermühle. Next stop. Passenger traveling on to Copenhagen should have their papers ready for customs and revenue inspectors. Crew and engine change here. Safe journey to you all."

Willy stood in the rear of his car, in no hurry to join the small press of passengers disembarking on the German side. Few passengers were remaining behind for the leg to Copenhagen, so customs inspectors wouldn't take very long to reach the last car. The stop would be a quick one. When the last passenger, save Willy, had stepped down, he paused for a moment and then stepped to the platform and then quickly dropped down on to the tracks behind the last car. No one was in sight.

He had intended to walk back down the tracks away from the station until he could find a private place to lie low for a while and consider his options. But as he studied the rear of the train, another idea flashed in his mind and before he had even considered the risks, he began to climb up the back of the railcar. It wasn't easy. There weren't any hand or footholds, possibly for this very reason. Once again his height helped as he could reach high enough to find a place to grab hold and haul himself up, his fingers and shoulders aching with the strain.

Once on top of the railcar, he crept on his belly to the very center of the roof and laid his thin body as flat as possible, wrapping an elbow and a strap from the rucksack around a ventilator. One quick peek all around told him that as long as no one made an effort to climb up to look down the roofs of the cars, he couldn't be seen from the ground next to the train. As he lay quietly, afraid the slightest move would resound loudly in the car below, the sun slowly rose in the east. It immediately started to warm the dark metal roof of the car, and Willy felt himself start to doze despite his discomfort and perilous situation. He'd managed only a few hours of catnap in the last forty-eight hours and caught himself several times, fighting to stay awake, but surrendering at last.

He was awakened abruptly by a tremendous crash. Disoriented, he first started to look up, and then caught himself and stayed flat, trying to listen to what was going on. An engine change: that was all. He was relieved and smiled at his own reaction. He had slept right through the tensest part of the process. His head rested on his outstretched arms and he could see his watch without changing positions: eight o'clock exactly and even as he considered it, the train started to move slowly away from the station.

The printed schedule said six more hours to Copenhagen, but Willy knew he couldn't remain on the roof the whole way. In the first large town buildings might be tall enough to overlook the top of the train. Someone would spot him and call ahead.

As the train rattled across the bridge spanning the Flensburg Fiord that demarked the actual border, Willy wondered whether the train would stop again for Danish customs on the opposite side. He knew he still couldn't move. He was at the end of the train that would be nearest any border guard station. Willy harbored no illusions that the Danes would help him, even if no German occupiers were nearby. In Munich the week before, he'd read in the newspapers how the Danes surrendered to the Nazis with hardly a shot and had been granted special status within the Reich as a protectorate state.

Prepared to wait it out, Willy was surprised when the train merely slowed through the Danish depot, blew its whistle several times and accelerated northwards towards Copenhagen. Willy spread himself out with legs and arms wide. No sleep now: he was certain that if he didn't stay alert he'd roll from the top of the car. As the train went faster and faster, Willy closed his eyes to try and recall the schedule folded in his jacket pocket. The train makes three stops before Copenhagen Central: where is the first? He remembered the name: *Tinglev*, but not the distance or time. He wanted desperately to check his schedule sheet but as the train swayed around a tight curve he was reminded of his precarious perch.

Forty minutes later, the engineer began to whistle almost continuously. Willy looked up and could discern ahead the outskirts of a small town over the treetops along the roadbed. He inched slowly towards the rear of the car roof. The whistle blew again and again. Lifting his head slightly to peer forward, Willy could see the station and its platforms. He thought the best strategy was to wait until the train slowed enough that he could jump safely and try to scamper away from the tracks. Later he could make his way to the station and try to get aboard the next train headed north, though he was concerned that tougher questions might be asked at the Danish stations. Denmark was an occupied country regardless its special status. If challenged for travel papers, he had nothing to show and would be taken into custody by either the Danes or the Germans, likely the same thing.

Willy reached the end of the car and sensed the train slowing as it approached the platform. Even before it stopped he began to lower himself down the rear of the car, hanging again by his fingers. His feet groped for a foothold of some sort. It was still nearly two meters to the ground and if he landed on a rail he'd break a leg for certain. Trying to pick his moment, the train suddenly lurched and he lost his grip and fell clumsily, landing on his side and sliding several feet across the rocks and gravel lining the track bed. The impact sent a lightning bolt up his spine and for a few difficult moments he thought he might not be able to get up again.

The train halted about twenty meters ahead and Willy could hear the brakes squealing. He looked around and there was no place to hide. There were several sets of parallel tracks and he'd have to make his way across a wide-open area before he'd have any cover at all. So he lurched to his feet and scrambled painfully to the back of the rear car, crouching just beneath and behind. He watched underneath as the folding stairs dropped to the platform and the conductor's feet stepped down and ambled off towards the station building. Willy peeked around the corner of the car. No one was in sight except for the back of the conductor. When the conductor opened the door and entered the building, Willy scooted around from the back of the car and climbed back inside, reclaiming his former seat. He spread out his books and tried to arrange things to look like he'd been settled there for awhile. Three other passengers in the car ignored him. Half a dozen new passengers wandered aboard the car and settled in similarly.

Twenty minutes later, after the train left Tinglev, the Danish conductor reached his last car, checking tickets. Willy was feigning sleep with his head cradled by his jacket. He had left his ticket for Copenhagen sticking from his sweater pocket. The conductor lifted the ticket carefully and examined it for validations. It didn't seem quite right. The ticket hadn't been punched properly at several of the transfer points. But the ticket *had* been purchased in Neumarket back across the border: another fucking German by his clothing, too. The conductor considered waking Willy to pester him about the discrepancies, but it was a beautiful spring morning, and his instructions were to treat Germans with kid gloves. The conductor decided it wasn't a day to screw with the master race.

Five hours later the train pulled into Copenhagen's central rail station.

Willy was convinced he'd been misled purposely. When he asked a shopkeeper standing outside his store for directions to Carlsberg House, he had done so in German. The man had looked him up and down and then sent him on a serpentine route. As Willy made the last turn he calculated that he'd walked twice the distance necessary from the central train station. It was nearly noon when he finally could see the walled complex just ahead. Willy grinned despite himself: while it was a very minor act of civil disobedience against German occupiers, he supposed, and hoped it had made the Danish man feel better.

The shopkeeper's shelves had been empty of everything except butter and eggs. With no exports to England, the Danes had more butter than they knew what to do with. A country with four million citizens, until four weeks ago Denmark had produced and shipped one hundred million dozen eggs to Britain every year. Now they had *an extra* three hundred eggs and thirty kilos of butter for every man, woman, and child. The stock was perishable and fragile and the German army had no interest, regardless the Danes' willingness to sell. But within weeks of the *invasion*, there was no coffee or cocoa. Rationing was going to be tough on the wealthy, comfortable Danes. Willy couldn't blame the shopkeeper, but he prayed for a friendlier reception by Professor Bohr and his associates.

Willy had only scraps on which to base a belief that Bohr could or would help. He was Heisenberg's mentor and friend, but that in itself implied an inconsistent and inexplicable attitude about the Nazis. Like Heisenberg, Bohr, with every opportunity available, had not tried to absent himself or escape from Denmark in the face of the Nazi threats, aggression, and occupation.

Next to Albert Einstein, Neils Bohr was arguably the most famous scientist in the world, and while Einstein's theories and teachings were esoteric and often abstruse, Bohr's theory on the structure of atoms and molecules was fundamental and unifying for both physicists and chemists like Willy.

Heisenberg had told Willy that Professor Bohr was as much a father figure as a colleague and friend. In Munich, Willy had heard that Bohr, like Einstein, Szilard, and others, had been active in finding academic positions in England and America for German-Jewish scientists fired under Hitler's civil service reforms six years before.

No matter how smart these men were, Willy wondered whether cloistered scientists truly comprehended the viciousness of the Nazis and the general apathy of most Germans regarding Nazi policies.

Professor Bohr lived and worked on the grounds of the Carlsberg Institute, an imposing cluster of buildings adjacent to the *Faelledpark* in the northeastern part of the city. His long route had brought Willy to the Institute from the north side through the park itself. Few private automobiles plied the streets: the Nazis had appropriated all the gasoline and motor oil stocks to help fight the battle in Norway. Makeshift horse-drawn taxis had been available for hire at the station.

All the shops were open despite the shortages and the cinemas were still showing American releases. Willy limped past theatres showing "Hollywood Cavalcade" and "Union Pacific." Willy saw few signs of the German army. A single squad of gray-uniformed troopers had been standing guard around the main station, and several empty army trucks had rumbled through the streets on some errand, but for the most part the Nazis were maintaining a low profile. Other than the line of huge staff cars parked outside, even *Wehrmacht* headquarters at the Hotel D'Angleterre was discrete. The German commander, General Kaupisch, had announced through the newspapers that Germans were in Denmark only to protect the Danes from Allied invasion. If the Danes felt humiliated by the ease at which the Germans conquered their country, for the first time in its long history, they limited their anger to their own military.

The park was crowded with children and their parents, teenagers playing soccer, bicyclists, and older people out for a stroll on a beautiful spring day. It was so unlike Germany that Willy felt a million miles away from Nazis and the war. If it weren't for the aching in his legs and in his heart, he might have been able to put everything out of his mind. He found a bench at the park's boundary, across the street from the Institute's rear entrance, intending to gather himself and go over what he was going to say when he got inside and considering his options if things didn't appear like they were working out. *They'll think I'm a Nazi spy. Other than my word and American passport, what proof do I have? Nothing!*

Rows of temporary food stalls had been erected nearby and business was good. Artists and booksellers had set up shop along the stone wall surrounding the park. Somewhere through the trees a band was playing Gilbert and Sullivan. Between gateposts above a park entrance a painted banner proclaimed *Forårfest*. That must mean *spring festival,* thought Willy. How could this be going on while the rest of the world is starting to burn? He began to imagine what the city might look like after a uranium bomb blast, but quickly steered himself back to his immediate problem. But it was hard to do.

Clothing was brighter and very casual. Everyone was enjoying themselves. He could hear laughter all around and realized that he hadn't heard this kind of free-spirited expression since he arrived in Europe. The humor and joking in the German beerhalls, his own included, he realized now to be dour, bitter, and sarcastic, colored by real fear and hopelessness. Here everything looked brighter and more cheerful somehow, the people, the park, buildings, everything.

That was how he spotted the plainclothes Gestapo agent.

A solitary man in a long black leather coat was leaning casually against the boundary wall smoking a cigarette. He was watching a side entrance to Carlsberg House. As he finished his smoke and crushed it on the sidewalk with a heavy shoe, he wandered over to a book display, picked up a volume and leaned back against the wall, pretending to read, but his attention really focused on the gate across the wide street.

Perhaps this man is part of routine security for the building, Willy told himself. But he knew it wasn't. If you wanted to keep people away, you'd use uniformed policemen. Every time someone walked towards the entrance, the man watched them intently. Surveillance. And he was watching people entering, not those leaving. Willy had no doubt they were looking for him. He had invaded a top secret Nazi atomic research facility two days ago and now there were undercover agents stationed at the entrance to Bohr's office and laboratory. Five minutes ago he had felt so pleased with himself. He'd managed to stay ahead of the Gestapo across northern Germany and into occupied Denmark. But he had been very wrong and had dangerously underestimated his pursuers. The Nazis had easily surmised where Willy might go and anticipated his movements, concentrating their forces at places where Willy might go looking for help.

What else did they know? Had they seen past the forged passport he'd presented at the *Gasthaus* in Ullem?

Do they know my name yet? How long will it take to track me back to Munich, to Lise and the Professor? How good a description did the technician give? Did Heisenberg recognize me from the description? Did he help the Gestapo set this trap? I believed Heisenberg wanted me to get the word out. Was I wrong?

Willy had been obsessed with the idea that if he could get to Bohr he would find a safe place to hide and get help escaping German territory. When he alerted Bohr about the weapons work, he was sure Bohr could get word to authorities in England and America.

Now these hopes had collapsed and Willy kicked himself for relying so heavily on this one chance. And Willy came to realize how he was a disease-carrier of sorts. Anyone he'd had contact with was in the same mortal danger as he: Lise and her father, his colleagues at the university, now even Bohr and his associates, though Bohr didn't even know Willy existed. People had entrusted him with their safety and hopes.

To avoid the agent, Willy made his way across the park, detoured several blocks, and cautiously approached the front gate of Carlsberg House. He deliberately stayed on the opposite side of the boulevard and kept his eyes straight ahead. At least four more men were watching from this side. The obvious ones. Willy had to believe there might be others, better disguised or hidden.

The streets were crowded and Willy found a passenger shelter halfway down the block where he could sit and watch the front entrance while pretending to wait for a trolley car. He picked up a section of a Danish newspaper left on the shelter bench and peered over the top edge as he pretended to read. He didn't know what he was waiting for, but he wasn't thinking very clearly at the moment. The situation was completely out of his control.

As he watched, a large saloon car pulled up near the corner across the street from the shelter. Willy twitched and flushed as the car horn blared three times. As its occupants climbed out, Gestapo agents up and down the street left their observation posts and converged on the car. Willy cringed as he noted that besides the four men he'd spotted, at least six others joined the group as they gathered at the back of the car.

Two uniformed SS officers and two leather-coated Gestapo men had emerged from the car and from an uncomfortable twenty-five meters away, Willy got a fairly good look at them. The major and lieutenant were both tall and erect, model German officers, immaculately dressed with gloves and high black boots, very much out of place on a Danish street corner. Danes brushing past made a point of ignoring the Germans.

The conference was brief and business-like. Both officers talked for several minutes, the senior man with great intensity and animation. A single piece of paper was handed all around, each field agent studying it for a few moments, before passing it along. The senior man asked several questions and looked from man to man demanding some sort of response or acknowledgement from each. Then everyone came suddenly to attention, and dispersed, returning to their posts.

The four men from the car continued to talk together for several minutes before climbing back inside. The car engine roared to life and it raced off down the street.

Cross Sections

Willy knew he had to get far away from Carlsberg House. That piece of paper could only be his description and after the visit from their officers, the agents would be all the more alert. Several trolleys had come and gone while Willy was sitting in the shelter: to linger longer would be suspicious. He waited for a group of passengers to alight from a trolley and merged with them as they walked off away from his last hope for help.

The early afternoon found Willy on a bench in *Faelledpark* with his scrap of unread newspaper in his lap. He was depressed and hungry. His ample supply of *Reichmarks* had worked and the previous evening he'd been able to purchase food from a vendor on the train between Hamburg and Neumünster, but that was eighteen hours ago. He'd learned to ignore the ache but Willy was concerned about the weakness in his legs. He couldn't tell how much might be from radiation poisoning and how much from hunger, fatigue, and tension. While food vendors here in the park would probably accept his German money, it would certainly call attention to him unnecessarily.

He discreetly counted his money and had nearly six hundred Reichmarks left, but little good it would do. He dared not go to a moneychanger or bank, buy food, or rent a room. He couldn't take the trolley or a taxi. The Gestapo would have feelers out everywhere and other than what Heisenberg had told him about Professor Bohr, Willy had no idea whether any other Dane would or could help.

He had been watching a large group of young men and women milling around in the park, college-aged and noisy. They were dancing and swaying with the music at the bandstand nearby, haggling with the street vendors, and flirting with passing girls. Several of the young men had long, unkempt hair, something that would stand out in Nazi Germany, and as Willy knew, would instantly engender a beating and crude barbering by SD thugs. Obviously Nazi discipline and regimen hadn't been introduced to the Danish student class in the first month of occupation. When Willy had first arrived in Munich in the fall of '38, there were still a few holdouts on the fringes of the university, but they had all disappeared by the time the war began eight months before. Intimidated by party thugs, converted by party doctrine, or drafted by the army, Willy had seen most of his colleagues and peers metamorphose into neat little soldiers or party functionaries. Those that hadn't, simply disappeared.

Children in cattle cars; the memory made his skin crawl. As Willy had told Lise, this war was going to be unlike anything before. The militarization of Germany extended to its children, to its education and science, to its very character. This was going to have a personal element unlike any before, where soldiers marched off and some didn't return. There would be no such dispassion or detachment this time. New atomic weapons would be used indiscriminately against cities and civilians; they would have little tactical value against formed troops. They would be used to terrorize and subjugate enemy civilians, with a lack of humanity so profound that when the war ended, *peace* would never mean the same thing again. Terror was the Party's weapon and so would be the uranium bomb. Terror was used on civilians who were more susceptible.

As an elderly flower lady paused near Willy's bench, one of the young revelers came over. As the two negotiated over the price of a small bouquet of bright flowers, Willy realized that the young woman wasn't Danish at all. With some difficulty and shuffling of currency a deal was made and the young woman ran back to her friends. Many of these young people must be tourists. Given the mood throughout the occupied countries, they could only be Finns or Swedes. Though nominal German allies, the Finns had just lost a war against the Russians, so they must be Swedes, and if they've come to Copenhagen as tourists there must be a means for them to return. Ferry service must be running again.

Pers Olsen was already drunk and for good reason. Ingrid had run off with some ass they'd met on the ferry Friday afternoon. He'd caught her making eyes at the man and then she'd been standoffish in the Copenhagen hotel on Friday night. Usually aroused by hotel rooms, she had brushed him off complaining of a stomachache. Pers was suspicious and when she disappeared on Sunday morning, he wasn't surprised but he was bitter. The last two nights he'd slept alone and miserable. He'd paid her fare from Malmö and expected *some* consideration. Tonight she'd be on the return ferry, probably with this other man. He hadn't decided what approach to take, anger, detachment and disdain, or disarming friendliness. Maybe drunk and pitiful would work. Pers was nursing his sixth liter of Danish beer: he wasn't sure about *pitiful*, but *drunk* was a real possibility! However getting drunk was difficult in occupied Denmark. The government had prohibited the sale of anything except weak beer and wine. Even *Aqua Vitae* was banned. The restriction was in place to prevent drunken, unruly Danes from hassling the damn Germans, but it did not take into account the acute needs of lovesick Swedes.

He was sitting on the grass in front of the bandstand where a small Danish band was butchering a favorite American Dixie tune. He tried to sing along: "Oh, ven der saints…..go marching in….., oh, ven der saints come marching in…."

A tall, skinny, yellow-haired man had stretched out nearby, and when Pers couldn't produce the next verse, the man picked up the lyrics in English: "Oh, I want to be in that number, when the saints come marching in!" Pers looked over with a smile and the man continued along with the band, "Oh, when those bells…begin to chime…oh, when those bells begin to chime…oh, I want to be in that number…when those bells begin to chime!"

As the band began to repeat the melody, the tall man shrugged and said in English: "Sorry, I believe there are other verses, but I don't know them. Sorry."

Pers had to change gears. He didn't have much occasion to practice speaking English, though he still read American and British newspapers, magazines, and books at the university library in Stockholm.

"Well, friend, you know more than I know," he said in English. "Are you an American?"

Willy nodded casually, still watching the band. "How did you guess?"

"Well, I suspect Englishmen would not be welcome in this tidy corner of the Third Reich. *QED*, you must be American. Leastwise, you don't sound like an Irishman, the only other possibility that I can think of. I read that all the damn Americans had already left Europe."

"Not many of us left, that's for sure. Your English is quite good," Willy offered. "Do you study here in Copenhagen?"

"Hell, no. All the Danes study is milk cows, bookkeeping, and our Swedish women. If their German friends will allow their universities to remain open, that is. Now they become experts at bending over and taking it up the ass! Just like Poles and Czechs!"

"Danes do brew passable beer, tasty if a little weak," Pers said lifting his empty glass to Willy. "Can I buy you a glass, my musical friend?"

"That would be great, thanks," Willy replied. As Pers struggled to his feet and made his way toward the pavilion, Willy pretended to concentrate on the band, but was watching the Swede as best he could. This was a moment of truth. If this man were not what he seemed to be, he would return with the police.

But two minutes later Pers was back with two liter beer glasses held at arms length to keep foam from dripping on his cloths.

They toasted and clicked, "*Skaol!*"

"How about you? I didn't see you on the ferry from Sweden. Do *you* study here in Copenhagen?"

"No, I'm actually a student in Bavaria. Just thought I'd run up here between sessions and see what Copenhagen is all about."

"I hear universities in Germany had shut down unless they were teaching marching, mayhem, or murder. Which is your field of study?" Pers challenged sarcastically.

"Oh, *mayhem* is my specialty," Willy teased back, "with a minor concentration in German women."

"A tough course for sure," Pers laughed. "The study of women is difficult and tedious enough: I have very recently failed one of my advanced classes. But *German* women, that is another thing altogether. I think I would choose something simple like Chinese algebra or Sanskrit poetry. I raise my glass to you. You are a strong and brave man!"

"And you?"

"I am a student of economics and complete my degree next year. Then I will work for father's meatpacking company, marry my cousin, and sire six boring, in-bred children. I will go to church every Sunday to be damned by the preacher and whatever money is left after the collection plate, I'll pay the state as taxes. Those taxes will be used to bribe the Nazis and British and Russians to allow Sweden to remain neutral. Our country will be neutral and so will be our lives.

"Sometimes I think a real war might be good for Sweden. At least it might be exciting for a while. Get us off our fat asses.

"Biggest concern right now is that naval blockades have cut off our supply of American recordings and gangster movies. They are the only bright spots in our otherwise neutral existence.

"Look at us! We spend our good money and vacation traveling great distances to a country occupied by a puritanical military dictatorship, looking for a good time. You must appreciate the irony.

Cross Sections

"I have to take a piss. How about another beer since I'm up? Wait here. I will be back in a minute." Pers stumbled to his feet this time and wove though the crowd.

By seven o'clock that evening, Willy had learned more than he needed to know about meatpacking, Swedish whores, and Baltic currency exchange. Pers had consumed a prodigious quantity of beer and improved his English vocabulary, though his annunciation suffered some. They were sitting together on the steps of the deserted bandstand. The park had emptied, with only a few stragglers and lovers lingering behind. The curfew would begin at nine o'clock. A partial blackout had been in effect for several weeks since the British first bombed the Luftwaffe's new airfield at Aalborg in northern Denmark.

"Willy, my friend, I am having a wonderful time. You are a good listener and fine man, even if you chose to live with the bloody Nazis and their cold-hearted women.

"But I now have a big favor to ask. The ferry for Malmö leaves from Saltholm at nine. I don't think I can walk right now. I need to take a nap for a few minutes: just twenty minutes or so and I will be fine. Let me just lie back for just a minute. I feel drunk, but I also feel good. It has made me forget.

"Please wake me up in twenty minutes? Thank you my friend, you are a scholar and a gentleman." With that Pers collapsed back, his legs still hanging down the steps. As Willy sat by, Pers, flat on his back, began to snore loudly. Willy was quiet for ten minutes before he moved, desperately tired and envious of his new friend. A minute later Willy was on his way to the harbor with a Swedish passport, some cash, and the return half of a ticket on the Swedish ferry *Sverige*.

Welcome to war, my Swedish friend.

S.23

Tuesday was the final evening of Copenhagen's spring festival. The ferry dock was crowded with young revelers returning to Sweden through Malmö from Saltholm at the northern end of Copenhagen's upper harbor. The *Sverige* was scheduled to leave at nine in the evening, though since this ferry was the last of the day, its crew usually allowed extra time for stragglers. And there would be many. Even under the new German occupation the Swedes continued to find Copenhagen a more vibrant and open city than Malmö and the other small, provincial Swedish towns along the coast. Service had been disrupted for several weeks after German troops arrived, but had restarted the previous week.

After less than a month of German occupation, there was little indication to a visitor that anything had changed. After all, Denmark was officially a Protectorate of the Reich, not an occupied country. Perhaps Danes were more guarded in their speech and were mindful of the curfew imposed by the occupation forces, but none of these things oppressed the Swedes. Though menu selections were limited, they had flooded the restaurants and bars and parks since Friday afternoon and were all waiting until the last possible moment before returning home. Now they packed the customs and police checkpoints at the ferry dock, pushing and shoving, and otherwise enjoying themselves fully.

This had caught the occupiers quite unprepared. Only a handful of German customs officials was on duty, supported by a single squad of troops, fifteen men with rifles and no crowd control experience. If this had been a hostile force, the small disciplined group of Germans would have maintained control. When confronted by crowds of drunken young men and pretty girls, they were helpless. Officially their duty was to carefully screen all the passengers to identify and detain any non-Swedes headed for Malmö without permission from the local German authority. Everyone from the occupied countries was trying to escape to Sweden: Danes, Dutchmen, Frenchman, and even Germans. Some were Jews;

others were communists, pacifists, intellectuals, and many simply fearful. Even German deserters had tried to sneak aboard the ferries in the past few months.

While the German soldiers tried to restrain the enthusiastic and boisterous crowd outside, it was left to Danish customs officers, now subservient to their German bosses, to check passports and transit letters.

Three hundred passengers descended on the customs house and all were cleared quickly, including a tall, gaunt man carrying a Swedish passport describing him as a foot shorter, five years younger, and brown-eyed. The Danish agent had examined the proffered passport, looked the fellow up and down, and said something unintelligible to him in Swedish. The man had just stood there, glassy-eyed, without responding. The agent took note of man's German clothing, smiled, applied his ink stamp, and handed him back the stolen passport. In German the official said with a chuckle, "Auf Wiedersehen, Herr Olsen, and good luck to you."

The young man was frozen in place. He didn't seem to comprehend. Then the next people in line elbowed him aside and away from the counter.

"Rolf," shouted the customs officer to an associate working the next section of counter. "If you get a Swedish fellow named Pers Olsen who claims to have lost his passport, let him go through to the ferry. Another man found his papers and ticket and showed them to me. I'm sure this guy will hold them on board for Mr. Olsen."

As the last of the passengers cleared customs and crammed aboard, a German staff car skidded to a halt in front of the customs building. The German soldiers, lounging and smoking now that the crush had passed, roused themselves to attention and one ran to find their officer. With his two grim-faced Gestapo sergeants clearing a path, Major Frick barged inside.

"You must hold the ferry," Frick demanded of the Danish customs men and a young German army lieutenant, without introduction or prologue.

"That will be difficult Major, very difficult," said the senior Dane, stalling as he watched through the windows as the ferrymen cast off lines. "The ferry and its captain are Swedes and they'll probably only follow instructions from the harbormaster."

"Lieutenant, get the harbormaster on the telephone immediately," ordered Frick and the officer quickly ran off. Glancing out the window behind him, now at last Frick realized that the ferry was starting to move away from the pier.

"Müller. Schmidt. Run. Get on board immediately. You understand your orders?" Smashing back through the door, Frick ran alongside his two men out along the quayside. "Find Petersen. Kill him. If you can't locate him, disable the ferry until we can get more men aboard for a thorough search. Do you both understand? Do not let Petersen get off the ferry in Sweden alive."

As the three reached the edge of the pier, the two Gestapo agents were just able to jump across the widening gap of open water to the lower deck of the ferry where bemused crewmen caught them. Frick, relieved that he had managed to get reliable agents aboard the ferry, hurried back to the customs office. The German lieutenant had not been able to reach the Danish harbormaster and within minutes the ferry's bright stern and deck lights were out of sight around the headland.

Frick confronted the two Danish customs men with Willy's photograph: "Did either of you pass this man through on tonight's ferry?" Though both shook their heads, Frick didn't miss the flicker in the fat one's eyes. Now they both knew that Petersen was aboard the *Sverige*.

"Lieutenant, are there any German naval units nearby? Quickly, if you value your commission."

"Yes, Herr Major. There are several patrol boats and inshore transports moored near the breakwater at Nyholm."

"You're coming to show me where," Frick said as he propelled the lieutenant bodily out the door ahead of him. Frick ran back to his car, the lieutenant in tow, and yelled to his driver, "Quickly, take me to the German navy headquarters. This man knows the way."

As the car raced back towards the city, the lieutenant gave the driver his instructions.

"Lieutenant. What is your name anyway?" demanded Frick.

"Lusser, Herr Major," stuttered the Lieutenant. His gray uniform and helmet looked two sizes too large.

"Lusser, tell me, how long does that ferry take to get to Malmö?"

"Three hours according to the schedule, sir."

"How many passengers went aboard?"

"They tell me the *Sverige* can carry over three hundred people, Herr Major. It looks like it was completely full this evening."

"How large is its crew?"

"I don't know exactly, Herr Major, but when the ship docks many of the crew disembark to shop and visit the bars near the dock. I've seen less than a dozen men myself. The entire crew can't be more than twenty."

Frick's mind raced. He considered attempting to contact the Swedish authorities at Malmö. He could warn them that a dangerous criminal was aboard who should be held. No good. The Swedes were unreliable drunkards and would probably go out of their way to help Petersen even if he truly were a criminal. It would take several hours to contact and rouse Gestapo agents or Nazi sympathizers in Sweden through headquarters in Berlin. The responsibility was his; he must follow through with the resources at hand.

The car whipped through a guarded gate at the Navy yard, slowing only enough for the sentry to see the major's collar badges. At a loss, the driver headed toward the water and the lights of a building next to some docks and piers.

The major was first out of the car and headed towards the dock. "Lusser, find me a naval officer. Bring him to *that* boat," he said, pointing to a sleek, low profile E-boat, a *Schnellboot*, tied at the end of the pier.

The E-boat was new, its light gray paint glistened in the damp air as if wet. *S.23* was stenciled in black on the bows and on the low cockpit combing. The *Schnellboot* was nearly thirty meters long. Frick had heard that the volunteer officers serving on these boats were all prima donnas and aristocrats. He could expect sassy resistance to his authority, but Frick was in no mood to tolerate any insolence, especially from amateurs.

Instead, Lieutenant Lusser turned up with a slow-moving, gray-bearded and rumpled petty officer in tow, smoldering pipe in one hand, coffee cup in the other. He was dressed in greasy blue coveralls and wore a crumpled watch cap.

'Good evening, Major," the navy man said, "What can we do for you?" His manner was disinterested and impatient.

"You are…?"

"Chief Warrant Officer Berg, Major. Sorry but I'm the senior man on duty tonight. We weren't expecting visitors."

"Who else is here?" asked Frick, trying to control his temper. These old veterans would resist threats.

"The are six of us. We're scheduled to make a patrol run around the harbor at midnight in the whaleboat over there looking for saboteurs, mermaids, whatever. Otherwise things have been pretty quiet here for the past few weeks." The Chief was just now beginning to realize that something unquiet might be in the making. "I'll send a man over to the officers' quarters and have him try and locate Captain Kraus, our division commander, or Lieutenant Von der Happel, this boat's skipper. Might take awhile. I suspect they're out having dinner somewhere in the city. So if you'll excuse me." He turned to make his escape.

"I can't do that, Berg. There isn't time," Frick mustered all the command and urgency he could into his voice. "A dangerous enemy of the Reich slipped aboard tonight's ferry to Sweden. I must commandeer this boat and intercept the ferry before it reaches Malmö. I need you and all the men you have available. This is an important duty. We need to leave immediately if we're going to catch that ship. Now."

"Major," the Chief pleaded, "no one from the E-boat crew is on duty."

"No matter. A man of your seniority should be capable enough or is undeserving of his current rank and privilege." This was the sort of threat even a senior non-com would consider. "Gather your men. Now, Chief."

Chief hesitated only a moment. There was of course, no choice. He was worried about what the major meant by "intercept," but he hurried back to the dock office to get his men. "Let's go," Frick ordered the lieutenant, "I need as many men as I can get, if we have to board and search that ferry. You, too," he said to the driver who was trying to be invisible and was edging his way back toward the car. Frick led them across the short gangplank down to the deck of the E-boat, dimly lit by partially masked flood lamps overhead along the dock.

Two torpedo launchers, one on each side, were sited well forward. A twenty-millimeter rapid-fire cannon, mounted near the blunt bow was fired from open pit in the forecastle. On the stern deck were several sets of empty racks Frick assumed were meant to hold mines or depth charges. The E-Boat had only a short radio mast, and its Navy ensign was furled and covered on a flagstaff amidships. In the center cockpit the controls looked simple enough. On either side of the cockpit were swivels for light machine guns. He could only wait for the Chief to return. He tried to look around below deck but the lights were off and he couldn't immediately locate a switch. Frick stashed his attaché case under the mess table and stood below alone in the dark trying to imagine how this might play out. His options were very limited.

It was several minutes before he felt the boat rock with the arrival of Berg and his men. He climbed up the companionway back into the cockpit.

"I brought seven men, Major, but that one there is just a boy, our mess steward."

"It will have to do. What is the situation in terms of fuel and munitions?"

"I know the boat was fueled after it returned from patrol this morning, Herr Major. As far as I know, no ammunition has been expended, except to test fire the guns."

"Small arms?"

"There are a dozen Mauser rifles stored below and several handguns with ammunition. Standard issue. My men are trained to use rifles as part of our harbor patrol duties."

"When you have a chance, show Lieutenant Lusser here where they're stored. Do we have enough skilled men to operate this boat?"

"Yes, sir. I can steer and navigate. Seaman Freund has experience with these types of engines and will tend them below. The others are all able seamen. Spitz and Hermann have been instructed in the use of the machine cannons, though to be honest, Major, we've never used any of these weapons in battle, only practice."

"Hopefully it won't come to that Chief," said Frick doubtfully. "It will depend on the Swedes. But first we need to catch them. Are we ready to go?"

"Yes, Major. What time did the ferry leave, sir?"

"Lieutenant?"

"At ten o'clock, Chief," Lusser answered.

The Chief thought for a few seconds. "It's going to be close sir, if we're going to catch up with them before they reach Swedish waters. In awhile I'll let Spitz take the helm and I'll try to calculate a more precise course and intercept point. Once we get close, it'll be easy enough to find her. The Swedes will have the ferry lit up like a party to keep the English bombers from mistaking her flag. If you're ready, Major, we'll start the engines and cast off."

"Hurry."

A moment later the twin diesel engines roared to life. Frick hadn't appreciated how loud they'd be, despite their underwater exhausts. The entire boat rumbled under his feet. It was very disorienting. As the crew went to work casting off and pulling in various lines Frick felt he was in the way and was concerned that he might hamper the boat's operation. He climbed out of the cockpit and as the boat accelerated away from the dock he braced himself against the aft cannon mount. Suddenly Frick and the whole boat were plunged into complete darkness, and it took several minutes before he could begin to make out building lights from shore. There was no official blackout in force in Copenhagen tonight, but most of the businesses and warehouses along the waterway were closed over the long weekend.

Five minutes later, the racing E-boat entered open water and began to pound up and down through the waves. Frick and Lusser stood together in the darkness clinging helplessly to the gun mount. Soon they could not see any shore lights at all. Frick was worried that they'd smash into some obstacle or another boat in the dark, but he recognized that he had to trust these navy men. This is their element, their duty. But if a crisis came, could he be sure they'd obey his orders? Could he give sensible ones? He felt seawater running over his boots and salt spray in the air made his face feel clammy.

Later the Chief came back to them and shouted over the engine sounds, "Come below if you wish, Major, I'll show you our problem. I can also show the lieutenant the small arms lockers."

Down below, the pounding of the boat was accentuated. Frick was dizzy from the motion of the speeding boat compounded by fatigue, hunger, and tension. While he wavered and wedged himself into the seat at the tiny navigation table, the Lieutenant stumbled after the Chief to the forward compartment. When the chief returned he switched on a red overhead light and pulled a rolled map out from a pigeonhole under the table.

"Major, I can't guarantee we'll overtake the *Sverige*. I know the ferry and her skipper very well. After the last war, before I was recalled to active duty, I served as a pilot on freighter runs all up and down these coasts. The ferry has a top speed of sixteen knots and I expect Captain Johansen will push his ship tonight since it's his last run and he won't expect any other traffic out here. The *S.23* is making around 38 knots and the seaway's fairly smooth tonight." *Smooth?* thought Frick!

"The *Sverige* has a fifty minute head start and it's 100 kilometers to Malmö from Saltholm." Berg was using the points of a pair of dividers to mark the ends of the route for Frick. "The *Sverige* had to stay below ten knots until they were around the point here, so when you add that all up, it will take them four hours point to point."

Frick had roughly calculated the transit time for the E-boat in his head. "Then we'll catch the ferry for sure, as long as you steer the boat straight," Frick said bitterly. He felt hot and sensed a rising gorge. He did not want to vomit in front of this enlisted man.

"Beg your pardon, Major, but it's not that simple. The Swedes claim a twelve-mile limit and we might not catch them until they're in Swedish national waters."

"That's no concern to you, Chief. Just see that we find that ferry as quickly as possible." Frick hauled himself up the companion ladder desperate to reach fresh air. As he moved aft back to his haven at the cannon mount he nearly fell over the quaking body of his driver, uniform front covered in vomit lying on the deck moaning. Frick stepped over him, took several steps, and then returned to kick the man solidly in the ribs with his boot.

"On your feet, you fool, or I'll throw you overboard this very minute." The driver pulled himself to a sitting position, then to his feet. Wordlessly he fled forward in the near darkness.

"Fool," repeated Frick. The kick had done himself more good than the pitiful driver. A sense of control and purpose was quickly returning. He reminded himself that he was a German officer, more importantly an SS officer. Such a man should have no feelings, no pangs, no self-pity, only duty.

He made his way back to the steering station. He was in command and this must be impressed on these men. Berg was steering with another seaman at his side. Frick watched for several minutes how the seaman played the engine speed controls evidently to smooth out the way the E-boat was smashing into the waves. Suddenly and decisively he stepped forward, shoved the seaman to the side and advanced both throttles to their stops. The boat accelerated noticeably. He stood his ground, hand on his holstered pistol, daring anyone to say anything.

Berg moved to protest. Running the engines unbalanced at full speed risked shaking the boat apart. But a single glance at Major Frick spoke volumes. Even in the dim light from the control panel, his stare was as black as his uniform, and looking away from the Major's face for a moment all Berg could see was the skull emblems on his collar tabs.

Todt. Death. Worry about what was going to happen when the *S.23* met up with the *Sverige*, was replaced by a morbid fear of what might happen right here now if Berg said or did the wrong thing. He concentrated on the compass and the faint horizon ahead.

"Lusser!" Frick shouted down the companionway. "Get up here."

"Sir!" said the Lieutenant as he came into the cockpit.

"Are you prepared to make up a boarding party?

"Yes, sir," Lusser replied with some uneasiness. "There are eleven of us in all, counting yourself and the mess boy. There are a dozen rifles with bayonets and ammunition below.

"The two light machine guns below are ready too, but there are no tripods or carrying straps. Sir, it would take two men to man each of the machine guns if we take them with us. I think we'll be better off with nine riflemen." Frick nodded his agreement.

"I found two Luger pistols but no bullets for them. The ship's officers probably keep them in their belts or have hidden them somewhere. You and I have pistols. I have three magazines for mine."

"Berg," demanded Frick. "Do you have any grapples aboard? The Swedes may not cooperate and lower ladders down to us."

"I don't know for sure, sir." Berg hadn't considered that. "Spitz, go and check the lazarettes fore and aft. See if you can find any grapples or small boat anchors. Fifty feet of throwing line for each. Hurry."

Frick looked at his watch in the light from the compass binnacle. "Lusser, make sure the cannons are properly manned. Mount the two machine guns here. Test-fire the guns when you're ready. We have less than sixty minutes."

The darkness was now almost complete, low clouds masking the stars. The E-boat was out of sight of any land and all the deep-water sea buoys had been extinguished to eliminate marks that might be used by English submarines trying to sneak into the target-rich Baltic Sea. For several minutes there was a bustle of men moving about the deck. Frick had to step aside in the cockpit as the light machine guns were mounted and tested. The throaty sound of the MG-34's was familiar and reassuring to Frick. He knew it extended his power out into the darkness. Several minutes later the forward twenty-millimeter cannon fired four rounds in quick succession. The muzzle flash temporarily caused him to lose his night vision, and before he had recovered, one of the seamen stationed at the starboard gun, was yelling to Berg. "Chief! I can see ship's lights ahead. Just off to starboard."

"I see them," Berg replied. Frick night vision returned slowly, but soon he too could make out the masthead lights of the *Sverige*. Berg momentarily turned the wheel to the right to line up his course.

"We're still nine miles away, Major. At night the distances are tricky."

"How long until we're up with him?"

"Twenty or twenty-five minutes, sir, unless they slow down. I can't tell how near he is to Swedish territory, but I'd guess he'll be close when we reach him."

For now the only sound was the engines and the hull pounding through the chop. All eyes were focused on the lights ahead. If Frick continued to stare unblinking at the lights nothing seemed to change from one moment to the next. But if he looked away for several minutes and then back, he could tell that the lights were getting brighter and more distinct. In ten minutes he could make out the ferry's stern light. In fifteen minutes everyone could discern the glow from deck and cabin lights. But Berg, looking further ahead saw something else.

"Major, we're too late. I can just now see the lights at Rock Point and the lighthouse at Stofdahl. We've already crossed into Swedish waters."

"Keep going," Frick commanded. His men aboard the ferry had failed, the fools. They'd been ordered to stop the ferry even if they failed to locate Petersen. Two trained and motivated men should have had no problems with the unarmed ferry crew. He wasn't going to give up now.

"Get us along side. We'll fire in the air and make them stop. Surely they won't resist, regardless the legalities. We'll let diplomats sort this all out later. We must stop the spy from escaping."

The ferry continued along, oblivious to its pursuer.

Fifteen more minutes and they were alongside. The bright lights from the crowded decks and open portholes cast a glow nearly half a mile wide. The Germans could see dozens of people running forward on deck and as they approached, many of the people along the side noticed the E-boat and could be seen pointing its way and shouting.

"Move up even with the bridge and match speeds," Frick ordered Berg. "Get close enough so they can hear me."

Berg steered the *S.23* as close as he dared under the bridge deck. The big ferry dwarfed the E-boat. The ferry's lowest deck was ten feet above the E-boat's masthead. No one on the *Sverige's* bridge had yet taken notice. Some sort of commotion had men running back and forth from the bridgehouse along the upper deck.

"Sound a horn blast," ordered the frustrated Frick who had not imagined being ignored like this. Berg pulled hard on a lever and an air horn blared three times. "Does your friend the captain speak German?"

"Yes, Major, his German is very good."

A mate aboard the ferry opened the bridge door and stared at the E-boat before leaning back inside to shout to someone. A bearded officer then came out onto the bridge wing and looked angrily down on the *S.23*.

Frick gathered himself and shouted, "I am Major Frick of the German Customs Department. I must speak to your captain immediately." Frick had so identified himself, figuring that Customs might be the only department a Swedish captain would wish to avoid crossing. Even using the hailing trumpet it was difficult to be heard across the gap between the two ships. At idle, the *S.23's* twin diesels bubbled loudly.

"I am the captain. What the hell do you want? I have no time for you now." The *Sverige's* skipper was short and very stout.

"Captain," Frick shouted, trying to sound both firm and friendly. A demand was not likely to sit well with this fat prick. "A German citizen, a murderer, boarded your ship in Copenhagen. He is armed and very dangerous. He's deranged. I want to come aboard your ship and find the killer and take him back with me."

"Rubbish! I already know there are *killers* aboard my ship and I'm sure you know all about it. Stand off!" replied the Swede angrily. "You have no authority here. This is Sweden. I've radioed ahead for help. They will find your man. Bureaucrats can decide whether to return him to you. And if you have anything to do with this, I see you in hell! Meanwhile, stay clear of my ship!"

"Captain, this man is a threat to your crew and passengers. I know what he looks like. It will take us only a few minutes to locate him. He's killed four people."

"Maybe it's more now. So what? Your whole country is full of bloody murderers. What's one more to you?"

Frick smiled to himself. If there had been shooting aboard the ferry there was a chance that Schmidt and Müller had found Petersen. But he had to know for sure. No room for lingering doubts. His orders were crystal clear.

In the lights from the ferry's deck, the Swedish captain recognized the E-boat's helmsman.

"Christian Berg! Is that you? What kind of fool's errand is this? Who is this black-hatted pig? Where is your captain?"

Frick turned on Berg and whispered, "Convince him. Get us on board. Once there we'll be able to get them to stop. At gunpoint if necessary." Berg passed the wheel to Spitz and climbed up on the bridge combing. His sea-trained voice carried easily between the ships.

"Matthias, the Major is right. The man he's looking for might start shooting aboard the *Sverige*. We can help protect your passengers. Please Matthias. It's for your own good."

"Christian, that's for me to decide. Someone has *already* started shooting. Best thing I can do is make port fast as possible and let the police sort things out. You know how things are. Explain it to your friend there. As for you, Major, if your story is true, you missed your chance in Copenhagen. I say again, back off. The Coast Guard will be here in a few minutes. Follow us in if you like, though you'll risk internment if you do!"

The Swedish captain looked forward and aft along his ship and turned to go back inside, bolting and locking the bridge door behind him.

"Captain! I must demand that you stop immediately," Frick shouted, "or I'll have to…." The Swedish captain was gone. Dozens of frightened, young passengers had crowded the railings listening to the exchange and now they too began to heap abuse and accusation on the Germans.

Frick sounded the horn several more times but was ignored by the ferry's bridge crew, and the blaring horn only seemed to bring more derision from the passengers looking down on the *S.23* from the crowded forward decks. Someone threw a deck chair over the railing towards the Germans but it fell way short, disappearing into the ship's wake.

The Major was fuming. "Lieutenant! Fire the forward 20-millimeter in the air in front of their bridge. Now!" Lusser ran forward and with the help of one of the seaman freed the Bofors gun and rapidly fired six rounds directed well forward of the ferry's bow. Startled faces appeared at the bridge windows. Many of the passengers at first ducked for cover and then panicked and ran aft diving into doorways. A few still paused to shout unintelligibly at the E-boat.

Frick was about to order Lusser to fire again when he realized that the ferry had turned sharply towards the E-boat. Spitz did not react quickly enough and the ferry came within only a few yards. The *S.23* was momentarily spun around, out of control, and for a brief instant they were close to being sucked into the ferry's propeller wash. It was a long minute before Berg and Spitz were able to regain steerage and accelerate away. At the last moment, they were sure they'd be crushed by the massive ferry, which hovered like a mountain above them.

As the Germans moved off, the *Sverige* returned to its original course and seemed to speed up, determined to reach Malmö as quickly as possible. The decks and bridge were cleared but the Germans could see that they were being watched from every window and port.

"Get closer, Berg. Now!" Frick commanded. Berg obediently swung the boat to port moving back to within fifty yards, parallel to the ferry bridge.

"Lieutenant. This time aim for the lights and structures above the bridge. They must understand. They must stop."

"Major," Berg meekly protested, "this is a neutral, civilian ship. You cannot fire on it. We'll all end up in prison. In Sweden. In Germany. I don't know. But you can't do this."

"Silence. Now Lusser!" Frick shouted forward.

The cannon fired, Lusser attempting to direct the shells high above the bridge. But the crew was inexperienced and the E-boat continued to roll dramatically in the ferry's bow wake. Shells smashed into the windows all along the bridge. Glass and shrapnel was flying everywhere, raining onto the deck and into the water alongside.

The ferry wavered left and right and then started to turn away. But it did not slow down. Within moments the stack started to spew heavy smoke as the *Sverige* began to race toward shore and safety at flank speed.

"Fire all the guns!" Frick ordered and moved himself to the MG-34 mounted on the cockpit combing. As Frick's light machine gun groaned, raking the bridge again, the aft 20-millimeter began firing. At first its crew purposely fired well above the ferry's structure, but when Frick paused and glanced back at them, they quickly lowered their aiming point and started firing ineffectively into the hull opposite them. When Frick's ammunition belt was exhausted, the others all stopped shooting at the same time and stood looking at the Major. As he stared at the ferry it again pulled slightly ahead.

"Torpedo!" Frick yelled. He turned to Berg, "Arm a torpedo and get in position to fire it."

"Sir, we can't. I mean I don't know how. None of my men do."

"You're lying. Ready a torpedo. We haven't any time left. Do what I say or I'll have you shot!"

Lieutenant Lusser had come back to the cockpit and overheard the orders. He joined the protest. "Major Frick, we can't sink the ferry. It's loaded with innocent people. Your own men are also on board."

"Please sir," pleaded Berg, "don't ask us to do this thing."

"Do you refuse my orders?" asked Frick looking at Lusser and Berg. They looked at each other in the dim light and began to straighten and face the Major. If they stuck together…

Frick lifted his right arm and fired his pistol point-blank into Lusser's face. The back of his head exploded. Berg felt for a moment that he'd been hit with sea spray; his eyes were misted and his face and beard were wet. But as he saw Lusser's body collapse and tumble down the companionway, he knew that he'd been showered by the lieutenant's brains, bones, and blood. He could now smell it and taste it. He wanted to scream but was petrified. Spitz was cowering, crouched in the rear corner of the cockpit, hands covering his ears, eyes tightly shut.

"Berg, I need you to steer the boat. Get ready to launch a torpedo. If you hesitate for a second, I will shoot the mess boy next. We don't need him."

"Spitz…. Spitz," Berg said, trying to rouse his man. "You and Herman set up the portside torpedo. Please, Spitz, please."

Without looking up to avoid the Major's stare, Spitz hurried out of the cockpit and ran forward.

"If you can't do this thing, I'll kill you right now!" Frick pointed his pistol at Berg.

"Please, Major, please," Berg begged as he advanced the throttle and started to swing wide to starboard to set up a right angle intercept course on the ferry. It took several minutes, but Berg maneuvered the *S.23* so it was two hundred meters ahead of the ferry's path. He slowed to wait for it to pass in front of its bow. Berg had vague plans to aim the torpedo at the ferry's prop and rudder, to cripple it. But he felt dizzy and helpless, like he had fallen off a cliff and hadn't yet hit bottom. Lusser's warm blood was now cold and sticky on his face. Spitz came back to the cockpit, wrench in hand.

"Christian, the torpedo is primed and ready. Herman will strike the firing mechanism when you order." He unobtrusively edged back to the rear of the cockpit, behind the Major, who, pistol in hand, was studying Berg's every action.

In the instant before Spitz could raise the heavy steel spanner, Frick instinctively spun to his right. Spitz's blow went wild, the wrench banged off the binnacle, and he fell to his knees and hands. Without hesitation, Frick leaned forward and shot Spitz once in the spine and once in the back of the head.

Frick stepped over the body and put the hot, smoking muzzle against Berg's neck, just below his left ear. Frick didn't say a word; he simply pressed the barrel harder. The ferry was now passing in front of the E-boat, holding course, not trying to avoid the attack they should have known was inevitable. Despite the faint light, the Swedes could surely see the man stationed at the port launcher and understand the significance, but they didn't slow or turn away.

Berg, gun to his head, edged the *S.23* closer until it was only fifty meters away. He could see bullet holes along the ferry's hull amidships. A few were leaking oil, he noted. For a moment he couldn't seem to remember how they got there. It was all like a dream.

"Now, Herman!" he yelled forward at the last possible second. Herman struck the manual trigger with a mallet and the torpedo's chemical motor roared to life and it was ejected from the tube that protruded through a notch cut in just aft of the bow stem.

Mesmerized, Berg watched as the ferry suddenly began to slow even as the torpedo dove under water then porpoised just before it struck the ferry a hundred feet in front of the rudder, several feet above the waterline. Instead of the watery spout from an underwater detonation, there was a fiery blast that extended out from the impact point enveloping the entire stern of the ferry and the nearby E-boat.

As a flame front and concussion overtook the *S.23*, the E-boat first pitched down by the bow, and then was raised steeply upwards. Everyone aboard the E-boat was bowled over by the force of the explosion or lost their footing, as the boat was tossed around like a toy. Frick who had been standing at the edge of the cockpit trying to watch the torpedo's path was thrown out of the low cockpit. He dropped his pistol as he grabbed desperately for a handhold on the deck. The lights had gone out on the ferry and he'd been plunged back into total darkness, broken only by an eerie glow at the point of torpedo impact.

Cross Sections

A fire had broken out on the ferry and as the flames quickly grew, the E-boat flattened itself out. The *S.23's* engines were shut-down and the crippled ferry's momentum continued to carry it forward.

Frick could neither hear nor see, but as his mind cleared, he felt a rush of excitement and gratification. By God, he'd gotten the ferry to stop. If it sank and Petersen drowned, so much the better. But he had to make sure and started to get to his feet.

Someone jumped on him in the darkness. At first it seemed just an annoyance as it someone had stumbled and fallen atop him, but as his assailant worked to improve his hold, Frick realized that he was being attacked. He felt several weak blows to his body absorbed by his heavy uniform jacket and coat, but finally a fist found his face and that blow was followed by another and another. The first strikes made him angry and he was flushed with rage until another stunned him and yet another bounced his head off the deck.

Now it seemed to Frick like everything was in slow motion: the blows came minutes apart and he could anticipate them. The pain was dull and suffocating. He wanted to stand up. It was his duty to stand up, to stand tall, fearless, and erect. His men should not see any signs of weakness, regardless how sleepy he felt.

The army driver sat limply leaning hard against the flagstaff. The pain in his hands was excruciating and in the faint light from the ferry burning several hundred meters away, he could see they were covered with dark stains: blood, his and the Major's. Many of the punches he'd thrown had missed and hit the deck. Now his fingers and knuckles were broken and useless. He shivered uncontrollably. When the flames flared, he looked up and could see the Major lying nearby. A seaman, both hands grasping the aft cannon pedestal, was standing on Frick's throat with one foot and kicking him in the head over and over again with the other. Every time a kick was dealt the seaman would sob and say "shit."

"Is he dead?" Berg asked coming aft from the cockpit. "Herman, is he dead?"

Herman gave a final kick and stepped off Frick's neck. "Yes, he's dead, Chief. But we're all dead men. Every one of us. Better we went quick like Johann. The Gestapo will garrote us like hogs. Better like poor Johann." He was now bawling like a girl.

The other sailors had come aft. "Chief, what are we going to do?"

"Look!" said another, "the ferry's going down." Illuminated by the flames on its stern, the Germans could see that the ferry was listing over to starboard. Suddenly, while they were all staring, the flames disappeared in an instant and there was nothing to see except the distant lights from villages along the nearby Swedish coast. The remaining crew stood together in the darkness.

"We should help them. All these people. The water's still freezing cold."

"What will we do with them, you fool. There'll be hundreds in the water."

"Someone on shore must have heard the explosion and seen the fire. They'll send boats."

"The ferry captain said the Coast Guard was on its way. They'll catch us if we stay here. I'd rather face things back home than rot in a Swedish jail for the rest of my life."

"Are you crazy? Don't you understand what's happened? We're dead whatever we do and wherever we go."

"Chief, you have to decide for us."

"I can't decide now. I can't think or see straight. Walter, get the engines restarted. We'll head back for Saltholm and try and decide what to do when we get there. But the best thing is to tell the truth, at least some of it. We followed the Major's orders. Tried to stop the ferry. Did what we were told. The Major was blown overboard by the explosion. Collect all his papers and throw them over the side. Our story must be all they ever know."

They all looked over to where Frick's body lay, a dark shape on the deck. Herman stepped over and started to push the Major's body over the gunwale. At the last second, Herman realized that the Major was still alive and was weakly trying to fetch hold of Herman's leg. Herman was as terrified as if some demon was clawing at him. He kicked and kicked, struggling like an animal caught in a steel trap. Then Frick was gone over the side.

The engines were restarted and the *S.23* slowly turned back towards Copenhagen.

Ferry *Sverige*

While it was simple enough to search open decks, the labyrinth of salons and cabins would take time. Working together, Müller and Schmidt made an initial sweep of all three decks, moving slowly, examining each man's build and face. Petersen was very tall and thin with yellow blond hair, spectacles, possibly wearing a blue woolen jacket and pullover. The battered and stained group photograph was not much more helpful and the Gestapo men had studied it only for a few moments. Within twenty minutes the two Gestapo men had reached the forward section of the uppermost passenger deck. They had paused four times to look over possible candidates, the last time doubtful enough to ask an innocuous question in German to get the man to turn around and face them. Neither German knew more than a few words in Swedish, all of them rude. They were convinced that none of these men was the spy Petersen.

The last man had upbraided the two in poor German. With their long leather coats and tough attitudes, no one would mistake them for anything but German policemen. Everyone had seen Gestapo men skulking around Copenhagen, trailing behind groups of Swedish revelers, trying to keep the Danes from getting too close. Playing tag with them had been an amusing game at first, a nuisance later.

"Get lost you pigs," the last man had offered generously, backed and emboldened by a half dozen friends.

"Yeah, go to hell."

"Fuck off, Nazis."

Müller started to boil over, but Schmidt gestured him away. There was no value or time to start something with these Swedish pukes. Schmidt knew they were trying to impress their slutty girlfriends.

The Germans agreed to begin searching the interior sections of the ferry starting with the lower deck near the stern ramp where everyone had boarded. But in case Petersen was watching them, dodging, managing to stay just ahead as they moved through the open areas, they separated and each made a fast sweep of one side of the ship, racing aft on the upper deck and forward on the lower deck. Nothing.

They tried the latches and handles of the hatchways leading below deck to the engine spaces and found them locked from inside, doubtless to keep drunken passengers from getting below, so now they would concentrate on the hallways, salons, and cabins.

It was nearly midnight and the ferry was scheduled to arrive in Sweden in two hours.

Willy was exhausted and disoriented, stunned to find himself aboard the ferry and apparently well on his way to safety in neutral Sweden. At the customs house, he had presented the stolen papers as a final act of resignation. While standing in line watching the Danish customs men, it appeared that they were not examining passengers' documents closely, but his were so patently false even the slightest scrutiny should expose him. Willy could only steel himself against an interrogation he knew was only minutes away. He had to concentrate on one thing only: don't tell the Gestapo about Lise. If he could just embrace or cling to that single thought whatever happened, he believed for now that he could take almost anything. The increasing pain and swelling in his legs suggested he might not have to hold out long.

Still distracted, he had stepped to the counter and handed over the stolen documents. Seconds later, instead of arrest, he found himself swept along with the rush of last minute passengers across the quay, up the ramp, and on to the stern of the ferry. In what seemed like an instant, the ferry had cast off its lines and was underway. Willy stood among the crowd and watched the dockyard lights begin to fade in the ferry's wake.

He needed to sit down and think and try to reorient himself, but he was still surrounded by rowdy Swedish passengers singing, dancing, and cavorting on the open deck. They didn't want the party to end. Willy realized that he too had reason to celebrate, but not just yet. Perhaps in a few minutes. From the stern deck, a double hinged door opened to a large salon.

A single oil lamp was lit, mounted on the wall beside the doors and the salon was comfortably warm. All the seats and the benches along the bulkheads were claimed. Small groups sat on the floor talking quietly. Several couples were cuddling in corners. But most passengers in the salon were already fast asleep stretched out on the benches or on the floor along the bulkhead opposite the doors. Stepping carefully over and around the bodies in the middle of the salon, Willy found enough space against the forward bulkhead to sit on the carpeted floor. As he gingerly stretched his legs out he thought about sleep but was sure if he let himself go, he wouldn't awaken until the ferry docked in Sweden. He had to clear his head enough to think about what might happen then.

His swollen legs itched like crazy all along his shins and ankles. Scratching with his nails made it feel worse not better. *Just ignore it: nothing I can do.*

Lucky so far, he still had to convince himself that he wouldn't be bundled back aboard and returned to Germany because of his false papers. He had no basis to judge how the Swedes would respond to a German demand for his return. At the very least he needed time and tools to cut his undoctored American passport from the lining of his jacket where Lise had so carefully sewn it. Without a visa for Sweden would they send him back regardless? He couldn't come up with a reason for the Swedes acting rashly but he was so tired and dull that he must be missing something. Right now, Willy wasn't being logical or scientific. If he could sit quietly for awhile, he'd be okay.

The burning itch in his legs was getting worse all the time. As long as he was moving or distracted, it was okay, but if he sat still like now, it was a constant and gnawing reminder of what had happened at the Institute and a terrifying promise that Willy hadn't yet paid full price.

Of course this was the real reason Willy could not consider returning to Munich, despite Lise's insistence and confidence and his passionate desire to stay close to her. He had known it from the first moment on the train from Potsdam when the tingling in his legs started. The effects of the radiation poisoning were going to get worse, how bad Willy couldn't guess. Even if the Gestapo wasn't already waiting for him in Munich, a point would be reached when his condition got bad enough where Lise would bring in a doctor, regardless the danger to them both. Word would get out and they would both be quickly arrested. Everything they had done and everything they had together would be wasted and lost.

In the end she accepted his other rationale without seeing through his deceptions and omissions. Willy wanted to leave Lise with hope that might sustain her for years: it was really all he had to give her now. He had to accept that she might be hurt by the hollowness of his reasons.

As the minutes passed, conversations around Willy died down, and before long it seemed like everyone in the salon was sleeping. Someone near the door reached up and doused the last light. Oblivious to the shouting and singing outside the open portholes, within a few minutes the salon was completely quiet.

Willy was thinking about Lise again. *Is she safely back in Munich? Could she really love me? Will I ever see her again? How long will this war last? How would it end? Can I write her? Maybe with our secret system? Shouldn't I have stayed with her? Couldn't I have forced her to come along? She'd be with me now, safe and free. Far away from war and Nazis and uranium bombs and moral dilemmas?* Willy was feeling self-conscious and guilty. After all they had done and risked together, he was safe and Lise was still in danger. He closed his eyes and tried to imagine Lise lying next to him.

When the wide doors swung open, noise from the party outside spilled into the salon. Willy looked up and in silhouette recognized the two Gestapo men instantly. It wasn't over yet. A surge of emotion caught in his throat but he managed to stifle any sound.

The first compartment they entered was dimly lit but even before their eyes had adjusted to the darkness, Müller and Schmidt could tell the room was crowded. Müller flicked his cigarette lighter and within its narrow arc of light the two could make out dozens of young men and women sleeping on the floor and benches all around the large room. Many had partially covered themselves with their jackets and coats. Lying down it was almost impossible to judge someone's height. Schmidt nodded to Müller and the two separated and began to work their way quietly through the room along opposite walls. It was slow going. Every face and build needed to be examined and considered. There was no time for mistakes or margin for error.

Several times one or the other German would inadvertently trod on someone's hand or step on someone's legs. Each time there was a momentary stirring. The Germans would wait patiently for a few moments and things would settle back down. Then they'd continue the search. Schmidt was relying on the light through portholes along the wall. Müller had his lighter. As Schmidt reached the furthest bulkhead, one man's face caught his eye even in the near darkness. Hair, spectacles, and dark jacket. Schmidt felt a small thrill: *I've seen this man before!* Was it in Petersen's photograph? He moved to get a closer look and stumbled over someone else sleeping on the floor nearby. She awoke cursing loudly. Schmidt ignored her and bent down to get a better look at his man. Suddenly a match was struck right in front of his eyes and he was completely blinded.

"It's those fucking Nazis again!" complained a voice on the other side of the flame. "I told you to piss off, you fucking creep!"

Schmidt, still disoriented by the bright light, tumbled on his face with a loud grunt when the angry Swede drew up a leg and kicked Schmidt's legs out from under him. Within seconds the whole room was in an uproar.

Müller moved quickly to help his comrade, plowing through the bodies, drawing more angry complaints and insults. He reached Schmidt's side just as Schmidt managed to get back to his feet. But now they were surrounded by angry Swedes who pushed and shoved both Gestapo men, shouting angry questions, curses, and challenges.

Müller was the first to pull out his Luger. He turned to the nearest person between him and the door and fired point-blank into the face. The face disappeared immediately from Müller's line of sight, replaced by another several feet beyond. He took two deliberate steps toward the door and when a new face, outlined by light from the doors, didn't move on its own volition, he shot again with the identical effect. Now no one stood between them and the doorway.

Müller turned to Schmidt who was standing at his back, pistol ready. "Let's go!"

The two walked back to back toward the doors, Müller kicking viciously whenever a body got in his way. In front of the doors Müller's legs became entangled with someone on the floor. Unable to see who it was, he lowered his aim and fired at a point just beyond his own feet. The next time he kicked out there was no one in his way. Then they were out the doors. Only now, as echoes of the two shots faded, did the two men notice the screams and shouting from behind the doors. When they came out, guns drawn, several passengers who had been celebrating on the stern deck started to run forward along both of the ferry's sides, both men and women crying for help. Others frozen in place too long to escape, threw themselves on the deck burying their faces in their arms.

Müller paused and reached in his pocket for a fresh pistol magazine. Schmidt had spun around and was looking for a means to bolt the salon door from the outside. As Müller snapped in his clip, they heard footsteps running from forward on the port side. Their eyes met in silent agreement and as a burly crewman turned the corner onto the stern deck, Schmidt shot him in the heart from four feet away, with Müller providing cover. The man continued to take two running steps before crashing into the deck face first, arms limply at his side.

Schmidt moved to look down the one side and Müller the other. For the moment there was no sign of anyone else from the crew coming aft, only desperate passengers falling over each other to get forward. It was unlikely the ferry crew had any firearms, but the two Gestapo men had only four magazines between them and would run out of ammunition before a concerted rush could be stopped if one were organized. They needed to push ahead quickly before officers could rally the crew, uncharacteristic as that might seem for pacifist and decadent Swedes.

The situation was different now. With all the commotion, the search for Petersen would be more difficult. They would have to halt the ship to regain the time needed to herd everyone forward and sort through the entire lot. Schmidt and Müller faced each other. Schmidt ordered Müller: "Engine room." No other discussion was needed. Müller nodded and started forward to find a way to get below deck.

Willy had pretended to be asleep, a childish idea, that somehow this would protect him from the Gestapo men, like parents at bed check. If they thought you were asleep they'd leave you alone. As he watched the shadowy figures working their separate ways around the salon, it was apparent they would come together again just where Willy was sitting against the forward bulkhead. There was no place to hide. His long legs were stretched out in front of him, telling anyone at a glance that *this* man is tall. Likewise he would have to roll himself completely around to stand up or to crouch prepared to make a dash for the doors. Except for the two Germans, the room was quite still. Any movement would draw attention to Willy instantly. His luck had run out this time and he tried to concentrate in the same way he had while in the queue at the customs house. He couldn't do it. He was so tired that he couldn't even find the fear that had helped drive him ahead over the last three days. There was just coldness and immediacy. He could neither remember nor plan ahead. Whatever was going to happen was outside his control. He was hypnotized by the flickering cigarette lighter.

Willy heard an angry shout in Swedish and then his eyes were drawn to his left by the light from a match. Other voices joined in the commotion and Willy watched as the first light started to move toward the second. People all around were sitting up and asking questions of their neighbors in the darkness.

"What the hell's going on?"

"People are trying to sleep here."

"Hey, shut the fuck up!"

People started to stand as the racket grew, afraid of being trampled. It sounded like some sort of fight had broken out. This was Willy's chance. He stood quickly and pushed his way clumsily through the melee toward the door. Once through and with the door closed behind him, he realized he had no plan, no idea of which way to go next. Suddenly there was a loud explosion from inside the salon and a moment later another. Angry complaints from the Swedes changed to screams of terror. A few of the passengers loitering on the stern deck started toward the salon door, curious as much as anything about what might be happening.

But Willy knew. He turn to his right and started to run along the deck, his legs as heavy as lead. Other passengers got the same idea and started after him. There was another explosion behind him. He felt naked and exposed on the open deck. He paused to try several of the doors but all were locked. By now a dozen Swedes, men and women had overtaken him. At forward end of the lower deck the panicked passengers were forced to climb stairs to the mid-deck. Everyone was trying to get up the narrow stairs at the same time, Willy jammed in the middle of the crush.

Someone pounded him hard on the shoulder and he turned in a flash of anger - he was doing the best he could - but fell down on top of a girl who seemed to have stumbled in front of him. He grabbed the girl by the arms to help her up. When he had wrestled her upright and pointed her body up the stairs, he yelled in her ear to "Hurry up!" Only then did he see that her face was gone. Surprised, he let her drop and she fell behind him down the stairs in slow motion. There was blood on his hands and right shoulder. He had never seen so much blood before: it was fascinating. He wiped his hands on his pant legs absently but when he tried to wipe the blood from his shoulder he realized that this was his blood, flowing from under his clothes. A bullet had passed through his shoulder and into the back of the girl's head. A loud bang and ringing of metal resounded as another bullet struck a stanchion on the stairs. The noise woke him up and he scrambled up the last steps. When he reached the upper deck he found himself alone, the other passenger had continued up a second flight of stairs to the bridge deck. He could hear someone pounding on a window or door trying to get the attention of those inside. Willy knew that if he followed, he'd probably be cornered again. He ran aft and cut across to the starboard side before the pursuing German made his way up the stairs. He tried several more doors. All were barred from the inside. Hide, he must hide. All along this deck running aft from just below the bridge was a line of covered lifeboats positioned inboard on their davits. He tried the cover of the second in the row. It was loose enough that Willy could climb inside and close it behind.

Müller used ten precious and frustrating minutes to find a way to get below. He finally found a hatchway on the lower deck with an accessible outside latch. Once opened, he hesitated for a moment. There was no sign of light and he was concerned that it was a deep bin or hold of some sort and he'd be unable to backtrack if it proved to be a dead-end. Flame from his lighter flickered in the sea breeze blowing across the deck. Müller thought he could see the floor of the lower compartment about fifteen feet below. Removing his trench coat, he transferred its contents, lighter, cigarettes, spare magazines, and stiletto knife, to his pants' pockets. Müller settled his Luger in its shoulder holster, sat on the edge of the open hatchway with his legs hanging, and twisted around to lower himself as far as possible to minimize how far he'd drop. No need to wait. He let go his hands and bent his knees to break his fall. It was farther than he thought and he hit the metal floor hard, breaking an ankle.

"*Scheisse*," Müller whispered exasperated: "Shit!" How could he be such a weak fool? With great difficulty he pushed himself up balancing on his good foot. He tested the broken ankle. It hurt like hell. *Pain is nothing*. With his lighter he found a hatchway in the aft bulkhead. It opened easily and he found himself at the end of a series of lighted, narrow corridors with companionways heading up and forward and down and aft. Müller began to make his way down towards the engine room, using handrails and wall brackets to keep weight off his bad ankle. Deeper into the ship he could first feel and then hear the ferry's engines and machinery. When he reached what appeared to be the last doorway, he leaned against it and listened. The engine sounds were clear. If word had come down from the bridge his way might be barred or the engine room crew alerted. He tested the door handle. It was unlocked. He took out his Luger, checked that a round was properly chambered, took a deep breath and turned the handle. The hatch opened inwards.

The Captain had called down to report some sort of trouble with the passengers and ordered the *Sverige* to Malmö as fast as possible. The Chief Engineer had rung the engines up to full speed and was studying his bank of temperature and pressure gauges when he heard the forward hatch clang open. *What clumsy fool?*

But instead of a crewmember, an armed man pointing a pistol at his heart confronted him. But he'd been Chief Engineer for twenty years and was used to having his say and his way.

"Who the hell are you? Get out of my engine room!" he yelled angrily at the intruder in Swedish.

"Stop the ship or I'll kill you," Müller yelled in German. Though the Chief spoke sailor's German, it was the last thing he expected to hear and he stood open-mouthed. Müller shot him in the chest: if the man couldn't understand him, he was just in the way.

The Chief's amazed expression never changed as he sank to his knees and then fell sideways. He tried to catch himself with his hands and just managed to prop himself upright until Müller, who had moved quickly towards the control station, shot him in the back of the neck, nearly decapitating the man. Foolish to waste precious bullets, Müller admonished himself.

Müller heard scuffling sounds that told him there are other crewmembers in the engine room space desperate to find someplace to hide. It might take several minutes to round them up and it was unlikely he'd find someone who would understand what he wanted them to do: *Stop the engines!* They would have to pass the control station to reach the door and upper decks. He was not concerned with them.

He scanned the dials and fingered the levers and the panel of switches at hand. Few had labels and many of the words were either Swedish or some foolish sailor jargon. Müller reasoned that if the ship was moving, reversing the position of all these switches and levers should have the opposite effect. Starting with the electrical switches, Müller methodically repositioned each one. He was disappointed when nothing appeared to change and the engines continued to roar.

He started on the levers. After several tries he discovered that many of the levers were interlocked and needed to be operated together. When he reversed the third set, the engines began to run rough and within a minute had stopped completely. It was like being struck deaf as the engines went silent. He looked at his watch: one-thirty. He and Schmidt would have time to hunt down the spy. At this point he would kill Petersen on sight and was willing to risk Major Frick's wrath.

His ankle throbbed like hell. He needed a few puffs before he started back to the main deck. Müller lit a cigarette, still wary of crewmembers he knew were hiding deeper in the engine spaces. He then knew he still had a problem: to deal with the engine room crew lest they restart the engines after he left. *Damn.*

Müller took out his knife and released the blade. He tossed his cigarette aside. It sizzled for a moment in the pool of blood still seeping from the Chief Engineer.

"Here, kitties, kitties, come out kitties," he called soothingly.

Schmidt was sure he had hit Petersen with his first shot. This time he had the right man, the man in the group photograph. He was a head taller than anyone else in the crowd fighting to get up the stairs. It had been a long pistol shot, nearly thirty meters along the deck. Petersen hadn't gone down but wasn't moving up the stairs. Schmidt ran half way to the stairs before he stopped and snap-fired again. Sparks flew off to one side: a miss. *Shit*, the last shot seemed to wake Petersen up and he fled up the stairs before Schmidt could get off a third round.

Schmidt was only seconds behind Petersen when he reach the foot of the stairs but he lost his footing when he stepped in the gore covering one of the treads. Damn. Schmidt clamored up the stairs using his hands ahead of his feet but as he reach the deck, pistol arm extended; Petersen was no where in sight.

The passengers were still pounding on the bridge door above. Schmidt ran up the stairs and at the top was face to face with frantic passengers who dove for the deck when they saw him. They didn't interest Schmidt in the least. Petersen wasn't among them. If they couldn't gain entry to the bridge from here, neither could he. Schmidt was still relying completely on Müller for his part of the plan. Complete trust between comrades. Schmidt climbed back down to the upper deck from the bridge. Petersen must have gone aft. Wary of an ambush, he paused at each corner as the deck wrapped around the stern and then started up the starboard side. Droplets on the deck and a fresh smear of blood on a handrail opposite told Schmidt he'd guessed right.

Schmidt hurried down the side of the ship until he reached the starboard stairs leading to the bridge. Luger extended and ready, he climbed until he could see up and down the narrow bridge deck. No one was there. Back down on the upper deck, Schmidt worked his way aft, checking doors along the way, searching for more blood sign. All were locked from the inside. When he reached the stern end of this deck he looked back towards the bow, studying the row of lifeboats. Stepping over to the nearest, he discovered that the canvas covers were loose. He had his spy now. There were five boats: Petersen was in one of them.

Schmidt moved around to the aft end of the first lifeboat. With his Luger in his right hand he tightly grasped the cover and tore it back as he moved quickly toward the bow. The covers were designed to be removed easily and didn't snag. The lifeboat was empty except for oars and crates of emergency supplies. Schmidt was not concerned: four more to go.

Ever cautious, before he checked the second boat he walked the length of the starboard deck to make sure no crewmembers or passengers were lying in wait or watching him from around corners. He checked his watch: a quarter past one in the morning. He walked to the rail to see if he make out lights from the Swedish coast, but before he could look forward he saw the most remarkable sight. Running parallel to the ferry, only fifty meters off the starboard side, was the dark shape of a patrol boat. He could hear its powerful diesel engines bubbling. As he peered out into the darkness alongside the ferry, the smaller boat passed forward through circles of light cast by the ferry's deck lamps. On the boat's stern transom flew the German navy ensign: a *Schnellboot*, and as it passed by Schmidt, he could distinguish its torpedoes and mounted machine guns. Schmidt was grinning widely. In an instant he and Müller had both help and a means of escape. To this point he'd pushed from his mind what he might have to face when the ferry arrived in Malmö.

He ran twenty meters forward and leaned over the rail. He didn't want to get too far from the lifeboats lest Petersen make a run for it. The patrol boat sounded three loud blasts on its horn. Schmidt could hear someone aboard the patrol boat hailing the ferry's bridge. As the patrol boat edged closer Schmidt recognized Major Frick speaking through a trumpet to someone on the ferry's bridge. Schmidt couldn't make out all the words but could guess what the Major was saying: *stop the ferry; reverse course; let us come aboard!* Surely the Swedes would comply.

358

Schmidt knew Frick very well. He would have neither compunction nor hesitation if it came to sinking the ferry with everyone aboard. Schmidt strained to hear the exchange. He realized that the Swedes were refusing to stop. He made a decision: if he could get to the bridge, perhaps his pistol would help convince the ferry's officers to comply with the Major's orders. As he ran forward to the bridge stairs, he heard the *Schnellboot's* horn blare several more times. At the foot of the bridge stairs, machine guns on the patrol boat started firing on the ferry. Schmidt ducked low and slunk back. He couldn't tell where the rounds were aimed: warning shots probably, over the bow. He needed to get Frick's attention and crept on hands and knees over to the railing, but the patrol boat had moved off and he could only dimly see it at the very edge of the ferry's bright lights. But when he started up the bridge stairs a second time, bullets from the patrol boat began raining onto the superstructure and fittings just above his head. Moments later more guns were firing and Schmidt flattened himself against the deck as far from the rail as he could get. Slugs were hitting the bulkhead inches above his head and he could actually feel the thunks of bullets striking the hull and bulkheads below him. After an eternity, the firing points seemed to work aft along the ferry's length, and Schmidt crept over to peer beneath the railings. The patrol boat had fallen astern and was powering off into the darkness. The ferry had not slowed down.

Müller and Schmidt were on their own again, but it was good to know that Frick was out there nearby. Schmidt knew Frick would not give up. Meantime, it was still Schmidt's responsibility to find the spy. There couldn't be much time left before the ferry reached port. Schmidt could now see the lights of the city ahead.

He turned his attention back to the lifeboats. Heavy caliber bullets from the *Schnellboot* had shattered two of them, the forward most boat nearest the bridge stairs had actually broken in half and was hanging limply from its davits. *Perhaps the Major has done the job for me.* Best to continue to be careful and thorough thought Schmidt. *No mistakes.*

He approached the second lifeboat, readied his pistol, and pulled back the cover. Again nothing. Looking into the boat, Schmidt could see the sea alongside through a series of holes shot in the boat's bottom. He reminded himself that when finished searching this side he should disable all the lifeboats on both sides in case Petersen tried to launch one to escape the ship. He should have thought of that earlier.

Cross Sections

As he stepped to the third lifeboat he noted blood specks on the deck near its bow. He relaxed. The hunt was over. He walked slowly all around the boat, gun ready. He put his ear to the boat's side and listened for movement, but couldn't hear anything. Cornered rats, especially wounded ones, can be unpredictable.

As he started to reach for the edge of the canvas covering the boat's bows, he suddenly felt the ferry lurch and slow. He could sense and hear the engine sounds dying down. Schmidt smiled: *good old Müller!*

Under the heavy canvas lifeboat cover Willy could only rely on sounds. Several times he heard someone walk slowly past his hiding place. Given the tumult aboard, only the Germans would be walking so deliberately. Another time he heard a single person hurrying aft. Willy cursed himself as an idiot: the lifeboats were such an obvious hiding place. Trying to lie still, the pain in his shoulder was almost unbearable. His clothes were soaked with sweat and blood and whenever he stopped pressing his fingers firmly against the shoulder, he could actually feel more blood trickling down inside his shirt. His back was wet with blood too, from the entry hole in the back of his shoulder just above his shoulder blade.

Willy would bleed to death without help. But he knew none was at hand. Everyone aboard the ferry was at the mercy of the pitiless Germans. His only chance was to remain undiscovered until the ferry reached port. Willy had lost all sense of time and couldn't read his wristwatch in the dark. He could only guess the ferry must be close by now. He knew the Gestapo would continue to search for him until the very last moment. Help still might be a long time coming.

When he heard the horns of a second boat come up along side the ferry, he sensed some relief, but still did not dare move or try to peek from under the boatcover. It was most likely a Swedish patrol boat sent from Malmö, but the few words he could make out in the shouted conversation were in German. Not a good sign.

Suddenly the world exploded with gun fire, at first just distant sounds, but only moments later accompanied by the rattling, thuds, and tearing sounds of bullets hitting all around him. Several rounds struck the hull of his lifeboat and sharp slivers of wood were thrown at him, stinging his face. Just as quickly the shooting stopped. Everything was quiet again except for the ferry's throbbing engines. Bless the Swedes!

But the emotional roller coaster took him back again to his concern for Lise and his dread that he might not be able to keep her secret. The Gestapo would beat it out of him. Willy had an old thought: the Gestapo would use drugs. How could he resist? The whole story would come out. Lise and her father would be arrested and executed; his friends suspected and tortured. And after all that, their sabotage would be discovered and would go for nothing. The Germans would build their bomb and seize all Europe, eventually the whole world.

He was out of choices, even if he could find the strength and will to make any. If discovered, he could fight and die, but now that all was like something in a silly movie. War was not like he had imagined. It was not a childhood game; it wasn't like sneaking around playing tag outdoors on a cool summer night. Nor was it playing cowboys and Indians with cap pistols and rubber cup-tipped arrows.

Willy had plotted their conspiracy like a series of college pranks with a semester's expulsion the expected punishment. Now he'd seen and heard innocent people die suddenly and horribly. No one had asked them if they wanted to play. No one had explained the rules to them. And he himself was responsible for death.

In this stark reality, Willy knew he could not fight it out with his pursuers. Nothing would work out the way he wanted, only the way they wanted. If they wished him dead, he would die; if they wanted him alive, he would live.

He could jump overboard and try to swim to shore. He would have to survive the fall and the ferry's propellers, but the shore couldn't be too far away. On a dare, he'd gone swimming in Lake Superior one teenage spring. But even without a bad arm and damaged legs, Willy was never much of a swimmer. As the idea ran through his mind he realized that this too was a cartoon. If he jumped overboard it would be making a decision to die, and that was the way he must face it. *Am I ready?*

He remembered Lise at the train station. He could still feel her hair and lips. As Lise had been swept away in the crowd, she looked so small, isolated, and vulnerable. The decision was not difficult at all. Despite everything, Willy smiled ironically and started to twist around to climb out of the lifeboat over its outboard gunwale. His resolution failed for a moment until he heard and felt the ferry's engines stop. No time left. No rescue now. As he slowly and carefully lifted the outboard edge of the cover, it was ripped out of his fingers and the bright yellow deck lights blinded him.

The torpedo had leaped out of the water and struck the ferry just behind the bridge thirty feet below Willy's lifeboat. Berg had aimed at the stern to disable the ferry rather than sink it, but as the ferry slowed, the intersect point moved forward. The ferry was no warship and the blast shredded it like so much paper. All the upper decks were ripped up from below. Sergeant Schmidt, gun in hand, arm raised, was torn in half from crotch to chest by a jagged iron plate. Schmidt could see his own insides dumping out even before he landed with a wet thump on the shattered wooden deck. The ferry immediately listed steeply to starboard, and Schmidt was still conscious as he slid down the deck into the chasm of twisted metal and fire below.

In the engine room, Müller had cornered one of the cowering crewmen when he was knocked off his feet by the explosion forward. He dropped his gun and knife on the grating. As he tried to stand the ferry began to pitch first aft and then rolled to starboard. With the engine silent, Müller could hear water pouring into the engine room from somewhere. The blast had sprung the propeller shaft seals aft. His pistol, he needed his pistol. He managed to find it on the grating nearby, just as a terrified young crewman raced past him toward the open door leading above. The crewman had to climb hand over hand up the deck grating as the ship continued to pitch over. Seawater started to flow over the sill.

Müller took careful aim and coldly shot the man in the back. The rush of seawater carried the body back into the engine room.

As the water started to rise, Müller braced himself against the control panel, straightened up as best he could, shouted *"Heil, Hitler!"* at the top of his lungs, and shot himself in the mouth, blowing off the top of his spine.

Willy's lifeboat had been thrown overboard by the blast below and landed upside down next to the ferry. He was trapped underneath, tangled in a jumble of ropes, lifejackets, and canvas, and fought and fought to free himself, now desperately fearful of drowning under the boat. *Fear* had returned and might now save him. With one last push he found himself free and clinging to some buoyant wreckage. It was barely enough to support him and whenever he tried to put more weight on it, it threatened to sink beneath him.

No sign of the ferry. He heard sobbing and splashing all around him. It was too dark and the waves too high to see anyone even close by. Kicking weakly Willy managed to turn himself around. On one horizon, back toward Germany, was only impenetrable darkness. Dense clouds were moving up from the south, and one by one, the stars in the sky above Germany were extinguished. Lise was back there under those clouds.

In the opposite direction Willy could clearly see the lights of the port and the glow of the city beyond. Even at this late hour, it seemed something alive and vibrant. He started to kick out with his useless legs.

Lund, Sweden

"I'm relieved you remained in town this week, Doctor Svendsen. The clinics in Lomma and Akarp are quite overwhelmed. A line of ambulances and private cars has been racing from village to village trying to find help for the victims. When I heard you were coming I had four of the more desperate cases brought here," the nurse said as she helped the clinic director out of his overcoat. Svendsen was young, square-jawed, and very efficient.

"So, Inge, what do we have?" He said as they hurried down the corridor toward the ward.

"All of the victims are suffering from exposure and hypothermia. The ambulance drivers told me that they might have been in the sea for three or four hours before they were rescued by fishing boats from the shore villages."

"What have you done so far?"

"We've only had time to wrap them up as warmly as possible. All are unconscious and probably in shock. We didn't even undress them: I didn't have enough help. They're still wearing wet clothing underneath the blankets.

"What a day for this to happen; the ferry must have been packed coming from Copenhagen last evening."

"A driver said fishermen have brought in about thirty survivors so far. There may have been three hundred passengers," she shuddered.

As they entered the ward, nurses and orderlies were hustling in with hot water bottles and dry blankets and bedclothes. The room was already oppressively hot and the doctor could smell the sea-wet clothes.

At the first bed, he pulled back blankets covering most of the face of a survivor and saw that it was a young woman, her lips cobalt blue, and skin as white as snow. Without a mirror he couldn't tell whether she was breathing, but when he checked, her pupils were still responsive.

"Take her temperature rectally; begin charting every twenty minutes.

Monitor her blood pressure and pulse. Get her undressed and wrap her again with hot water bottles under her arm pits and beneath the small of her back," he ordered. "I believe this one will live."

On to the second bed in the row: a large-boned, middle-aged man with long hair and a beard. Again no sign of breathing, even when the doctor held the back of his hand in front of the man's mouth. The eyes were dead and so was the man. "Leave the body dressed," said the doctor, "It will help the police to identify him."

At the third bed, the orderlies and nurses, anticipating the doctor, had begun to strip the survivor, a very tall, thin young man with blond hair. He was unshaven and a black and yellow contusion beside his left eye was prominent against his frozen pallor. The doctor could see by the shallow rise and fall of his chest that he was alive and as the staff struggled to remove the young man's trekking boots and trousers, the doctor felt for a pulse. It was weak and thready, but this man would probably survive, the doctor thought.

"Doctor, look at this," a nurse pleaded. She had managed to get the young man's boots off and his wet trousers pulled down to his ankles. "He's been badly burned."

Svendsen moved down to examine the young man's legs. He had oozing suppurations on his legs below the knees and on parts of his ankles and feet. They appeared to be second degree burns and very recent. The ankles were swollen with edema.

"Let me see his trousers," the doctor demanded. There were no signs of any burning or scorching on the outside and when he turned them inside out he found signs of skin and flesh that had sloughed off onto the lining. "These burns are recent but apparently happened prior to his immersion. Cover them with salve for now. We need to get his condition stabilized and his core temperature raised before we can treat his legs."

Svendsen continued to examine the burns. They were *unusual*. They were severe and deep but there were no indications of charring. The hair on his legs near the wounds was unsinged. He thought they must be injuries caused by scalding steam. Perhaps the young man had been near the ferry's boiler when it went down.

The orderlies who had continued to undress the young man removed his jacket and pullover. The shirt below initially appeared to have been dyed red.

Cross Sections

"Doctor!" said one of the orderlies in amazement; "This man has been shot!"

"Heavens!" said the doctor, "What next?" The gunshot wound was in the right shoulder, entering from the back and exiting in the front just above the clavicle. Evidently the bullet had missed any vital blood vessels or else the young man would have been dead hours ago. Indeed it was likely the cold water and hypothermia might have saved him. In the absence of massive bleeding, the wound would not have been fatal, though it must have hurt like hell. Seawater had washed the wound, but it was apparent that this injury was also very recent. It was hard to imagine a connection between a bullet wound and the ferry disaster. A gunshot was a matter for the police. An orderly was holding out the young man's jacket with his fingers sticking though what was apparently matching holes.

The doctor turned to the nurses, "Watch the shoulder wound for sign of renewed bleeding as this man warms up. We'll clean the holes out and stitch him up later. Compression for now."

"Eric," he asked one of the orderlies, "when you have time later on, walk over to the constable's office and ask him to stop by and see me as soon as he can. If he's not in, please leave a message."

The doctor moved on to the last survivor, who was now semi-conscious and shivering wildly. This man at least was fortunate enough to be suffering only from a near drowning. Svendsen shook his head in amazement.

It was two days before the constable, Mr. Borg, could come to the clinic. He'd been lending a hand down at the shore villages. The toll was horrendous: two hundred and twenty dead or missing; fifty-two survivors, not all of whom were expected to make it. Few were lucid enough to say anything meaningful about what happened. None of the crew of fifteen had been found alive. Apparently the ferry had sunk suddenly and without warning. The best theory was that it had struck a floating mine, though none were known to have been laid in this part of the straits since the war began. Perhaps it had drifted in from the North Sea; maybe it was left over from the Great War. There was anger and rage among the villagers against foreigners who must be responsible for the explosion. German or British: it didn't matter to them.

Regardless, there had been no time to launch any rafts or lifeboats and few of the survivors or victims were wearing life jackets. Bodies were still washing up on the beaches every day, by now as far south as Falsterbo at the northwest end of the Baltic Sea.

The shores of both Denmark and Sweden were being combed, though the search by now was for bodies only. Even the Germans had expressed their sympathies and volunteered soldiers and sailors to help with the searches. The Swedish authorities did not allow any German soldiers onto its soil, but several senior observers were allowed to join the search teams ostensibly to help find and identify survivors and victims from Germany. The observers, escorted by Swedish police officers, went from hospital to hospital taking photographs of the bodies of unidentified victims, visiting bedside unconscious and unidentified survivors, and interviewing any survivors who had begun to recover.

Dr. Svendsen had transferred two of his patients to the hospital in Malmö. The young man with the burns and gunshot wound had not yet regained consciousness and though his body temperature and blood pressure were up, his burns seemed to be getting progressively worse.

"Constable, thank you for coming by," said Doctor Svendsen, offering his hand. "Eric said you were down at the coast. It must have been very bad."

"I pray never again to see anything like it," said the Constable. "The worst part is the families, especially the mothers and wives, as they search among the bodies lined up in each town along the quay. I'm afraid that some of the bodies will never be found and others never identified. There were Swedes, Danes, Germans, and Finns among the passengers. Half the crew was Norwegian, so we've had bureaucrats from all these countries fumbling around and getting in the way. As you might expect, the Germans act like their people are the only ones that matter. They want to look at every body, at all their personal effects, and want to talk to every survivor, asking about other survivors and victims."

"Well, we're lucky enough not to have them visit here for whatever reason. We've been trying to keep our last remaining patient as quiet as possible. His injuries are very bad and I must admit that I don't understand why.

"The reason I've called you is the simple fact that this patient, a young man about twenty-five years old, has recently been gunshot. The wound is not dangerous and will heal. He also has very bad burns on his legs possibly from a steam explosion, but I suspect the burns came some days prior to the ferry's sinking."

"This is very interesting. What else?"

"The young man is from America, at least according to the passport he's carrying. We found the passport sewed *inside* the lining of his jacket. One of the nurses had been trying to dry the jacket over a radiator when she made the discovery. The passport itself was badly damaged by seawater. The ink has run and smeared and we can't read anything like a name or address. But the photograph matches the patient."

"This is quite remarkable. You have an unconscious American with burns and a bullet wound who survived the ferry disaster. Does anyone else know about this business?"

"Just the clinic staff, though I'm sure everyone in the village knows something by now. I didn't ask them to be discreet, but for now it's just one of the hundreds of stories circulating about. I just wanted to wait for you to take charge since this is such an unusual case."

"I appreciate everything you've done. What's the boy's condition?"

"He is still unconscious as I said. We've patched up the bullet hole. He's recovering steadily from the exposure. It's the burns on his feet and legs that I'm most concerned about. I've sent a note to Doctor Palme, the chief district surgeon from Eslöv, to drive over as soon as possible to take a look."

"Please inform me immediately if the boy regains consciousness or when Doctor Palme arrives. Meantime, I like to see the boy and look over his personal effects. Please request that your staff be discreet about this matter until we know more. There are entirely too many foreigners traipsing around the countryside already."

"Come along and I'll show you where his things are locked up."

Doctor Palme had never seen burns like these before. When he arrived later that day, early signs of tissue necrosis had appeared. The swelling was extreme. Doctor Svendsen had been applying sulfa powder to fight infection. The young man was still unconscious and was now developing a fever, though whether the cause was the gunshot, the burns, or some other aftereffect of his exposure was unknown. His condition was grave. Constable Borg had walked over to the clinic from town hall.

"These burns are very unusual, Doctor Svendsen. They appear to extend underneath otherwise unmarked tissue and are uniformly distributed all around his legs. If his feet had been burned to the same extent I would speculate that he'd been dropped feet first into some sort of corrosive chemical agent.

"I've seen similar types of tissue damage coincident with hospital patients receiving radium treatments for cancer but it's always isolated to a limited area immediately surrounding the radium seed. I doubt there's enough radium in all of Sweden to account for these burns if indeed they stem from radiation."

"Could they be from overexposure to Roentgen rays?" Svendsen offered.

"Excuse me doctors, what are these rays you speak of?" asked Constable Borg.

"They are produced by electrical devices used to examine bone fractures and malformations," Svendsen explained. "They penetrate through solid objects and leave an image on photographic plates showing differences in the density of objects. The equipment is available only at the largest hospitals around Europe. I understand the roentgen rays produced by the equipment are relatively harmless if used correctly.

"That's also my understanding," said Doctor Palme, stroking his chin. "But I met a German woman several months ago at the Medical Institute in Stockholm, a Jew who made her way to Sweden several years before the war. She's supposed to be an authority on radiation. Many of these scientists, even Professor Curie in Paris, die from the effects of long-term exposures. Perhaps this woman has seen something similar before. As I recall her name is Meitner, Lise Meitner. I'll make the call when I get back to my office. Meanwhile your patient seems to be as well off here as anywhere else."

Palme turned to the constable, "Perhaps you should discreetly contact the American Consul in Stockholm. Perhaps they will find the means to get this poor young man back home again, even if only to die."

Berlin: June 4, 1942

"Gentlemen, I need your honest appraisals," demanded Reichsminister for Industry Albert Speer, young and handsome: the quintessential businessman. "Regardless what we have heard today from Professor Heisenberg and his associates, it is our responsibility to decide whether to continue their program. The resources they request are substantial, however both the military and industrial sectors have long lists of needs and an existing set of priorities."

A new series of updated presentations and lectures by Heisenberg, Von Weizsacher, Otto Hahn, and other members of the Uranium Club had lasted most of the day. Held in Harnack House at the Kaiser Wilhelm Physics Institute, the audience comprised high ranking, invited representatives from industry, the military, the party, and the SS. Students and other outsiders had been excluded this time. The scientists had been dismissed and the senior representatives met privately in the Institute's boardroom.

"For myself," began General Fromm, senior military man present, "Heisenberg's promises are irresistible and the costs paltry to this point. If he can actually succeed with development of an atom weapon, the war would be over within days. The threat itself would force the Allies to the peace table on our terms."

Speer nodded to the next man along the table, Admiral Rhein, a former U-Boat commander. "Heisenberg and Hahn suggest they might be able to build power systems that would not require our U-Boats to surface or return to base for refueling. The impact on the naval situation should not be underestimated. With the Americans now in the war, we need to carry the sea battle to their doorsteps and interdict the resupply of England and Russia. These atom power units would reduce our reliance on disguised supply ships and *milch* cows. These are having increasing difficulty getting through the English blockade of the French coast.

"However if this is going to work we need to know *now* so that redesign and engineering can begin. Our shipbuilding resources are

---

already stretched and since the English bombing campaign began, schedules are frequently disrupted," Rhein finished.

"General Platin, your considered opinion?" Speer asked.

Dieter Platin had studied advanced chemistry at the Technical High School in Dortmund. Of all present he was the only man who might be expected to comprehend some of the physical and mathematical principles presented. Though Speer and his assistants were engineers and technicians by inclination and experience, most had been businessmen in the years prior to the war. While they could readily grasp the practical applications of atom splitting, their immediate burden was to evaluate whether theory could be brought to reality.

Platin, father of six and devoted husband, was in charge of the Ordnance Research project for poison gas weapons. His factories were spread all across the Reich; his highly efficient experimental laboratories were sited within the barbed wire of concentration camps in Poland. His promotion to general was recent.

"I have been considering the use of radioactive materials as poisonous agents for the battlefield. Even if this Heisenberg cannot provide us with a new explosive weapon, his work seems to suggest we could use his atom pile to manufacture persistent radioactive chemicals. While I will requisition enough of his radioactive uranium oxide for tests on subjects at my laboratories, I have very serious doubts about practical application of these agents. It would seem that while the effects are irreversible and dramatic, depending on exposure levels, debilitating injuries might take weeks to manifest. Enemy soldiers exposed are not even aware of their jeopardy and might continue to fight for many days. Enemy soldiers who understand the implications of their exposure might even assume near suicidal aggression. This all brings an uncertainty to the battlefield that we must avoid at all costs.

"However we might develop these radioactive agents as defensive weapons, laid down as our troops retreat, sort of invisible razor wire. When enemy soldiers comprehend the dangers, they will not cross through contaminated areas."

General Fromm interrupted, "I see a problem. This would require *us* to educate the *enemy* about the dangers. While this might work against English soldiers, do you seriously think any Russian peasant, lead by their ignorant officers, could be made to understand the danger?"

"I agree," said Speer, leaning back to address to his secretary who was taking minutes, "Delete reference about General Platin's comment on 'defensive weapons.' The *Führer* is rarely in a mood to read about preparations for *defense* and it might render *all* our considerations as equally inappropriate. Agreed?"

Everyone nodded. Speer turned his attention to the next man.

"Reichsminister," said Major Kreb from the SS, uncomfortable and unsure of how this was all playing out. "Many in the SS's Technical Section have voiced the opinion that Professors Heisenberg and Von Weizsächer may be playing a very dangerous game. We are faced with the same dilemma as this group: can these theories be applied practically? But is it possible that these people are purposely *underestimating* both the potentials and the chances of success? Perhaps they do not wish the Reich to have such weapons. They all worship the pacifist Jew Einstein like he was God himself. We must consider whether these men are actually holding back, exaggerating the difficulties and obstacles."

This was a remarkable idea, quite opposite to everything they'd been lead to believe.

"Herr Mark, how does the Education Ministry stand regarding this research?"

"Reichminister, we have funded and followed this work since its inception a decade ago. In the last two months on orders from Minister Rust, I have been studying all the available reports and data. We greatly appreciate the assistance we received from the Army, Luftwaffe, and the Gestapo," he said, looking around the conference table for allies.
"I make no claims to understand even one percent of the physics involved, but I have endeavored to evaluate the sources from the standpoint of trust and credibility. These characteristics derive from motivation and personality.

"That Heisenberg and Hahn and the rest are men of great science is no doubt. But during war motivations change. In peacetime, these scientists strive almost desperately for the recognition and approval of their peers. They will do almost anything to be first to publish word of their discoveries. I have come to believe that all this theoretical nonsense has become popular in the last twenty years as a means for researchers who are poor or lazy experimentalists to by-pass the need to spend time in the laboratory. I do not doubt for a minute that this is a further manifestation of Jewish influence on our science that we have tried so hard to root out over the last ten years.

"These men, Heisenberg and the rest of them, are all known to be sympathetic to Jews, as Major Kreb noted. The Gestapo has sufficient documentation to bring capital charges against Hahn for abetting the escape of Professor Meitner three years ago.

"Although insufficient corroborated evidence has surfaced, the Gestapo believes that Heisenberg has traitorously communicated critical information about our program to Professor Bohr in Copenhagen. This Professor Bohr, whom Heisenberg and Von Weizsächer both mentioned worshipfully during their presentations this morning, is known to actively aid Jews in Denmark. Intelligence suggests Bohr has regular contacts with England and America through that woman Meitner in Sweden. Unfortunately, Bohr is protected by his connections to the Danish monarch and is currently beyond the reach of the Gestapo. We know Heisenberg met secretly with Bohr in September of 1940, managing to elude the agents following him for some number of hours.

"In my researches I came across a report to Admiral Canaris at the *Abwehr* from a secret agent returning to Germany soon after Heisenberg's visit to America in 1939. The agent reports overhearing a conversation with the Hungarian Jew Teller where Heisenberg suggests he would remain in Germany through any war in order to protect his students and associates from conscription.

"There you have it. With one more piece of evidence I will discuss in a moment, I believe I can prove that this atom splitting is all *Quatsch*: nonsense! So with apologies to my friend Major Kreb and the SS, it is my considered belief that Heisenberg and his group are purposely *overstating* the chances of practical success from their research. Yes, they hem and haw about this difficulty and that problem, but I think the truth lies elsewhere. Heisenberg has managed to keep several hundred men away from war critical jobs, so if saving himself and his friends is his goal, he has achieved it so far."

"Tell us about this other evidence," Speer asked thoughtfully.

"In going through files secretly copied at the Physics Institute by Army Intelligence, I found a lengthy report written by Herr Professor Ernst Wagner at Munich University…in 1939! I recognized the name immediately. He is a legend: strict and no nonsense, Prussian to his core, unquestionably loyal to the state and party. He was a master experimentalist renowned around the world for his insight and forthrightness.

"Sometime in late 1938 or early 1939, Professor Wagner was asked to review mathematical calculations fundamental to the same technical issues we heard about today from Heisenberg. One of the crucial elements, as you recall, is a determination as to the quantity of active uranium needed for a self-sustaining reaction and for generating explosive forces. Professor Wagner's calculations yield quantities that *exceed ten times* the values reported today by Heisenberg. Accepting Professor Wagner's calculations, a power system for a U-Boat would be thirty meters square and an atom bomb would be so heavy no Luftwaffe plane could deliver it. There is hardly enough uranium in all of the Reich to provide for a single atom weapon. Again this report, from one of Germany's greatest scientists, has existed for nearly three years, buried in Heisenberg's files. *The 1939 review was requested by Heisenberg himself.*"

"This is most disturbing," said Speer. "Can we talk to Professor Wagner to see whether his opinion has changed based on recent research?"

"Reichsminister, I had hoped to have Professor Wagner here today to listen to Heisenberg and confront him directly. He is perhaps the only man in Germany, outside of Heisenberg's cabal, with the reputation and authority to do so. Unfortunately, Captain Posen returned yesterday from Munich with word that Professor Wagner died six months ago during an English air raid on Munich that partly destroyed his home. This is a tragic loss."

"But he speaks eloquently from the dead," Speer said, standing to signal the end of the meeting, "Gentlemen, I now have a clearer picture regarding today's conference. I am angry that our valuable time was wasted. I am also quite concerned that the activities and motives of these people have been selfish at best and traitorous at worst. Major Kreb, I will leave it to you and your Gestapo associates to decide whether legal action against these men is warranted. I am having dinner with the *Führer* this evening, and hopefully he will not ask me again about this matter. Our conclusions will disappoint him greatly. Thank you all for your attention and counsel."

Speer swept out of the room followed by his personal staff. The meeting broke up quickly, the matter settled by the highest authority. Four men held back until the others had all left.

Fromm, Kreb, Rhein, and Mark relaxed back into their chairs. They had come to know and trust each other over the last several months, as ethereal as trust might be in Nazi Germany.

"Well, Kreb, what will you do?" asked Fromm of his SS friend. "Mark's argument is very persuasive, but I can't help but think that even if Heisenberg and Hahn have only a chance in a thousand of success, the money dedicated and the few men needed, is a pittance. You've met many of these scientists, will they make good soldiers?"

"On the contrary," said Kreb. "My personal opinion is that a permanent solution is most appropriate. But we can't forget that Herr Heisenberg remains under special protection. *Reichsführer* Himmler's father grew up with Heisenberg's father. Heisenberg's mother is friendly with Himmler's mother."

"Himmler has a mother! That might be the most amazing thing I have heard today," said Mark irreverently.

"Ah, the Chief certainly hasn't spoken of it himself," laughed Kreb, "but as men of science, we must accept the possibility. Regardless, the subject of *Herr Professor Heisenberg* is not one *I* choose to raise with the Chief."

"And we all know of Von Weizsächer's family connection within the Foreign Ministry. Action against him at this time might be equally perilous to his executioner," Admiral Rhein added. The group sat thoughtfully for several moments.

"Can we agree among ourselves," General Fromm said finally, 'to let sleeping dogs lie? For my part I will not authorize any increase in the Army's funding for the physics institute. They'll have to make do with what they have. Heisenberg can have all the heavy water he needs now that the Norwegians have increased production under German control. He'll have no such excuses to throw back at us."

Rhein shook his head. "I have my own concerns about that. It's true enough. But for some reason the British have launched several unsuccessful air raids against the heavy water plant in Norway, each more determined and violent than the last. Collaborators suggest partisan saboteurs might also be planning an attack. The timing is suspicious. Do we indeed have a spy or traitor in our midst?" He asked rhetorically.

"Please keep the Gestapo apprised," Kreb requested, gathering his notes and papers. "If we reach a point where success seems impossible, it's best to make the whole thing disappear. I can have the entire operation cleaned out in twenty-four hours. It will be as if they never existed."

"Maybe it will come to that," said Fromm. "Meantime, like the Reichsminister, we all have other things to do."

Munich: July 20, 1945

Lise's arms and hands felt leaden, so heavy and numb she wasn't sure she'd be able to raise them from her lap to scratch an itchy nose. Her fingers and wrists were stiff and she couldn't make a fist or retie her bootlaces. A labor of love had quickly become simply labor.

News had gone around the city by word of mouth that the nuns were asking for help at the *Frauenkirche*. The papal delegate from the Vatican who arrived in Munich in the wake of the American Third Army had pledged Rome's support in rebuilding and restoring the great church. Allied bombs had reduced the two distinctive onion-domed spires and great buttressed vaults to a disperse pile of individual blocks and red-brown bricks. American Army engineers were using heavy equipment to reopen streets around the city and tank-mounted plows and bulldozers were sweeping loose bricks and blocks from near the demolished church into bigger and bigger piles increasingly distant from the blackened skeleton.

The sisters were asking for anyone able to come help by sorting through the piles and returning the distinctive red blocks and bricks back to the church site. A promise of extra food rations for volunteers brought out hundreds the first day.

Despite all her loss, Lise recognized how fortunate she was. The family's house on the western side of the *Englisher Garten* was habitable despite bomb damage to the study and parlor. At night she could return to its relative serenity and comfort, even if she, like everyone else in the city, lacked electricity, gas, running water, and hope.

She had taken in several of her bombed-out neighbors but they'd left her the undamaged upstairs rooms. Among all this loss and desolation and death, trivial formalities had taken on exaggerated importance. Everyone went out of their way to be polite and civil even to strangers. All semblance of social status had vaporized; Germany was now ironically and truly a classless society.

Everyone's shoe were equally worn, everyone's stomach equally empty. Everyone smelled the same. You could meet people on the street you'd known all your life and you wouldn't recognize them, and the only emotion expressed was dull amazement that they were alive. You could also look into the broken shards of a mirror and not recognize yourself, not see yourself as an individual distinct from everyone else.

Lise wore threadbare ski pants and a greasy wool sweater. Her hiking boots, so carefully maintained over the years, were failing at last, as the stitching rotted and the outer soles separated. She was twenty-three years old, looked forty, and today, felt seventy.

For three days now Lise had worked on a single, enormous pile of debris about two hundred meters across a roughly formed plaza near the *Frauenkirche*. Today with a morning rain and unsummerlike cold, the number of volunteers had dwindled to a handful. Some sympathetic GI's had lent a hand several days previously and in the matter of a single afternoon had reduced the height of the pile by half. Their energy and industry was otherworldly. Watching them work, Lise had felt she was in a dream where her feet were stuck in clay and she couldn't keep pace with the rest of the world. Yesterday and today the GI's were off somewhere else.

As she wearily rested, seated on a block with her arms drooping nervelessly to her sides, she watched as a jeep picked its way through the piles of debris towards the church foundation. Beside the driver rode a bespectacled civilian and behind them were two soldiers with machine guns. As the jeep stopped and the passengers dismounted, the stout and well-dressed civilian approached a group of nuns supervising distribution of rations to a long, patient line of homeless people. After several minutes of conversation, Sister Agnes pointed the men in Lise's direction. Trailed by his escorts, the civilian stumbled toward her, unsteady over the muddy and broken ground.

"Fräulein Wagner?" the man said in German, with an indistinct accent. "Fräulein Lise Wagner?"

For nearly six years during the war Lise had expected soldiers or police to arrest her. Sometimes she dreamed they would smash down the door, other times they would knock politely. Either way she would be rousted from bed and pushed naked into the street. She's always awakened at this point, but she didn't need fantasy to know what would happen next. She had been witness often and closely enough to have very distinct and vivid images more detailed than she'd ever conjure in her dreams.

She was paralyzed where she sat. In the two months since the Americans arrived, the dream had become less frequent and despite all the devastation around her, some semblance of peace had settled. But for Lise, any uniform was still the symbol of fear. What remained except resignation?

"Fräulein Wagner? Lise Wagner?" the man repeated patiently, unsure whether this girl matched the description he'd been given. He was stocky and balding and dressed too well to be a German. His voice was high, almost bird-like, unthreatening. As she slowly was able to focus on his face, she could see laugh and smile lines around his mouth and eyes.

"My name is Lise Wagner," she offered tentatively.

"I am so glad we were able to find you," he said, cheerfully, clapping his hands. "We first stopped at your father's house on *Königenstrasse*. An elderly woman there, Frau Erna, suggested you might be here helping with the church. I have visited Munich many times but even with a map it was very difficult to find our way around the old city."

He scanned the horizon and noted the cloud-draped Alps in the distance. Ordinarily from this plaza one would see only the facades and eaves of tall, elegant buildings. Nothing remained standing tall enough to obstruct the view.

The little man frowned, "I'm very sorry...about this. But I can reassure you: I've come to know these Americans very well in the last ten years and I believe that with their help, in five years this will all be as good as new." His sweeping gesture encompassed the entire city. Lise feared the man might be insane.

"Fräulein Wagner, we've never been introduced but I met your father many times while I was a student in Germany. You were just a baby then, I suppose. I'm sorry to hear of his death.

"My name is Leo Szilard and I've come from America. I've been sent by a mutual friend who has asked me to find you and bring you to America, if you're willing to come. I'm afraid I can't say anything more at this time. Secrets, you understand. Dickie Groves sent this officer and these soldiers along to make sure I don't flap my mouth too much or try to sneak off to the Russian sector," he said impertinently.

The man didn't seem to be afraid of these uniformed soldiers, indeed they all looked at one another, laughed, and smiled, the kind of friendly, open, honest, sincere smiles Lise had forgotten existed. Then she

remembered. Lise suddenly felt warm and flushed. She trembled.
   "I know this is very mysterious and sudden, but will you come?"
   "Yes," she said at length with a smile and a single tear.

As further reading consider...

The Making of the Atomic Bomb by Richard Rhodes, Simon and Schuster (1986)

Heisenberg's War by Thomas Powers, Knopf (1993)

Gestapo, Instrument of Tyranny by Edward Crankshaw, Da Capo Press (1994)

Berlin Cabaret by Peter Jelavich, Harvard University Press (1993)

Scientists Under Hitler by Alan Beyerchen, Yale University Press (1977)